17/10/16

Books should be returned or renewed by the last
date above. Renew by phone **03000 41 31 31** or
online *www.kent.gov.uk/libs*

Libraries Registration & Archives

CUSTOMER
SERVICE
EXCELLENCE

Kent
County
Council
kent.gov.uk

no further. Murphy is your man' – *ICLR*

'Peter Murphy's novel is an excellent read from start to finish
and highly recommended' – *Historical Novel Review*

'This beautifully-written book had me captivated from start to

'An absorbing read, and one which will make you think, and consider yourself fortunate to be living in a world which has moved on' – *Mystery People*

A MATTER FOR THE JURY

An utterly compelling and harrowing tale of life and death – *David Ambrose*

'One of the subplots… delivers a huge and unexpected twist towards the end of the novel, for which I was totally unprepared' – *Fiction Is Stranger than Fact*

'In *A Higher Duty* Peter Murphy wrote more about the barristers themselves. Here the spotlight is on the defendants, the witnesses, the judges, and even the hangman since this is 1964 and capital murder means what it says' – *Counsel Magazine*

'*A Matter for the Jury* is a page-turner' – *Historical Novel Society*

'gripping courtroom drama' – *ICLR*

'a rich and absorbing read' – *Mrs Peabody Investigates*

AND IS THERE HONEY STILL FOR TEA?

'An intelligent amalgam of spy story and legal drama' – *Times*

'a story that captures the zeitgeist of a turbulent time in British history' – *Publishers Weekly*

'A gripping, enjoyable and informative read…Promoting Crime Fiction loves Peter Murphy's *And is there Honey Still for Tea?*' – *Promoting Crime Fiction*

'Murphy's clever legal thriller revels in the chicanery of the English law courts of the period' – *The Independent*

'The ability of an author to create living characters is always dependent on his knowledge of what they would do and say in any given circumstances – a talent that Peter Murphy possesses in abundance...Arnold Taylor loves *And Is There Honey Still for Tea?*' – ***Crime Review UK***

'There's tradecraft of the John le Carré kind, but also a steely authenticity in the legal scenes... gripping' – ***ICLR***

'Digby, the real protagonist, will keep you guessing until the very end' – ***Kirkus Reviews***

TEST OF RESOLVE

'Peter Murphy presents us with a truly original premise and a set of intriguing characters then ramps up the pressure on them all. *Test of Resolve* is an aptly named, compelling read with a nail biting conclusion' – ***Howard Linskey***

'a gripping political thriller' – ***ICLR***

Also by Peter Murphy
Removal (2012)
Test of Resolve (2014)

The Ben Schroeder series
A Higher Duty (2013)
A Matter for the Jury (2014)
And Is There Honey Still for Tea? (2015)

THE HEIRS OF OWAIN GLYNDŴR

A BEN SCHROEDER NOVEL

PETER MURPHY

NO EXIT PRESS

First published in 2016 by No Exit Press,
an imprint of Oldcastle Books Ltd,
PO Box 394,
Harpenden, Herts,
AL5 1XJ
noexit.co.uk
Editor: Irene Goodacre

ISBN
978-1-84344-786-3 (print)
978-1-84344-787-0 (epub)
978-1-84344-788-7 (kindle)
978-1-84344-789-4 (pdf)

2 4 6 8 10 9 7 5 3 1

Typeset in 11 on 12pt Garamond MT
by Avocet Typeset, Somerton, Somerset TA11 6RT
Printed in Great Britain by Clays Ltd, St Ives plc

For more about Crime Fiction go to www.crimetime.co.uk / @crimetimeuk

For my brother, Paul Murphy: scholar, explorer,
genealogist of our Cymric family, a lover of Cymru.

I fy mrawd Paul Murphy: ysgolhaig, fforiwr,
achydd o'n teulu Cymreig, cariad o Gymru

Glendower:
Three times hath Henry Bolingbroke made head
Against my power; thrice from the banks of Wye
And sandy-bottom'd Severn have I sent him
Bootless home and weather-beaten back.

Henry IV, Part One
Act 3, Scene 1

THE HEIRS OF OWAIN GLYNDŴR

PROLOGUE
PROLOG

1

Monday 4 May 1970

It was the kind of morning all police officers had from time to time, but even so, PC Hywel Watkins of London's Metropolitan Police was feeling a bit hard done by. For one thing, he was short of sleep. He had worked a busy night shift and, even before he went on nights, his new baby, Gaynor, had made sure that he wasn't getting enough rest. Not that he begrudged her the attention – he loved her to death – but it all took its toll. Then, this morning, when his shift had ended and he was looking forward to breakfast, followed by a nice long lie-in while his wife Mary looked after Gaynor for a few hours, his desk sergeant had had other ideas. Sergeant Lees had ordered him to take himself off home at the double, change out of uniform into his best suit and tie, and present himself at the Old Bailey in time for a trial set to begin at 10.30.

It wasn't the first time this had happened, just one of the more inconvenient. PC Watkins had a skill the Met and the courts in London had need of from time to time. He was a native Welsh speaker. Welsh speakers who had dealings with the police or the courts in England were generally quite capable of speaking English, but they sometimes chose not to – usually without giving advance warning. On such occasions, PC Watkins would find himself in demand at short notice, and this morning was such an occasion. To make matters worse, he was going to be late.

When he arrived in the Old Bailey's famous court one, just after 11 o'clock and slightly out of breath, he was surprised to see a scuffle taking place in the dock, to the accompaniment of loud shouting, some in Welsh, some in English. He was even more surprised to see that court was fully assembled: a High Court judge, resplendent in his wig and red robes, on the bench; barristers in their wigs and gowns; a jury of twelve citizens, ten men and two women, in the jury box; an array of clerks, ushers and other court staff; and one or two men in suits who, to Watkins' practised eye, looked like plain clothes police officers. But none of them seemed inclined to lift a finger to intervene in the fracas in the dock; they all seemed somehow resigned to watching from a safe distance, and there was an almost eerie silence in the courtroom.

The scuffle appeared to involve one of three defendants, a male, and two male uniformed prison officers. The two other defendants, one male, one female, and a female prison officer were trying to stay out of it, huddled against the bullet-proof glass in the right-hand corner of the dock. Sergeant Lees had not told him what case he would be dealing with, but as soon as he heard that a Welsh interpreter was needed in court one at the Bailey, he knew. He considered briefly what to do, whether to report to someone, or just make his way forward. He could see no point in standing back. He would be needed in the dock eventually, if he was to interpret, and if there was a scuffle to sort out before he could interpret anything, he might as well take himself there sooner rather than later.

'PC Watkins, Welsh interpreter,' he said loudly, holding his warrant card up high in his right hand, and making his way forward from the courtroom entrance to the dock, as quickly as he could without actually running. He repeated what he had said, in English and Welsh, several times, and saw that he had the attention of those in the dock. Some conversation began at last among those in court, and some semblance of normality was restored. The female prison officer quickly unlocked the door of the dock, opened it just wide enough to allow him to enter, then closed and locked it again hurriedly. The scuffle was winding down as a result of his appearance. The two prison officers released the defendant with rough final shoves and all three of them started to adjust their clothing and tentatively feel the places where blows had landed. All three men had red marks on their faces, where bruises would begin to show before long. Watkins stepped between the defendant and the prison officers, to ensure that it did not kick off again. He touched the defendant's left arm and guided him to the left-hand wall, where he stood still. He turned towards the front of the court to address the judge.

'My Lord, I am PC Hywel Watkins, Welsh interpreter. May I have a few moments to introduce myself to the defendants?' He repeated what he had said in Welsh.

The judge nodded. 'You should take the oath first, please, Officer.'

It was all Watkins could do not to laugh out loud. This was getting surreal. He had just broken up a fight in the dock in court one at the Old Bailey when an entire courtroom of people seemed willing to let it take its course, and the only thing the judge could think of before resuming proceedings was to ask him to take the oath. He quickly reminded himself of where he was, and what Sergeant Lees would have to say about it if he were to be reported for undue levity in court.

'Yes, my Lord.'

A female usher was making her way to the dock carrying the card with the words of the oath inscribed on it. She held it up to the glass for him to read.

'I swear by Almighty God that I will faithfully interpret and true explanation make of all such things as may be required of me to the best of my skill and understanding.'

He turned to face the judge again. 'My Lord, I am Police Constable 246 Hywel Watkins, attached to Holborn Police Station. The language is Welsh. It would assist me if I could speak briefly with the defendants to introduce myself and explain my function to them.'

'Yes, very well,' the judge replied. 'As quickly as you can, please, Officer. I and the jury are waiting.'

Watkins looked down at his feet and took a deep breath. It would be much easier if the judge left the bench and gave the jury a coffee break, just long enough to allow him some chance to assess the situation. He had no idea what was going on, what had led to the strange scene he had witnessed when he entered court. He did not even know how many of the defendants had requested his services, or whether their lawyers spoke any Welsh. It would help if he could have a few minutes to establish some such basic facts, but apparently the judge saw no need for that. He would have to do what he could.

'Yes, my Lord.'

Watkins decided to start with the defendant involved in the scuffle. For the first time, he looked at the man closely. He was a strangely imposing figure, rather over six feet in height; a slim build; age hard to read, late thirties perhaps, Watkins thought; black hair, beginning to turn grey and worn long, tied in a small knot behind his head; a moustache and beard, short and tidily trimmed. He wore an open-necked shirt and dark trousers and, around his head, a thin white bandana, with a small image of the *Y Ddraig Goch* – the Red Dragon of Wales – in the middle of his forehead. His eyes were blue. Watkins felt their suspicious scrutiny of his face.

'I am going to speak quietly to you in Welsh,' he began. 'I don't know how long we will have before the judge orders me to translate what is being said. But I want to explain my role as interpreter. What is your name?'

The defendant looked at him in silence for some seconds, before replying in Welsh.

'Why should I talk to you? You're a police officer – one of *them*.'

'I have no connection with this case,' Watkins replied. 'I was called in this morning when I finished night duty because they needed someone to interpret. I am here to help you, but I can't do that unless you cooperate with me. What is your name?'

Another searching silence.

'Where are you from?' the defendant asked.

'Bridgend,' Watkins replied. His patience was fraying at the edges. Being cross-examined by a Welsh nationalist on trial for conspiracy to cause explosions was not something he was going to put up with for long. But the court needed him to do what he could to establish contact. 'I grew up in South Wales. I moved to England because I wanted to join the Met – and also because of a girlfriend at the time, as a matter of fact – but Wales is still home.'

Why Watkins had volunteered this information about himself, he was not sure, but to his surprise, it drew a smile.

'Porthcawl, in the summer, was it?' the defendant asked.

'And Barry Island,' Watkins replied, returning the smile.

'The fish and chips are better in Porthcawl.'

'No comparison, man.'

'My name is Caradog Prys-Jones.'

'Thank you. Was it you who asked for an interpreter?'

Prys-Jones laughed. 'None of us asked for an interpreter,' he replied. 'All I did was to tell my gaolers that I intended to speak in Welsh, which is my language. It was the judge who decided I needed an interpreter.'

'Which of the barristers is yours?'

'I haven't got one. There's very little I want to say to this court. What I have to say I can say myself. I don't need a barrister to say it for me.'

'What about the other two defendants?'

'They won't need you. My sister Arianwen and Dai Bach have

decided to recognise the court, and they will speak English. The barristers are for them. Good luck to them.'

Watkins nodded. 'All right. I will interpret what you say, and what the court says to you. But it would help if I knew what was going on. Has the trial started? Why were you fighting with the prison officers?'

'The so-called trial is about to start. As you see, they have a jury of English people ready to convict me. The judge and the lawyers were talking among themselves before these goons attacked me, but I played no part in it. When the judge asked me something, I told him that I refused to recognise the court. I was speaking in Welsh, so he didn't understand me. That is not my fault. We have an English judge who doesn't speak Welsh, even though we have any number of judges in Wales who do. He's a bad-tempered bastard, too. He shouted at me for a while, and then these prison officers took it upon themselves to try to persuade me to speak English, which I refused to do. Eventually one of them assaulted me and I defended myself – which was where you came in.'

'All right,' Watkins said. 'Are you ready?'

Prys-Jones renewed his searching scrutiny of Watkins' face.

'I want you to interpret exactly what I say.'

'You heard me take the oath,' Watkins replied. 'Besides, you understand English just as well as I do. You'll know whether I'm interpreting properly or not.'

'It could get loud again,' Prys-Jones said. 'It might even lead to those monkeys jumping on me again, too. Just so you are warned.'

'Just so *you* are warned,' Watkins replied, 'I *am* a police officer, and I've already had a long day. You kick off again, boyo, and you'll have *me* jumping on you as well as them.'

He turned back to the judge.

'We are ready, my Lord.'

2

MR JUSTICE OVERTON HAD been on the bench less than a year, and the last thing he had expected was to be sitting at the Central Criminal Court to try such a high profile case. Even the press seemed bemused that the Lord Chief Justice had not chosen to try the case himself or, at the very least, assigned it to a very senior High Court judge. Most of Overton's friends, over dinner at his club, had suggested smilingly that he had been chosen as a sacrificial offering, the prospective scapegoat to bear the guilt if, God forbid, such an important case were to go wrong — and God knew that if this case went wrong, it would go spectacularly wrong. One or two kinder souls tried to reassure him that it was a sign that those higher up had confidence in him, and that if all went well, as it surely would, a seat in the Court of Appeal would be in his future. Overton was not reassured.

The case against the defendants looked strong enough on paper. But he had Evan Roberts prosecuting, a selection made, presumably, because of the man's Welsh origins. Evan Roberts had made his career as Civil Treasury Counsel. No one doubted his ability as a lawyer, but he had hardly ever set foot in a criminal courtroom before. True, he had a very able Welsh junior, Jamie Broderick, to assist him, and Broderick was making quite a name for himself in crime in Cardiff. But this was not a case for beginners, and Roberts would have formidable opposition to contend with.

All three defence counsel came from the chambers formerly headed by his long-time rival Bernard Wesley, a guarantee of high quality in itself. Gareth Morgan-Davies QC and his junior Donald Weston represented Dafydd Prosser. Gareth had been in Silk for only three years, but he was known as one of the best criminal advocates in London. He was now Head of Chambers at 2 Wessex Buildings, because Bernard Wesley had been appointed a High Court judge at about the same time as Overton. Gareth was also the only barrister involved in the case who was a native Welsh-speaker.

Ben Schroeder, who represented Arianwen Hughes, was a junior of some seven years' experience, who had already built a reputation as a skilful and determined fighter for his clients. Overton had learned a lot about Ben when they had been on opposing sides in the case of Sir James Digby, a leading Silk who had been unmasked as a long-term Soviet spy, and had fled to Moscow on the eve of the libel trial which was supposed to clear his name. Ben had worked tirelessly for his client while it still seemed that he had been falsely accused, but when the truth began to emerge, he had not hesitated to secure and reveal the evidence which exposed his client for what he really was. Overton had a high opinion of him and had wondered, sometimes aloud, whether Evan Roberts could survive in this company in a criminal case. He was about to find out.

Overton had been warned that Caradog Prys-Jones was likely to cause trouble, but that was something that did not trouble him in the slightest. In the course of a professional lifetime spent arguing, and usually winning, the most challenging of cases, Overton was well used to litigants throwing tantrums to get what they wanted. Caradog Prys-Jones was nothing new. If he insisted on speaking Welsh, he would have an interpreter. If he continued to disrupt the proceedings, Mr Justice Overton, after giving him every chance to change his mind, would reluctantly have him sent down to the cells. He would then be brought back up to court at key moments of the trial and again invited to participate, and would be taken back down when he refused. If he refused to have counsel to represent him, Mr Justice Overton would bend over backwards to make sure that the jury heard everything that could be said on his behalf. And the jury would be present to see and hear it all for themselves. They had to judge Caradog Prys-Jones, and they would see for themselves what kind of character he was. It would all be perfectly fair.

'Mr Prys-Jones,' the judge began, 'you have an interpreter, and you may speak in Welsh if you wish. We are about to begin the trial. Do I understand that you still wish to represent yourself?'

Standing next to Prys-Jones, PC Watkins watched the man raise himself to his full height, which, by the sheer force of his presence, he somehow managed to make appear even greater than it was. He started to speak quite slowly.

'I refuse to recognise this court. I demand to be tried in Wales, under Welsh law, by a court conducting its proceedings in Welsh. I demand to be tried by a Welsh judge and a Welsh jury.'

Mr Justice Overton waited patiently for Watkins to finish his translation.

'Mr Prys-Jones, whether or not you recognise the court is irrelevant. The Central Criminal Court has jurisdiction to try you, and you have been properly indicted. That, I am afraid, is a fact, whether you like it or not. You will be tried under the law of England *and* Wales, which is the law to which we are all subject. The proceedings will be conducted in English because that is the language which everyone in this court understands but, as I have said, you may speak Welsh if you wish.'

Prys-Jones began to speak again before Watkins had the chance to finish his translation of the judge's reply. He reached out a hand to touch Prys-Jones's arm to ask him to wait, but the defendant pulled away. He was speaking quickly now, and the pace was increasing. It took every ounce of concentration for Watkins to keep up with him.

'This is just another chapter in the subjugation of Wales by the English, and the cultural genocide being committed against the Welsh people. Ever since the days of Edward I, you have assumed the right to do what you like in our country. You have killed our people. You have replaced the true princes of Wales with your imported Saxon royalty, and you demand that we recognise them as our rulers. You threaten our language...'

By now, the defendant and his interpreter were shouting at the same time, and Watkins was struggling to make himself heard. Watkins held up his hands to the judge to indicate that he was doing his best.

'Mr Prys-Jones,' the judge was saying, 'all this has nothing to do with the case. You must confine yourself to speaking about the case.'

'You flood our valleys, you take our money, you take our coal, and then you throw our miners out of work when your English bankers decide that the mines are no longer profitable enough for them.'

'Mr Prys-Jones, you will stop this immediately, or I shall have you taken down to the cells.'

'You have sown the wind, and you shall reap the whirlwind. The people of Wales will rise up as one and drive you out of Wales.'

'That's enough,' the judge said. 'Take him down.'

The two prison officers once again approached Prys-Jones, who lunged at them violently, catching one officer on an already red cheek. His colleague punched Prys-Jones in retaliation. Watkins intervened to prevent further violence and, with his assistance, the officers soon pinioned Prys-Jones's arms behind his back, and began to drag him towards the door leading down to the cells. He had to be dragged every inch of the way, as he continued to rant.

'I am a member of a legitimate military force. We are freedom fighters. I am a prisoner of war. This is an illegal tribunal. I demand my rights under the Geneva Conventions. I do not recognise this court. I demand to be taken back to Wales.'

By now, two more prison officers had made their way upstairs from the cells, and the four officers finally subdued him. As he disappeared from the dock, he gave one piercing final scream.

'We are the Heirs of Owain Glyndŵr!'

Suddenly, there was silence in court. Watkins turned round to check on the others in the dock. Dafydd Prosser, the second male defendant, was sitting with his head in his hands, looking down at the floor. The female officer was standing by his side, looking thoroughly shaken. Arianwen Hughes, the female defendant, was sitting next to Dafydd. She seemed composed, but there were tears in her eyes.

'Everyone all right?' Watkins asked in English, then, out of habit, in Welsh.

All three nodded.

'Mae'n ddrwg gennyf i,' Arianwen whispered. 'I am sorry.'

He shook his head. 'No, don't worry. Not a problem.'

As if it had been a perfectly normal morning and nothing untoward had happened, Mr Justice Overton turned towards the jury. Glancing in their direction from the dock, Watkins thought they were looking a bit shell-shocked. If the judge noticed the same thing, he did not acknowledge it at all.

'Well, there we are, members of the jury. These things happen. Nothing for you to worry about. Let me just say this. It is my duty, and yours, to treat Mr Prys-Jones fairly, and he will receive a fair trial despite his absence. I will ensure that all the points that can be made in his favour as the trial proceeds are brought to your attention, and it will be your task to give his case the same fair consideration you would if he were in court, and had someone representing him. It is his choice to absent himself, but I will give him a further chance to participate in the trial, and we will see what happens then. We are now ready to begin the trial.'

He looked towards the dock.

'PC Watkins, even though the two remaining defendants have not asked for an interpreter, I think it would be advisable for you to remain throughout the trial. There may be a need for a Welsh speaker to interpret or to translate documents as we go along. I will make sure that your senior officers are informed, of course, so you needn't worry about your other duties. You may leave the dock and sit behind prosecuting counsel for now.'

Watkins bowed to the inevitable. Well, at least he would be on days for a while, now, which would make things easier for Mary and Gaynor.

'Yes, my Lord.'

Gareth Morgan-Davies stood.

'My Lord, my learned friend Mr Schroeder and I are concerned that the jury have witnessed this display by Mr Prys-Jones, and that they may hold it against our clients. It would be a natural enough reaction. I am sure your Lordship will direct them not to do so in the summing-up, but I would like the opportunity to make it clear now that neither Mr Prosser nor Mrs Hughes had anything to do with Mr Prys-Jones's outburst, neither do they agree with what he said.'

The judge paused, and Gareth saw him fight to keep his temper in check.

'Very well, Mr Morgan-Davies,' he replied. 'Members of the jury, of course, this has nothing to do with Mr Prosser or Mrs Hughes. You will consider the case of each defendant separately. The fact that Mr Prys-Jones has chosen to behave in this manner does not affect the case of Mr Prosser or Mrs Hughes in any way. You will bear that in mind.'

Gareth was smiling reassuringly at the jury, and they nodded in return.

'You may begin, Mr Roberts,' the judge said.

Gareth leaned across to Ben.

'God, this is going to be a long trial,' he whispered.

3

'MAY IT PLEASE YOUR Lordship, members of the jury, my name is Evan Roberts, and I appear to prosecute in this case with my learned friend Mr Jamie Broderick. As you have just heard, the defendant Caradog Prys-Jones has chosen to represent himself. The defendant Dafydd Prosser is represented by my learned friends Mr Morgan-Davies QC and Mr Weston. The defendant Arianwen Hughes is represented by my learned friend Mr Schroeder. With the usher's kind assistance I am going to give you four documents.'

Geoffrey, the black-gowned usher, a tall, silver-haired man wearing a dark suit and a tie emblazoned with the coat of arms of the City of London, quickly took the documents from the prosecutor's outstretched hand, and distributed them to the jury.

'The first document is a plan of the centre of the town of Caernarfon in North Wales. The second is a plan of Caernarfon Castle. The third is a floor plan of a book shop in Caernarfon called, in English, the Prince Book Shop. My Lord, I understand there is no objection...'

'That is correct,' Gareth said.

'I am obliged. In that case, my Lord, may these become Exhibits 1, 2 and 3?'

'Yes, very well,' the judge replied.

'We will come to those when the evidence gets underway. The fourth document is a copy of the indictment, which you have already heard read to you by the learned Clerk. It has one count, which is in these terms. The statement of the offence is conspiracy to cause explosions. The particulars of the offence are that:

Between a date unknown and 1 July 1969, Caradog Prys-Jones, Dafydd Prosser, Trevor Hughes and Arianwen Hughes conspired together and with others unknown to cause explosions.

'Members of the jury, you will hear that the four defendants plotted together to commit as grave and as heinous an offence as could possibly be imagined. They plotted to plant an explosive device in Caernarfon Castle on the morning of the 1 July 1969. That was the day on which Her Majesty the Queen performed the ceremony of Investiture of her son, His Royal Highness Prince Charles, as Prince of Wales. You will hear evidence that, if the defendants' plan had succeeded, it might well have resulted in death or serious injury to a large number of people gathered together that afternoon in the Castle for the Investiture, perhaps even, in certain circumstances, the Queen or the Prince of Wales.'

Roberts paused to allow this to sink in before continuing.

'You will have noticed, members of the jury, that although four defendants are named in the indictment, we only have two in the dock. You know why Caradog Prys-Jones is not here. But another defendant is missing from the dock. That is Trevor Hughes. Trevor Hughes is the husband of Arianwen Hughes, and the prosecution say that he played a full part in the conspiracy, together with his wife. But when the other three defendants were arrested in the early hours of the 1st of July, Trevor Hughes somehow managed to evade arrest. When police officers went to his home and his place of work shortly after the arrest of his wife, they fully expected to find him at one or the other of those places. He was not at either.

'The prosecution assume that in some manner he found out that the plot had been uncovered and that his fellow conspirators either had been, or were about to be arrested, and that he seized the chance to make good his escape. He has not been seen since. There were reports at the time that he had fled to Ireland, but whether or not that is true, his whereabouts are not known at present. We have every confidence that he will be arrested in due course, and when that happens, he will be brought before the court to answer this charge. But he is not here today, and he will play no part in this case.'

Roberts paused for a sip of water.

'Who are these defendants?' he asked, suddenly raising his voice. 'Who are these people who planned such a heinous crime designed to cause such mayhem and havoc on a day of national celebration, a crime which so callously and viciously threatened the safety of our reigning Monarch and of the Heir to the Throne, and which represented an attack on the very foundations of our country?'

Ben looked at Gareth, his eyebrows raised. Gareth shook his head, briefly. He knew what Ben was asking. Roberts' rhetoric would have been more suited to the Old Bailey of 1890 or 1910 than to the court of 1970; it betrayed his lack of experience of criminal cases. It would have been quite proper to object to such an attempt to play on the jury's emotions. Some judges would have intervened even without an objection, would have told Roberts to stop it and get on with what he should be doing – which was to provide the jury with an overview of the evidence they were about to hear. But Gareth could not see Miles Overton doing that; he had heard Overton use some pretty robust language himself during his days at the Bar. Besides, Roberts was entitled to make the gravity of the case clear to the jury. There was no point in picking a fight about it unless it got out of hand.

'Caradog Prys-Jones is a graduate of the University of Bangor,' Roberts continued. 'He graduated in 1955. His degree was in Welsh literature and history. After graduation, he based himself in Caernarfon, living in what, until their deaths, was his parents' home in Pretoria Terrace. He had a conventional job as a senior administrative officer in the Office of the Inspector of Ancient Monuments for Wales. Outwardly, there was nothing to suggest that he was anything other than a young man beginning to make his way in the world. He had been known as a radical spirit as a student at Bangor, attending a few demonstrations in support of the Welsh language. But once he had graduated, he avoided the public gaze completely and seemed to lead a quiet life. He performed his work well, and he aroused no suspicion. He did not express any extreme views publicly. But he did have such views, and they seem to have evolved in his mind over a period of several years until they became an obsessive hatred of all things English.

'Caradog Prys-Jones, members of the jury, as he told you himself this morning, regards the English as the invaders and occupiers of Wales, and he is willing to resort to force to drive them out. He was the intellectual and moral leader of the conspiracy, and its ideological guru. He was the man who conceived the idea of planting an explosive device at Caernarfon Castle on the day of the Investiture, and he it was who recruited the others, and persuaded them to join the conspiracy.

'It was Caradog Prys-Jones who gave this group of conspirators its name, the Heirs of Owain Glyndŵr. Members of the jury, you will hear that Owain Glyndŵr was a Welsh prince, regarded by many nationalists as the last true Prince of Wales. He was born in the period 1349 to 1359 and was believed to have the blood of the two great Welsh princedoms of Gwynedd and Powys running through his veins. In September 1400, Glyndŵr led a revolt against King Henry IV, which continued spasmodically for several years, but which was ultimately unsuccessful. He died in 1415. From the nineteenth century onwards, Welsh nationalist organisations have regarded Glyndŵr as an iconic figure and the Father of Welsh nationalism. You will hear that the Queen's decision to make Prince Charles Prince of Wales, and to hold the Investiture at Caernarfon Castle, was regarded by many as an affront to the people of Wales, and the prosecution say that it was the trigger for the plot with which you are concerned in this case.

'This may be a convenient moment, members of the jury, to mention that this was not the only plot of its kind. Some of you may know that a number of bombs were found in and around Caernarfon in the day or two before the Investiture. Only one device was successfully detonated, and that device was in a place where it posed no threat to the Royal Family, although tragically it caused terrible injuries to a young boy who was on holiday in the area. Some of you may also know that, just last month, in April of this year, a man called John Jenkins was convicted of a number of offences involving explosive devices committed during the same time period, and that he was sentenced to a term of imprisonment. Members of the jury, it is not suggested that the defendants in this case had any connection with Jenkins, or indeed with any others who may have committed other such offences. I want to make that clear here and now. The Heirs of Owain Glyndŵr acted on their own, with no known connection to any other individual or group. But they were no less dangerous for that.

'Dafydd Prosser, known to the others as Dai Bach – members of the jury, I am told that Dai Bach, meaning "Little David", is an affectionate form of address in Welsh – is an expert in chemistry. He studied for his degree in chemistry at the National University of Wales at Aberystwyth, and graduated in 1956. After graduation, he accepted a job teaching chemistry at the Menai Strait Grammar School in Bangor, where he became a popular and well-respected teacher. Like Caradog Prys-Jones, Dafydd Prosser used a respectable position to conceal his extremist beliefs. Neither his colleagues nor his pupils had any idea that this well-liked teacher had another side to him, and indeed was leading a double life. But in fact, Dafydd

Prosser is also a nationalist extremist, and a member of the Heirs of Owain Glyndŵr. He played a vital role in the conspiracy.

'We come next to Arianwen Hughes, the younger sister of Caradog Prys-Jones. Like her brother, Arianwen Hughes graduated from Bangor University, but in 1957 and with a degree in Welsh and music. Until her marriage to Trevor Hughes in 1963, she lived with her brother in the house in Pretoria Terrace in Caernarfon. She was a private music teacher, and taught piano and cello to local children, and indeed, adults. After their marriage, Trevor and Arianwen Hughes lived together above the Prince Book Shop until their son Harri was born in 1965. They then moved to larger premises in a street called *Penrallt Isaf*.

'The prosecution say that Arianwen Hughes agreed with her brother's nationalist views, and was fully prepared to play her part in the conspiracy. As an indication of her dedication to the cause, members of the jury, you will hear that at a crucial moment, when it came time to carry out the plan to plant the explosive device, she had her four-year-old son Harri with her, strapped in his car seat in the back of her car, giving the impression of a perfectly innocent mother driving her child for some perfectly innocent purpose through the streets of Caernarfon. No doubt this was intended to deflect the attention of any police officer who might be suspicious about what she was doing. Apparently she had given no thought to the safety of her young son, or, for that matter, her own.

'Lastly, members of the jury, we come to Trevor Hughes. Trevor Hughes was the owner of the book shop I have already referred to, the Prince Book Shop in Palace Street, in the heart of Caernarfon. Its name in Welsh is the *Siop Llyfrau'r Tywysog*. Trevor Hughes arrived in Caernarfon and took the shop over in October 1961. The Prince is quite a large shop, covering two floors, with a third-floor flat above which came with the shop, and in which Hughes lived until after his marriage and the birth of his son. The Prince stocked a large selection of books, in Welsh and English, on a large number of subjects, both fiction and non-fiction. But there was also a basement room which the vast majority of customers never saw, and probably never knew about.

'In the basement, more controversial items could be purchased. Some of these were books, magazines, and other materials of interest to Welsh nationalists, and some of these were of a violent, and even a terroristic nature. The basement room also served as a meeting place where nationalists of various hues could get together and discuss their plans without fear of being overheard or interrupted. Trevor Hughes provided such people with sanctuary in the basement. We say that it was in the Prince Book Shop that Trevor Hughes first met Caradog Prys-Jones and Arianwen Prys-Jones, his future wife; where he became their friend and a member of their family; and where he eventually became a member of the Heirs of Owain Glyndŵr, and joined the conspiracy. When the police visited the book shop on the morning of the 1st of July, Trevor Hughes, as I said before, was gone.

'I hope not to take too long, members of the jury, but I must now outline the history of the conspiracy as far as we know it, until the moment of the arrest of the three defendants who are before you. The story begins in Caernarfon in late October 1961.'

PART 1
RHAN 1

4

AFTER SOME FORTY YEARS, it was not easy for Madog to hand the shop over to anyone else, especially to someone about whom he knew so little. The *Siop Llyfrau'r Tywysog* had been his life for so long that he could hardly imagine any other, including the life of retirement he was about to embark on. Throughout those long years, on six days of every week, barring Christmas, New Year and short family holidays, he opened religiously at 9 o'clock in the morning. He chatted with delivery drivers, the postman, and customers, ate a sandwich for lunch at his desk, and sometimes even sold a few books. Once or twice a week, he took the contents of the till to the bank, barring a few pounds and some change for a float. When he closed the shop at 6 o'clock, he climbed the stairs to the flat above the shop, where he lived. When he looked back over those years, much of the time was a blur. There were special days which stood out. But there were also so many days, spent in the same way, of which he had no memory at all, which ran together and merged into each other without differentiation, like paints on a watercolour left out in the rain.

Nonetheless, he could boast of a life's work well done. The shop was a modest enough establishment. The faded brown sign above the front window offered only the most basic information – the name of the *Tywysog* itself, Madog's name as the proprietor, and a telephone number. But in an age of struggling independent book shops, the *Tywysog* was alive and well, and known far and wide, even to many outside Wales. Even after all those years, his spirit willed him to carry on. But he was getting older, and his arthritis was making it more difficult to get around, especially to climb the steep flight of stairs up to the flat. If Rhiannon had still been with him, he might have managed for longer, but she had been gone for almost ten years now. His daughter and son-in-law had more than enough space for him in their house in Cardigan, and they had been trying to persuade him to sell up and come to live with them there ever since Rhiannon had passed. He had resisted for as long as he could, but he had always known that, eventually, the time for resistance would end, and now it had.

The speed with which the sale went through came as a surprise, though, if he was honest, not a wholly welcome one; a stubborn part of him secretly hoped that the process of sale would drag on and allow him to linger for a little while longer. Still, the ease with which the sale was accomplished, and the absence of any haggling over the asking price, came as a relief and seemed to him to be some vindication of the work he had put into the shop over so many years.

When he first met Trevor Hughes, Madog was not sure whether he was the man the *Tywysog* needed. He certainly had the credentials. He had worked for many years at Foyles in London, and his knowledge of books and the book trade could, therefore, be taken for granted. He spoke Welsh, of course. That was essential. Welsh was the language of everyday discourse at the *Tywysog*. English was tolerated politely when spoken by tourists, and even when spoken by transplanted newcomers to Caernarfon; and with commendable broad-mindedness, the shop sold books in both languages. But Welsh was the heart and soul of the *Tywysog*, and Madog would never have sold the shop to anyone who was a non-speaker. Trevor's Welsh was not the best or the most fluent Madog had ever heard, and he had a South Wales accent, which sometimes meant you had to concentrate on what he was saying if you were a native of the North. But you couldn't blame him for that. His parents were from Cardiff and they had been moved away from Wales during the War, when his father worked for the Home Office. Trevor had spent most of his life in England and, given that history, his Welsh was by no means bad. After a few weeks, he would be speaking as though he had lived his whole life in Caernarfon. The locals would see to that.

All the same, Madog had a doubt at the back of his mind. It was a doubt which concerned, not Trevor's ability to run a book shop, but his commitment to what the *Tywysog* stood for: its willingness to provide a platform for voices raised in support of controversial and uncomfortable causes, voices outside the political mainstream, even voices raised in support of the grail of independence. It was a commitment which had always been low key and understated and which mainly inhabited the shop's basement. But it was real, and if that commitment left the *Tywysog* with Madog, there would be some who would not forgive him for selling to the wrong buyer. It was a doubt he could not raise with Trevor directly, and one he certainly could not raise with his agent, who was absurdly pleased with himself for landing a buyer who wanted to complete as soon as possible and who did not even need a loan to fund the purchase. Madog reassured himself with the thought that Trevor could not possibly be ignorant of what the *Tywysog* stood for. He was knowledgeable about the shop and he was obviously very keen to take it on. That would have to be a sufficient guarantee.

When it came to the painful procedure of moving out, Trevor put no pressure on Madog at all. He had travelled to Caernarfon a week before he was due to take possession, and had installed himself at the Black Boy Inn, just a couple of hundred yards along *Stryd y Plas* – Palace Street – from the *Tywysog*. He told Madog to take all the time he needed. He allowed Madog to give him his personal tour of the shop, even though he had seen all there was to see when the agent had showed it to him; and he listened attentively to Madog's stories of the special days, days when Welsh politicians, writers, international rugby players, and celebrities such as Richard Burton, had visited him to buy a book, or simply to hear Welsh well spoken. He even offered to help with the packing, if needed, but Madog had his daughter to help him, and he preferred to keep that last intimacy within the family. When the day came, Madog took one last look, remembering the day when he had first entered the shop with Rhiannon, then turned his back and walked away.

5

AFTER 5 O'CLOCK ON the afternoon when Madog left, when it was already dark and there were storm clouds moving in from the Menai Strait, Trevor Hughes walked unhurriedly along *Stryd y Plas* from the Black Boy Inn to the *Siop Llyfrau'r Tywysog*. He took his new set of keys from his coat pocket, the key ring still bearing the agent's tag with the address written on it, opened the door of the shop, switched on the lights, then turned and locked the door. He looked around him. The shelves were still fully stocked, and the notice board by the door was still filled with notices advertising local events, from theatrical productions and concerts to readings of Welsh poetry and harp recitals. Others advertised Welsh lessons and rented accommodation. As promised, Madog had left his directory of phone numbers, suppliers, other book shops, publishers, and important customers. The space at the back of the shop for making tea was still fully equipped. But there was an emptiness, a profound silence, about the place, and he wished very much that it was already 9 o'clock the following morning, when there would be daylight and when the *Tywysog* would have people browsing and chatting again.

He began at the top, with the flat. As he had expected, there was no trace of Madog left, but there was a card with red roses on the front, in which someone, the daughter, he suspected – the hand was too young for Madog, and in any case did not match the phone directory – had written a warm message of welcome in Welsh. Standing beside it was a bottle of white wine. He put the card up on the mantelpiece in the living room, and the wine in the small fridge in the kitchen, a recent acquisition Madog had made at his daughter's insistence and against his better judgment, he having lived without such a contraption for most of his life. The living room and bedroom were just about large enough for Trevor's needs. The kitchen and bathroom were small, but functional. There was a very small storage area off the bedroom. Trevor had made no decision about how long he would occupy the flat. Nowhere near as long as Madog had: that was certain. It was a pleasant enough flat, and obviously convenient, but he would lose his mind eventually. He could not comprehend how the old man could have endured being cooped up in such a small place for so many years, with no home away from work. Inertia, perhaps? Being there so long that moving somehow seemed impossible? He would not fall into the same trap. But there was time enough to think about that.

Locking the door of the flat, he walked downstairs to the upper floor of the shop. This, according to Madog, was where the more serious books were kept. A large section was devoted to Welsh historical and literary works, with dictionaries, grammar books, and books about topics of cultural interest, such as national monuments, the National University of Wales, and Welsh music, including a history of the National Anthem. Another section contained poetry and novels in Welsh. But there was also a decent-size English section with English and American literary classics from Dickens to Scott Fitzgerald, and a smaller collection of philosophical works, translations of Plato and Aristotle, works by Locke, Hobbes and John Stuart Mill. In the middle of the room stood a large rectangular table and several chairs, where customers could sit and read a variety of Welsh and English periodicals.

On the ground floor was a wide variety of books of general interest, including travel books, biographies and autobiographies of well-known personalities, books about sports and hobbies, cooking and diets, and crime and espionage novels of every kind. Opposite the desk at the front of the shop was a selection of records featuring Welsh music, from traditional choirs to brass bands, operatic soloists to contemporary rock groups.

A door at the rear, which was kept locked, led down to the basement.

Madog had taken him down to the basement, but he had seemed reluctant to talk about it in any detail, almost as if he assumed that Trevor already knew what was to be found there. To some extent, in a general sense, he did. It was no secret that the *Tywysog* catered for those with nationalist views, including some at the extreme end of the spectrum. Trevor was aware that it was a favourite haunt of activists, some of whom had interests that went beyond conventional politics. So, somewhere, there had to be some books, periodicals and pamphlets which would be of interest to this kind of customer, the kind of stuff Madog presumably thought was better locked away in the basement – and certainly there had been no sign of any such materials on the two floors above. That made sense. You wouldn't want to risk upsetting the more conventional customers, he reflected. It was rather like having a stash of pornography. You would keep it hidden away in a discreet place, to be revealed only on request.

Madog had whisked him around at such a speed that he had not been able to study the contents of the basement to confirm his assumptions. Now, he took his time, going slowly from bookcase to bookcase. The basement was less organised than the two above-ground floors. It had no signs to divide it into sections, or to provide a customer looking for something specific with a hint about where it might be found. Trevor speculated that those interested in the materials in the basement had to ask Madog to show them. In any case, there was no access to the basement unless Madog unlocked the door.

Two large bookcases held books and privately printed pamphlets about Welsh nationalism dating from the nineteenth century and going forward. Many were in a poor condition, some even bearing traces of mildew, and looked as though they had been stored in the slightly damp atmosphere of the basement for rather too long. In two more bookcases were treatises dealing with historical subjects. A number concerned the historic princes of Wales – fair enough, given the shop's name, Trevor thought – and the princely houses of Gwynedd and Powys. There were biographies of Owain Glyndŵr, some professionally published, and others which might have been someone's doctoral thesis, or papers published by a private society. Several volumes were diatribes against Edward I for his military invasion of Wales, his use of the castles at Caernarfon and elsewhere in North Wales as bastions of English power, and his blatant treachery in foisting his new-born infant son on the Welsh as their prince. A quick glance inside suggested that the authors' opinion of the British monarchy since Edward I was not a great deal better than their opinion of the invader himself. A number railed against the Investiture of the future Edward VIII at Caernarfon Castle in 1911 as a further violation of the integrity of the Welsh nation.

A handsome wooden cabinet stood against the back wall of the basement. It had three drawers, all of which were locked. Trevor examined his key ring again. He had wondered what the smallest of the four keys he had been given was for but, despite reminding himself several times, he had somehow forgotten to ask either Madog or the agent. Now he knew. He opened the cabinet gingerly and began to sift through the contents. These contents did not exactly come as a surprise, but they were disturbing, nonetheless. The cabinet contained a number of military-issue technical documents for weapons, mostly high-velocity rifles and side-arms, but also one or two devoted to hand grenades. There were also some items, quite obviously not military-issue, privately and badly typed on cheap paper, which contained some very specific instructions for making your own explosive devices. They were mostly in English, although one or two were in German. He spent a few minutes flicking through them. Trevor was no expert on such things, but even to his eye the diagrams seemed crude and simplistic, the kind of thing which would be at least as dangerous to someone making or activating the device, as to anyone against whom the maker might try to use it. Yet there they were, in a cabinet in what was now his basement. He locked the cabinet before making his way back upstairs.

6

HE DID NOT ACTUALLY see her come in. He was dealing with a telephone inquiry at the time, and he had turned his swivel-chair away from the door. But he noticed her as soon as he had replaced the receiver and turned back. She was scanning a small stand which featured books by local authors. She was tall, with long black hair, beginning to turn grey, though she did not look at all old enough for that to happen. She wore a blue blouse, an ankle-length black skirt, and a thick grey woollen shawl around her shoulders. She had picked up a book from the stand, and had turned in his direction; at which point he saw her soft blue eyes, and his mind stood still.

He had been open for a week. For much of that time he had seemed busy, certainly if you judged by the influx of visitors. The shop had a steady stream of local people coming in and out each day, far more than he had anticipated. But sales remained at the modest level Madog had warned him to expect. For the most part, they were there out of curiosity. Madog's departure was a significant event in the life of Caernarfon. It was talked about in the pubs and cafés, and in the market. Almost all the town's inhabitants had known Madog for as long as they had been alive; he was as much a fixture at the *Tywysog* as the statue of David Lloyd George was in the *Maes* – the town square. Some refused to believe that Madog had really gone until they came into the shop to see for themselves, and even then they prowled around each floor in turn, just in case he might by some chance be hiding somewhere. Eventually, most of them introduced themselves, and Trevor listened politely to all manner of reminiscences and eulogies of Madog, stories of acts of kindness and of great wisdom, stories of a local hero. After a day or two, he would not have been greatly surprised if a statue of Madog had spontaneously appeared alongside that of David Lloyd George. Although they were polite to him and uttered a few formal words of welcome, he had no sense yet that the people of Caernarfon were ready to accept him as Madog's successor. With all this going on, he still had to cope with the business of running a book shop. He was beginning to feel slightly overwhelmed.

But now, her eyes held him and made his mind stand absolutely still, and for an instant there was no *Tywysog* and no Caernarfon, there were no books to sell, no orders to place, and no visitors lamenting the departure of Madog. There were only the eyes. He began to regain his composure only because she was saying something to him with her gentle voice, in a beautiful formal Welsh, a Welsh quite different from the guttural conversational language he was getting used to hearing day by day. As his mind began to work again, he wondered whether she was speaking in that way as a kindness to him, as if she were afraid that he might not yet have adapted to the local speech sufficiently to understand her. He could not recover fully in time, and had to ask her to repeat what she had said. With a smile, she approached and stood next to where he was sitting at the desk.

'It's not important. I was just wondering whether you have heard of this writer, Glenys Gower, and whether she has written anything else.'

He stood and took the book from her.

'No, I'm afraid not. I haven't been here very long, and I haven't had a chance to investigate the local authors yet. I am sure Madog would have known.'

She laughed. 'Madog would have given me her phone number.'

He laughed too. 'Yes. All I can offer is a catalogue. It's upstairs, on the big table. It should have some information about all the authors we sell. At least, that's what Madog told me. Why don't you have a look at that, and if you can't find anything I will make some inquiries for you.'

'I will,' she replied. 'As I said, it's not important. I only picked it up because you were on the phone. I came in mainly to introduce myself. My name is Arianwen Prys-Jones.'

'Trevor Hughes,' he replied and they shook hands, warmly, neither in any hurry to release.

'What made you come all the way to Caernarfon to take over the *Tywysog*?'

'All the way?'

She smiled again. 'I heard you came from London.'

'Yes, that's quite true. I lived in London for many years. I worked at Foyles for a long time. I don't know whether…'

'Yes,' she replied, 'of course I know Foyles. My parents took us – my brother and myself – to London a number of times when we were much younger. Foyles was one of the places we would always visit. Most parents visiting London would take their children to Buckingham Palace and the Tower of London, but not my parents. My parents took us to Foyles and the British Museum.'

He laughed. 'I take it they were keen on education?'

'That would be an understatement.'

'Do they still live in Caernarfon?'

'No. They died about two years ago,' she replied.

'I'm sorry.'

'Thank you.'

There was a silence.

'You were about to tell me why you left such a glamorous life to take over a book shop in Caernarfon.'

'So I was. Well, my parents were Welsh – South Wales, I'm afraid…'

'I picked that up from your voice. It is part of Wales, it still counts, you know…'

He smiled. 'I think so. But I'm not sure everyone around here would agree with you.'

'No,' she laughed, 'there are some who wouldn't.'

'We were from Cardiff. But my dad worked for the Government and they were ordered around during the War. Somehow they never made their way back to Wales. But I always wanted to come back if I could, and now seemed like as good a time as any. I thought, "If I don't do it now, when *will* I do it?" I was keeping an eye on the trade journals, and when the *Tywysog* came on the market – well, I just couldn't resist it. I know Madog is a hard act to follow…'

'Yes,' she replied, 'but someone has to, so why not you? You will get used to us in time. We are not such a bad lot.'

A group of three customers had entered the shop and were hovering.

'I mustn't keep you,' she said.

'Thank you for introducing yourself,' he replied. 'Dare I hope that you may be a regular customer?'

She smiled. 'I will be back,' she said. 'You will probably meet my brother next. I don't think he would survive without visiting the *Tywysog* at least once a week. It's almost his second home.'

'He is a keen reader, is he? Well, I suppose, with the kind of upbringing you both had, spending holidays at Foyles, you would hardly have much choice, would you?'

'My brother is Caernarfon's own self-styled intellectual,' she said. 'He will buy some books, but he will browse his way through many more, and ask endless questions, and generally make your life a misery. I'm surprised Madog didn't ban him.'

'Tell him to introduce himself,' he said.

'I will. His name is Caradog.'

They shook hands again.

'If you are interested in Glenys Gower, and you can't find anything about her in the catalogue, let me know.'

'I will.'

Trevor had begun to venture out to the local pubs for a pint after work, as part of his plan to introduce himself to his new local community. Often, he stopped for an early dinner somewhere. But on this evening, he chose to sit upstairs in the flat and subsist on beans on toast. After washing up, he opened a bottle of whisky and sat at the table in the living room, in the dim light of the single bulb which hung down, encased by a white paper light shade, from the ceiling above his head. He thought for a long time about Arianwen Prys-Jones, and did his best to write her off as a passing fancy. It had been some time since he had been involved with a woman, at any rate in any serious way, and it was not his intention to become involved now. It wasn't the right time. It's one of those things that happens, he told himself. You got talking, there was an attraction between you. But you know nothing about her. You don't even know when, or if, you will see her again. Don't make it into something it's not. It will all die away. He convinced himself for a few moments. But the trouble was, he knew otherwise.

7

IT WAS THREE DAYS later when the man approached him. It was late in the afternoon and the shop was quiet. He was tall and striking, with a trimmed black beard, and long black hair in a ponytail, held by a clip at the back of his head. He wore a casual grey jacket and black slacks with a white shirt, open at the neck. Trevor had noticed him immediately when he entered and had seen him make his way upstairs, where he had remained for almost an hour. When he came back downstairs he walked across to the desk.

'You met my sister the other day,' he said.

Trevor stood. 'You would be Caradog, then?'

'I would indeed.'

They shook hands.

'It's Trevor, isn't it?'

'Trevor Hughes.'

'I'm glad you're here,' Caradog said. 'I wouldn't have wanted to see the *Tywysog* close. It's been too important to Caernarfon for too many years. We are grateful to you for keeping it going.'

'Even though I've come from England?'

Caradog laughed.

'Yes, despite that. You're a Welsh man, and that's all that matters. I hope we locals haven't been too unkind to you.'

'No, not at all. You have made me feel quite at home.'

He gestured to Caradog to sit at the side of his desk, and sat himself.

'Tell me. Do you really think the *Tywysog* would have closed if I hadn't come along?'

Caradog shrugged. 'I don't know. It might have. I suppose Madog would have found someone to buy it. It's hard to imagine him walking away otherwise. But it's a strange way of life running a small book shop in North Wales, and it wouldn't be to everyone's taste. I can't think of anyone round here who would want it.'

'I'm surprised you didn't think about it yourself,' Trevor said. 'Arianwen explained about the childhood visits to Foyles. She said you were a regular visitor here during Madog's time. You must like books a great deal.'

'Very true,' Caradog smiled. 'But I like to *read* books. I'm not sure I want to sell them, and I'm certainly not sure I have the kind of head for business you need to keep a place like this going.'

He paused.

'I probably shouldn't have said that. It's none of my business. But I know about the turnover and all the rest of it. Madog wasn't any good at keeping secrets.'

'There is no need for secrets,' Trevor replied. 'I know the *Tywysog* is not going to make me rich. That's true of any small book shop. I learned enough about the trade at Foyles to know that. Even the big ones have to be careful these days. Small ones are always balanced on the knife edge. But this is a good shop. There is no reason why it shouldn't do well.'

'I'm sure it's in good hands,' Caradog said. 'The main thing is to have someone who will love the place just as much as Madog.'

He looked at his watch.

'You'll be thinking of closing up soon, I daresay.'

'I'm in no hurry,' Trevor replied. 'Take your time. If you want to go back upstairs, that's fine.'

'No. I'll get out of your way. But look, I'm going around the corner for a pint or two. Why don't you join me when you've locked up?'

Trevor nodded. 'Thank you. I'd be pleased to. Where will you be?'

'The Four Alls, in Hole in the Wall Street.'

'I know it,' Trevor said. 'I'll see you in about fifteen minutes.'

'Whenever you're ready,' Caradog replied.

Trevor locked up as the last lingering customer left, and made his way the short distance to the Four Alls, walking to the end of Palace Street, emerging into the illuminated view of the Castle, then turning left into Hole in the Wall Street, dark and narrow, barely wider than an alleyway. The Four Alls was on the left, a short distance down the street. The pub had low ceilings and was dimly lit. It was not crowded, but in the smoky atmosphere it was almost half a minute before Trevor's eyes adjusted sufficiently to enable him to see Caradog seated at a corner table on the far side of the bar. He had a pint in front of him. Trevor bought one for himself, before walking over to join him. Caradog raised his glass as he sat down.

'To the *Tywysog* and to Madog,' he toasted.

'Indeed,' Trevor replied, clinking his glass against Caradog's. 'The *Tywysog* and Madog. May they live for ever.'

They both drank.

'So, you're living in the flat, are you?' Caradog asked. 'Not much room, is there? Madog took me up there once or twice.'

'No. I can't stay there for ever. But it's a start. Once I've got the hang of the shop, I will start to look around for somewhere a bit bigger.'

'I don't know why Madog didn't do that,' Caradog mused, 'especially being with Rhiannon. It was bad enough for one, but for two… well I can't imagine it. Not that she ever complained. Perhaps if she had, he would have done something about it. But anyway, that's Madog for you. He's a strange fellow.'

'Where do you live?'

'Arianwen and I still live in our family home in Pretoria Terrace, just outside the city walls, past the Black Boy,' Caradog replied. 'Did she tell you that our parents are dead?'

'Yes. I'm sorry.'

'Thank you. It was a huge loss to both of us. Having the house is some comfort, but we still miss them. The house is more than big enough for us, fortunately. One of these days, no doubt, Arianwen will get married and we will probably sell it then. But we shall see.'

'You might even get married yourself,' Trevor smiled.

'No one would have me,' Caradog replied. 'I'm too immersed in my books and thoughts. I would drive a woman mad. I drive Arianwen mad at times, as it is, but she puts up with me, fair play to her. But she has to, if I'm her brother, doesn't she?'

They laughed together. Trevor took a long drink from his glass and replaced it on the table. He leaned forward confidentially.

'Caradog, listen, can I ask you about something that's bothering me?'

'Of course.'

'I take it you have been down to the basement in the *Tywysog* at some point?'

'Why would you assume that?'

Caradog picked up his glass and drank. He then held the glass close to this chest. Trevor waited silently. Eventually, Caradog replied.

'Yes, I have been in the basement. Madog took me down there several times. What's the problem? Damp getting to the books? Woodworm in the bookcases? Wouldn't surprise me at all.'

Trevor swirled the remains of his beer around in the glass for some seconds.

'Caradog, I'm talking about the materials Madog had stored down there. Look, so that you know where I stand, I have no problem with books on any subject, whether it's politics or anything else. I'm against censorship. The public should have access to all shades of opinion, however controversial. What else are book shops and libraries for? In fact, most of the stuff down there I would be happy to have on display upstairs in the shop itself. That's what we would do at Foyles. I can't see any reason to keep it hidden away in the basement.'

Caradog had not moved. 'Fair enough,' he said.

'But there are some materials down there which are different. They are different not just because they are controversial, but because there may be a question of whether it is even legal to have them at all. I don't know. I'm not a lawyer, but I'm concerned about it.'

'We have one or two decent solicitors in town,' Caradog said. 'Why don't you ask them?'

'I'm sure you do, and I can find them for myself. The reason I'm asking you is that Madog had these materials locked away in the cabinet in the basement. I assume he had a reason for doing that. I think it means that he sometimes had customers who were interested in seeing those materials discreetly.'

Caradog shrugged.

'Perhaps he did. What does that have to do with me?'

'Nothing. But there is obviously a chance that the same customers may contact me, now that Madog is gone, and I want to know what to do about it, how to deal with it, if they turn up one day and ask me to let them loose in the basement. You were a regular visitor to the *Tywysog*, and you knew Madog as well as anyone. It occurred to me that you might be able to give me some hints.'

Caradog drained his glass.

'I seem to need another pint,' he said.

8

THE BAR WAS BUSIER now, and it took Trevor several minutes to buy two more pints and return to the table. Caradog was seated in exactly the same pose, as if he had not moved at all.

'There are some things which are not to be talked about in the pub,' he said, acknowledging the pint with a nod. 'Besides, I'm expecting someone to meet me here. He's coming to supper at the house. You should come as well. It will give us the chance to talk.'

'And your friend?'

Caradog smiled. 'Dai Bach? No need to worry about him. He's heard me talk about such things many times before.'

'All right,' Trevor replied. 'Thank you. As long as I'm not imposing. Are you sure Arianwen won't mind?'

'She won't mind. There is always room for one more. And, if I'm not mistaken, here's the boy himself now.'

The boy himself was a short, heavily built man, probably mid-to-late twenties like Caradog, Trevor thought, but with chubbier cheeks and younger looking, wearing an off-the-peg brown suit, a blue shirt open at the neck, and a brown and yellow tie hanging loosely down below the top buttonhole. He had an unruly mop of black hair, and his chin showed signs of a dark late afternoon stubble. He was carrying a pint, expertly, no danger of spilling even a drop.

'I saw you were both all right,' he said, 'so I just got one for myself.'

'Quite right,' Caradog said. 'Dai, this is Trevor Hughes. He's just taken over the *Tywysog* from Madog.'

'Nice to meet you,' Dai Bach said. 'I've heard a lot about you, of course.'

'This is Dai Bach.'

They shook hands.

'Good to meet you too,' Trevor said.

'Dafydd Prosser I am, really,' Dai said, 'but Dai Bach they call me. It's because of my slight, lithe build, see.'

They laughed.

'I will try to remember,' Trevor said.

'So, how is it going at the *Tywysog*?' Dai asked. 'It's hard to believe that Madog is gone. I remember him there from when I was a little mite.'

'It's early days,' Trevor replied. 'Everybody is being very nice to me. We shall see.'

'I haven't been in there as often as I used to, lately. I live in Bangor, see. I teach chemistry there, Menai Strait Grammar School.'

'That must be a challenge,' Trevor smiled.

'You can say that again. I spend most of my time trying to make sure the little bastards don't blow the bloody school to smithereens. You can't turn your back for a minute when they're in the lab. If the parents had any idea how many dangerous chemicals their children have access to, I don't think they would allow them to take chemistry, or even come to school.'

'He coaches the under-15 rugby team, as well,' Caradog said.

Dai Bach laughed. 'I'm not sure "coach" is the right word. Stand on the touch line and swear at them, mostly, that's what I do. I can't run around as much as I used to. I'm past my playing days now. I used to be a tight-head prop, though, in my day, and I could give as good as I got.'

'Difficult position, tight-head,' Trevor commented.

'Did you play?'

'Inside centre for my school, not that I made much impression. But tight-head is another story. That's a very physical position. You don't come out of that without a few cuts and bruises, do you?'

'It's the worst of all, man,' Dai agreed.

'What kind of level did you play?'

'I played a few games for the university when I was at Aberystwyth, and I've played a few for the club here, but I'm a bit past my prime now. Put on a bit too much weight, see, a few too many pints.'

'I bet you could still make a loose-head's life a misery.'

Dai smiled happily. 'Aye, I bet I bloody could, too.'

'You'd need to knock off the beer for a week or two,' Caradog said. 'He needs a wife to take charge of him, keep him under control.'

'Aye,' Dai said. 'Perhaps I do. Anyway, I won't ever pull on the red jersey myself, I've resigned myself to that now. But I'm always there at the Arms Park for the home games, and I can still give the under-15s a few tips.'

'I'm sure you can,' Trevor smiled.

'Come on,' Caradog said, finishing his pint. 'Drink up. We should go. We don't want to keep supper waiting. Trevor is coming home with us.'

'Right you are, then,' Dai Bach said.

9

SHE WAS GENUINELY PLEASED to see him. Trevor noticed that at once. He made an apology for taking her by surprise, but she waved it aside. She had made a lamb stew, and she always made enough to have some left over. Caradog brought Dai Bach home often enough without warning, she explained, and she was used to having to cook for at least one more than expected.

The house on *Rhês Pretoria* – Pretoria Terrace – was the last in a row of terraced houses. Pretoria Terrace itself was just outside the town wall, a comfortable five-minute stroll from the *Tywysog*. It was set above the main road leading from the town to Victoria Dock, and each of the well-kept houses had a small garden in front, on an incline leading down to the road. He noticed that the rooms seemed heavy in tone, dark wallpapers, dimly lit by floor lamps covered with grey shades with tassels, and cumbersome old furniture. On the mantelpiece stood china figurines, a motley collection of people and animals with no obvious theme. A Welsh grandmother clock, eighteenth century by John Roberts of Wrexham, gave the house its heartbeat with its soothing rhythmic tick, and chimed lightly on the hour.

'We have three bedrooms upstairs,' she said. 'This is the living and dining room, and the room at the back is my music room.'

He had heard music playing, a fugue for cello, when they had entered the house.

'Oh, was that you? Do you play cello?'

'Does she play?' Dai Bach asked. 'That's like asking Cliff Morgan whether he played rugby.'

She laughed. 'Hardly.'

'She's played for an orchestra, man. You should hear her. Marvellous, she is.'

'I played with the orchestra when I was at University at Bangor,' she said, 'and for a short while with an orchestra in Cardiff after

I graduated. But the travelling was too much. I teach now. I have my own pupils, cello and piano. They come to the house. School children, mostly, but some adults as well.'

'But do you still play?' he asked. 'Publicly, I mean?'

'Not much any more,' she replied, and he sensed a sadness in the reply. 'I play for the children's carol services and things like that, but there's not much call for it in Caernarfon.'

'I've encouraged her to audition,' Caradog said. 'We have other good orchestras in Wales. You don't have to go all the way to Cardiff. But she won't, and she's as good on the cello as anyone I've ever heard.'

'He hasn't heard many people,' she was saying in a stage whisper, smiling.

She placed Trevor on her left during supper, and he noticed that the beautiful formal Welsh in which she had spoken to him in the shop came naturally to her. If it was for his benefit, she was prepared to continue for as long as he wished. After they had eaten, she excused herself, saying that it was time for her nightly practice. After a few moments, the soft sound of scales and arpeggios on the cello, and then a suite for solo cello, percolated into the dining room. Caradog had produced a bottle of whisky.

'I will answer your question about the basement, Trevor,' Caradog said, pouring for everyone. 'But please try to understand, I may go around the houses a bit. It's not as simple as you might think.'

'Ask him the time,' Dai Bach said, 'and he will give you the history of clock-making. Born lecturer, he is. At the university he should be, not the Ancient Monuments.'

Caradog laughed indulgently.

'Take your time,' Trevor said, smiling.

Caradog finished his pouring of whisky.

'Nationalism in Wales,' he began, 'is a unique creature. It is very different from nationalism elsewhere. Take Ireland, for example. Ireland is a divided nation. So nationalism in Ireland has a tangible goal – the uniting, or re-uniting of the country.'

'A rather unlikely one,' Trevor suggested.

'Do you think so? The Irish Free State was a compromise, a temporary solution at best. It got the British Government out of a difficulty at the time, but it was no basis for a permanent solution. The Government can never be quite sure how far the Free State supports nationalists in the Six Counties, or how far they would go in that support if push came to shove. That was all the doing of our local MP, as you know – dear old David Lloyd George. Not his finest hour.'

They were sitting close together at the end of the table by the front window, Caradog at the top of the table, Dai Bach to his right and Trevor to his left. Caradog had placed the open bottle in the middle between them.

'There is the religious question, too, of course. I don't see any permanent solution until someone finds a way to make the Catholics and Protestants at least tolerate each other.'

'I don't think they'll ever do that,' Dai Bach observed, with a shake of his head. 'Too extreme about it, they are, that's the problem. No sense of compromise about them at all.'

'Then you have the social structure. The English have spent centuries taking land away from the Catholics and giving it to the Protestants, so the Protestants see themselves as a different social class, and look down on the Catholics accordingly.'

Trevor smiled. 'The legacy of Oliver Cromwell.'

'It started long before Cromwell,' Caradog replied. 'The only Englishman ever to be Pope – Adrian, his name was – purported to give Ireland to the English 500 years or more before Cromwell, and that shaped the English attitude. The idea that England owned Ireland lock, stock and barrel, was firmly entrenched long before Cromwell. No, it's an historic grievance, and from time to time it spills over into violence. It has before, and it will again.'

He poured himself another large glass of whisky and pushed the bottle across the table to Dai Bach.

'But my point is that Wales is different. We are not a divided nation, and there is no religious divide between us and the English. We have an historic grievance, of course. Edward I invaded our country and annexed England in the thirteenth century, and ever since then Wales has been part of England, politically speaking.'

'He bloody deceived us too,' Dai Bach jumped in. 'Told us that he would never make a man Prince of Wales who spoke English, didn't he? Then he shows off his infant son at our own Castle here in Caernarfon, before he's old enough to speak any language at all, and says, "Look, here's your Prince. I kept my word. He doesn't speak a word of English." He didn't speak a word of anything. In our own castle, right under our bloody noses. Duplicitous bastard.'

Caradog smiled tolerantly.

'Yes, Dai Bach, as you say: a duplicitous bastard. But he was also a powerful bastard, and there was nothing we could do to stop him. Much later, there was Owain Glyndŵr.'

'Aye, we had a leader in those days,' Dai Bach said.

'Yes,' Caradog agreed. 'But what you have to understand about Glyndŵr is that he didn't set out to be a rebel.'

He paused to refill his glass.

'He was a country gentleman, a prosperous farmer, and a soldier who had served in an English army. He had no enmity towards the English. He lived among the English. He had English family. He even went to London to study at the Inns of Court. I don't think he wanted conflict. But his blood was his undoing, you see. He had the blood of the two princely houses in his veins – Gwynedd and Powys. He was a lightning rod. There were those who did want conflict, and Glyndŵr was forced into the role of leader because of who he was, and what he represented. Once his hand was forced, he did his best to throw off the English yoke. To no avail. Henry IV was too strong for him, just as Edward I had been too strong for us in his day. But anyway… since then we have never tried to take up arms, and now there has been so much inter-marriage, so much day-to-day commerce, so many Welsh men like Lloyd George taking up important positions in public life, that people don't even think about it. We have become one country.'

Trevor smiled.

'And the basement?'

Caradog returned the smile. 'I'm coming to the basement. I told you we would go round the houses, but I am coming to it.'

It had started to rain earlier. The rain was beating more persistently on the windows now. Caradog turned round briefly, looked out of the window, and turned back.

'The fact that there has been no violence in Wales in modern times doesn't mean that there is no Welsh nationalism. But the roots of Welsh nationalism have never been in political independence. If you look back to 1925, when Plaid Cymru was founded, they weren't concerned with that. They were concerned with preserving the language, cultural questions. They knew that it's cultural independence that makes sense for Wales.'

'Plaid Cymru backs political independence now,' Trevor pointed out.

'Yes, now they do, and there have always been those who have advocated it. But they know it's not going to happen – not unless there is a shake-up of Great Britain as a whole, and there's no sign of that. On the other hand, they also know that the survival of the language, the survival of our culture, is possible. That's what Madog always believed.'

The whisky bottle made another circuit.

'That is what the *Tywysog* has always been about. Madog believed that if the language and culture are to survive, two things have to happen. One, our language, literature and history must be taught in our schools, and two, there must be book shops and libraries which make them available to the people. He saw the *Tywysog* as part of that.'

'All right, I see that,' Trevor said. 'But, as I said before, most of the stuff Madog had in the basement ought to be upstairs on public display. I mean, if you want to reach the people, why not have it out on the shelves, where the people can see it? That's what I would do. In fact, that's what I'm going to do. I'm not sure quite where I will put it all. I may have to squeeze another bookcase in upstairs somehow, but that's just a detail.'

He paused.

'But the other stuff…'

'The other stuff is there,' Caradog said, 'because there are some people who haven't totally rejected the idea of armed resistance.'

There was a silence for some time.

'Bunch of bloody comedians, most of them, if you ask me,' Dai Bach said. 'No idea what they're doing. Bloody fools.'

'Bloody fools they may be,' Caradog replied, 'but they have to be reckoned with. Madog knew that. Every once in a while, one or two of them would come into the *Tywysog* and start asking for materials – the kind of materials that would be useful for violent resistance. Madog had no interest in getting that kind of material for them and he had no way of getting his hands on it even if he wanted to. But after a while, something rather strange happened. People started coming in, not to buy, but to *donate* materials.'

Trevor raised his eyebrows.

'You've seen it for yourself. Some of it is idiotic nationalist ranting. Some of it is smuggled military output – there have always been members of the military with nationalist sympathies. Some of it is – well, God only knows where it comes from – but it gives home-made designs for bombs.'

'You're saying they *brought* this stuff *to* Madog?' Trevor asked.

'Exactly. They asked Madog to store it for them, and he did. And no doubt other people would come in from time to time and look at it. Perhaps he shouldn't have done it, but he did. Perhaps he was afraid of them, or perhaps he agreed against his better judgement. Or perhaps there is a part of Madog that believes that the day may come when the culture is so threatened that violence becomes justifiable, or even inevitable. I don't know the answer to that, Trevor. I'm speculating. But that was what happened.'

'So, the *Tywysog* became an information exchange, as well as a book shop?'

'Yes, that's one way of putting it. And now you have to decide what to do with it all, because it is not going to go away, and neither are the people who brought it.'

'He might have warned me,' Trevor mused.

'He may have thought you would run a mile, and the deal would fall through, if he did. In any case, you were bound to find out for yourself at some point. I'm glad you have had the sense to ask me before one of them turns up at the shop one fine day.'

'I could just make a bonfire of it all,' Trevor suggested. 'Then, when the nationalists come calling, I can just say I have no idea what they are talking about.'

'That would be one way,' Caradog agreed. 'But whatever you do, don't forget one important thing. The urge to resort to violence is getting stronger, not weaker. It's going to become an issue.'

'Look around you, Trevor. We're in the sixties now. We've stopped looking backwards to the War, and we've started to look forward to the kind of world we want to inhabit in the future. The War was a great leveller. A lot of people who were ignored and looked down on and discriminated against before the War suddenly became indispensable to the War effort, and now it's over, those people want recognition. They want the rights they were denied before their country needed them. It was a fight they postponed in the interests of winning the War. But how long do you think black people in America will put up with being treated as second class citizens now? And in Europe, the students – the new generation of students who weren't part of the War and who resent the political system that could inflict two world wars on their continent, and want to bring it down – what about them? They are the people you really need to watch, if you're the government. They're the ones with new visions, who will carry the fight forward. They have causes of their own, and some of those causes are to do with changing the political landscape forever, and some of that landscape will have to do with nationalism.'

'Oh. Come on,' Trevor replied. 'Students are always protesting about something or other. It's a right of passage for students to give the authorities a hard time. Then they graduate and join the club, as we all do. It's a fad; it will pass, like everything else.'

'Will it? I'm not sure. I see a new desire to recreate the world in their own image, a new willingness to embrace political protest, and even political violence, as a means to an end. America certainly won't be able to escape it, but neither will Europe and neither will Britain. Ireland has unfinished business, and so does Wales. Wales will come under the same pressure, which means that eventually we will all have to decide where we stand. Just like Owain Glyndŵr.'

As Trevor stood to leave, he heard the dying notes, sweet and confident, of the piece which marked the end of Arianwen's practice. She left the music room and came into the hall just as he was putting on his coat. She saw him to the door, pressing an umbrella into his hand against the pouring rain. As he left, she kissed him on the cheek.

10

'THERE IS A WELSH custom,' she said, without raising her head from his chest, 'according to which women are just as entitled to propose marriage to men as men are to women.'

'Really?' he replied, also without moving. 'I never knew that.'

'Oh, yes. It goes back to the laws of Hywel Dda, so it's many centuries old. Under Hywel Dda men and women were equal, or at least, women had many more rights than they do now.'

'No wonder Welsh women are so forward,' he smiled.

They had first made love at the house on a cold night earlier in the year, in March, when Caradog and Dai Bach were away, attending a meeting of Plaid Cymru supporters in Carmarthen. The meeting was expected to end late, and they had arranged to stay away overnight. By that time, Trevor had become a friend of the family and a regular visitor to Pretoria Terrace. Often he came for dinner, but sometimes he would drop in just to listen when she played her cello in the evening. Sitting in an armchair, closing his eyes, and allowing the smooth tones of her music to wash over him, he could go far away in his mind to a place where the stresses of the day no longer bothered him. Sometimes, he was so far away that he did not even realise she had finished playing; she would come and touch him on the shoulder, laughingly accusing him of falling asleep during her recital, although to Trevor, it did not feel like sleep.

He started to take her out, at first for a meal or a drink, or to see a film locally, but then to other events, classical concerts in Bangor and further afield. But that night in March was a simple supper on a work night, and by that evening, the friendly kisses at the end of their times together had taken effect, and there was no doubt in either of their minds that they would make love. It was simply that there was no reason to delay it any longer. Yet he still felt nervous as they kissed at the bottom of the stairs.

'What if Caradog comes back tonight instead of staying over in Carmarthen?' he asked, to give voice to the nervousness.

'What if he does?' she countered. 'Caradog is my brother, not my guardian.'

They went upstairs together, hand in hand.

After that night they were open with everyone. Often, she came to stay with him in the flat above the *Tywysog*, and if Caradog had any reservations about their relationship, he did not express them.

'Have you thought about what marriage will mean?' he asked.

'Marriage generally, or marriage to you?'

'Both.'

She considered.

'I've often thought about marriage in the abstract,' she replied, 'as an idea. But you can't think about it the way it really is until you meet someone you want to marry.'

'So, you've thought about marriage to me?'

'Of course.'

'What have you thought?'

She smiled. 'I have thought that when two people feel about each other as we do, they are already married. The ceremony and the festivities are for the benefit of others, so that they know about it, and can celebrate it too. I don't think it changes anything between the people who are getting married.'

He sat up in bed.

'Arianwen, what if we get married and you find you don't really know me, that I am really someone else?'

'We are all someone else,' she replied.

They were married in April 1963 and, after enduring the cramped conditions of the flat above the *Tywysog* for some time, they went to live in an old house in *Penrallt Isaf*. Their son, Harri, was born in May 1965.

11

ONCE THE NEW YEAR festivities had subsided, Trevor re-opened the *Tywysog* to begin another year of its life. He had enough experience by now to know that business would not be particularly brisk until people had convinced themselves that the holiday period was finally over, and had resigned themselves to resuming their daily routines. He was a part of the daily life of Caernarfon now. People still remembered Madog, but Trevor's presence as the owner of the *Tywysog* was now accepted without rancour. It had required a lengthy diplomatic struggle, but the struggle had paid off. The time for curiosity was over, and his English past had merged into his new Caernarfon identity. It was noted that he was not above attending rallies in support of Welsh causes, and that he had expressed a cautious support for Plaid Cymru, and these things had gone down well. As had his marriage. Arianwen and Caradog were liked and respected in Caernarfon, for their own sake and for the sake of their parents, who had had many friends in the town.

Trevor was by no means as religious as Madog about staying open until 6 o'clock when business was slow, and at just after five on this evening, as he watched the wind and rain pound the windows and the street outside, he had decided to call it a day. But as he was reaching for his jacket and keys, he looked up to see two men approaching the door of the shop. They were tightly bundled up against the weather, but he knew them at once by their size and gait. He opened the door and beckoned them inside.

'You look like a couple of drowned rats,' Trevor said. 'Take your coats off. Hang them up by the door.'

'It's the flood, man,' Dai Bach said, struggling to extricate himself from his sodden raincoat. 'It's the bloody biblical flood, I tell you. It's a judgment on us, aye. It's going to rain for forty days and forty nights, and we will all be swept away. God, I'm soaked.'

They shook hands warmly.

'How's Harri?'

'Doing very well, Dai, thank you.'

'He's a good boy. I can't get over how well he speaks in Welsh for his age. I enjoy just listening to him talk and, as a teacher, that's not something I say about children every day. A bard he will be by the time he's ten, aye.'

Trevor smiled.

'He gets that from Arianwen. But it helps that we are keeping him on the one language for now. We both feel he should have a solid start with Welsh at home. He will have plenty of time to learn English once he starts school.'

He took Caradog's heavy coat and draped it over the top of the tree-like coat rack which stood in the corner behind the door.

'What are you two doing out in this weather? Do you want a cup of tea?'

'Aye, that would go down a treat,' Dai replied.

'Yes, please,' Caradog added.

Trevor walked to the tea area and put the kettle on to boil.

'We have come out because we need to talk to you,' Caradog said. 'And it's not a conversation we can have at home. But we can wait until you've closed the shop.'

'That sounds intriguing. Actually, I was just about to close up anyway. Five minutes and you would have missed me. No one is going to come out to buy books in this weather.'

He walked to the door and locked it, turning the sign from 'Open' to 'Closed'.

As the kettle approached boiling, he warmed the teapot and added three good size scoops of tea.

'Do your own milk and sugar.'

'If you don't mind, I'd prefer to talk in the basement.' Caradog said. 'You could turn the lights off in here, so that we won't be disturbed.'

Trevor looked at Caradog for some seconds.

'Yes. All right. Are we going to be some time? If so, I'll phone Arianwen to tell her I've fallen in with bad company and I may be home a bit late.'

'Yes, that would be a good idea.' Caradog said.

12

'WHAT HAPPENED TO ALL those materials Madog had locked away in the cabinet when you took over?' Caradog asked. 'Are they still here?'

There were only two old, unstable chairs in the basement, so they were leaning against the bookcases in the dim light provided by four naked yellow bulbs hanging down from fixtures in the corners of the room. Trevor did not reply immediately.

'They are still in the cabinet,' he said eventually.

Caradog was also taking his time.

'It's just that you did say, at one time, that you might destroy anything you didn't want to put on display in the shop. You weren't even sure it would be legal to possess some of the materials.'

'That's right. But I never got round to doing anything about it.'

'I warned you that certain people – nationalists – might come in and ask for them.'

'Yes. I remember.'

'And did they?'

Trevor shifted uncomfortably and looked down at the floor.

'Do you mind my asking why you want to know?'

'It's because of the Investiture, man,' Dai Bach jumped in.

'*What* is because of the Investiture?'

'The harassment. And it's only going to get worse.'

Trevor shook his head. 'I'm sorry. You've lost me. What are you driving at?'

'I don't like to use the word "Investiture",' Caradog said, 'but whatever we call it, on the 1st of July the Queen is going to foist her son, another member of their Saxon Royalty, on us as our Prince.'

'I know that, Caradog,' Trevor replied. 'It's hardly news. They announced it over a year ago.'

'Yes, but now it's getting close, and they are worried because they have suddenly woken up and realised that they don't have the whole-hearted support of the people of Wales. In fact, they think that some of us may have something to say about it, or even something to do about it.'

'*Do* about it?'

'Protests, demonstrations,' Dai Bach interjected, 'or even some direct action to prevent it from going ahead.'

'Well, of course there will be protests,' Trevor agreed. 'But the police are used to dealing with things like that. What is there to get excited about?'

Caradog paused again.

'The word is,' he said, 'that they have already placed people from MI5, people from Special Branch, here in Caernarfon.'

Trevor laughed.

'Oh, for God's sake.'

'What? You don't think they would do that?'

'It seems a bit far-fetched, if you ask me. During the Investiture itself, during the week or two beforehand, yes, I'm sure security will be tight, but that's true whenever the Queen goes somewhere. So what?'

'The word is,' Caradog replied, 'that they have people in place already, to try to ferret out anyone who may be planning something more than your basic peaceful protest, and then infiltrate them, and neutralise them.'

'If they do discover anyone planning anything,' Dai Bach added, 'they will arrest them on some charge or other and even put them on trial, to keep them out of the way.'

Trevor laughed again. 'Where are you getting this from?'

'Contacts,' Caradog replied.

'Contacts. And you don't think these contacts may be just a little bit paranoid?'

'No, I don't,' Caradog said firmly.

'They have already arrested a few people,' Dai Bach continued. 'Public order charges, or some such nonsense. Some of them are supposed to go on trial in Swansea, and they say it could be a long trial. It could even last until after the Investiture. Now, there's a coincidence for you.'

'All right,' Trevor said. 'Let's assume for the sake of argument that you're right. Why are you telling me this? What do you want me to do about it?'

'We don't want you to be caught in possession of the stuff you've got in there,' Caradog replied, nodding in the direction of the cabinet.

Trevor looked up sharply. He did not reply immediately.

'You think they might arrest *me*?' he asked, after some time.

'No, probably not,' Caradog replied. 'I think it is more likely they would see you as a source of information. They know that the *Tywysog* is a gathering place for Welsh-speaking intellectuals, and they know that the people likely to cause the most serious trouble are Welsh-speaking intellectuals. So I don't think they would want to close you down. But I would expect them to be very interested in who comes and goes here, and I would be very surprised if they don't stop by for a chat once every so often.'

'I see,' Trevor replied thoughtfully.

'Which is why we are interested in who may have been coming to ask about the materials in the basement. They may not have been who you thought they were.'

'And we wouldn't want them to catch you with that stuff, would we?' Dai Bach said. 'You might have a bit of explaining to do, like.'

Trevor ran his hands through his hair.

'I've only had two or three approaches in all these years,' he said. 'Two of them were definitely FWA, Free Wales Army.'

'How do you know that?' Dai Bach asked.

Trevor smiled. 'They might just as well have been wearing badges with FWA on them. They make no secret about it. They strut around as if they own the place, and you get the impression they have no sense of basic discretion, let alone security.'

Caradog laughed. 'You're absolutely right. The police don't have to worry about the FWA. If they ever get organised enough to do anything, they will probably call a press conference, or put a notice in the *Western Mail*, just to make sure everybody knows where and when it will happen.'

'The third time,' Trevor continued, 'was two or three months ago, two far more serious gentlemen. I thought they were probably with the Movement, the *Mudiad*. They could have been *Cymdeithas*, the Language Society, but they have already announced plans for peaceful protests, haven't they?'

'That's not necessarily the whole story, though,' Dai Bach said.

'What did they ask you?' Caradog asked.

'They asked whether I still had any materials which Madog might have stored in the basement. It was all very cryptic. They didn't say in so many words what they were interested in, but I knew what they were talking about, and they knew that I knew.'

'What did you tell them?'

'The same thing I told the FWA, that when I took over from Madog I cleared out the basement, and that any doubtful documents, which I might get in trouble for storing, were destroyed.'

'Did that satisfy them?'

'It had to. They weren't going to force their way into the basement in broad daylight.'

'They might try at night,' Dai Bach suggested.

'Possibly,' Caradog said. 'But they would have to recruit a real professional for a job like that in the middle of town, when the premises are alarmed. That's on the assumption that they were *Mudiad*, not Special Branch or MI5.'

'You're getting me worried now,' Trevor said.

'You should be, boyo,' Dai Bach said. 'Look, forget about the *Mudiad*. Just think about the Government. The way this is going, they are going to get extremely paranoid between now and the 1st of July. They are going to start imagining that there is a threat to the Royal Family on their big day. Believe me, there is no telling what they might get up to.'

'Well, what do you think I ought to do? Perhaps it's time to do what I thought of originally, take the whole lot out and make a bonfire of them.'

'That's one approach,' Caradog replied. 'Another is that you let us take them to a place of safety.'

Trevor stared at him.

'Why would you want them?' he asked.

'Why would *you* want them? Caradog countered.

'Who says I want them?'

'Well, you haven't destroyed them,' Caradog replied. 'Have you?'

13

THERE HAD BEEN A long silence.

'Cards on the table?' Caradog asked.

'Cards on the table,' Trevor agreed.

Caradog raised his eyes to the ceiling, and took several deep breaths.

'I'm speaking to you, not only as a Welsh man, but also as my brother-in-law,' he began. 'And I hope, as a friend.'

'Of course.'

'You know where I stand on questions about Wales. I resent everything England has done to us since Edward I. But I am a realist. I know that after so many centuries of living as one country, after so many centuries of inter-marriage, of business and social connections, we can't just turn the clock back. So I have never insisted on political independence. I have no hatred for the English people, though I despise their imported Saxon Monarchy, and I don't like the way their politicians and military leaders still act as though they own most of the world.'

Dai Bach laughed. 'All those pink places on the map. I remember from being a boy at school. "We own all of this," my teacher used to say. Imagine!'

'Yes. But now we participate in government ourselves, and we have the opportunity to influence the law and the Government's policies. If Plaid Cymru wins a few more seats, we may be within reach of a substantial measure of self-government, which will look and feel almost like independence. What we have to do in the meanwhile is preserve our language and our culture intact.'

'That's what you've been saying ever since I've known you,' Trevor said.

'Yes,' Caradog agreed. 'But now I say more.'

'You mean you have changed your mind about something?'

'Yes.'

'Why? Because of the Investiture? The Queen announced that she was going to make Charles Prince of Wales over ten years ago. She announced the date at least one year ago. And it's not as though it's the first time. George V made the Duke of Windsor Prince of Wales in this very castle, here in Caernarfon, in 1911. None of this is exactly new, Caradog.'

'No, but there is Tryweryn too,' Dai Bach said.

'Tryweryn was four years ago,' Trevor said.

'Does that mean we should just forget about it?' Caradog asked.

'No. Of course not. Look… what I'm trying to say…'

'Trevor, listen to me. It was Tryweryn that led to the only serious armed resistance we've ever had. It wasn't the Investiture of the Duke of Windsor, or anything else. It was Tryweryn that gave birth to the *Mudiad Amddiffyn Cymru*, the Movement for the Defence of Wales.'

'There's some serious people for you,' Dai Bach said, shaking his head.

'They are very serious people, and in their day they did some serious things. Emyr Llewelyn Jones detonated a bomb near a transformer at the site of the dam. That was five or six years ago now. He was convicted and sent down for twelve months. On the very same day Emyr was convicted, Owain Williams and John Jones blew up a pylon, and then they were both convicted too. John Jenkins took over, and he is suspected of being responsible for the bomb at the Clywedog dam three years ago. But because of all that they have a track record. Tell me, Trevor, where does that leave the *Mudiad* today?'

'With the police keeping a careful eye on them.'

'Exactly. They know that the *Mudiad* has not forgiven them, and never will forgive them, for Tryweryn, for Capel Celyn.'

'That would explain why the *Mudiad* might pay a call on me,' Trevor suggested. 'It might explain why they are interested in what Madog had stashed away in the basement.'

He looked up.

'Is that why you want the materials? So that you can pass them on to the *Mudiad*?'

'No,' Caradog replied. 'I don't see how they can function now. They would like to do something to mark the 1st of July, I'm sure. But the Government will be watching them like hawks between now and then. They may even have infiltrated an agent. If there is going to be an effective response to the 1st of July, it will have to come from someone else.'

Trevor snorted. 'I can't think who that would be, unless you count the *Cymdeithas*, or perhaps some mavericks on the fringes of Plaid Cymru. I'm not counting the FWA.'

'Neither am I,' Caradog replied. 'With the level of surveillance there is going to be from now on, I think we can rule out anyone who is already on the Government's radar. The only possible hope of a response on the scale the *Mudiad* would have in mind is a group whose members are not on the radar – a group composed of men there is no reason whatsoever to suspect.'

'A group that is small and well-disciplined,' Dai Bach added. 'Like a well-coached rugby team.'

Trevor felt his stomach churning. He waited a few moments before he spoke.

'I still don't understand what has changed for you, Caradog', he said quietly. 'I am married to your sister, you are my friend, we see each other every other day. In God's name, why haven't you said something before?'

'I don't like to express my thoughts until they are fully formed.'

'So, now that they are fully formed, explain them to me. Because I'm not sure I like where this is going.'

Caradog was silent for some time.

'Trevor, the Government tried to portray Tryweryn as nothing more than a planning decision, an engineering project. By going through the motions of debates and public inquiries, they made it all seem so normal. It was a technical problem, no more than that. The English city of Liverpool needed a huge new reservoir to provide for its water supply. What was the solution to this technical problem? Simple. The solution was to flood an entire Welsh valley, to destroy a living Welsh village, Capel Celyn. No matter that they had to remove the village's inhabitants by force. No matter that they had to destroy their family homes. No matter that they had to destroy the valley's entire history. Who cares? It's only a few Welsh people, after all. Who are they compared to the English population of Liverpool?'

'We protested at the time,' Trevor said. 'We all did. We were at the rallies; you two, Arianwen, me. We supported Plaid Cymru. We campaigned for them and we got our first Plaid MP, as a result.'

'Yes, and Gwynfor is a good man. But he is one voice out of more than 600 at Westminster, and if they decide to flood another valley tomorrow, there will be nothing he can do about it.'

He paused.

'Tryweryn was not just another event; it was not just a political question.'

'What was it, then?'

'It was an act of rape…'

'Come on, Caradog…'

'No. That's what it was. It wasn't just another annexation of our land for the benefit of England. That would have been bad enough. But this… this was an assault on our people and our culture. More than that, it was an assault on our soul, our sense of self-worth, our identity. This was England saying: "You're ours, and we can do what we like with you, and there is nothing you can do about it". It was about our right to survive as a people.'

He paused again.

'And now, the English are sending their Saxon Queen to foist yet another false Prince on us – another act of rape against our culture. Perhaps either of those things individually, in isolation… perhaps we could look the other way, even though it would make us sick to our stomachs. But, taken together… they cross the line.'

'The line? Whose line?'

'Anyone's line who has any sense of national pride.'

'Anyone's line who has any sense of decency, man,' Dai Bach added.

'And… the line having been crossed…?' Trevor asked.

'The line having been crossed,' Caradog replied, 'the situation calls for a response. I can't rely on the *Mudiad* to make that response for me, not any more, and in any case, I have no right to rely on them. It is something every Welsh man has to decide for himself, but I see myself as having no choice. I have to do something.'

'But we are four years on since Tryweryn, Caradog,' Trevor pointed out. 'Why this sudden change of heart now?'

'It's personal,' Caradog replied quietly. 'I'm not sure you will understand.'

14

'TRY ME,' TREVOR SAID.

Caradog hesitated.

'Trevor, Capel Celyn was our home, our family home. The family had lived there for at least two hundred years. My great-grandparents had a house there. And do you know what happened?'

'Of course I know what happened. You had family who lost their home. I have met them.'

'"Lost their home?" No. That's the journalist's way of putting it. That's the sanitised way of putting it, so that no one sees the reality of it, because the reality of it is too disturbing, and it might offend someone's conscience if they actually stopped to picture it, if they actually had to think about it.'

'Caradog...'

'They treated Capel Celyn as if it were just a collection of buildings. It wasn't just a collection of buildings. It was a living community where people lived and worked, and worshipped, and celebrated. And when you talk of people losing their homes, what you mean is that some English civil servant turns up at your door one day and offers you money, and says "We need your home. We are going to flood it, flood the whole village, flood the whole bloody valley, come to that. It's in the name of progress, except it's not your progress, but never mind that, because we are offering you money, so how could any reasonable person possibly object?"'

Trevor nodded.

'You say no, at first, but they make it clear that they will turn you out, whether you say no or not, and: "If you resist too much," the civil servant says, "maybe the money will go down or even go away altogether, but don't quote me, because I'm not supposed to say that". And one day, they give the chapel one last chance to marry somebody, or bury them, to have their last service. They give you one chance to take a last look at the home your family has occupied for two hundred years. Take a few pictures as a keepsake, to show the grandchildren, they suggest. Then walk away. Go wherever you can, but don't come back here.'

He shook his head.

'It's like bringing a condemned man his last meal. It's a planned, staged execution, and you have no choice but to play the part of the condemned, and you have to pretend you are happy with their money, which you would like to take and stuff up the Government's collective arse, if you had the chance to do it.'

He was silent for a moment.

'And then you go and live wherever you can until you die of a broken heart. But the Government won't care about that, because Liverpool has its water, and all's right with the world. And who gives a damn if a few Welsh people have their lives torn apart for it?'

'I do understand, Caradog,' Trevor said. 'But you need to think carefully about taking serious decisions for personal reasons.'

'Personal or not, I don't reach such decisions lightly,' Caradog replied. He raised his voice for the first time. 'For God's sake, Trevor, you have known me long enough. Who do you think I am? Do you think I am a violent man by nature? I tell you, I have a horror of violence. I would much prefer to remain in my ivory tower, looking down on the majority of the world that doesn't speak Welsh, glorying in the unique culture of my nation. But when the enemies of my nation are so determined to destroy it, to commit cultural genocide without any remorse at all, it is my responsibility to stand up and say: "No. Enough."'

'Just like Owain Glyndŵr,' Trevor said. 'You would prefer the quiet life, but you feel yourself compelled to lead.'

'He *is* Owain Glyndŵr, man,' Dai Bach said. 'Well, his heir, anyway. Taking up his legacy, putting on his mantle, so to speak.'

'I think that those of us who stand up for Wales have the right to call ourselves the heirs of Owain Glyndŵr,' Caradog said. His outburst was over now, and he was speaking again in his usual moderate voice. 'We are the *Etifeddion Owain Glyndŵr*. It's not just a name. It is who we are, or who we have been forced to become.'

Trevor looked at Dai Bach, who was smiling happily.

'And you're a part of this, Dai, are you? You are one of the heirs of Owain Glyndŵr?'

Dai Bach stood and straightened himself to his full height.

'Aye,' he replied, 'bloody right I am. And this time we will give the Queen of England a black eye, boyo, I'm telling you.'

Trevor exploded.

'For God's sake, Dai!' he shouted. 'Do you have any idea what you are getting yourself into? This isn't a game. You're not at bloody Cardiff Arms Park watching Barry John beat England on the rugby field. You're talking about causing an explosion that might endanger the Royal Family. Do you have the faintest bloody idea what you will be up against if that happens? Do you have the faintest bloody idea what will happen to you if you get caught even thinking about something like causing explosions which could endanger the Royal Family?'

Dai Bach shrank back down a little, but still tried to look defiant.

'I understand the risks,' he protested.

'Do you indeed?'

'Causing explosions, Trevor?' Caradog said calmly. 'I don't remember saying anything about causing explosions.'

Trevor pointed a finger.

'No. Don't give me that bloody nonsense. What do you take me for, Caradog, an idiot? You come here asking about plans for making explosive devices, you tell me you're taking up where Owain Glyndŵr left off, and you don't think I can work out what the two of you are up to?'

Caradog smiled.

'No, I certainly don't take you for an idiot, Trevor. But I do take you for a Welsh man. And I don't believe for a moment that you feel any less strongly about Tryweryn, and about the 1st of July, than I do.'

Trevor rounded on him.

'Perhaps I do feel those things. But that doesn't mean I want to go around planting bombs.'

'I think you want to make a response,' Caradog replied. 'Otherwise, we wouldn't be having this conversation.'

'A response is one thing. What makes you think I would want to get mixed up in something like this?'

'Well, you kept the materials in the cabinet, didn't you?' Caradog replied gently. 'Have you ever honestly asked yourself why?'

15

'HOW IN GOD'S NAME would you do it, anyway?' Trevor asked, after a lengthy silence. By common consent, there had been an interlude to allow the atmosphere in the basement to subside. Dai Bach seemed subdued. Caradog seemed frustrated.

'You won't be able to get anywhere near the Castle. The security at the Castle, and in the town centre, will be unbelievable. Or don't you care about hitting the Castle? Is it enough to set off an explosion somewhere in town, anywhere you can, just to make a point?'

'No, it will be in the Castle,' Caradog replied.

'That's madness. It can't be done. You would be bound to get caught.'

'Not necessarily. What if I had a job there?'

'A job at the Castle?'

'Yes.'

'How are you going to get a job at the Castle?'

Caradog smiled. 'It's actually very simple. They are going to close the Castle to the public on 1 February until after 1 July, so that they can have the place to themselves to get all the work done to make it ready. As you say, there will be security in place. But who do you think is going to be *doing* the security during those four months?'

'I don't know.'

'Well, I do. The usual staff will be on duty during the day time. But they are recruiting watchmen for duty at night. I have applied.'

Trevor laughed.

'You? You've applied to be a night watchman?'

'Why not? I'm not your average night watchman, I agree. But, as it happens, I'm perfect for this particular role.'

'In what way?'

'They think it would be a good idea to have one watchman on each shift who has a detailed knowledge of the Castle and the perimeter. Actually, it is a good idea. During the daytime, there are plenty of people to ask if something goes wrong in a particular area of the Castle. They can get expert advice within minutes just by picking up the phone. But not at night. All the experts have gone home. So they want to make sure they have at least one person on site who knows what he is talking about, just in case something comes up. I work for the Inspector of Ancient Monuments for Wales. I am just what they need, and the Inspector is happy to release me for duty.'

Trevor shook his head.

'All right. Let's say you are a watchman on duty at the Castle at night. What's the plan? Would you work every night?'

'No. Four nights on, three nights off.'

'So you can't pick and choose?'

'No, I would be assigned to certain shifts, but I am sure there will be some give and take, opportunities to swap shifts with somebody if necessary. The main object would be to work on the night of 30 June, the night before the event, or as close to it as I can get. I will try to schedule that with the management. If that doesn't work, I will try to swap duty with someone else to work that night.'

'And when you are working, you would do what exactly?'

'I have to find a place where I could plant a device of some kind with a reasonable chance of it not being discovered. The only real chance is to plant it the night before in a very good hiding place.'

'Even then, they are going to have specialist teams, sniffer dogs...'

'I know. But at least, that way, I would have a chance, and I would not be implicating anyone else. It would be down to me on my own.'

'I doubt that very much,' Trevor replied.

'They can't link me to anyone in the *Mudiad* or the FWA.'

'Perhaps not, but they are not going to believe that you built a bomb on your own. You don't have the background for it.'

'The devices the *Mudiad* used were pretty crude. I think anyone with a modicum of intelligence could work it out.'

'Well, thank you very much for that, I'm sure,' Dai Bach said, with a nervous laugh.

'They won't believe you,' Trevor said. 'And where would you get the raw materials for the device, for this person with a modicum of intelligence to use?'

Caradog did not reply.

'So that's another link to someone else, isn't it?'

Again, Caradog remained silent. Trevor allowed some time to pass.

'Assuming that this hare-brained scheme could actually work,' he said at length, 'what is the goal? Are you actually intending to cause harm to members of the Royal Family, or to the guests, or to members of the public – many of whom will be Welsh? What is the goal, exactly? What do you expect to achieve?'

'The goal is to make a response,' Caradog replied. 'There is no specific intention of harming any particular person. But a response must be made.'

'That's not good enough. Your bomb maker would need to know exactly what the goal is. If all you want is to make a point, you don't want a device which would reduce the entire Castle to rubble and take most of the Royal Family with it, do you? And how do you know what size device you could hide successfully? What dimensions does your bomb maker have to work with?'

'You seem to know a few things about bombs all of a sudden, boyo,' Dai Bach said. 'How come? Been doing some reading in the basement, have you?'

'No, Dai,' Trevor replied patiently. 'I'm just asking questions any reasonable person would ask if they thought about it for five minutes, questions you should be asking if you are really thinking of doing this. And I'm not getting any answers that make sense. Do I take it that you will be building the device?'

'Why not?' Dai Bach asked petulantly. 'A chemist I am, after all. Why shouldn't I bloody build it? Don't you think I can?'

'I have no idea whether you can or not,' Trevor replied. 'But you'd better think of the possible consequences and be sure about it before you start. And you'd better make bloody sure you know what kind of device Caradog expects you to give him.'

'We will work all that out once I am in place,' Caradog said. 'I can't give you answers now. It depends on the conditions I have to work with.'

'God in Heaven,' Trevor said.

'As I said, the goal is to make a response.'

'Why? What do you think will happen if you explode a bomb at the Castle? Do you really think the English will throw their hands up and say: "All right, we give up. The Welsh have exploded a bomb. Now we have to give in to whatever demands they have"? Because, historically, that has not been the reaction of the English to the use of violence. In fact, from my knowledge of history, the reverse is true. They will dig their heels in as never before. They may take away the few things we have gained.'

'I'm sure you are right, Trevor,' Caradog replied. 'I have no illusions about the English. But I can't worry about that. I can only do what I have to do to make a response to their endless rape of Wales. As to the outcome, if there is an outcome, I can hope for nothing at all.'

He paused.

'And now, the question is: are you with us?'

'I don't even know how anyone decides to be a part of something like this,' Trevor said.

'Sometimes simply by taking over a book shop,' Caradog replied. 'Don't tell me you picked the *Tywysog* out of all the bookshops in Britain by sticking a pin in a list over a cup of coffee in your office at Foyles, because I'm afraid I won't believe you.'

Trevor turned his back on Caradog and Dai Bach. He leaned his forehead against the wall between two bookcases, his eyes closed. He remained in that posture, silent, for a long time. Caradog showed no impatience. Suddenly, Trevor slammed his hands down on the shelves of the bookcases, straightened up and turned back to face them again.

'Arianwen must be kept completely out of this,' he said. 'She must know nothing. Is that clear?'

'Agreed,' Caradog said.

'Is that *clear*?'

'Clear,' Caradog and Dai Bach replied together.

'Because if she is not kept out of it, you will answer to me – both of you.'

'We understand,' Caradog said.

Trevor looked at Dai Bach.

'You're definitely going to build it, are you?' he asked.

'I *am* a chemist,' Dai replied.

'I think there may be a bit more to it than just being a chemist.'

'I know some people we can consult, if we have to,' Caradog said.

'We should move the instructions out of the cabinet now, tonight,' Dai said. 'I will keep them at my house.'

'No,' Trevor said firmly. 'Not in your house, not in anyone's house. Find a garage for rent somewhere in Bangor, and I will take a lease on it. Call me with the landlord's number. You're going to need a workspace anyway, and it should be in Bangor, well away from Caernarfon, but definitely not at your house. As soon as you've taken possession, then we move the documents. Not before.'

He looked at Caradog. 'Do you agree?'

'Completely,' he replied.

16

March 1969

'I'VE HIT A BIT of a blank wall, see,' Dai Bach admitted.

The garage was small and cold, with off-white walls pock-marked with holes where some previous tenant had put up a shelf or hooks for tools, all of which had long since disappeared. Damp patches on the floor, which sloped downward towards the rear of the structure, suggested that the door, resting flimsily on the uneven concrete surface beneath, was powerless to keep the rainwater at bay. The garage was lit by stark tubular yellow lights which hung down from the centre of the ceiling. Trevor had seen it only once previously, on the day he rented it on a monthly cash basis from a local bar manager who had been disqualified from driving for a long time and had sold his car.

The only item of any size in the garage now was the large metal trestle table which occupied the central area. Two bright desk lamps were connected by a long extension cable to a socket on the wall. On the front section of the table were quantities of electrical wire, several pairs of pliers and screwdrivers, and a small battery-powered alarm clock with its back panel missing. The remainder of the table was covered by several sets of instructions for assembling home-made bombs, which had previously been stored in the basement cabinet at the *Tywysog*. Two smaller tables had been set up along the rear wall, on one of which were three large cardboard boxes and two metal cases containing materials and tools for use in the assembling of the device. The second table held an electric kettle, a jar of instant coffee, a bowl containing lumps of white sugar, a bottle of doubtful milk, and several unwashed cups.

'How are the ingredients?' Trevor asked.

'Fine.'

'Do you know that?'

'I know as far as I can know,' Dai Bach replied. He sounded frustrated. 'They came from a reliable source.'

Trevor looked at Caradog.

'Some friends had access to a military base some time ago, and helped themselves. This was surplus to requirements.'

'Caradog...'

'And that's all I'm going to say. Even to you, Trevor. No offence. I had to give my word. This is serious business.'

'That's fine,' Trevor said. 'But its quality is important. You're storing it in less than ideal conditions.'

'Dynamite is relatively stable,' Dai Bach said, 'as explosives go. Obviously, you have to be careful handling it, but it's not going to deteriorate and start leaking nitro-glycerine in the time it's going to be here. It comes from a military source. I'm not worried about the quality.'

'I'm worried about everything,' Trevor said.

'I am satisfied that we couldn't have done any better,' Caradog said.

Trevor nodded slowly.

'All right. So, what's the problem?'

Dai Bach waved an arm over the table.

'It's setting up the timing mechanism, see. Your basic timed detonation is easy. One clockwork alarm clock, remove the minute hand, insert a screw as a point of contact, and when the hour hand touches the screw it completes an electrical circuit, allowing current to flow from the battery; child's play, really, once you get the idea. But the maximum time you can get from that is twelve hours.'

'Not enough,' Caradog said. 'Once I've found my spot, I have to plant it as soon as I can. I need a longer delay.'

'So then,' Dai said, 'we have to think about a battery-operated clock, again ideally an alarm clock. In theory, that should give us up to 24 hours, but the instructions we have are not clear about the wiring. The best diagram is in the German booklet, but I can't understand what the instructions say. I suppose I could get a German dictionary and do my best. The English instructions are not clear at all.'

'You have to get the timing right,' Caradog said. 'Otherwise it's useless.'

'It's not useless I'm worried about, man,' Dai Bach replied. 'It's blowing myself to kingdom come I'm worried about. It's bloody dangerous to fool around with timing devices. If anything goes wrong when I put it in place with the dynamite, the whole lot could go up. I'm scared to do it, to be honest with you. I'm not sure what I'm doing.'

Trevor walked around the table and perused one of the instruction documents. He glanced over at the table.

'The general principle seems the same, whatever you are using. You have to fix it so that the timer completes the circuit.'

Dai Bach shook his head.

'Yes, thank you, Einstein. I had got that far. But a battery-operated clock is not the same as a mechanical clock. I'm sure it's easy if you've done it before. But I haven't. And then…'

He paused, seemingly reluctant to continue.

'What?' Trevor asked.

'One set of instructions says you can set the timer in such a way that after the set time, the device becomes unstable. That would mean…'

'It would detonate if someone tried to move it or tried to disarm it,' Trevor said.

'Yes. The trouble is, you need more equipment for that. I think you might need a mercury tube, and I don't know where we would find one of those, and even if I did, mercury makes the whole thing much more volatile. And whatever we assemble, I have to test it safely before Caradog tries to put it in place.'

'Well, obviously, you mustn't test anything you're not sure about,' Trevor said. 'Otherwise, I will have some explaining to do to Mr Watts about what happened to his garage. And it's no good asking me.'

'There are some people we could ask,' Caradog suggested.

'Who?' Trevor asked. 'The FWA? The *Mudiad*? You said it yourself, Caradog. We can't risk that kind of contact with all the police activity going on now. We have to stay below the radar. I'm not sure I would trust them anyway. Are they clever enough to build what Dai wants to build?'

'I wasn't thinking about them,' Caradog replied.

'Well, who, then?'

Caradog fingered the alarm clock gently.

'You remember some time ago, a few Irish lads came over and threw green paint all over the statue of the Blessed David Lloyd George?'

Trevor laughed. 'I remember. It didn't strike me as the most intelligent protest in the world, I must say. I assumed it was the result of a few too many pints on the ferry from Dublin to Holyhead.'

'It was a bit more than that,' Caradog said. 'I was watching in the *Maes* at the time. They struck me as serious people. Just out of interest, I kept an eye on them and tracked a couple of them down later in the night, and we had a couple of glasses. One of them, name of Seán, told me he was with the IRA, which we are hearing so much about now. He called himself a unit commander, or something of the kind.'

'And you don't think that was the Guinness talking?'

'It would have been the Bushmills talking if it had been anything, and no, I don't think it was that. This wasn't his first visit to Wales, Trevor. He knew his way around, and he knew some people. He had met with some of the boys from the FWA. He had much the same opinion of them as we do. Amateurs, he called them. He said he wouldn't trust them far enough to work with them.'

'Well, at least we can agree on that.'

'Yes, but he said he was open to meeting some more serious people in Wales, if there were any. He gave me a phone number. I still have it.'

There was a long silence.

'You don't know who you are dealing with,' Trevor said. 'He could be Garda, Special Branch, Army even. If he is IRA, why should he want to get involved with us? If we contact him to say we can't work out how to make an efficient timing device, and can he please help us, he's going to lump us in with the FWA. It will just reinforce his view that everyone in Wales is useless.'

'I don't think so,' Caradog replied. 'His problem with the FWA is the same one we have – it's their lack of discretion. It's security he is concerned about. I think we could convince him that we are serious about security.'

'How would you propose to do that?'

'By going to see him, not asking him to come over here, and doing it very quietly.'

'Where did he claim to be based?'

'Belfast.'

'Where, particularly?'

'West Belfast, the Falls Road.'

Trevor considered for some time.

'That's a high-profile place at the moment.'

'It would be more high-profile for us if he came over here.'

Trevor nodded.

'You're really sure you need help, Dai?'

'Aye. I'm out of my depth, man. You were right, see. I *am* just a chemist.'

'All right, Caradog. Call Seán,' Trevor said. 'See if the number is real. But don't tell him what we want over the phone…'

'Of course not…'

'And listen very carefully to what he has to say. We don't move unless we are sure we are not walking into a trap.'

She asked him later that night. She was already in bed by the time he got home.

'You've been spending a lot of time with Caradog and Dai Bach lately. You've had quite a few late nights. What on earth do you get up to, the three of you?'

'We have a few drinks,' he replied, 'and put the world to rights.'

She made a face at him.

'Actually, we are talking about the demonstrations to come before the Investiture. I'm trying to make sure they don't get out of hand. You know what Dai Bach is like after three or four pints.'

She scoffed.

'We have all been on demonstrations before, Trevor.'

'Yes, but these will be bigger.'

'We will see about that,' she said.

He laid her back down on the bed. Harri was sleeping peacefully in his bed in the small bedroom across the hall. The door was open and the sound of his gentle breathing floated into the room. She looked incredibly beautiful to him in her simple white night dress, and her hair had that wayward look it had when she had just woken up, which could drive him mad.

'I didn't understand how strongly Caradog felt about Tryweryn,' he said. 'He only told me recently.'

A sadness crossed her face.

'Yes. It was my grandparents' generation, and those who came before. Well, you've met Uncle Stan and Aunt Jenny.'

'Yes, but I never understood how personal it all was, all the time we were going to the demonstrations, all those years when we were fighting to stop them flooding the valley.'

She nodded.

'It was very hard. We tried not to make it be about us, we tried to keep it political, to oppose them as a matter of principle. But that was very hard to do. It changed Caradog, I think. It's strange how things like that can change you even when it doesn't affect you directly.'

'It's the idea that your family was violated,' Trevor suggested.

'It's the sense of being powerless,' she replied.

'What would you think?' he asked, 'if I took the two of them away for a day or two of drinking and general trouble-making, get them away from this obsession with the Investiture?'

She laughed.

'That might be a good idea. Did you have anywhere in mind?'

'I thought we might take the ferry over to Ireland,' he replied.

'You should be able to find some trouble to make there,' she said, with a smile.

She turned on to her side and settled, to go back to sleep.

'Will you bring Harri to the shop tomorrow?' he asked. 'I miss you both during the day.'

17

SEÁN RAISED HIS GLASS as a toast.

'So, welcome to West Belfast, gentlemen,' he said. 'Make yourselves comfortable. We want you to feel at home. We are going to chat for a while before we talk business. I think that's the accepted way of discourse in civilised societies, isn't it? Certainly in Ireland, and Klaus, I know that's true where you come from also.'

'We are a very polite people in Germany,' Klaus said. He was a tall, thin man wearing a black and white checked shirt and blue jeans. He wore thick black-framed glasses and his long black hair was swept back. He fidgeted constantly, twirling a lock of his hair between his fingers.

'Klaus knows the likes of Mr Baader and Miss Meinhof, you see,' Seán continued, 'so he has clearly mixed in the best of circles. We are among friends here, so there's no reason to be nervous about us, no reason not to say whatever you wish. Nothing gets back to the Royal Ulster Constabulary from the Ring of Kerry, I assure you. But we do like to know who we are dealing with before we go into too much detail. You were very hospitable towards us when we were with you in Wales, Caradog, and I appreciate that very much. But you've brought two friends with you now.'

The Ring of Kerry was a dingy pub in a side-street off the Falls Road. Miniature Republican flags decorated the bar. Hanging proudly on the walls were photographs of St Patrick's Day parades of years gone by and, in pride of place, behind the bar, a photograph of the landlord as a younger man shaking hands with Éamon de Valera outside Leinster House in Dublin. At 8 o'clock in the evening, the bar was crowded and boisterous, the air thick with tobacco smoke. It already seemed an age since they had left Caernarfon to board the overnight ferry from Holyhead to Dublin. They had little more than two hours of snatched sleep before they disembarked into the fresh early morning air. There followed the almost 100-mile trip by road to Belfast in a left-hand drive Volkswagen Beetle which had seen better days, driven by a taciturn middle-aged man called Padraig, who had been sent by Seán. Although they negotiated the border and entered Northern Ireland without any apparent incident, they found themselves looking around anxiously when they entered the city. The route to their ultimate destination in West Belfast took them through unwelcoming, and sometimes overtly hostile areas, and did nothing to lift their spirits. The city was outwardly quiet, but there was an unmistakable tension and aggression in the air which was compounded by Padraig's relentless silence. By the time they were seated in the Ring of Kerry waiting for Seán to appear, their nerves were frayed. They were questioning the wisdom of the trip, but they knew it was too late for that.

'I feel I know you already, Caradog,' Seán was saying. 'And you know what I like? The idea of a man employed by the Inspector of Ancient Monuments taking a swipe at an ancient monument. I like that a great deal. Are you sure you've no Irish blood in you, Caradog? Because there's something very Irish about that. I think James Joyce himself would have approved of that, I really do. Don't you, Klaus?'

Klaus was sitting on a stool nursing a beer, and gave no sign of having heard.

'Well, Klaus wouldn't know about that,' Seán laughed. 'I don't know whether they read James Joyce in Germany, especially if they have to do it in English. On the other hand, God help anyone who has to translate him into German, or any other language for that matter. So, what about your friends, Caradog? Dafydd, isn't it? What account do you give of yourself?'

'They call me Dai,' Dai Bach answered uncertainly. 'It's a short form of my name in Welsh.'

'Is it indeed?' Seán said. 'I'm not sure that's such a good name for someone who wants to make bombs. Dai? Sounds just the same as "die" – D.I.E. – doesn't it? Just a tiny bit pessimistic, to my way of thinking. But only if you are speaking English, of course, and you would be speaking Welsh. So, I understand, and if you are known as Dai in Wales, you shall be known as Dai in Ireland. You're a teacher of chemistry, then?'

'Yes.'

'And a philosopher like Caradog?'

'Not like Caradog, no.'

'No, well, Caradog is a thinker, you can tell that about him. He can tell you every reason a Welsh man ever had to hate the English since the dawn of time, and every reason of logic why you are justified in doing whatever you have to do to drive them out, and when he puts all of this together, it becomes a storm in your mind of hurricane force that you can't resist; you just have to lie down and let it roll over you. We have such thinkers in Ireland too, and God bless them, because someone has to remind us why we do the things we do. But I don't think that's how you got there, Dai. What makes you so anxious to harm the Queen?'

'I haven't said anything about our intentions,' Caradog said.

Seán laughed.

'Quite true, you haven't. Well, then, we will just have to try to guess, won't we? So, let me review the situation. The Queen is going to create her son Prince of Wales in July, and here you boys are in Belfast in April not liking that idea one little bit and asking for our help in making a bomb. So, let me see. What could you possibly have in mind? Come on now, Caradog, give me some credit, please. I've done one or two laps of the circuit in my time, so please don't insult my intelligence. We were getting on so well. Don't be spoiling it, now.'

Dai Bach looked at Caradog, who nodded.

'I apologise. I didn't mean to insult your intelligence. I was just being careful.'

Seán nodded. 'Very well, then. Dai, what have you to say for yourself?'

'They have raped our country,' Dai Bach replied, 'and they have taken everything they want from us for hundreds of years. No, I can't give you a lecture like Caradog, but I feel it just as much. You have Oliver Cromwell to remember England by, don't you? I don't need anybody to tell me why we have to stand up against people like that. We've had the same kind of people in Wales, I assure you. Many of them, over the centuries, and even today it goes on. They won't stop – not until they have killed our language, wiped out every last trace of our culture, and stolen as much as they can from us.'

Seán looked at him thoughtfully.

'Aye, we have had Oliver Cromwell and many others since. That's true enough, Dai. And you have had the same. And you want to do something about it. As do we. As would anyone who gave a damn about his nation.'

Seán turned towards Trevor.

'And Trevor, what account do you give of yourself?'

'I keep a book shop,' he replied.

'Do you, now?'

For the first time, Klaus seemed to spring to life. He sat up, drained his beer, and slammed his glass down on the table. He suddenly laughed out loud.

'My God, he is the most dangerous of all these Welsh men,' he said. 'Anyone can make a bomb and blow a few people up. But with a book shop you can destroy whole civilisations.'

Seán stared at Klaus for several seconds. He then started to laugh also, and eventually the laughter spread to everyone.

'Conor,' he shouted, in the direction of the barman. 'Set up another round for us, there's a good fellow. These mad Welsh men are in town. Anything can happen. It calls for a drink.'

'Klaus will take Dai into a room in the private area of the house,' Seán said. They had moved to a table away from the main throng in the bar, and were quieter now. 'He is the real expert here. I'm telling you, these Baader-Meinhof boys – and girls too – are far more advanced than we are. We ask their advice ourselves, I don't mind telling you. He will show you what you need to know.'

He leaned across the table towards Dai Bach.

'Make notes if you want, but make sure it's nothing that could be understood if you were to get yourself arrested on the way home. Nothing in writing leaves here unless Klaus and I both approve it. So listen to him very carefully and commit as much as you can to memory. Not that you're going to get arrested, of course. But we have to guard against every contingency, don't we? We are giving you some high-grade information here, state of the art, you might say.'

'What about us?' Trevor asked.

'You and Caradog can have another drink and keep me company,' Seán replied. 'You can tell me all about your book shop.'

'Have you boys thought through all the consequences of what you are doing?' Seán asked, when Klaus and Dai Bach had returned, over an hour later. 'I mean, do you understand the forces you are calling down on your heads with this?'

'We know there will be a big reaction, regardless of how far we are successful,' Caradog replied quietly.

'A big reaction? Well, that's one way of putting it, I suppose, if you like under-statement. Caradog, if you harm one hair of Her Majesty's head or one hair of Prince Charles's head, they will pursue you to the ends of the earth and they will not rest until they have destroyed you; do you understand that?'

Caradog nodded.

'They will spend any amount of money, employ whatever resources are needed, to hunt you down. Even if you don't harm them, the attempt itself will be enough. They will make sure there is no place for you to hide.'

'We are aware of the consequences,' Trevor said.

'Are you, now? Well, I'm glad to hear that. You see, Trevor, the reason I'm bringing this up is that I don't want myself or my friend Klaus being dragged into it. I don't want our names being bandied about, if you take my meaning. I have to think about the people I represent, you see, and things are getting hot enough for us in Belfast as it is. We already have enough of a British presence to worry about in our fair city, thank you, what with our Loyalist friends over in the Shankill Road and the RUC backing them up. We don't want you bringing them down on our heads in even greater numbers. So I strongly advise that you have your escape plan set in stone before you make your move.'

'I understand,' Trevor said. 'You're telling us not to come to you if things go wrong.'

'I'm saying, don't come to Belfast,' Seán replied. 'I'm not casting you adrift altogether. You are comrades in arms, after all, and I have to admire your spirit in taking on the target you are aiming at without any prior experience. I think I speak for Klaus and myself in saying that we are in awe of your ambition.'

He took a small folded piece of paper from his pocket.

'If you choose to come in the direction of Ireland, which would be a natural enough choice from Caernarfon, go to Cork and find the pub named on this piece of paper. You will have to memorise it. I'm not giving you anything in writing. There are people there who will be on the lookout and will try to steer you safely to the Continent. You won't be able to stay in Ireland. It will be too hot for you here. But these gentlemen have some experience of helping folks on their way safely. You must understand that getting into Ireland in the first place will be the real challenge. You had better build yourselves a good legend.'

After they had left, Seán and Klaus sat quietly together in the bar.

'So, did our friend Dai learn something?' Seán asked.

'Yes. But whether he will blow up the Queen or only himself cannot be predicted. The chances are about even.'

Seán laughed. 'Ah, so he is an own goal waiting to be scored, is he? Well, you can't blame yourself for that, Klaus. There is only so much any of us can do.'

They were silent for some time.

'What did you make of our book seller?'

'He is a serious man,' Klaus replied at once. 'The most serious of them. The stakes are higher for him for some reason, I think.'

18

CARADOG LIFTED THE DUFFLE bag gingerly from the trestle table and tried to sling it over his left shoulder. It still felt too heavy for him. It fell back on to the table, and all three men in the garage jumped involuntarily.

'Damn it!' Caradog said. 'Why can't you help me? I'm going to set the damn thing off.'

'No you won't,' Dai Bach replied patiently.

They had been attempting the manoeuvre for some time, and Caradog was showing signs of frayed nerves. From his first night at work as a watchman at the Castle, Caradog had made the large duffle bag part of his legend. As he arrived for work each night with the bag slung jauntily over his shoulder, its vivid design – red, yellow and black shapes on a grey background – became familiar to those on duty, and after three or four nights it became routine, nothing to be questioned or examined. It was an effective way of taking items into the Castle. But the device Dai Bach was building posed a problem.

The device would fit snugly inside the large bag with careful placement, but for stability it was housed in a heavy steel carrying case. Its weight made it difficult to lift on to the shoulder and hold there for any length of time. Caradog had begun with light items, sandwiches and magazines. Gradually, he had started practising with books, and most recently with five heavy tomes supplied by Trevor from the *Tywysog*. But the practice had not prepared him for the reality of the device. It was now ready, and the Investiture was only two days away. Two days later he would have to walk from the far end of the *Maes* to the Castle, and then to the site he had chosen to plant the device, all without giving anyone reason to suspect him. He had to master the bag, with its increased weight, and so far he was not succeeding.

'It's dynamite. I can't just throw it around.'

'I've told you, man. It's not armed. There is no way you will make the connection by accident, and you're not going to make this stuff detonate by dropping it on the table. It's stable and it's in good condition, and it's in its carrying case, so it's not going to be flopping around. You just need to concentrate on getting it up on your shoulder.'

'You jumped just as much as I did, the pair of you, when I dropped it,' Caradog said.

Dai Bach smiled. 'Aye. Well, let's not pretend we're not nervous. It's hard not to react when you see it come down. It is safe, though.'

'It doesn't *feel* safe.'

'Couldn't he just carry it like a shopping bag?' Trevor suggested.

'No. It's too heavy for that. He would be changing hands every few seconds, and with the distance he's got to cover, it would be far too obvious. Besides, he goes in every night with it over his shoulder. That's what they're expecting. He must look the same as he always does.'

'It's too heavy to be over my shoulder,' Caradog protested. 'Even when I get it up there it's almost pulling me over backwards. Besides, I don't think the bag will take the weight. It's going to fall out and smash all over the floor at the entrance to the Castle.'

'No, it's not,' Dai Bach replied. 'I've strengthened the bag. Look here, now. All the straps have stitched-in supports. It's not going to come apart that quickly. It's not much heavier than it was with those books you've been practising with.'

'It feels much heavier. It weighs a ton.'

'You should have played in the scrum for a couple of years.'

'Well, I didn't, and it feels as though I'm going to drop it.'

'That's because you're scared of dropping it. You need to throw it around a little more, get used to it, get some confidence in it. Throw it like you did when it had the books in it. Come on. Let's try it again.'

Caradog tried it again, with the same result. The bag fell back on to the table with a bang.

'Look,' Trevor said, 'why can't you help him, Dai? You are both going to be there for the handover.'

'I can help him at the handover, but not if he needs to re-adjust it on the way. The bag could start to slip off his shoulder at any moment. He's got to be ready to put it back in place. Let's try again.'

This time, Caradog threw the bag over his shoulder so violently

that it almost spun him round, and he had to fight to keep his balance.
Trevor reached out both hands to steady him. Dai Bach applauded.

'There you go, boyo. How does it feel now?'

'As if it's going to yank my shoulder out of its socket.'

'It won't. Try raising your shoulder a bit, to support the strap, like.'

Caradog took a few tentative steps.

'How do I look?' he asked.

'Like a night watchman carrying a bomb,' Dai Bach replied.

19

at 11.45. Ης.

30 June 1969, 18.30

'LET'S GO OVER IT again,' Caradog said.

'We've been through it three times already,' Dai Bach protested.

'Yes, and we are going to go through it a fourth time, because we
are not going to meet again before the event, so we need to be sure
we are all on the same page,' Caradog replied.

They had gathered at the house in Pretoria Terrace. They were
seated quietly around the dining table now, and the mood was tense.

'We are going to spend the evening separately. The police have
already started picking up people they have identified as trouble-
makers. If we are on that list, there is nothing we can do, except to
keep out of sight and hope for the best.'

'I haven't noticed anyone paying attention to me,' Dai Bach said.

'You wouldn't,' Trevor said. 'Not until it is too late.'

'I agree,' Caradog said. 'But we have been careful not to give
them a reason. I don't think I would still be working at the Castle
if they had any suspicions about me, and you two have been posing
as peaceful protesters for the last week, so if they've noticed you
at all, they should put you in that category. Hopefully, they will be
preoccupied with arresting assorted members of the FWA, and the
Mudiad, and you will pass unnoticed.'

'So Dai and I put in an appearance in the *Maes,*' Trevor said.

'Yes. The regular evening protests are dying down. Most of the
protesters are leaving town for the duration now, so I don't think a
lot will be going on there. But you should put in an appearance. Let's
say between 8 and 10. The rehearsal at the Castle should be over by
then, so there will be people around. I will be on my way to work of
course. After that...'

'After that, Dai and I go our separate ways,' Trevor said. 'I pick
Dai up in the car outside the Castle Hotel at 11.45. We drive to

Bangor, collect the device. You leave work, bringing the duffle bag with you, and meet us at the corner of New Street and Chapel Street at exactly 1.15.'

'Correct,' Caradog confirmed. 'Dai arms the device, we put it in the bag, and the rest is up to me. We go our separate ways to await developments.'

'And don't forget to wipe your fingerprints off everything you touch,' Trevor added.

'What about clearing out the garage?' Dai Bach asked.

Trevor shook his head.

'I don't want to draw attention to the garage. We can clean up any time in the next few weeks. I'm going to continue renting it for a few more months yet, as cover.'

'And you've checked the dimensions of the space where you're going to plant it?' Dai Bach asked.

'Several times,' Caradog replied.

'Well, excuse me for being anxious,' Dai Bach said. 'Better safe than sorry.'

'That's it,' Trevor said. 'We don't need to sit around all night asking the same questions and making each other even more nervous than we already are. There is no more we can do now until tonight.'

20

DAI BACH FELT COLD as he stood alone outside the Castle Hotel in the *Maes*, with his watch indicating 11.35. The evening had gone as planned so far. Caradog had left for work, the duffle bag over his shoulder, after the miserably small demonstration had ended some two hours earlier. An understanding had grown up among the protesting population that leaving Caernarfon not later than the eve of the Investiture was the only form of protest still left to them, and many had already done so. The town would be abandoned to the English for the day as a token of their disgust. Most of those who had stayed to stand in the *Maes* in the earlier part of the evening had dispersed, having made a futile attempt to make themselves heard in the Castle during the final rehearsal for the ceremony to take place the following day.

There was a strong police presence in town, but that was only to be expected. It would all die down by the time he and Trevor returned from Bangor, and they were going to do nothing to attract suspicion. Arming the bomb was the work of half a minute if he didn't get too nervous about it, if he was systematic and didn't panic, if his hands didn't shake. Caradog and Trevor would keep a look out while he did it. It would take the Devil's own bad luck for anything to go wrong up to that point. After that, it was up to Caradog and his shoulder.

Even with his protest placard beside him as a prop, Dai felt uncomfortably exposed, standing there by the entrance to the hotel. There were fewer people in the square now, but there were several police officers, a few taxi drivers who would continue work until the town centre was closed to traffic at 3 o'clock, and one or two stragglers who, for whatever reason, still had not made their way home. Increasingly, he had the feeling of being stranded centre stage in the glare of the spotlight when the rest of the cast had exited for the interval. He suddenly could no longer remember the explanation he was going to give to police for his presence, should they ask. He cursed and forced himself to concentrate. Of course, he was waiting for his friend to give him a lift home. His friend would be arriving in just a few minutes. It was almost true, as far as it went.

This thought prompted him to look at his watch again, and when he did, he saw that 11.45 had come and gone, and there was no sign of Trevor. The panic started instantly. Dai Bach had no right to criticise anyone for lack of punctuality; his own failings in that department were legendary. But not tonight. Tonight he had made an effort, and even he, Dai Bach, had arrived early. For Trevor to be late was like Big Ben being five minutes slow. It didn't happen. Trevor was precise and self-controlled. How could this be? There might have been traffic, he reasoned. At this time of night? A police check-point, perhaps? Nobody had said that was going to happen, but you never knew. Or perhaps something more prosaic? He had to stop for petrol, or his car had developed a fault. None of it seemed very likely. He had no way of contacting Caradog. There was nothing for it but to wait. Surely, Trevor would not be long.

When 11.55 had come and gone, he could not endure waiting any longer. Leaving his placard outside, he walked quickly into the hotel. Reception was quiet. Testing the steadiness of his voice, he asked the night clerk if he could use the phone, muttering an excuse about his friend having mixed up his times. The clerk agreed indifferently and returned to the football magazine he was reading. Dai dialled a number. A female voice answered.

'Arianwen, sorry to disturb you, like.'

It took her a second or two to place him at that time of night.

'Dai? Hello.'

'Hello.' He didn't really know what to say to her. He was groping his way along, word by word. 'I'm sorry to disturb you so late, but is Trevor there?'

'No. He's not back yet. I thought he was with you and Caradog.'

'He was. Caradog went to work, of course. But... no, actually, I haven't seen Trevor for a while, but he said he would pick me up in the *Maes*.'

'Oh, yes?'

'Yes. Well... the thing is, I made arrangements to stay with a friend for a day or two, but I have to collect a few things from

Bangor and bring them back here, before they close the town to traffic, you know. Trevor said he would give me a lift there and back. It wouldn't take long, you know, but I'm worried now that he might have forgotten.'

'That's not like Trevor,' she said.

'No.'

'Hang on a minute, Dai.'

She was gone for some seconds.

'Well, the car is here, so he would have to come back here first.'

She thought for a few seconds.

'Where are you, Dai?'

'Outside the Castle Hotel.'

'All right. Stay where you are. I'll come and get you myself. Give me five minutes.'

Dai Bach almost passed out. No, he wanted to scream. You can't do that. That was Trevor's one rule. Arianwen must be kept out of it. Arianwen must not know. He tried to make his voice work, tried to think of some excuse, any excuse, for refusing her offer. But she had hung up.

She was as good as her word. Five minutes later she pulled up outside the hotel, and reached across to open the front passenger door.

'Arianwen, you don't have to do this. It's late.'

'Don't be silly,' she said. 'It won't take long.' She nodded towards the rear seat. 'I had to bring his nibs, of course, but it won't do him any harm to have a night-time adventure. He might even take in all the lights on the Castle and remember them when he's older... well, he might if he was awake.'

At the sight of Harri sleeping peacefully in his car seat, Dai started to feel sick.

'Let's go back to your house,' he suggested. 'Trevor is probably back by now and wondering where the car is.'

She laughed.

'No need. I'm going to give him a good talking to when I get back, forgetting his friends. What can he have got up to?'

'I don't know,' Dai replied. 'Found a place to have a couple of drinks, I shouldn't wonder, and just put it out of his mind.'

As he said this, he was imagining Trevor in a police cell. What would that mean? Would they all be lost? Should he abort the whole plan now? He could go to his house, take an innocent suitcase, leave

the device in the garage to deal with later, return to town, send
Arianwen home with his thanks. Caradog would be beside himself,
but he could hardly blame Dai. Trevor would be the one in trouble,
when he showed up, if he showed up. But on the other hand, even
if Trevor had been arrested, it might have nothing to do with the
plan. It might have been just because he ran the *Tywysog*. The police
would be bound to assume that he had a lot of contacts. They might
not even have arrested him. They might just want to ask him about
people they couldn't find. There would be nothing Trevor could do
about it.

In any case, Caradog would be angry if Dai abandoned the plan
just because of that. If Trevor couldn't be there, Caradog would
expect Dai to use his initiative, take a taxi… 'Oh, for God's sake,' he
suddenly scolded himself. 'Why didn't I just take a taxi? I didn't have
to involve Arianwen. I could have…'

She was asking him something.

'I'm sorry. What did you say?'

She looked at him strangely.

'Where are you meeting your friend? Where does he live? Or she,
perhaps, is it?' she grinned, raising her eyebrows suggestively.

'No, he,' he replied, hearing his voice echoing in his head. 'I'm
meeting him near the *Maes*, just after 1 o'clock.'

She glanced at her watch. The grin remained, as if she didn't quite
believe him about the friend being male but wasn't going to press
him further.

'We will make it,' she said. 'We won't have traffic.'

As they entered Bangor, he directed her, not to his house, which
she knew well, but to the garage.

'How long have you had this place?' she said, pulling up outside.

'It's just for storage,' he replied. 'I've got too much stuff at home,
see, running out of storage space.'

Before she could say anything else, he jumped out of the car and
unlocked the garage door. The device was on the big trestle table,
where he had left it – in its gleaming steel carrying case, which didn't
look anything like a suitcase you would take to spend a day or two
with a friend, male or female. If Trevor had been with him, that
wouldn't matter, but… There was nothing to cover it up, nothing
to put it in. Too late to worry about that now. He would have to try
to keep her in the car. He picked it up, and looked outside. She was
sitting in her seat, turning round to look at Harri. He locked the

garage door. She saw him, but did not seem to react to the carrying case.

'The boot's open,' she called out to him.

With a sigh of relief, he opened the boot, and laid the device down carefully. There was an old green blanket lying at the back of the boot. He picked it up and threw it casually over the device. He closed the boot, and climbed into the passenger seat.

'Got everything you need?' she asked.

'I hope so,' he replied.

When they arrived back in Caernarfon he directed her into the centre of town, and asked her to stop on New Street, near the corner with Chapel Street. It was exactly 1.15 and, at that precise moment, the world as Arianwen Hughes knew it, ended. From that time all she had left to connect her with that world was a series of memories, memories of events which made no sense and which happened in lightning quick succession.

Stopping the car.

Dai Bach getting out of the car.

Dai Bach walking across Chapel Street and disappearing from view.

Two men approaching from the same direction.

Realising that one was Dai Bach.

And that the other was Caradog, carrying his brightly-coloured duffle bag.

Why is he here, not at work in the Castle?

Caradog seeing her, suddenly very agitated.

Caradog screaming at Dai Bach.

Caradog and Dai Bach walking around the car to the boot.

Where is Trevor?

Getting out of the car.

Walking to the boot.

Suddenly seeing a metallic case.

Seeing Dai Bach open it.

What the…?

Horror. A thousand questions, but no words to ask them.

Two men approaching very fast.

Shouting and screaming, horribly loud.

The two men pinning Caradog and Dai Bach to the car.

A third man approaching.

Being thrown against the car like a limp rag doll.

Pain as her head and body hit the hard metal.

Handcuffs being forced on to her wrists.

Where is Trevor?

A fourth man, very big, screaming into a radio.

'Bomb squad… Evacuate the area…!'

Dai Bach crying. 'No, it's safe. There is no danger.'

Someone screaming: 'There's a kid in the car! There's a kid in the car!'

Seeing Harri through the car window, still sleeping peacefully.

Where is Trevor?

PART 2
RHAN 2

21

GARETH MORGAN-DAVIES QC TURNED towards Sir Bernard Wesley to conclude his short speech of congratulation.

'Bernard, you have presided wisely over our Chambers for many years now and we will miss you, but our loss is the High Court's gain. You will be a glittering addition to the High Court bench, and we wish you many happy years in your new career. Amélie, we are so pleased that you are with us this evening to celebrate Bernard's elevation. I hope that, as a true French woman, and therefore, a dedicated republican, you will not be too distressed about being known as Lady Wesley. With your permission, we will still call you Amélie when you visit us, which we hope will be often.'

He held his glass up high.

'Ladies and gentlemen, I give you the newest judge of the Probate, Divorce and Admiralty Division, Mr Justice Wesley.'

The members of Chambers and their guests raised their glasses and toasted Bernard Wesley. It was a big day in the life of the barristers' chambers at 2 Wessex Buildings. Bernard Wesley had been Head of Chambers for more than fifteen years, ever since his predecessor, Sir Duncan Furnival, had left on the occasion of his own appointment to the bench. Now Gareth Morgan-Davies, in silk for only three years, would take over the helm. By the standards of the Temple it was early in his career to assume such a huge responsibility, even for a set of chambers which deliberately kept itself small in number. Gareth had a substantial practice in serious criminal cases, and was greatly respected by judges, solicitors, and the members of Chambers alike. There was no reason to think that Chambers would not continue to thrive under his leadership. But such mercifully rare days always represented a time of transition, and for a profession which loved stability and continuity, it was inevitably a nervous time.

'Thank you, Gareth,' Bernard replied. 'I have enjoyed every moment as Head of Chambers, but it is time for me to move on. I do so in the knowledge that Chambers is in good hands. I do hope you will invite me back for Chambers parties and the odd dinner if I won't be in the way. And now, I will do what every outgoing Head of Chambers ought to do, namely, to shut up and let you enjoy your champagne without having to listen to any more speeches. Let me just add that Amélie and I are grateful for your friendship, for your understanding and support over the years, and for your kind hospitality this evening. I ask you to raise your glasses again and toast Chambers.'

The toasts completed, those assembled rushed to refill their glasses and sample the *hors d'oeuvres* and sandwiches.

Ben Schroeder had been a member of Chambers for more than six years. He was a good-looking man, with thick black hair, and dark brown eyes set rather deep in his face because of his prominent cheek bones. He was almost six feet in height, and his naturally thin figure was showing the first signs of filling out in response to his body's age. As always, Ben wore an immaculately tailored three-piece suit, dark grey with the lightest of white pin-stripes, a thin gold pocket watch attached to a gold chain threaded through the middle button hole of his waistcoat, and a fluted white handkerchief in the top pocket of his jacket. As a young Jewish man from the East End of London, he had not found it easy to gain a place in the most waspish and conservative of professions, but he had already played his part in a number of important, high-profile cases as junior to both Bernard and Gareth, and his long-standing self doubt had now receded. He was making his mark at the Bar.

'Many congratulations again, Bernard,' Ben said. 'Don't give us too hard a time when we appear before you, will you?'

'As long as you behave yourselves,' Bernard smiled.

Ben kissed Amélie lightly on both cheeks.

'*Félicitations*, Lady Wesley.'

'*Mais non, non*. Lady Wesley is still Amélie, and she will be continuing her work at the university as usual.'

She stepped forward.

'Jess, I am glad you could come. How are you?'

Jess was almost as tall as Ben, her hair and eyes brown and, although she dressed formally as a barrister in the mandatory dark grey suit, when she was not in court she could not resist adding touches of colour, with a bracelet of bright beads on one wrist and a multi-coloured band holding her luminous hair in place behind her head.

'Very well, Amélie, thank you.'

They hugged affectionately.

'I haven't seen you since you became Mrs Ben Schroeder, *n'est-ce pas*? It was a wonderful day.'

'More than a year ago now,' Jess replied.

'Too long,' Amélie said. 'We must get together again soon.'

'How are things going at the Bar?' Bernard asked.

'Really well,' Jess replied. 'I've been a member of chambers for about 18 months, and I'm starting to get some decent work of my own.'

'Family, mostly?'

'Yes. I leave the crime to Ben. One of us doing crime is enough.'

'It is strange how time passes so quickly,' Amélie said. 'When I first met you, you were still working for a solicitor, *n'est-ce pas*?'

'Barratt Davis,' Bernard said. 'Of course, that's what you were doing when we both first met you. The Middle Temple was giving you and Ben such a hard time about "consorting together" when Barratt was sending Ben work.'

'They called it "touting for work",' she replied. 'And if it hadn't been for you and Miles Overton talking some sense into them, it would have been disastrous for us. Thank you again for that, Bernard.'

She kissed him on the cheek.

'I'm just glad it worked out so well,' he replied.

'It was only the other day Miles Overton was appointed, wasn't it?' Ben said. 'You have scaled the Olympian Heights together.'

'Yes. Well, not quite together. I am slightly miffed that I let him beat me to it, but there it is. He will never let me live it down, you know.'

They laughed.

'Bernard, I must dash.' Mr Justice Furnival came over briskly to take his leave.

'Thank you for coming, Duncan.'

'Not at all. Always happy to call in when there is champagne on offer. Many congratulations. I couldn't be more pleased, and Chambers is in good hands with Gareth. Amélie. Schroeder. Ah, and Miss Farrar. You were in front of me the other day, weren't you?'

'Last week, judge.'

'Yes, of course. You were telling me that what the Court of Appeal said in that wretched *Staunton* case was a load of complete poppycock.'

'I hope I didn't put it quite like that, Judge.'

They laughed.

'No, of course you didn't. You put it very well. I'm only sorry I couldn't agree with you. But they outrank me, as you know, so you will have to go up there and try to persuade them, rather than me.'

Merlin was hovering quietly, but with intent.

'I am sorry to interrupt, sir,' he said to Ben. 'But can I drag you away for a moment? I need a word with you and Mr Morgan-Davies.'

'Sorry, Bernard.'

'No, it's quite all right, Ben. When your senior clerk calls, you must obey. I've known Merlin long enough to know that, haven't I, Merlin?'

'Indeed you have, Sir Bernard.'

'In any case, I see Aubrey hoving into view, so we won't be lost for conversation. Enjoy the rest of your evening.'

Merlin appeared to hesitate.

'Actually, Miss Farrar, I need you as well, if you don't mind.' He caught her look of surprise and smiled. 'I know your clerk isn't here, but perhaps I can take his place for this evening? Steven and I have known each other for a long time. I'm sure he won't mind.'

'This is all very mysterious, Merlin,' Ben said.

'All will be revealed, sir,' Merlin replied.

22

THEY GATHERED IN WHAT would still be Gareth's room for a few days, until Bernard Wesley had finally removed the last traces of his occupancy from the Head of Chambers's room and ceded it to Gareth. Barratt Davis was waiting for them, with a man Ben did not recognise. Ben knew Barratt well. He was a partner in the firm of Bourne & Davis, which sent its work in the courts to Chambers, much of it to Ben.

'I'm sorry to interrupt the party,' Barratt said. 'How is Mr Justice Wesley? I haven't seen him since the *Digby* case. He was most impressive, I must say. I would think he will be rather good on the bench.'

'I agree,' Gareth said. 'I am sure he will. And you're not interrupting at all, Barratt. What can we do for you?'

'Well, first I must introduce someone – Eifion Morris, an old friend, and a solicitor practising in Cardiff. We did our solicitors' finals together at Guildford, more years ago than either of us cares to remember. Eifion, may I introduce Mr Gareth Morgan-Davies QC, Mr Ben Schroeder, and Miss Jess Farrar of Counsel.'

'Very pleased to meet you all,' Eifion said, shaking hands.

'I haven't quite got used to saying "Miss Farrar of Counsel" yet,' Barratt grinned. 'She used to work for me, you see,' he added. 'Apparently, the experience was enough to make her desert the solicitors' profession in favour of the Bar, but it doesn't seem to have done her too much harm.'

'It was an essential part of my training,' Jess smiled.

'Well, let me come to the point,' Barratt said. 'Eifion arrived in my office unexpectedly this afternoon. It's probably best if I let him tell you why.'

They took seats.

'I'm sure you all remember this quite well, with it being so recent,' Eifion began hesitantly. 'Three people, two men and a woman, were arrested in Caernarfon on the eve of Prince Charles's Investiture. It is alleged that they were planning to plant a home-made bomb in the Castle, timed to detonate during the ceremony.'

'I remember it very clearly,' Gareth replied. 'The papers said they planned to hide it under a flagstone, not far from where the ceremony would be taking place.'

'Yes, that's right. At this precise moment, my firm represents them – well, two of them, anyway. I've known Caradog and Arianwen Prys-Jones for years. My wife and I were close friends of their parents, God rest them. Arianwen asked me to come to see her at the police station, just after she had been charged. Caradog is representing himself. He told me he will refuse to recognise the court, so what will happen with him, God only knows. But Arianwen is my client, as is the third defendant, Dafydd Prosser. I don't know him really. He came to me through professional colleagues in North Wales who knew I was representing Arianwen. I would like to continue, but...'

'They have already decided to move the trial out of Wales,' Barratt said, 'to the Old Bailey. Apparently they were afraid there might be too much local feeling in Wales, or that there was too much danger of public disorder and the like. Or perhaps they just couldn't trust a Welsh jury to convict. In any case, the Bailey has it now.'

'It would have been a huge headache in Wales, politically, in addition to everything else,' Eifion said. 'Anyone in any position of power in Wales would be glad to wash their hands of it.'

'Is it too much of a headache for you too?' Gareth asked.

'No. It might have caused some resentment against us in certain quarters, but that wouldn't have stopped me. We can't back off just because the client's cause is unpopular, can we? They couldn't have kept it in North Wales – Caernarfon, Mold and so on, obviously. That would have been asking for trouble. But they could have moved it down to South Wales, Cardiff or Swansea, and if they had, I would have done it using my local counsel.'

He paused.

'But in England, you know, with a London jury... I just think it would be in their best interests to have London solicitors and counsel. Of course, you are well-known in Wales yourself, Mr Morgan-Davies. You are fluent in Welsh, I understand?'

'It's my first language. Is there any conflict of interest between the two?'

Eifion shook his head. 'Not for the solicitors, but we will need separate counsel.'

'Wasn't there a fourth suspect?' Ben asked. 'Another man?'

'Yes. Trevor Hughes, Arianwen's husband,' Eifion replied. 'He seems to have disappeared without trace. Arianwen and Dai Bach – that's what they call Dafydd – both tell me they have no idea where he is, and I believe them. It's possible the police may find him before trial, but we will just have to wait and see about that.'

'Mr Morris tells me that the trial will not be before the spring of next year,' Merlin said.

'Yes. The prosecution has a lot of exhibits to submit for forensic testing, and they have to take a lot of witness statements. I was told that April or May is the earliest we can expect.'

'That is good for us, in the sense that we can accommodate it,' Merlin said. 'My understanding, Mr Davis, is that you were suggesting Mr Morgan-Davies for Dafydd Prosser and Mr Schroeder for Mrs Hughes?'

'That's correct,' Barratt replied. 'I'm sorry, Gareth, but from what Eifion tells me, I'm not sure your man has much of a defence.'

'They're accused of trying to kill the Queen and Prince Charles,' Gareth said. 'I'd be very surprised if any of them has much of a defence.'

'I'm told Dai Bach made highly incriminating statements to the police, including one in writing,' Eifion added, 'though, fair play to him, he does say that it was beaten out of him.'

'It's not the first time a defendant has alleged he was beaten up by the police,' Gareth smiled. 'There are even times when it is true. I've dealt with that one before.'

'And by MI5, actually, in this case,' Eifion said, 'as well as the police. And he says there is medical evidence.'

'Really?' Gareth said thoughtfully. 'Well, that ought to make it interesting.'

'But even if we keep his statement out, they say they have a lot of circumstantial evidence against him. I don't know what that amounts to, yet.'

Gareth nodded. 'Well, we will just have to wait and see. I will need a junior.'

'I was going to suggest Mr Clive Overton, sir,' Merlin said. 'Someone relatively junior would do for this, I think.' He smiled. 'But I am told there is a problem with that.'

'The case has already been assigned – to Mr Justice Overton,' Barratt said. 'We don't think it's a good idea to have him appearing in front of his father, even as a junior.'

Gareth laughed out loud.

'Miles Overton would have a heart attack if we even suggested it,' he said. 'Who else is there?'

'I've got Mr Weston, sir,' Merlin said.

'Perfect,' Gareth agreed.

'I'm not sure about Arianwen, Mr Schroeder,' Eifion said. 'I'm told that her statement to the police protests her innocence, and the only evidence against her is that she was driving the car, accompanied by Mr Morgan-Davies's client, when the police found the bomb. She says she had no idea what she was carrying. It's early days, yet, obviously, but you may have some chance in her case.'

'All right,' Ben replied. 'That gives me something to work with.'

'So, where do I fit into all this?' Jess asked with a smile.

'Well, Miss Farrar,' Eifion replied, 'we are going to need your expertise too. When she was arrested, Arianwen had her son Harri with her in the car. He is four years old, so he was in a child's seat in the back of the car.'

Ben took a sharp intake of breath.

'She had her four-year-old son in the car while she was carrying the bomb?' he asked.

Eifion nodded grimly.

'I'm afraid so. Of course, the boy was taken to a foster home immediately, and he is being well looked after. But it's a problem for her defence.'

'You can say that again,' Ben said.

Eifion smiled thinly.

'I didn't mean that only in the obvious sense. It presents us with another problem, as you will find when you see her. I'm afraid she is obsessed with seeing Harri, and with getting him back. I've tried to talk to her about it, but she is not rational at the moment. She is heart-broken about being separated from him, and I don't use the term lightly, Mr Schroeder. I'm not sure I knew what "heart-broken" meant before I saw her. But she is really heart-broken. She is almost out of her mind with grief. It's difficult to get her to concentrate on the criminal case at all, and it worries me.'

Jess shook her head.

'Well, obviously, getting him back is something we can't even consider unless, and until, she gets a "not guilty" in the criminal case. Even then, the local authority may want to delay returning him until she has proved herself to be a fit parent, and if they think she really did put him in the same car as a bomb, it may not be easy to satisfy them. Remember, there's no need for proof beyond reasonable doubt in child welfare cases. It's just a question of what seems more likely, so she doesn't have the same protection she does in the criminal case, and even if she is acquitted, getting Harri back won't be automatic.'

'I agree, Miss Farrar,' Eifion replied. 'But I believe it is essential to involve family counsel now, so that we can reassure her that we are not forgetting Harri, we are making sure nothing bad happens to him, and that we are waiting in the wings to apply to the court for him to be returned to her when the moment arrives. She is going to be a very difficult client, and we are going to have to support her, be patient with her. Mr Schroeder, I hope you agree with that strategy.'

'Absolutely,' Ben replied.

'I will talk to Steven tomorrow, Miss Farrar,' Merlin said, 'and explain what we have discussed this evening.'

'Thank you, Merlin.'

'Well, there we are,' Gareth said. 'It would be helpful for us to have a conference with the clients as soon as possible. Even though we have some time before trial, this is going to be a difficult case, and it's going to take a lot of preparation. She is in Holloway, I imagine. Where is he?'

'Brixton,' Eifion replied.

'I will work out a date for that with Merlin,' Barratt said.

'Good.' Gareth looked at his watch. 'Well, what do you say to a glass of champagne before you go?'

'That would be very welcome,' Barratt replied.

'Right. Come on, both of you, and you can give Mr Justice Wesley your congratulations personally.'

23

Thursday 24 July 1969

'HAVE YOU HEARD ANYTHING more about Harri? Are they going to let me see him?'

The words were spoken quietly but urgently, and they were the first she spoke as they entered the conference room in Holloway Prison.

'He's very well, Arianwen,' Eifion assured her. 'He is with a very good foster family, and we are doing our best to bring him to visit you. I don't have any news today, but I have brought your family barrister, Jess Farrar, who is going to be working with us.'

Jess stepped forward and shook Arianwen's hand.

'Thank you,' Arianwen said.

'I'm going to do everything I can,' Jess replied.

'Arianwen, this is Barratt Davis, my friend who is a solicitor here in London. You remember I said last time we met, I thought it would be better to have a local solicitor and barrister?'

'Yes. But you will still be involved, Eifion, won't you? You understand my anxiety about Harri, and that means so much to me.'

'Of course I will. I will be involved for as long as it all takes. But Mr Davis will be in charge of things for the trial.'

She shook his hand. 'Thank you, Mr Davis.'

'It's my privilege,' Barratt replied. 'And please call me Barratt. This is Ben Schroeder, the barrister who will be representing you in the criminal trial.'

As he shook her hand, Ben took in the tall, gaunt figure. She must have lost weight since her arrest, he thought. She looked unnaturally thin, and her brown and white, ankle-length Indian cotton dress hung about her frame too loosely. Her long hair was untidy, as if it had been combed hurriedly and indifferently just before they arrived. But it was the eyes he noticed most. They looked haunted, as if she really were, as Eifion had said, heart-broken. But at the same time, behind the heartbreak, he saw just a flash of resolve and a sense of dignity that had not deserted her. She was still ready to fight. The eyes also had another effect on him, a far more personal one. For a moment he could not catch his breath, and he could not look away. By the time he did, he knew something had changed. In the space of a few seconds she had changed for him. She was not just another client. He felt an irrational determination, an intense desire to save her, whatever the cost. The feeling took him by surprise, and he could not immediately understand it.

They took their seats around the small table, crowded together in the small conference room with its harsh fluorescent lighting, with a watchful prison guard prowling up and down in the corridor outside, and peering in through the glass panel in the door from time to time to remind them of her presence.

'We've received a copy of the statement under caution you made to the police,' Ben said. He produced a copy of the statement from his briefcase and perused it slowly. 'You say that you knew nothing about what was going on. Dafydd Prosser – Dai Bach – phoned you and asked you to drive him to Bangor. He told you a story about having to collect some personal belongings because he was going to stay with a friend. You drive him there, he picks up his suitcase, as you believed it was, from the garage. You drive him back to the square. But then your brother Caradog appears unexpectedly. You see what is really in the boot of your car, and you are arrested. Will that be the evidence you give if I call you at the trial?'

'Yes. That's the truth.'

Ben nodded.

'Arianwen – may we use first names…?'

'Yes, of course.'

'Arianwen, I'm going to play devil's advocate for a moment. Do you know what I mean?'

'Yes, I think so.'

'I'm going to look at it from the prosecution's point of view, because that is what you are going to hear when you are cross-examined.'

'All right.'

'The first question is this. This plan to make a bomb and place it in the Castle wasn't hatched overnight, was it? It must have taken a considerable time. They had to decide that they were going to do it. That alone…do you see? Then, somehow, they had to work out how to actually make a bomb. They had no prior experience of doing anything like this. They needed a workshop, they needed the materials, and they needed assembly instructions. Then they had to decide how to get the bomb into the Castle at the right time, and put it somewhere they had some hope it would not be discovered.'

'Yes.'

She was starting to cry.

'I'm sorry. You must forgive me. I keep thinking about Harri.'

'I understand,' Ben said. 'But we have to talk about your trial.'

'I know. It's just that I still can't believe any of this is happening.'

She put her head down on the table. Jess reached across to take her hand.

'Arianwen, we all want to help you get Harri back. That's why we're here. We are going to do whatever it takes. But we can't get him back for you if you go to prison, so first we have to make sure that doesn't happen. We have to make sure you are found not guilty. That's why we have to talk about this now. I know it's hard, but we do.'

'I know. I will do my best.'

'All right,' Ben said. 'Let us know if you need to take a break for a minute.'

'Thank you.'

Ben allowed some time to pass. Eventually she lifted her head and returned her attention to him.

'I was saying that it must have taken them quite some time to plan what they were going to do to disrupt the Investiture. You were close to all three men. Trevor most of all, of course. You were married to him, and living with him. But you were also close to your brother Caradog, and I imagine you saw quite a bit of Dai Bach. So the question the jury will have is…'

'How could I not have known?' she smiled through her tears.

'Exactly.'

'I ask myself that question every day.'

She stood and walked over to lean against the wall to the left of the door, away from the prying eyes of the prison officer.

'Looking back now,' she said, 'I even question myself. How could I not know? But I didn't. I've known Caradog all my life, and it doesn't make any sense to me to think of him carrying a bomb which could kill or maim people. That's not the Caradog I know. He is a gentle man, a kind and gentle man. If you knew him… it just doesn't make sense. He lives in a world of his own, yes, but it's a world of ideas, a world of books. He likes to keep himself to himself, and he likes to sit around reading, or thinking, or brooding. But violence? This kind of violence, especially, I just can't picture in him. He is an intellectual, a dreamer, but he's not an anarchist. It's not possible. There are days when I am convinced it is all a bad dream, and I'm going to wake up and find that everything is normal again. I have to think that. It just doesn't make any sense.'

'He *is* a nationalist,' Ben pointed out.

'We are *all* nationalists,' she replied, 'me, Trevor, Caradog, Dai Bach. We vote Plaid Cymru and we work for the Party. We go to demonstrations. But those are just political activities. I know there are some people on the fringes of the Party who are capable of violence, but none of us ever had anything to do with them. Caradog in particular would have nothing to do with them. He had nothing but scorn for them.'

Ben thought for some time.

'Well, something led him to do what he did. Could anything have shifted for him? Did you see any change in him over the years, however slight it might have seemed at the time?'

'If there was a change,' she replied, 'it would have been at the time of the flooding of the Tryweryn Valley. We fought the Government for years over that. I don't know whether you remember. They flooded an entire valley and destroyed a village called Capel Celyn, just to provide more water for Liverpool. It wasn't right. It was a huge injustice to Wales. We went to all the demos, wrote letter after letter to our MP, letters to the newspapers. We did everything we could. We held it up for a long time. But of course, it didn't stop them in the end. Nothing ever does. I did sense a hardening in Caradog at that time. Our family owned land there, a house, you see. But I still can't believe it's come to this.'

She hesitated.

'The Tryweryn Valley was where our family came from originally, you see, generations ago. Our great grandparents were the last in our immediate family to own land and live there. Their home was in Capel Celyn. So both Caradog and I had a particular attachment to the area, and it was very hard for us when we lost that fight. We had relatives who had to move when the fight was finally over. It's possible that Caradog changed then, but to me, it just seemed that he stayed lost in his own private world even more than usual. Perhaps he was covering up the hurt, and didn't know how to deal with it. Perhaps if he could have talked to me about it… I don't know.'

There was silence for some time.

'What about Dai Bach?' Ben asked.

She laughed.

'Dai Bach is totally different from Caradog. He's a clever enough man. He is a chemistry teacher, after all. But he's not an intellectual in the sense Caradog is. He's not a philosopher. He admires those qualities in Caradog. He looks up to him, almost like an elder brother. Actually, it's more than that. He is like Caradog's puppy dog in a way, following him around, hanging on his every word. But still, he has his own life. He enjoys people; he's a complete extrovert, and he can be very funny.'

'Would he be likely to do whatever Caradog asked of him?'

'In general, perhaps. But I can't see him doing something like this.'

'Is he capable of violence?'

She shook her head.

'He is quite impulsive. We have had to pull him back from the front line at demos a few times for his own safety. If you told me that he threw a placard at a police officer at a demo, or if you told me that he had a few pints after an international at Cardiff Arms Park and punched some English rugby supporter, I would believe you. I can see him doing that. But making a bomb to kill or injure people? No.'

'What about Trevor?' Ben asked.

She began to cry. Jess again reached over and took her hand. They waited for her to compose herself.

'Trevor came into my life unexpectedly when he bought the *Tywysog*. It was one of those things that happen. I think we both knew straight away. There was something between us – an understanding. He was very gradual with me. He came to the house for dinner. He took me out. He was interested in my music, which no one in the family ever was, much. He would sit and listen to me play the cello – for hours, sometimes. He found concerts to take me to, and there are not all that many near Caernarfon – not classical concerts. And when we agreed to marry, it was the most natural thing in the world. I never questioned it at all. He is a wonderful husband, and he loves Harri just as much as I do. He adores him.'

She cried again. Ben sat back, pen in hand, and allowed her time.

'Arianwen, do you have any idea why the police haven't been able to find him? Do you know where he might be? Whatever you tell us here is privileged. We can't tell anyone. But it is something that's bound to come up during the trial, and we have to give the jury a believable answer.'

She shook her head.

'Dai Bach told me that Trevor was supposed to take him to Bangor and bring him back to the *Maes*. It was because Trevor didn't show up that he called me. Trevor told me that he was going to the *Maes* earlier in the evening to join in the last demo before the Investiture. Caradog wouldn't be there because he was working at the Castle, but he was expecting to see Dai Bach. No one thought the demo would last very long – a lot of people had decided to protest by leaving town – and then I was expecting him home. I didn't go with him that evening because I didn't want to take Harri and I had no one to look after him, so I stayed home.'

'Were you worried when Dai Bach called?'

'Not really. I thought it was a bit odd if he had forgotten, because Trevor doesn't forget things like that. But I assumed he had met someone and gone for a couple of pints. Dai Bach sounded a bit anxious and it was getting late, so I thought the easiest thing was to drive him myself.'

'And you didn't think it was strange that you were taken to a garage rather than Dai Bach's house?'

'It seems strange looking back now, I suppose, but at the time, no. He said he had rented the garage for storage, and I didn't think anything of it.'

Ben finished the note he was making.

'I know this isn't easy, but how do you feel now about Trevor being gone when you have to face trial?'

She cried again.

'I know there is some simple, logical explanation. If I could just sit down and talk to him, I am sure it would make sense.'

'I take it that it's not the kind of thing you would expect him to do – to run out on you, I mean?'

'No. No. We have always been so close. I suppose he must be afraid about getting into trouble himself. He would be prosecuted if the police arrested him, wouldn't he?'

'Yes.'

'So, I think that must be it. He's afraid of being prosecuted, even though I'm sure he couldn't have had anything to do with it.'

Ben allowed some time to pass.

'Arianwen, is there anything about Trevor at all that makes you think he might have been involved?'

'Such as what?'

'I don't know. Anything. You must feel you know him very well by now. Is there anything that strikes you as odd now, even if it is only with the benefit of hindsight?'

She considered.

'The only thing that ever struck me as strange about Trevor is that he has never talked about his family very much. He told me that both his parents died long before we met, and he is an only child, so perhaps there wasn't very much to talk about. He didn't invite any family or friends to our wedding, but then, it was a very quiet affair – we both wanted it that way. I always had the feeling that when he came to Caernarfon, he was deliberately putting his past in London behind him. But I assumed that he was just tired of working too hard at Foyles, and he mentioned a relationship with a woman that hadn't ended well, so I didn't press him. I was just glad that he had come into my life, and I am sure he felt the same way.'

'He was re-discovering his Welsh identity too, perhaps?'

'Yes. I'm sure that was part of it.'

'And I must ask the same question I asked about Caradog and Dai Bach. Did you ever have any reason to think him capable of violence?'

'No. He can be firm, and there is a kind of brooding silence about him sometimes, which comes on for no apparent reason. But he is very controlled. I've never seen him lose his temper. And I can't believe he would put me and Harri at risk by being part of something like this. I just don't believe that, and I will never believe it. Never.'

24

THEY MET IN GARETH'S room at the request of Eifion Morris. After one final visit to Arianwen Hughes and Dafydd Prosser the next day he intended to return to Cardiff until the trial, but he was reluctant to leave before hearing what the barristers thought about the case after their conferences. Gareth Morgan-Davies and Donald Weston had spent much of the day at Brixton prison with Barratt Davis, talking to Dafydd Prosser. They had made a tentative inquiry of Caradog Prys-Jones using the good offices of the prison officers, but he had declined to see them or even send a message back. It was time to assess where they stood.

'Our interview last Thursday went well, on the whole,' Ben said. 'As you warned us, Eifion, Arianwen is very emotional when it comes to the subject of Harri, but she understands what the issue is going to be at the trial, and she is adamant that she knew nothing about any plan to plant a bomb.'

'Do you believe her?' Eifion asked.

'I think so. Whether a jury will believe her is another question.'

'Well, I believe her,' Jess said.

'Why?' Barratt asked.

'Just meeting her, watching her. If she had got wind that anything remotely like this was going on, she would never have kept quiet about it. I have no doubt about that. She would have been screaming bloody murder.'

'You think she would have turned them in?' Barratt smiled.

'She wouldn't have had to turn them in. She would have made them listen to her. She would have made it impossible for them to carry on.'

'Why would she have done that?'

'She would have done it for Harri, if for no other reason. She would never have placed him in danger of losing both his parents at the same time. And she certainly wouldn't have had him in the car if she knew she was carrying a bomb. Not in a million years.'

'I agree with you, Jess,' Eifion said. 'That's my reading of her too. Don't be fooled by that quiet demeanour. She is quite capable of making herself heard when she needs to. She would have been the voice of reason, and I can't see any of those men standing against her – certainly not Caradog or Dai Bach.'

'If she can give the jury that impression, then she has a chance,' Ben said. 'But she is going to have to survive some brutal cross-examination. We must support her as much as we can about Harri, as you said before. We must also remember that we haven't seen much of the prosecution's evidence yet. They may have something we are not expecting.'

'Agreed,' Barratt said. He turned to Gareth. 'And now for the bad news.'

'Oh?' Ben said. 'How so? Is Dai Bach being difficult?'

'No, on the contrary,' Gareth replied. 'Dai Bach is being very easy indeed. He is quite happy to admit that he was part of the conspiracy, that he built the bomb in his rented garage, and that he was delivering it to Caradog at the time of his arrest, knowing that it would be placed in the Castle, where it might well cause death or serious injury to people later in the day.'

Ben's jaw dropped.

'He admitted that to you?'

'In so many words.'

'Which means…'

'Which means that we can't represent him, except to the extent of challenging the prosecution's evidence on the ground of admissibility, and making any other legal arguments he is entitled to have made for him. I can't present a positive case, and I can't call him to give evidence.'

'You can try to keep his confession from the jury, presumably?' Ben suggested.

'Yes. Actually, that's the only part of the case where we might make some progress. He did somehow sustain some injuries at the police station, enough to make them call the police surgeon, who insisted that he be taken to hospital to be examined. So we do actually have a shot at keeping his confession out. But beyond that, there is not much we can do.'

They were silent for some time.

'Why doesn't he just plead guilty and get it over with?' Ben asked.

'He's worried that if he pleads, it will reflect badly on Caradog and Arianwen,' Gareth replied. 'I've told him it is unlikely to have any effect on them at all, but he is not listening to me at present. Still, trials concentrate the mind wonderfully. He may think more about it and change his mind as the trial approaches. But there's no sign of it yet.'

'What does he say about Arianwen?'

'He supports her story completely. He insists that she knew nothing about it, and she only sprang into action to drive him to Bangor when he couldn't find Trevor. And no, he doesn't know where Trevor is. I am sorry I can't call him to support her case in front of the jury. He would be quite happy to do it.'

'It's not Dai Bach I need,' Ben replied.

25

Monday 30 March 1970

AT ALMOST 7 O'CLOCK in the evening, Ben was still working in his room in Chambers, the files containing the prosecution's witness statements and the exhibits covering almost the entire working surface of his desk. The trial had been fixed for 4 May, which was now just over a month away. Ben felt as though he was going around in circles. The more he read the evidence, the more clearly he saw that everything hinged on how well Arianwen Hughes performed as a witness. The issue in her case was simple: did she know? Try as he might, he could find nothing more complicated than that in the morass of papers on his desk. The case still felt disconcertingly personal. He had begun to feel that he was as well prepared for trial as he would ever be, a strange and unfamiliar feeling so long before a trial. It was a feeling that in theory should have brought him comfort, but instead it had left him feeling more anxious than ever.

His chambers room-mate Harriet Fisk, who had a complicated civil case ahead of her the next morning in the High Court, yawned audibly from across the room and banged her pen down on her blotter.

'That's quite enough of this nonsense for one day,' she said.

'Calling it a night so early?' Ben grinned. He and Harriet had always got on well. As pupils they had shared a long, hard struggle to be taken on as members of Chambers, she as a woman, he as a young Jewish man from the East End. The victory had taken its toll emotionally and for a while, until their practices took off, had drained their self-confidence; they had supported each other loyally throughout and ever since. They had shared the room in Chambers ever since becoming tenants, and Harriet was building a good practice in the civil and family courts.

'I know. I have no staying power. But there's only so much I can read about incompetent building repairs, however expensive, in any given period of 24 hours without losing my mind. I will come in early tomorrow morning and make one final effort to tie it all together, and after that, the chips will fall where they may. How does your trial look? Do you have a shot?'

Ben sighed.

'Yes, we have a shot. But it all depends on how good she will be in the witness box.'

'No sign of the husband still?'

'No sign at all. Certainly not in time for this trial.'

She picked up her briefcase and walked over to stand in front of his desk.

'I don't understand how people talk themselves into doing something so dreadful,' she said. 'Planting a bomb and timing it to go off when there is almost certain to be a loss of life and terrible injuries. I understand that they have a political point to make, but how could this kind of violence help them? Do they really think we will all roll over and give them everything they want?'

Before Ben could answer, there was a knock on the door, and Gareth entered.

'Sorry,' he said. 'I hope I'm not interrupting anything.'

'No,' Harriet smiled. 'I was just telling Ben that I don't understand why people plant bombs in support of political causes.'

'I'm not sure they necessarily understand it themselves,' Gareth replied. 'If you want to hear my grand theory of it all…'

She reached out a hand and touched his shoulder.

'Much as I would love to, Gareth, it will have to be a pleasure postponed. I have a heavy couple of days coming up, and if I don't get out of here now, I will be in no condition to put a brave face on it tomorrow. Good night.'

'I, on the other hand, would be very pleased to hear about it,' Ben said, when Harriet had closed the door behind her. 'Have you finished for the night?'

'Yes. I've sent Donald off to do a bit of legal research for me, since that's likely to be my only role in the trial.'

'Does Prosser really understand that you can't present a case for him?'

'Oh, yes. To be honest, he doesn't seem too concerned. He seems resigned to his fate, in a strange way, as if he is already reconciled to the inevitable. At least that takes the pressure off Donald and myself to some extent. But I wish there was more we could do for him.'

Ben waved Gareth into a seat.

'So, do you really have a theory of why people like Caradog and Dai Bach are taking to setting bombs off, Gareth? Is it because they really think it will bring about change?'

'No. I don't think they were labouring under any delusion that the Queen and her Government would hoist the white flag at the first sign of trouble. Anyone who thinks a bomb or two will have that result is woefully ignorant of British history. These are intelligent men, and they know just as much about British history as you or I – perhaps even more.'

'But there are cases where governments have given in to violence, aren't there? The bombing of the King David Hotel, for example.'

Gareth laughed.

'Well, I wasn't going to bring that one up with you. But yes, of course, you are right. The Irish Free State is another example. But those were cases where change was demanded by the population at large, and the bombers were reflecting popular opinion. In Wales, you don't have that set of conditions at all. The nationalist cause is confined to a small minority, and there is virtually no support for nationalist violence.'

'The Welsh Nationalist Party has been doing well in elections lately.'

'Plaid Cymru has one MP, Gwynfor Evans – a good man, actually, I know him quite well. But if it becomes a real force, I think even Plaid Cymru will have to moderate its demands, perhaps accept some measure of home rule short of actual independence, because there simply isn't the support for breaking away from England altogether. I mean support for the idea itself – before you even stop to think about the practical implications, and ask whether Wales could even survive as an independent country.'

'But still, they may think that bombs are one way of influencing public opinion?' Ben suggested.

'In that case, they are misreading the Welsh public,' Gareth replied. 'All the evidence is that things like that drive people away from the nationalist cause rather than attracting them to it. It may be different elsewhere, but I'm fairly sure that's true in Wales.'

'Then, why do they do it?' Ben asked.

'They do it because they have developed an obsession with their history. If you grow up hearing about England subjugating Wales, and you never hear anything else, and you brood about it for long enough, eventually you develop an obsession that defies logic and reason. You start to look at your whole life through the prism of hatred towards England. There are those who can't control it; their emotions spiral out of control, and before they know where they are, they wake up one day and see nothing wrong with planting a bomb where it will kill and injure a lot of innocent people. That's how out of touch with reality you can become when you have tunnel vision about your history.'

Ben thought for some time.

'I would really like to understand that kind of obsession. I understand what you are saying, up to a point. But I have no real feeling for what I'm dealing with. Arianwen said that their family lost land in the Tryweryn valley, which I'm sure was an awful experience, but even so… I'm just not getting the idea, Gareth. Is it because I'm not Welsh? Is it beyond me?'

Gareth did not reply immediately.

'What are you doing for the rest of the week?' he asked eventually. 'You're not in court, are you?'

'No. I asked Merlin to keep me out of court so that I could concentrate on the trial. But I'm not sure I really need the time. I…'

Gareth stood.

'Good. In that case, go home and pack, and tell Jess that you are going to be away for a few days from Wednesday. You will be back on Sunday evening.'

Ben stared at him blankly.

'What?'

'You heard. Nothing formal, you won't need to dress up, but you will need warm clothing where we are going, even at this time of year.'

'Gareth, where am I going?'

'You're coming with me,' Gareth said. 'I am going to Wales. We are going to Wales together, and I'm going to try to show you why people like Caradog Prys-Jones and Dafydd Prosser and Trevor Hughes plant bombs.'

26

EVEN WITH AN EARLY start at Euston station, the train journey took most of the day, and by the time they had settled into their rooms at the *Gwesty'r Castell*, the Castle Hotel, they were tired and hungry. The hotel's dining room was quiet, and they relaxed with a hearty plate of lamb casserole, washed down with a bottle of a quite respectable French *vin ordinaire*.

'A good decision not to venture out tonight,' Ben smiled. 'I think I might have fallen by the wayside if we had tried to do any sight-seeing now.'

'We will have plenty of time tomorrow,' Gareth agreed. 'Caernarfon is not a big town. You can see it all in an hour or two. But we are not here as tourists. I want you to get a feel for the place. If you can begin to see the case through Arianwen's eyes, or Dai Bach's, it may help. My vote is that we get a good night's sleep and venture out early tomorrow. I want you to see the Menai Strait in the early morning light.'

'That sounds good. Actually, I've noticed one thing already.'

'What's that?'

'You booked us into our rooms, and ordered our drinks in Welsh. Everybody here really does speak Welsh, don't they? Arianwen told me, of course, but somehow, you don't take it in until you hear it.'

'Exactly.'

'I mean, obviously, if you go to France it seems natural to hear people speaking French, but if you don't go abroad... or are we abroad?'

Gareth laughed.

'Well, now you're asking the question. To you and me, no, we are not abroad. We crossed no national border today, we haven't been asked for our passports, we can use the same money here as we use in England. We think of ourselves as being in the same country. But the Welsh see Wales as a nation. I'm not talking about nationalists now, Ben, I'm talking about Welsh people in general. There is no hostility to England or the English, or anyone else. The waiter didn't mind you ordering dinner in English just now, and he spoke to you perfectly politely in English, didn't he?'

'Yes, but obviously, the language is an important part of the national identity,' Ben said. 'It's something you are proud of – quite rightly.'

'Yes, and of course, you will find a few people in Caernarfon who will pretend they don't understand you, and will insist on trying to make you feel uncomfortable by speaking Welsh, knowing you can't understand a word they say. But that's not peculiar to Wales. You find that sort of behaviour the world over, don't you? It's not nationalism; it's just rudeness, and fortunately, in Wales at least, it's a minority sport. So, my answer would be: no, we are not abroad, but we are in a different nation, and as long as people respect that, I am satisfied.'

They stood and left money for the bill and the tip on the table.

'Though if I had my way, I would do away with the use of the words "Wales" and "Welsh", at least while I am here.'

Ben looked at him blankly.

'You're going to have to explain that one to me.'

'"Wales" and "Welsh" are English words derived from Germanic sources, and they mean "foreign" or "foreigners". In our language, we call the nation *Cymru* and our language is *Cymraeg*. Those are words which signify members of a community, family, friends and colleagues. Much better, don't you think?'

'Much better,' Ben smiled.

'Right, well, sleep well. I'm going to knock on your door early tomorrow morning. We will have a walk to get some fresh morning air, and then come back for breakfast.'

27

Thursday 2 April 1970

IT WAS A FINE, brisk morning, and they set off at a good pace, turning left outside the hotel and making their way along the same side of the town square, the *Maes*. The Castle confronted them immediately, and Ben stopped dead in his tracks to stare at it.

'Yes, it makes quite an impression, doesn't it?' Gareth said.

'It's incredible. It's so massive. It dominates everything.'

'Yes, and that's today, in a modern town. Imagine what it was like in an early mediaeval settlement where there was nothing else even approaching that kind of scale. It wasn't just a castle in the military sense, to provide a defence to the area, and give warning of impending attacks, and so on. It was a statement, an assault on the psyche, designed to convey the idea that the local people were powerless to resist an invader capable of building a fortress like that. And, you know what, I bet it worked.'

'I bet it did,' Ben replied.

'And it wasn't the only one. Edward I built them all over North Wales.'

They walked on, more slowly, as Ben took in as much detail as he could.

'Statue of you-know-who,' Gareth smiled, gesturing to his left as they were leaving the square.

'David Lloyd George,' Ben replied. 'Even I know that one.'

'We will do a tour of the Castle after breakfast,' Gareth said. 'For now, we are going to walk right past it and head out of the walled town towards the docks.'

'This is magnificent,' Ben said, as their walk took them outside the ancient walls. 'I didn't know that Caernarfon was a complete walled town. I knew about York and Chester, but I had no idea.'

'It's every bit as fine as York or Chester,' Gareth replied, 'even if on a smaller scale, obviously. It compares with anything I've seen, here or in Europe. You can't walk around town on the walls, sadly. They are in a state of disrepair. Hopefully, someone will do something about that, eventually. It is a shame. You would get a wonderful, panoramic view of the town from up there.'

He put a hand on Ben's shoulder and stopped him.

'Oh, since we are here, let's go back a few yards just for a moment.'

They back-tracked for a short distance, and stopped outside a building with a faintly ridiculous Greco-Roman frontage supported by pillars in the classical style, the dimensions of the frontage out of all proportion to the size of the building as a whole.

'This rather silly building here, on the corner of Shirehall Street,' Gareth said, 'is used as a court. Whoever had this entrance built just opposite the Castle must have had an inflated idea of his own importance, don't you think? But more to the point for our purposes is that the name of the street in Welsh is *Stryd y Jel*, which I'm sure I don't have to translate.'

'Jail Street.'

'Yes. The jail is attached to the court, a not uncommon arrangement and a convenient one, of course. It was in there that DCI Grainger and his colleagues beat the living daylights out of Dai Bach, if you believe him – which I do.'

'And where Arianwen was separated from Harri and cried her eyes out for days,' Ben added quietly.

'Yes.'

They walked on towards the dock. It was fully light now, the soft, tentative mixture of light grey, light blue and light gold ushering in a new day. They stopped at the dock and looked out over the Strait. The water was calm and unhurried, with no tell-tale sign to show where the River Seiont ended and the Menai Strait began, its course gentle enough to suggest that it might have required no more than the light itself to evoke the ripples on its surface. Gareth pointed to the mass of land in the near distance, where they could clearly see light green fields, woodland copses, and a few cottages scattered along the shoreline.

'You know what we are looking at, of course?'

'Anglesey.'

'Yes, *Ynys Môn* in *Cymraeg*.'

'It's…'

'No. Don't say anything yet. Just take it in.'

They surveyed the sight in silence for almost ten minutes before Gareth resumed their walk, eventually turning right to take them back into the walled town.

'Many people feel that *Ynys Môn* is the heart of Wales,' he said. 'It's always been a mysterious place. There are many legends about it. It is felt to be a place of magic; it has many druidic associations and so on. It is the heart of *Cymru* as far as the language is concerned.'

Ben nodded. He looked back towards the water as they turned the corner.

'That's how it feels this morning,' he said. 'Mysterious. Even to me. Why is that?'

'I have no idea,' Gareth replied enigmatically.

28

BY THE TIME THEY had done justice to a hearty breakfast the day had become warmer, and when they emerged from the hotel again on to the *Maes*, the square was filling up with people criss-crossing it, going about their daily work. The market stalls were open for business, selling everything from fruit and vegetables, to cheap clothing, to office supplies, and a short line of taxis waited for custom outside the hotel itself. Gareth took Ben to the right as they left the hotel, and they walked a short distance away from the Castle.

'We are now on Chapel Street,' he said, 'and just ahead, to our left, is New Street. I'm sure you recognise those names.'

'Of course.'

They crossed the street and stopped on the corner. Gareth pointed.

'That is where Arianwen and Dai Bach came from in the car. They stopped just a few yards from where we are standing, on the other side of New Street.'

He pointed again, straight ahead, and moved his hand in an arc, left to right.

'The main road to Bangor is just up there, and they were travelling left to right as we look at it. I would guess that they turned off on *Stryd y Llyn* – Pool Street – which runs parallel to Chapel Street where we are now. Then all they had to do was turn left on to New Street, and there they were, in position. Caradog would have left work at the Castle, timing his walk to coincide with their arrival at 1.15. I suspect he might have taken the route past the back of our hotel along *Fford Santes Helen* – St Helen's Road – which would have been a bit quieter than walking the way we did through the *Maes*, and it would have fitted in with his story of leaving work to join in a patrol of the perimeter of the Castle. He would have turned up towards where we are at the last moment, and he would have come out on Segontium Terrace, where it joins New Street. That would fit in with Dai Bach's account of it, according to which he and Caradog approached the car from that part of New Street.'

Ben nodded. 'That's what Arianwen said too. And at that point, Caradog gets the shock of his life.'

'Seeing his sister? Yes. But he has no time to react, and Dai Bach has no chance to explain. They have a bomb in the car, and they have to get on with it. The problem is that Special Branch and MI5 are all over the place, lying in wait for them. They must have been parked just along here on Chapel Street, or perhaps on New Street itself to our right, between here and Segontium Terrace.'

'So Caradog probably walks right past them.'

'Yes.'

'And no Trevor Hughes,' Ben mused. 'Where on earth did he go?'

'That's the question,' Gareth agreed.

They were silent for a few moments.

'Come on,' Gareth said. 'Since we are here, let's walk up and see where they lived. It's not far. You can see what a small place Caernarfon is. Nothing is more than a short stroll from anything else. Then we can bring ourselves back into the centre of town.'

They made their way back to the square, crossed to the other side, and walked up Bridge Street, which within a short distance led them to *Penrallt Isaf*, and to the house where Trevor and Arianwen had lived.

'If you turn right, you come straight to the Bangor Road,' Gareth observed, 'very convenient if you are doing the drive regularly.'

Ben stood and observed the house for one or two minutes. It was an unremarkable two-storey terraced house, painted in a dark brown. It had once been the centre of an apparently normal and happy family life. Now it stood silent, with no trace of life left in it, deserted. The sight chilled him. Gareth did not rush him.

'Just to complete the picture,' he said eventually, 'let's walk back up in the direction we walked before breakfast, though we are a fair distance from the water here.'

They walked in silence along Bangor Street until Gareth suddenly prompted a left turn, heading down towards the dock.

'These houses to our right,' he said, 'are *Rhês Pretoria*, Pretoria Terrace.'

'The Prys-Jones family home,' Ben said.

'Yes. They are rather pretty houses, aren't they? Much more

colourful than *Penrallt Isaf*. I like the way those small front gardens point downhill towards the water. And they are so well kept, including the family home – at least for now. Somebody must have been looking after the garden, but I imagine some weeds will begin to show before long.'

They stood together for a while and looked at the house where Caradog and Arianwen had grown up.

'I can almost hear her cello,' Ben smiled.

'Yes. It's strange the way we can imagine what must have been going on in places we hear about in our cases, isn't it? And now, if we turn left, we will arrive back inside the walled town. You can see how compact it all is, can't you?'

'That's why they chose Bangor for the place to build the bomb, isn't it?' Ben asked suddenly. 'It wasn't just because Dai Bach was living there, was it?'

Gareth shook his head. 'No, I'm sure you are right. It's too small here, too much risk of someone making the connection between the various addresses. Bangor gave it some distance. And they knew there would be a heavy police presence by the time the day of the Investiture arrived.'

They walked back to the gate leading into the walled town.

'The Black Boy Inn,' Gareth smiled. 'Sixteenth century, and the most famous hotel in Caernarfon by a long way.'

'Which, I take it, is why we're not staying here?'

'Yes. I thought the Castle would be a bit more low profile. That's not to say someone won't make the connection from our names in the hotel register, but there's slightly less chance that anyone will try to ask us questions we don't want to answer. When we visit one or two hostelries later in the day, I will be surprised if we don't overhear some conversation about the case.'

'I won't know, will I?' Ben smiled.

'I will translate for you,' Gareth said.

They walked on.

'We are on Palace Street now,' Gareth said, as they crossed the High Street, 'so coming up on our right is the *Tywysog* book shop.'

The shop was locked and dark. Trevor's final display of books could still be seen dimly, gathering dust, behind the now grimy windows, and again Ben had the sense of desertion he had felt at the house in *Penrallt Isaf*.

'It's a pity we can't go in,' Ben said. 'I would like to look around, and I would especially like to see the basement.'

'We would have to ask the police,' Gareth said, 'and that would blow our cover here once and for all. It's probably still a crime scene, technically. In any case, there won't be anything to see. They would have seized anything of any possible interest on the day of the arrests.'

'I wonder if he came back here that night,' Ben mused. 'I wonder if there was anything he hid – anything he took with him.'

'The elusive note for Arianwen? It's becoming a bit like the quest for the Holy Grail, isn't it?'

'I can't believe he didn't leave her something to give her some clue about where he was.'

'Ben, if he had left a note, the police would have found it. They would have left no stone unturned. He might have left something more subtle, I suppose but, as things turned out, she had no chance to find anything, did she?'

'That's what I mean. I'm wondering if we should ask the police to let Eifion in to take a look around.'

'That could be very dangerous,' Gareth said.

'Why? The worst that could happen is that he finds nothing.'

'I disagree. Remember, Ben, the police have no evidence that she knew anything except for her presence in the car at the time of her arrest. The last thing you need is something which might create additional suspicion.'

'But still...'

Gareth laughed.

'There's a French saying, Ben. *Les absents ont toujours tort.*'

Ben grinned. 'The absent are always wrong.'

'Yes. Or "the absent are always to blame" may be a better way of putting it. I heard it in French from Amélie, Lady Wesley as she now is. I think, in America, they call it the empty chair principle. But the idea is as old as Demosthenes or Cicero.'

'So, contrary to what I have been thinking all this time, I may actually not want Trevor Hughes at trial. Is that what you are suggesting?'

'No, I wouldn't go that far. If we give Trevor the benefit of the doubt, if we assume that, given the chance, he would do the gentlemanly thing and tell the jury his wife had nothing to do with it, your first choice would be to have him there. No doubt about that. But your second choice is not too bad. While he is missing, presumed to have flown the coop, he can't say anything bad about her, and he can't be cross-examined by the prosecution – not to mention that his leaving her in the lurch is bound to buy her some sympathy with the jury. Meanwhile, you can blame him all you want, and he can't say anything to contradict you.'

He put a hand on Ben's shoulder.

'On the other hand, if he left something behind which the jury think confirms the prosecution's suspicions about her, it may be the worst of all worlds. It helps the prosecution case, but you have no one to cross-examine about it. I know you would like to have him in the trial – so would I in your position – but at least count your blessings that it isn't any worse than it is.'

Ben smiled. 'I'm glad I still have my pupil-master to keep me on track.'

'I'll send a fee note for my advice when we are back in London.'

'How about a couple of pints later?'

'Done,' Gareth said. 'Come on, let's go and take a look at the Castle.'

29

THEY STOOD TOGETHER FOR some time just inside the King's Gate, the main entrance to Caernarfon Castle. Ben looked around slowly, as he absorbed the sheer scale of the place, the majestic space it occupied, the massive solidity of the stone walls, the dominating height of the towers, the sudden quiet of an ancient fortress from which the bustle of a modern town was abruptly cut off the moment you walked through the gate.

'You can just imagine the effect of a network of castles like this across North Wales, can't you?' Gareth asked. 'As we were saying, in the Middle Ages it must have been an incredible statement of royal power.'

'It must have seemed impregnable,' Ben replied. 'But it wasn't always, was it? There were successful Welsh uprisings.'

'There were, but they didn't last very long, and whatever was destroyed was rebuilt, even stronger than before. You can't blame the king, in a way. It was difficult to keep control over distant parts of the country in those days. Travel and communication were slow at the best of times. That's why the king had to leave reminders of his power, like this. It's also why he had to leave such powerful nobles in charge of key places like Chester and Durham, and hope to God he could trust them not to go over to the other side.'

'The king must have resigned himself to having subjects, but not friends.'

Gareth laughed.

'I think that's part of being king,' he replied. 'You remember what Shakespeare said about it: "Uneasy lies the head that wears a crown", or something like that.'

He pointed across the Castle grounds slightly to his right.

'That's where the great hall was. It is long gone, but you can tell how big it was from the way they've marked out where the walls stood. You can almost see it, can't you? A hundred or more packed in there for dinner, with minstrels playing and the wine flowing freely. You can imagine them carrying dishes from the kitchens, behind us to the right there, across to the hall for banquets, can't you? It would have been interesting to be a fly on the wall during some of those dinners, I'm sure.'

They turned left and started to walk slowly. It was a quiet day in the Castle, with only one or two tourists occupied in photographing the Eagle Tower on the far side to their right. No members of the staff were to be seen in the grounds.

'That was where the Royal Party entered the Castle,' Gareth said, pointing towards the tourists. 'The Queen received the keys from the Constable as a symbol of welcome and submission, though of course she was expected to hand them back. The grassy space at the top of the rise to our left is where the royal dais was, and where the ceremony took place.'

They walked up the incline to the spot.

'After the ceremony, the Queen led the new Prince of Wales to the Queen's Gate, just over here, to present him to his people. It is the one part of the Castle that was never properly finished but, as a result, you can stand here and wave to the people down in the square, and be seen by everybody.'

'What some people thought of as the final insult,' Ben said.

'Yes. No doubt.'

They stayed, looking down, for some time as the square carried on with its daily life, the market stalls still in full swing.

'And if we walk back this way we come to the Black Tower, and the Chamberlain Tower is the next one down.'

'So, it was in here, somewhere, that Caradog was going to plant the bomb,' Ben observed.

'Yes. Let's go inside and walk around.'

'I suppose it's too much to hope that the site will be marked in some way,' Ben said.

'They might have left a chalk mark,' Gareth replied. 'But they would have put the flagstone back in place and cemented it shut after they photographed it. Well, they would have to, wouldn't they, with visitors coming and going all the time? It wouldn't be safe to leave it exposed, not in the dark like this. They would have to keep a guard here all the time, just to make sure visitors didn't break an ankle.' He smiled. 'Were you expecting yellow tape and a notice saying "crime scene" and warning people to keep away?'

'Well, it *is* a crime scene, isn't it? What if we wanted to take a look at it?'

'I'm sure we could ask the police to open it up for us. Perhaps that would be a good idea, once we've seen the photographs. We can ask Eifion to arrange it if we need to. But I would like to get an idea of approximately where it is, now, if we can. Let's see what we can find.'

'So we are looking for…?'

'Chalk marks and new cement. It's a pity we didn't think to bring a torch.'

As they entered the tower, Ben felt chilled to the bone. The Black Tower itself was a small, dark space, and the staircase leading up to the battlements was roped off, with a sign declaring it to be closed to visitors. They moved slowly along the corridor towards the Chamberlain Tower, feeling their way and searching the darkness with their eyes. It took time for their eyes to begin to adjust and, even then, progress was slow. The flagstones were uneven; and it would certainly have been easy to trip and sprain an ankle, Ben thought. But what he noticed most was the cold. On the outside wall, the sun's rays penetrated only through the occasional narrow arrow slit in the walls. The front was open to the grassy area, but somehow the heavy stone seemed to suck any hint of warmth out of the air. He had expected the interior to be colder than the grounds outside, but the chill he felt seemed more intense than simply a sudden absence of sunlight, more like an almost total absence of heat.

He tried to focus his eyes and his mind on the likely site. What would Caradog have been looking for? Undoubtedly, a quiet spot where he could work unseen. He would have to prise the flagstone out of its space without anyone noticing. True, he could do it a bit at a time, and replace it as often as he wanted. It was unlikely that anyone would notice markings in the cement unless he was very unlucky. But every time he worked on it he would be taking a risk, that would be unavoidable. The bomb Dai Bach was building was not huge. He would have to put it somewhere reasonably close to the front wall if he wanted to do anything more than make a big bang, and the nearer he got to the front wall, the more risky the work was.

They stopped.

'We are almost half way to the Chamberlain Tower,' Gareth said. 'We can't be too far away.'

They turned to their right and walked over the huge flagstones which covered the floor in front of the low front wall.

'It could be any one of these, couldn't it?' Ben asked.

'He wouldn't be digging right next to the wall,' Gareth replied. 'In fact, the witnesses say it wasn't up against the wall, don't they? But anywhere here, two or three flagstones back, has to be a possibility.'

'He's taking quite a chance on being seen.'

'Yes, although if he works in the hours of darkness, he has a good chance, doesn't he? He has a clear view of anyone approaching, and it's easier for him to see out into whatever light there is than for someone to see in. And you can't walk silently in here. He would have warning of anyone approaching from one of the towers.'

They looked in vain for chalk marks and new cement.

'Perhaps it doesn't matter,' Gareth said. 'All will become clear when we see the prosecution's photographs. It's not hard to see the most important thing, is it? There were seating stands right outside the wall, and beyond the seating stands, the Royal Family and their guests on the dais.'

'He was out to cause mayhem,' Ben said. 'It wasn't just about making a scene, was it? If you plant a bomb here, you are certain to kill and maim people. A lot of people. He knew that. He must have known.'

'I am now going to take you to the most interesting pub in Caernarfon,' Gareth said, as they left the Castle.

'It's a bit early, isn't it?' Ben smiled.

'It's work,' Gareth insisted, 'part of your case preparation. We are here to give you a feel for Wales, Caernarfon in particular, and you can't get that without visiting a pub or two.'

They crossed the street and walked towards the square.

'This is Hole in the Wall Street,' Gareth said, as they turned left into what looked like a narrow alley, 'so called for the obvious reason that it in fact begins with a hole in the town's wall. If you look at the wall, you can just see the remains of what, at one time, was a stone staircase leading up to the top of the battlements.'

'It looks rather colourful.'

'It was more than colourful in its day. It boasted several houses of ill repute, and the sale of alcohol has always flourished, even in the heyday of the Welsh Temperance Movement.'

'The Four Alls,' Ben smiled, indicating a pub to his left. 'Is this where we are going?'

'Strange name, isn't it? But I wasn't going to take you there – well, perhaps we will have a second pint there on the way back. But for the moment, we are going a few yards farther down the street. Let me do the talking here, Ben. This is one of the places where it's definitely better to speak Welsh.'

'I will stand mute of malice,' Ben grinned.

They turned into a small tavern on the right, where Gareth ordered two pints and some peanuts, and they found a corner table in the tiny snug bar.

'This is the Hole in the Wall, as you see,' Gareth said. 'By reputation, it's a real hotbed of nationalist sentiment. This is where the locals like to come. They are quite happy to leave the tourists to enjoy the Castle Hotel and the Black Boy. It's a safe place to talk, so it has the reputation of attracting people who need a safe place to talk, which can include some pretty unsavoury types, at least from the point of view of the authorities. If you come in here not understanding Welsh, you will stick out like a sore thumb, and they will find a way to get rid of you in short order.' He grinned. 'Don't worry. You will be all right as long as you stick with me.'

They took a deep drink of beer. It had been an intense day, and they were both tired, but the pleasantly cold shock of the beer and the saltiness of the nuts slowly revived them.

'So, tell me, what is your impression of Caernarfon so far?'

Ben thought for some time.

'It's really been fascinating. Not just seeing where various events in the case took place, but, as you say, getting a feel for it. It's been… well, it's hard to define.'

'Try.'

Ben sat up in his chair.

'It started this morning, when we had our early-morning walk to see the Menai Strait. It was so beautiful and peaceful, but I had the strangest sensation… no, it's silly, I'm embarrassed, I shouldn't be asking you to listen to this…'

'No. Go on.'

He hesitated. 'Well, I had the strangest sensation that Arianwen was standing by my side, and somehow directing my eyes to what they needed to see.'

'That's interesting,' Gareth replied. He adopted an outrageous stage-German accent. 'Tell me, *Herr* Schroeder, for how long have you been experiencing these symptoms?'

Ben laughed.

'I'm not psychotic, Gareth – well, at least, I hope not. I'm not seeing visions or hearing voices. It's just a sense of having her with me in spirit.'

'And what did she direct you to see, in spirit?'

'The place, that's all. I don't know how to describe it. It was as if she just wanted me to see what she sees when she looks at Caernarfon, so that I can understand what she feels for it.'

Gareth nodded.

'Are you sure it's not because there is some attraction between you, rather than an attraction to Wales?'

'Gareth…'

'There would be nothing strange about it. It happens to all of us from time to time, and Barratt tells me that there is something bewitching about her, that she is something of an elemental force.'

Ben laughed uncomfortably, feeling himself blushing.

'Yes, I suppose she is, in a way.'

'Yes, well there you are. It's an occupational hazard, nothing to worry about. All the same, discretion being the better part of valour, probably best not to tell Jess that Arianwen's following you around town, don't you think?'

'She will understand,' Ben replied, without hesitation.

Gareth looked at him keenly. 'If you say so. But if I said something like that to Margot, I would be in for a very thorough cross-examination, believe me.'

They laughed.

'How are things with Jess?' Gareth asked. 'Has your family forgiven you for marrying a Gentile girl?'

Ben nodded. 'It was only ever my father, really. My mother was always understanding. Both she and my grandfather liked Jess the first time they met her. It was when my grandfather had his heart attack while I was doing that capital case in Huntingdon with Martin Oldcastle. Jess drove me home and was a pillar of support for everyone. My father has very entrenched views, but he was overruled by the rest of the family. They are very proud of their Jewish heritage, but they don't want to run their children's lives.'

Gareth laughed.

'That's the grandfather who always calls you "Viceroy" in honour of Rufus Isaacs?'

'Yes.'

'Well, I'm glad it worked out so well. In my case I would have been in real trouble if I hadn't married a Welsh girl, but fortunately I fell in love with one.'

'You've had a very happy marriage, haven't you, Gareth?'

'Yes. We would have liked to have children. Margot can't, you know. We did think of adopting, but somehow we never quite did. But, yes, we've been very happy, despite that.'

He looked briefly around the snug.

'Well, let's drink up. We will have one at the Four Alls on the way back, and then we will seek out an early dinner. We have to be up betimes tomorrow to catch our train to Cardiff.'

Ben smiled.

'And what awaits us in Cardiff?'

'The second part of your initiation into the mysteries of Wales,' Gareth replied. 'Actually, we are meeting Donald for dinner tomorrow evening, and then on Saturday – well, let's just say we have very special plans for Saturday.'

30

GARETH HAD BOOKED THEM into the Angel, a striking Victorian hotel in the heart of Cardiff city centre. Donald Weston was waiting for them in the bar when they arrived just after 6 o'clock, tired after a slow train journey from Caernarfon.

'I'm glad to see you've made a start, Donald,' Gareth said.

'I didn't know what time you were arriving,' Donald grinned, 'so I decided it was better to wait here with a pint than in my room without one. What can I get you?'

'Quite right. A pint of whatever you're drinking,' Gareth said.

'Same for me,' Ben added.

'How was Caernarfon?' Donald asked, when they were all seated with their drinks. 'Do you feel any more Welsh now than you did before, Ben?'

Ben laughed.

'I'm not sure I can answer that. Was that the objective, Gareth?'

'No,' Gareth smiled. 'You can't *become* Welsh. It was about soaking up the atmosphere and getting inside your client's head to some extent, which I think we achieved.'

'Yes, I think we did,' Ben agreed. 'Caernarfon is an odd place. Have you been there, Donald?'

'No, never.'

'It's amazing. It's such a small town, dominated by such a grand castle. That gives it an incredible atmosphere.'

'And if you are born and bred there,' Gareth added, 'that is part of your psyche. You grow up in the shadow of the Castle, and you know its history and its associations with the English domination of Wales. You grow up surrounded by all of that, and you can't escape it. It's mother's milk. It's not surprising that, in some cases, it turns into an obsession, and obsessions can get out of hand, and that's what we are dealing with now. But it's one thing to understand that intellectually, and it's another thing to feel it for yourself.'

'I think I did feel something of it,' Ben said. 'And if it made an impression on me in a couple of days, I can only imagine what it must be like to be aware of it every day of your life.'

'Yes. In Caradog's case you are probably dealing with an intellectual who sees everything in black and white, and if you see everything in black and white you tend to see conspiracies against you everywhere, and from there it's a short journey to outright paranoia. And one day, it suddenly seems perfectly logical to you to build a bomb and plant it where it will cause enormous loss of life, and it doesn't bother you at all because it is a necessary and proportionate response to the evil done to you. And because you then have an absolute belief in yourself and your convictions, you can easily recruit a follower like Dai Bach, who is looking for a cause to make some sense of his life, and has been waiting all his life for someone to lead him to it. How Arianwen fits into that I don't know, but if the prosecution are right, she fits in somewhere. Your job is to work out whether he recruited her too, or whether she managed to stay on the right side of sanity.'

They were silent for some time.

'How are you looking forward to the second part of your indoctrination tomorrow?' Donald asked.

'I haven't been told about that,' Ben replied. 'Gareth has been very mysterious about it.'

'You haven't told him?'

'No,' Gareth smiled. ''He's a devotee of the round ball game, a West Ham fan. Well, who isn't, after the last World Cup? But I didn't know how he would react to being exposed to football in its true form.'

'You're taking me to a rugby match?' Ben laughed. 'That game with the funny-shaped ball?'

Gareth feigned outrage.

'Now then, now then… in the first place, Ben, if you are to have any hope of understanding Wales, you have to understand that rugby is not a game with a funny-shaped ball – it is the *only* game, and the ball is exactly as it should be. Rugby is not a sport in Wales; it's a religion. If you don't grasp that, you haven't grasped Wales. Dai Bach is the perfect example, but I bet you even Arianwen can tell you how many times Wales have beaten England, and give you the score in quite a few of the games, to boot. In the second place, I am not taking you to just *any* rugby match.'

'Wales versus France at Cardiff Arms Park,' Donald smiled.

'Yes,' Gareth added, 'and I want you to know that I had to mortgage my soul to get three tickets for this match. Do you know how hard it is to get international tickets for Wales?'

Ben laughed.

'I will take it seriously, then,' he said. 'You're going to have to explain the rules to me as we go along. I know you have to ground the ball behind the other team's line, and you can't pass the ball forward, but all this business with the scrums and line-outs is very mysterious.'

'It does get a bit esoteric,' Gareth agreed. 'Donald can tell you all about the finer points. He's played enough. My main concern is that you experience the atmosphere of the Arms Park on international day. I guarantee that it will be quite different from anything you've felt at Upton Park.'

'Of course,' Ben said. 'You got your blue at Cambridge, didn't you?'

'I did,' Donald replied. 'Actually, we have two members of Chambers who got their blues the same year, Clive Overton and myself. That must be something of a record.'

'So you must have had ambitions of playing here yourself at one time, or perhaps you still do?'

Donald shook his head.

'I wasn't quite that good, unfortunately. I would have loved to play for England, but it wasn't going to happen. I decided to call it a day to concentrate on my practice. It's an incredible time commitment to play rugby at that level, or any serious level, really.'

'But you must miss it.'

'I do.' He paused. 'Now, Clive was a different story. He could have played for England. The selectors were looking at him while he was still up at Cambridge. If it hadn't been for... well, you know, the prank that went wrong after the rugby club dinner, that chap dying, and his father sending Clive to America...'

'Yes,' Ben said. 'I suppose that put an end to it.'

'Yes. It's a shame. He would have been a source of tickets for Twickenham.'

Ben laughed.

'Well, that's one way of looking at it, I suppose. So, Gareth, what's at stake tomorrow – other than national pride in beating France, obviously?'

'If we win, we will share the honours of the Five Nations for this season. They may just pip us to the post on points difference if we don't run up a decent score. It would be nice to win outright.'

Donald laughed.

'He says that,' he said, 'but it's already been a successful campaign, hasn't it, Gareth, regardless of what happens tomorrow?'

'Certainly.'

'In what sense?' Ben asked.

'We beat England,' Gareth replied. 'At Twickenham.'

31

IN CAERNARFON, LOOKING OUT over the calm of the Menai Strait, and standing in the *Maes,* awed by the majestic towers of Caernarfon Castle, it was the silence that had entranced Ben. Now it was the sounds. Even an hour before kick-off, when they took their seats in the North Stand, there was an air of expectation, a steady hubbub among the spectators. A male voice choir, its members dressed in identical smart navy blue blazers with the three feathers of the Prince of Wales emblazoned on the top pocket, was warming up in the centre of the pitch, players in track suits running around them, also warming up, as if the choir were just as much at home on the pitch as they were.

'Quite a sight,' Ben said. He felt unaccountably nervous, butterflies in his stomach.

'The Park is changing, isn't it?' Donald asked. 'When is the new National Stadium due to open?'

'Any time now,' Gareth replied despondently. 'It's been some time since I was here last, but you can see the construction going on all around us. We may be seeing the last Five Nations in the old Arms Park. I hope the new stadium can keep the atmosphere alive.'

The crowd grew steadily in size and became more vocal, chants and shouts began to drift across the stadium towards them. Gareth smiled.

'You can just imagine Dai Bach over there, in the South Stand, getting his voice warmed up, can't you?'

'I'm sure he wishes he was here,' Donald said.

'So do I,' Gareth said.

As Ben looked around him, the butterflies grew stronger. It was not an unpleasant sensation. It reminded him of how he felt when he was waiting to go into court, feeling the surge of adrenalin

through his body which made him ready to perform. He felt almost
as though he was waiting to play in the match, and smiled inwardly
at the thought. It was not the stadium itself. He had grown up as
a regular at First Division matches at Upton Park. He was used to
big stadiums and big matches and the crowds that went with them,
and to the singing, chanting and cheering which accompanied them.
None of that seemed strange at all, but there was something about
this place that made today's experience different from anything he
had known before. As he watched the legion of fans, with their red
scarves, rapidly filling the stadium, there was a tangible feeling of
ever-increasing excitement in the air.

Suddenly, there was only half an hour to go to kick-off; an
announcement was made; and the choir suddenly formed their
serried ranks and were ready to begin. A conductor with a long, thin
baton, took his place in front of them. He held the baton aloft. He
had the choir's full attention, and there was a momentary silence.
Then they began. Within seconds, the many rows of fans had joined
in, making one massive choir of thousands of voices, effortlessly
picking up the bass and tenor lines, as if they sang together every
day.

The first song was in Welsh. Ben turned to Gareth to ask for a
translation, but was only just able to make himself heard as the waves
of harmonious sound swept over them from all around the ground,
and those around them joined in.

Mae bys Mari Ann wedi brifo,
A Dafydd y gwas ddim yn iach,
Mae'r baban yn y crud yn crio,
A'r gath wedi scrapo Johnny Bach.

'It's called *Sospan Fach*. It's a nonsense song,' Gareth almost
shouted. 'It's all to do with saucepans boiling, and a baby crying, and
the cat scratching little Johnny.'

'Those are strange lyrics for a rugby song,' Ben shouted back.

Sospan fach yn berwi ar y tan!
Sospan fawr yn berwi ar y llawr!
A'r gath wedi scrapo Johnny Bach!

Gareth laughed.

'It's not so important what words they sing. It's the tune that
counts, and how they sing it. They will come on to a couple of hymns
in a moment, and not everyone would associate hymns with rugby,
either.'

'No, but you did tell me that rugby is a religion in Wales.'

'Yes. There you go. Now you're getting the idea.'

As the strains of the cat scratching little Johnny died away, the choir eased off the volume a little, and the tone became sweeter for a moment as they launched into *Calon Lân*.

Nid wy'n gofyn bywyd moethus,
Aur y byd na'i berlau mân;
Gofyn 'rwyf am galon hapus,
Calon onest, calon lân.

'This is one of our great Welsh hymns,' Gareth said. 'They learn it in chapel, and all the male voice choirs sing it. It's all about having a clean heart.'

Then the choir broke into the chorus, and once again the volume soared, wave after wave of pulsating chapel fervour sweeping across the Arms Park.

Calon lân, yn llawn daioni,
Tecach yw na'r lili dlos,
Dim ond calon lân all ganu,
Canu'r dydd a chanu'r nos!

'Only a clean heart can sing,' Gareth was saying, 'singing by day and by night... well, it's very poetic language, and a translation doesn't really do it justice.'

Ben nodded, but he was only vaguely aware of Gareth's voice. The music had almost engulfed him. Other verses were sung, and they were followed by a deafening final chorus.

As the time arrived for the presentation of the players and the national anthems, the choir had time for one more: in English this time, and Ben needed no translation. Two verses of *Guide me, oh thou Great Jehovah*. The stadium was now one huge choir, and as the bass chorus rose as one man to the famous arpeggio on the line *Feed me till I want no more*, Ben found himself lost in the stadium in the midst of the crowd, overwhelmed by a physical wall of noise.

Finally, the anthems. A good crowd of French supporters, sporting blue scarves and black berets and placards bearing the legend *Allez Bleu!* had established themselves in one corner of the stadium, and gave a hearty rendition of the *Marseillaise*, but when the Welsh anthem started, Ben felt light, as if the music itself might carry him away of its own accord.

Mae hen wlad fy nhadau yn annwyl i mi,
Gwlad beirdd a chantorion enwogion o fri,

Ei gwrol ryfelwyr, gwladgarwyr tra mad,
Tros Ryddid collasant eu gwa'd!

Gareth was too busy singing to translate, and it was much later, in the hotel bar, that Ben understood the references to the land of bards and singers, about their love for the language and the country. At the time, no translation was necessary. The passion echoed through in every word. The wall of noise was physical, making the whole stadium reverberate.

Gwlad! Gwlad!
Pleidiol wyf i'm gwlad,
Tra môr yn fur, i'r bur hoff bau,
O bydded i'r hen iaith barhau!

Afterwards, Ben remembered little about the match. At half time he asked Donald one or two token technical questions about what he had seen, but Donald was preoccupied with the game, and Gareth was anxious about the outcome. When the final whistle blew, with Wales ahead 11-6, Gareth gave a triumphant shout. They waited for the crowds to clear before beginning the short walk back to their hotel. The singing and the roar of the crowd had dissipated now, but Ben continued to hear it until much later, when he eventually drifted off to sleep in the early hours of the morning.

Just before 4 o'clock he awoke with a start. He had the impression that he had been shouting something, but he could not recall what it was. He suddenly realised that he was in a cold sweat, and he pulled the bedclothes tightly around him. When the shivering finally subsided, he tried to reconstruct the dream, or nightmare, from which he had awoken so abruptly. There were only fragments, and only one fragment made any sense. He was in Caernarfon, walking slowly from the *Maes* towards the Castle, holding a brightly-coloured duffle bag. There was a thick fog, and the towers of the Castle were only visible by its lights, high above the ground. Through the fog, in the fragmented light, he could just make out the shapes of some shadowy figures clothed in black. These people were calling out to him, but he could not see who they were, or even whether they were men or women, and he could not hear what they were saying. He walked on, but however much he walked, he never seemed to get any closer to the Castle.

He had to be up before 7 o'clock to ready himself for the journey home. He decided not to try to go back to sleep.

When he arrived home Jess noticed that he was distracted, and tried to draw him into conversation about his short visit to Wales. But he seemed to find it hard to give a coherent account of it. He made an effort to describe what he had felt at Cardiff Arms Park but, as he had not yet understood it himself, what he said made no sense to her, and little enough to him.

'Well, do you at least feel you understand Arianwen any better?' she asked eventually.

'Yes,' he replied. 'I think so. I think I am beginning to see Wales through her eyes.'

'Does that make you want to rush out and bomb something?' she asked.

'No,' he replied. 'But I've only lived with it for three days.'

PART 3
RHAN 3

PART 3

32

'DEREK PARKER, DETECTIVE SERGEANT, currently attached to the Metropolitan Police Special Branch, my Lord.' The officer nodded briefly in the direction of Mr Justice Overton, and folded his hands behind his back.

Evan Roberts' opening statement had occupied almost the whole morning of the first day of trial. It had been far too long and extremely repetitive; the entire court – including the jury – had found it a challenge just to stay awake, much less take in everything he was saying. It was, Ben thought, just another indication of his lack of experience of criminal practice. Anyone who practised in the criminal courts learned early on that you couldn't afford to lose the attention of the jury – twelve members of the public with no legal training and no training in the art of listening attentively to a speaker for hours on end. When it finally ended, to audible sighs of relief from the defence side of the courtroom, a frustrated Mr Justice Overton adjourned court until after lunch. It was now time to see how well Roberts would do with a witness.

'Detective Sergeant,' Roberts began, 'did you make any notes about the matters you are going to deal with?'

'I did, sir.'

Roberts looked across counsel's row towards the defence.

'I don't know whether my learned friends have any objection to the officer refreshing his memory from his notes?'

Gareth whispered to Ben. 'I'm not sure I have the patience today. Why don't you explain it to him?'

Ben stood.

'My Lord, that rather depends on what reply the Sergeant gives to the usual questions,' he replied. 'I suggest that my learned friend should follow the usual practice and put them to him.'

'I am surprised that that should be necessary, my Lord.'

The judge closed his eyes and shook his head slightly as his anxiety over Roberts began to increase. Why in God's name they couldn't have given this to criminal Treasury Counsel, or at least a Silk with a decent amount of experience of crime, he would never understand.

'I can't see any reason for surprise, Mr Roberts,' he replied as patiently as he could. 'It is for the prosecution to demonstrate that the officer is entitled to refer to his notes to refresh his memory.'

'As your Lordship pleases,' Roberts replied ungraciously. 'If your Lordship would allow me a moment.' He turned to consult hurriedly with Jamie Broderick.

Ben sat down with a shake of his head, glancing over at Gareth.

'Surely to God he is not asking Broderick what the usual questions *are*?' Gareth asked.

'It looks like it,' Ben replied.

'I wish he would just let Broderick get on with it. It would save us all a lot of time, wouldn't it?'

'Officer, when were your notes made?' Evan was asking.

'About eight hours after the event, at Caernarfon Police Station, sir.'

'Eight hours? Was that the first practicable opportunity you had to make your notes?'

'It was, sir, yes. It had been a very busy day up to that point.'

'In what way?'

'Well, in addition to arresting three suspects, we – my colleagues and I – had to convey them to the police station, and make arrangements to take care of Mrs Hughes' young son. We were then assigned to assist uniformed officers in evacuating a large area around the scene of the arrests so that the Army bomb disposal officers could work on the bomb we found. It was quite a while before I had time to sit down and make notes. I did it as soon as possible, of course.'

'When you made your notes, were the facts fresh in your memory?'

'Yes sir, they were.'

Jamie Broderick was still whispering to Roberts urgently from the row behind him.

'Did you make your notes alone, or with other officers?'

'I wrote my notes alone, sir, but I checked my memory of certain events with DC Owen and DC Swanson subsequently, and I did make one or two changes based on my discussion with them, which I indicated by initialling them in my notebook.'

'And what was the purpose of discussing your notes with those other officers?'

'To make sure we had the best possible recollection of events, sir. Everything happened very quickly that day, and there was no way all of us could have remembered everything that happened.'

Roberts looked over at Ben once again. Ben stood at once. It must already have become clear to the judge that he had every reason to look at the officer's notes later if he wished. There was no point in giving Roberts any more of a hard time now, just for the sake of it.

'No objection, my Lord.'

DS Parker produced his notebook from the inside pocket of his suit jacket, opened it carefully at the page he wanted and placed it in front of him.

'Detective Sergeant, in the early morning of 1 July 1969, were you on duty as a member of a team of officers assigned to duties in Caernarfon in connection with the security of the Investiture of the Prince of Wales?'

'I was, sir. I am usually based in London, but I had been assigned to Caernarfon about three weeks before the Investiture.'

'What were your particular duties on that day?'

'I was part of a small mobile unit with my colleagues DC Owen and DC Swanson. We had no definite assignment, but we had to be available for immediate deployment to anywhere we might be needed at very short notice. We were under the command of DCI Grainger, who, I was given to understand, was working with a senior officer of the Domestic Security Service, MI5.'

'Were the members of your unit in uniform or plain clothes?'

'Plain clothes, sir.'

'And is there any other detail it might be relevant for the jury to hear?'

'All the members of my unit are trained in the use of firearms, sir, and we carried side arms whenever we left the police station.'

'At what time did you begin duty on that morning?'

'In fact, sir, we had been on duty since about 11 o'clock the previous evening. We replaced colleagues who had been on duty until then, liaising with the Earl Marshal's team, and who had been extremely busy.'

'Yes, I see. And at about 12.30, did the unit receive any information? Just answer yes or no, please, Sergeant.'

'Yes, sir, we received some information from DCI Grainger.'

'As a result of that information, did you do anything?'

'Yes, sir. We immediately checked our side arms out of storage, and made our way in an unmarked police car to the junction of New Street and Chapel Street, not far from the *Maes*, the name given to the town square, and also not far from the Castle.'

'Yes. Sergeant, you should have before you a copy of a plan of the town centre. My Lord, that is Exhibit 1.'

'Yes,' the judge replied.

'And on Exhibit 1, would you please point to the junction of New Street and Chapel Street, and hold the plan up so that My Lord and the jury can see it.'

'Yes, sir, it's just here.' The sergeant made a broad sweep of the court, the forefinger of his left hand resting firmly on the spot.

'Thank you. What did you do on arriving at that junction?'

'We parked the car a short distance away from the junction, and remained in the vehicle, from where we had a good view of the street. Shortly after our arrival, I saw DCI Grainger arrive in an unmarked car, and park nearby. I saw that he was in company with two officers of the Domestic Security Service.'

'At about 1.15, was your attention drawn to anything in particular?'

Sergeant Parker looked down at his notebook for the first time.

'Yes, sir. At about 1.15 I noticed a vehicle approaching the junction in a southerly direction on New Street. As the vehicle approached the junction, it seemed to slow down, and it stopped at the junction, about fifty yards from our position. I was able to see that the vehicle was a grey Austin 1100 car, registration number EVF 421D.'

'Were you able to see who was in the vehicle?'

'Yes. I was able to see that the driver was a female, who I now know to be Arianwen Hughes. In the front passenger seat was a male I now know to be Dafydd Prosser.'

'Did the driver get out of the car?'

'Not immediately, sir. She remained parked, with the engine running for, I would estimate, about three minutes.'

'Then what happened?'

'Dafydd Prosser got out of the car and walked along New Street to the junction with Chapel Street, crossed the road, and continued down New Street in the direction of Segontium Terrace. I lost sight of him. Mrs Hughes remained in the car with the engine running.'

'Did you see Dafydd Prosser again?'

'I did, sir. After two minutes or less I saw Prosser approaching, walking along New Street, coming back the same way he had gone. He was in company with another male, who I now know to be Caradog Prys-Jones. Mr Prys-Jones and Mr Prosser seemed to be having an animated conversation, though I was unable to hear what they were saying. Mr Prys-Jones was carrying a brightly-coloured duffle bag. They crossed Chapel Street and walked towards the rear of the car. At this point, Mrs Hughes got out of the car, closed the driver's door, and also walked around the car to the rear.'

'Was any of the three of them doing anything you could see?'

'Yes, sir. Mr Prosser appeared to bend down as if examining or looking for something in the boot. Mrs Hughes and Mr Prys-Jones were standing next to him.'

'Did you do anything at that stage?'

'Yes, sir. We were in radio contact with DCI Grainger's car and, at this stage, I heard the DCI shout "Go! Go!" several times, very loudly. Together with DC Owen and DC Swanson, I left our vehicle. I drew my weapon and ran towards the boot of the Austin, shouting as loudly as I could, "Armed police! Put your hands in the air! Now!" I repeated this several times as I ran towards the car, and I heard DC Owen and DC Swanson shouting similarly. They also had their weapons drawn.'

'Tell the jury, please, why you had drawn your weapon.'

'I couldn't see the suspects' hands. From the direction we were approaching, my view was blocked by the lid of the boot, so I couldn't see whether one of the suspects might have been reaching into the boot to retrieve a weapon. The situation was unclear, and could have been dangerous to myself, other officers, or members of the public.'

'Yes, I see. What happened when you reached the rear of the car?'

'All three suspects appeared to be taken completely by surprise, sir. None offered any resistance. DC Owen and DC Swanson got there a moment or two before I did, and I saw them holding Mr Prosser against the boot of the car so that they could handcuff him. They then dealt similarly with Mr Prys-Jones. I went over to Mrs Hughes and put her up against the rear passenger side of the car, and handcuffed her by her wrist to the door handle. She said something about her son. I looked into the rear of the car, and saw a male child who appeared to be four or five years old strapped to a car seat in the rear driver's side seat.'

'What did you do about the child?'

Sergeant Parker shook his head. 'Well, sir, I did a whole series of things in a hurry at that point, because just as Mrs Hughes pointed out the child, I heard DC Owen shouting loudly from the rear of the car.'

'What was he saying?'

'He was saying that there was a bomb in the car, that we had to evacuate the area now, and call in Bomb Disposal. By that time, DCI Grainger had arrived on the scene and had seen the bomb for himself, and he was already on the radio.'

'Go on.'

'I instructed DC Swanson to arrest Mr Prys-Jones and take him to the police station. I instructed DC Owen to keep Mr Prosser in cuffs, and to remove him to a place of safety away from the vehicle. I immediately took the cuffs off Mrs Hughes and instructed her to follow DC Owen in company with a uniformed officer. She declined to move until she knew her son was safe. I judged that she was not a flight risk, and rather than wasting time arguing with her, I left her where she was. I then opened the rear driver's side door and removed the child from the car seat. I handed the child to Mrs Hughes. We then took her and the child to the police station.'

'Do you now know that the child was Mrs Hughes' son, Harri?'

'Yes, sir.'

'Sergeant, why was Mr Prosser not taken immediately to the police station?'

'Based on information we had received, sir, I had reason to believe that Mr Prosser would have information useful to Bomb Disposal in making the device safe. We needed to have him at the scene so that we could ask him to assist.'

'And is it within your knowledge that he did in fact assist in that way?'

'I wasn't present, sir, but I believe he did.'

'Did you actually see the bomb yourself?'

'No, sir, there was no time. We had to get Mr Prys-Jones, Mrs Hughes and the child into the police cars and take them to Caernarfon Police Station. I was in one car with Mrs Hughes and her son. DC Swanson accompanied Mr Prys-Jones in another car. On the way, I informed Mrs Hughes that she was under arrest on suspicion of the unauthorised possession of explosives, and cautioned her. She made no reply to the caution.'

Roberts paused again. Broderick was whispering to him from the row behind.

'Yes. I am much obliged. Sergeant, as this is the first time the jury has heard a reference to the caution, please tell the jury the words of the caution.'

'Yes, sir. The words of the caution are: "You are not obliged to say anything unless you wish to do so, but what you say may be put into writing and given in evidence."'

'Sergeant, after delivering the suspects to the police station, what did you do?'

'We immediately returned to the scene to assist uniformed officers in evacuating a considerable area around where Mrs Hughes' vehicle was parked. This included the Castle Hotel in the square, which had many guests, so it was a major undertaking. In fact, within a fairly short space of time, we received word from Bomb Disposal that the device was safe, and officers informed members of the public that they were now free to return to the buildings from which they had been evacuated. As soon as I received word that it was safe, I joined DC Owen, who had arrested Mr Prosser and was still detaining him, and we conveyed Mr Prosser to the police station. By now, it was after 2.30 in the morning, sir.'

'Thank you, Detective Sergeant. With the usher's assistance… please look at the object the usher is going to hand you. Can you tell my Lord and the jury what that is?'

'Yes, sir. This is the duffle bag Caradog Prys-Jones had with him at the time of his arrest.'

'Exhibit 4, my Lord, please.'

'Yes.'

Evan turned round and whispered with Jamie Broderick for some time. Mr Justice Overton coughed loudly enough to get his attention.

'Yes, thank you, Sergeant,' he said. 'Wait there, please.'

33

'SERGEANT,' GARETH MORGAN-DAVIES BEGAN, 'Mr Prosser was fully cooperative with the police, was he not?'

'At all times when I saw him, sir, he was.'

'He made no attempt to escape, did he?'

'No, sir.'

'He was carrying no weapon when he was arrested, was he?'

'That is correct, sir.'

'And when DC Swanson and DC Owen discovered the bomb, did he not immediately shout out that the bomb was safe and was not armed?'

'I did not hear that myself, sir. I was busy with Mrs Hughes. But I can say that DC Owen later confirmed that Mr Prosser had told him that the bomb was not armed. When exactly he said that, I do not know.'

'Thank you, Sergeant. Of course, I understand that in any case, you could not take his word for it…'

'No, sir, we could not…'

'No, of course. But he said everything he could, before Bomb Disposal arrived, to indicate that he would cooperate with them?'

'I would accept that, sir, yes.'

'And he did in fact assist them when they arrived, didn't he?'

'I believe so, sir, yes.'

'Yes, thank you, Sergeant.'

'Sergeant, as you have told us, you were the officer who dealt with Arianwen Hughes at the scene.' Ben said.

'I was, sir.'

'When DC Owen and DCI Grainger started shouting that there was a bomb, what was her reaction?'

DS Parker looked down at his notebook.

'I have not recorded this in my notes, sir, but I do recall that she looked extremely shocked.'

'What did you notice about her that led you to think that she was extremely shocked?'

'Her whole body was shaking, sir. I saw her turn to look at Mr Prys-Jones and Mr Prosser, and she seemed to have difficulty speaking at first. It was only when I had her handcuffed to the car and was preparing to arrest her that she spoke.'

'And that was when she refused to leave the scene without her son, Harri?'

'Yes, sir.'

'Mrs Hughes was not carrying a weapon of any kind, was she?'

'No, sir, she was not.'

'How did she behave while you were taking her to the police station?'

'She was quiet most of the time, but she did ask me questions once or twice about what would happen to Harri, and of course I had to explain that he would be taken into the care of the local authority until matters were sorted out.'

'And how did she react when you told her that?'

'She was bitterly distressed, sir,' the Sergeant replied, 'bitterly distressed.'

'Well,' Evan Roberts said, jumping to his feet before Jamie Broderick could reach out a restraining hand, 'you say that she was extremely shocked at the discovery of the bomb. But isn't it just as likely that what you saw as shock was simply distress, because she knew she had been caught?'

Ben was half way up to object when he saw the look that DS Parker gave Evan Roberts, and on seeing it he sat down quietly. Jamie Broderick glanced in Ben's direction and shook his head.

'I have given my evidence, sir,' the Sergeant replied, 'and I have nothing to add.'

DC Swanson and DC Owen were called next to describe the arrest of the suspects, and their evidence followed the same path as that of DS Parker. Neither Gareth nor Ben had anything to add to what they had already established through their cross-examination of DS Parker, and they let the witnesses pass. As if fatigued by the exertions of the day, Evan Roberts handed over abruptly to Jamie Broderick to deal with the few remaining items of business for the afternoon. It came as a relief to all present. Jamie was not only a great deal more confident in the courtroom, but was also far more pleasant in his manner. He was by no means tall, but he had handsome dark features and his open face always seemed ready to break into a smile. Once he was underway, some of the tension in court disappeared, and everyone, including the judge, relaxed for the first time that day.

'My Lord,' he began, 'the next three witnesses will deal with events at the Castle. They are all coming from Wales, and we had not expected to reach them today. So I am not in a position to call them now, but they will be available first thing tomorrow morning. May I invite your Lordship to release the jury for the day now?'

Mr Justice Overton agreed readily, and the jury left for the day. When they had gone, Gareth stood.

'My Lord, once those three witnesses have given evidence, matters of law arise, and I will have to ask your Lordship to hear evidence in the absence of the jury. I'm afraid it is likely to take some time; indeed, I think we may not get any further with the jury tomorrow.'

The judge raised his eyebrows.

'I take it this is to do with the written statement under caution made by Mr Prosser to the police?'

'Yes, my Lord. There is one other short matter also, but I will come to that in a moment. Mr Prosser made a number of oral statements to the police while being interviewed, and made a written statement under caution, which the jury, if they see it, might well think to be highly incriminating. I am sure your Lordship has read it?'

'I have, Mr Morgan-Davies, and I agree with you – the jury may well find it extremely incriminating. I take it you are going to ask me to keep it out?'

'Yes, my Lord. We say that it was obtained by the use of force, and I will be inviting your Lordship to keep it from the jury. The proper time for that to be done is tomorrow morning, before DCI Grainger gives evidence in front of the jury, and I have invited my learned friend to call him, and another officer, to give evidence then. I have also asked him to make available the custody sergeant on duty at the relevant time, and the medical officer who examined Mr Prosser while he was in custody.'

'All those witnesses will be available,' Jamie said.

Mr Justice Overton nodded.

'Very well. You said there was one other matter, Mr Morgan-Davies.'

'There is. My Lord, as Queen's Counsel I feel some responsibility to raise matters which might be raised by counsel on Mr Prys-Jones's behalf, if he were represented. I won't try to deal with every such matter, of course. Mr Prys-Jones is unrepresented by his own choice, and he must live with the consequences of that choice. But if there is a matter which might affect the interests of justice or the fairness of the trial, would your Lordship hear me?'

'That is in the best tradition of the Bar, Mr Morgan-Davies, and I would be very pleased to hear you if it is an important matter.'

'My Lord, I am much obliged. There is one matter which arises now. The prosecution is going to give the jury a translation of the statement under caution made by Mr Prys-Jones. The original, of course, is in Welsh. I invite the prosecution to look at it again, to make sure that the English translation is accurate. I am in some difficulty, because I am a native Welsh-speaker and there are some passages which strike me as questionable. But as counsel I can't give evidence, and that is all I can say about it. I wonder whether PC Watkins might be asked to look at the original and the translation this evening, to see whether he would suggest any changes?'

'Mr Broderick?' the judge asked.

'My Lord, I see no possible objection to that,' Jamie replied, without even glancing in the direction of Evan Roberts. 'My learned friend is quite right to raise it. It is important that, if there are any errors, they are corrected before it is placed before the jury. I will ask PC Watkins to look at it tonight.'

'I am much obliged,' Gareth replied.

34

Tuesday 5 May 1970

'I SWEAR BY ALMIGHTY God that the evidence I shall give shall be the truth, the whole truth, and nothing but the truth.' The voice had a lyrical Welsh accent, very different from that of the Met officers who had given evidence on the first day of the trial. The speaker, who was in uniform, returned the New Testament to the usher. 'Superintendent Stanley Rees of the Gwynedd Constabulary, based at Caernarfon Police Station, my Lord.'

Ben had wondered whether interest in the trial would be as intense as it had been on the first day. His question had been answered as soon as he and Barratt fought their way into court, pushing past the hordes of reporters and members of the public. The same Welsh observers had returned, queuing up early in the morning outside the Old Bailey and taking their places as soon as the courtroom doors were opened, to make sure that they were not excluded. They were quiet, but flashes of red, in handkerchiefs and scarves were noticeable whenever they turned their heads.

'Thank you, Superintendent,' Jamie said. 'First, can I ask you generally, was the Gwynedd Constabulary in overall charge of security in the period leading up to the Investiture?'

'The Chief Constable was responsible overall, sir, yes, in consultation with the Ministry of Defence.'

'Thank you. Were you on duty in uniform on the early morning of 1 July last year?'

'I was, sir.'

'And at about 1.30 that morning, were you given some information and asked to do something?'

'Yes, sir.'

'Were you informed…?' Jamie glanced across at the defence side.

'No objection,' Ben and Gareth replied in unison.

'Much obliged. Were you informed that Special Branch officers had discovered an explosive device, and that the Security Services believed that there might be a continuing threat to Caernarfon Castle?'

'Yes, sir. I was told that, although three suspects had been arrested, at least one more was still at large, and the Security Services could not exclude the possibility that there might already have been a breach of the Castle's security, or that a breach might be imminent.'

'What were you asked to do?'

'I was asked to undertake an immediate and detailed search of the Castle to determine whether there was any evidence of a breach of security, and deal with the breach appropriately.'

'And how did you do that?'

'I immediately called for every available uniformed officer assigned to duty in the town to report to the Castle without delay. I made my way to the Castle myself...'

'And, just so that the jury will understand, if they look at the plan of the town centre, Exhibit 1, is the police station in effect joined to the court building, which they will see bottom left at the corner of Castle Ditch and Shirehall Street?'

'That is correct, sir.'

'So you were not far away?'

'I only had to cross the street.'

'What else did you do?'

'I asked my duty sergeant to contact the Earl Marshal's office and wake someone up if he had to, to let them know what was going on. I also called for the bomb disposal squad to be deployed at the Castle in case of need, and for military assistance in making the search. Once I arrived at the Castle, I gathered all the night watchmen together, and I ordered all the lights to be turned on. Fortunately, in addition to the usual floodlights which would be on at night, many extra lights had been added for the purposes of the Investiture, and with them all switched on, it was brighter than day. This made the task a great deal easier than it might have been under normal circumstances. There were still some dark areas inside the towers, but far fewer than there would have been otherwise.'

'Yes, I see. How was the search undertaken?'

'I first divided all the officers and night watchmen I had – which made about twenty men in all, at that time – into four groups, and I ordered them to commence a systematic search of the towers. When that search ended, the teams carried out a search of the outside perimeter of the Castle. After the search had begun, further officers and a number of soldiers arrived to assist so, in due course, we had at least fifty men involved.'

'Yes.' Jamie looked up. 'If the usher would kindly show the witness our Exhibit 2, the plan of the Castle.' He paused to allow Geoffrey time to do this. 'As the jury have not really looked at this before, can we take a minute or two to orientate ourselves? Looking at the plan, is it fair to say that the Castle is laid down roughly in the shape of a figure eight?'

'Yes, sir.'

'The narrowest part is by the King's Gate, the main entrance, which is at the bottom of the plan in the middle. Yes?'

'Yes, sir.'

'Then if we were to go left from the King's Gate, we are heading east or north-east at that point, aren't we?'

'Yes.'

'And we would come, in order, to the Granary Tower, then the North-East Tower on that corner, then turning the corner the Watch Tower, and then to the Queen's Gate on the east side of the Castle?'

'Yes, sir.'

'I think it was at the Queen's Gate that the Queen presented Prince Charles to the people standing in the *Maes*, the town square, immediately after the ceremony. Is that right?'

'It was, sir.'

'As we were walking the route we have just taken, we were walking alongside the lawn of the upper ward, and that is where the dais was placed and where the ceremony of Investiture took place. Is that right?'

'Indeed, sir, yes.'

'And if we continue in the same direction, we come to the Black Tower and then the Chamberlain Tower, and we find ourselves opposite the King's Gate, where we started.'

'Yes, sir.

'And continuing on, passing the site of the Great Hall, which no longer exists, we would come to the Queen's Tower, we would turn right slightly, and we would come to the Eagle Tower on the west side of the Castle. And I think the Eagle Tower is of special importance, is that right?'

'Yes, sir. It is the biggest and most developed of all the Towers.

It has a basement antechamber which, traditionally, was the Royal entrance to the Castle, and above the antechamber are three floors with apartments. This tower houses the office of the Constable of the Castle, Lord Snowdon, and during the Investiture preparations, also housed the office of the Earl Marshal, the Duke of Norfolk.'

'And did the searchers walk through each area in turn?'

'They did, sir, and as new men arrived I assigned them to one of the four teams.'

'Yes. Now, taking this shortly, is it right to say that, after a thorough search, no explosive device or hazardous material was found anywhere in the Castle or on the perimeter?'

'That is correct, sir.'

'Were there any reports of any unauthorised intrusion into any part of the Castle?'

'No, sir.'

'But was one matter of potential interest brought to your attention?'

'Yes, sir. An army officer who was assisting with the search of the area surrounding the Black Tower found that a large stone in place on the ground had been loosened and then put back in place, leaving an empty space under the stone of about a foot in depth, and the dimensions of the stone itself being about three feet by two feet.'

'And why was that significant?'

'Because it provided a potential hiding place for an explosive device.'

'Did you examine the stone and the space underneath it personally?'

'Yes, sir.'

'Can you indicate to us, using the plan of the Castle, where the stone was?'

The witness peered at the plan. 'Yes, sir. To the right of the Black Tower as you look at it from the main entrance, the King's Gate, you will see a low corridor which leads to the Chamberlain Tower. The stone was in this corridor, roughly a third of the way from the Black Tower to the Chamberlain Tower, and close to the front or inside wall.'

'The wall by the upper ward lawn, where the ceremony was to take place later in the day?'

'Yes, sir.'

'What, if anything, did you do about that situation?'

'I brought it to the attention of the Ministry of Defence security team. I believe they arranged with the engineers to have the stone put back securely in place.'

'Yes. I will deal with that further with another witness. Thank you, Superintendent. Please wait there. I am sure there will be further questions.'

35

'SUPERINTENDENT,' GARETH BEGAN, 'WHEN you first received word that a bomb had been found on the edge of the *Maes*, a very short distance from the Castle, that must have been very alarming?'

'Of course.'

'Of course. Because, with at least one suspect at large, you must have feared that a device had already been placed in or around the Castle, or that something of that kind was about to happen?'

'Indeed.'

'If a device had somehow been planted in, or anywhere near, the Castle, immediate steps would have to be taken to deal with it?'

'Yes.'

'You would have had to evacuate the area and call in the bomb squad, wouldn't you?'

'Yes.'

'You would have had no way of knowing how much time you had to make the device safe?'

'That is correct.'

'Or even how great a danger it posed?'

'I would have made the assumption that it was extremely dangerous.'

'Yes, I'm sure you would. Quite rightly. I'm not criticising at all. My point is that in the situation you were in, time was of the essence. You had to act as quickly as you could?'

'Yes.'

'And the more information you had about what you were dealing with, the better, would you agree?'

The Superintendent paused for some time.

'I'm not sure what information we could have had, except for the device itself, sir. Even then, I would have had to leave it to the bomb squad to deal with. I didn't have any expertise of that kind available to me. It would have been up to them.'

'Yes, of course. But I'm sure they would have appreciated any assistance the police might have been able to give.'

'I don't see how we could have helped.'

'Superintendent, you knew, didn't you, that one of the three suspects arrested by your colleagues in Special Branch was a man called Dafydd Prosser, who was suspected of having designed and built the explosive device found earlier in New Street?'

Another pause.

'I'm not sure I was told his name at the time.'

'Perhaps not. But you knew that this man was in custody, just a few yards from the Castle, didn't you?'

'I did, sir.'

'And did it not occur to you how useful it would be if Dafydd Prosser could be persuaded to tell the police whether any more explosive devices had been planted, where they had been planted, and what would have to be done to disarm them?'

'I can't say I gave any thought to that.'

'Did you not, Superintendent?'

'My concern was to get on with searching the Castle.'

'But if the search turned up a bomb, you gave no thought to how to deal with it, other than to leave the bomb squad to do their best with whatever information they could get from the device itself?'

The witness did not reply.

'Superintendent,' Gareth said slowly. 'You may find it difficult to believe what I am about to say, given your long experience as a police officer, but I ask you to accept that what I am about to put to you is not intended as a criticism of you at all.'

The Superintendent smiled. 'One does get used to being criticised, sir.'

Gareth returned the smile. 'Yes, of course. But in this instance, you had every reason to believe that an explosive device might have been planted in or around the Castle, which had the potential to cause loss of life or serious injury. Is that not correct?'

'Yes, sir.'

'And I venture to suggest that no one in England, and very few in Wales, I suspect, would criticise you if, in those extraordinary circumstances, you had sanctioned methods of obtaining information which you would not for one moment contemplate in any other circumstances?'

Jamie Broderick was on his feet instantly. So was Evan Roberts.

Jamie put a hand on Evan's shoulder and pushed him down. He was going to deal with this one himself.

'My Lord, I don't know what my learned friend is suggesting?'

'That is because my learned friend interrupted before I could suggest it,' Gareth replied.

'Well, what *are* you going to suggest?' Mr Justice Overton asked.

'I am going to suggest that this witness sanctioned the use of force against Dafydd Prosser in an effort to discover information of the kind we have just been discussing,' Gareth replied.

'That is outrageous,' Jamie protested.

'It is not outrageous at all. I have even made it clear that I don't criticise the witness for what he did in the circumstances. But what he did may have certain legal consequences, which I will not refer to with the jury present, and I am entitled to ask about it.'

'I think that must be right, Mr Broderick,' Mr Justice Overton replied, recalling cross-examinations of his own during his career at the Bar, when he had made equally serious allegations against police officers with far more venom than Gareth was likely to use. 'If there are allegations of violence against a suspect, surely counsel is entitled to ask about it.'

'If there is a proper basis for it,' Jamie replied.

'I will demonstrate a basis,' Gareth said, 'if I am allowed to continue.'

'We shall see, Mr Broderick,' the judge said, 'shall we not?'

'As your Lordship pleases,' Jamie said, resuming his seat with a flourish.

'Do you need me to repeat the question, Superintendent, or are you…'

'No, I don't need you to repeat the question. No, I did not sanction the use of force against Prosser or anyone else. I would not have considered it.'

'Really? Not at all? Not even if the life of the Queen were to be threatened?'

'If we thought that Her Majesty's life, or the life of Prince Charles, or anyone's life, for that matter, was under threat, I would have advised the Earl Marshal to delay the ceremony of Investiture until such time as we were sure it was safe, and I am sure he would have accepted my advice.'

'Oh, really?' Gareth asked. 'After all the years of planning, all the money that had been spent? You would let one criminal Welsh nationalist stand in the way of a British state occasion?'

The Superintendent did not reply.

'Well, let me ask you this. If you didn't sanction the use of force against Dafydd Prosser, do you know who did?'

Jamie was on his feet again. 'Isn't that like asking him when he stopped beating his wife?'

'Or in this case, when they stopped beating Dafydd Prosser.'

'Oh, really, my Lord…'

The judge was smiling. 'Rephrase the question, Mr Morgan-Davies.'

'Yes, my Lord. Let me ask this. You do know, do you not, Superintendent, that while in custody at your police station, Dafydd Prosser suffered two broken ribs and multiple lacerations to the back of his head, his nose, and around his mouth?'

'I was told of that later by Sergeant Griffiths.'

'Sergeant Griffiths being the custody sergeant on duty at the time of the arrests, who was responsible for the welfare of any person arrested and kept in custody at your police station?'

'Yes.'

'And do you also know that, on the recommendation of Dr Markey, the police surgeon, Mr Prosser was taken to hospital to receive treatment, and was later returned to custody after being discharged?'

'So I was told.'

'So you were told? Did you not investigate for yourself? Was it of no concern to you that a man in custody at your police station had suffered serious injuries while in custody?'

'You keep saying "my police station"…'

'Were you the senior officer on duty at that time?'

'Yes, I was.'

'I am going to ask you once more, Superintendent, and I say again that I do so without criticism. Is it not true, that with your sanction, or at least with your knowledge, police officers beat Dafydd Prosser in his cell, while he was in custody in your police station, in an effort to gain information from him?'

The Superintendent stood silent for some time.

'I am not aware of that,' he replied.

'Do you know how he received his injuries?'

'I was told that he was injured while being restrained after he had assaulted two officers who were interrogating him.'

'Were you indeed?' Gareth said, looking around towards the dock and inviting the jury to follow his eyes to Dafydd Prosser. 'He assaulted two officers, did he? And who told you that?'

'It would have been Sergeant Griffiths.'

'And who were the unfortunate officers who were assaulted?'

'DCI Grainger was one,' the Inspector replied. 'And I believe DS Scripps was the other.'

'Did you authorise the presence of any person who was not a police officer in Mr Prosser's cell while he was being interrogated?'

'Such as who?'

'Such as an officer of the Security Services.'

Jamie was on his feet again.

'The witness cannot be allowed to answer that question, my Lord. It is not a proper question. The Crown has a privilege not to disclose matters of that kind. If my learned friend persists with it, I shall have to ask that the jury retire so that I can address your Lordship on the law.'

Gareth nodded. 'I do not persist with it for now,' he replied. 'But I may return to it at a later stage, and no doubt we can take advantage of a time when the jury is absent to discuss the law. I have no further questions for this witness.'

'I have no questions,' Ben said, but he had the impression that almost nobody was listening to him.

36

'MY LORD, I NOW call Alan Siddell,' Jamie announced.

Alan Siddell, a short, precise-looking man in his early forties, wearing a grey three-piece suit, a light blue shirt with a dark blue tie, and spectacles with clear plastic frames, climbed nimbly into the witness box, took the oath, and gave the court his full name.

'Mr Siddell, please tell his Lordship and the jury what you do for a living.'

'I am a senior administrative officer in the office of the Building Surveyor for Wales. The Surveyor's office is a sub-department of the Ministry of Public Building and Works. We are based in the Central Office for Wales in Cardiff.'

'What responsibilities, if any, did the Building Surveyor have for the Castle in connection with the Investiture?'

'The Surveyor was responsible to the Project Manager for almost everything relating to making the Castle ready and installing necessary equipment. This included seating stands for the guests, extra flagpoles, facilities for the television and radio personnel and the press, platforms for the military bands and other musicians. Everything, really, down to making sure that the grass was in perfect condition on the lawns. Obviously, we weren't doing all this ourselves. We had contractors who did the actual work, but we were in overall charge. You name it, we were involved in it.'

'What about security? Were you responsible for security in and around the Castle?'

Siddell thought for a moment. 'Partly. We had overall responsibility for the site, which did include security. But our job was to implement the security measures rather than decide what measures should be taken. The Chief Constable was in charge of that, and we took our lead from him.'

'What security measures were in place generally, in the period leading up to 1 July?'

'Well, first of all, you must understand that the conditions were very different from what they would be in normal circumstances.'

'In what way?'

'Well, for a start, the Castle was closed to the public for five months before the big day. We closed it on 1 February, and it remained closed until just after the Investiture. That had nothing to do with security. It was just that we needed the place to ourselves to get all the work done. We could never have done it with visitors roaming all over the place, and in any case it would have been too dangerous. It was like a building site in many ways. There were a lot of hazards.'

'What impact did that have on security?'

'It decreased the risk from members of the public, and it focused our attention on people working for contractors, sub-contractors, and different Government departments, the Earl Marshal's office, the Constable's office, the local authority. We issued passes of various kinds to allow those who needed access to the Castle to have access, and hopefully keep any others out. We issued about 600 passes in all during the project, so it was a complicated operation.'

'Did you have security guards in place?'

'Of course. Always. The day time security was provided by the Custodians of Ancient Monuments. At night, we had our own watchmen, who we employed specially. We also had police officers keeping an eye on the perimeter and the streets around the Castle.'

'Who was responsible for checking the passes of people who had reason to enter the Castle during this period?'

'The security staff on duty. They were given some training and they should have been very familiar with each kind of pass. Of course, as time went by they got to know the people who were coming in and out regularly.'

'Did the night watchmen you employed have written contracts of employment?'

'Yes, they did. We had to have their photographs on file, and all personal details, full name, date of birth, nationality, address, and so on.'

'Yes. If the usher would be so kind… Mr Siddell, I would like you to look at the document I'm going to give you, and tell me whether you recognise it.'

Siddell took the two-page document from Geoffey and studied it for some moments.

'Yes. This is a contract of employment issued to one of our night watchmen.'

'Thank you. Exhibit 5, my Lord, please.'

'Yes,' the judge replied.

'There are copies for the jury. Mr Siddell, who is the man referred to in this contract?'

'Caradog Prys-Jones.'

'The jury will see that his photograph is there, his date of birth and address are given. I assume you cannot recognise the signature?'

'No.'

'But has the contract been signed on behalf of the Surveyor's office?'

'Yes it has, and it is within my knowledge that Mr Prys-Jones was employed with effect from 1 February, as the contract states.'

'Leaving aside the salary and so on, which we can see is marked as declined…'

'Mr Prys-Jones was a permanent salaried employee of the Office of the Inspector of Ancient Monuments for Wales, and so continued to be paid by that office. We had one or two watchmen who came from other departments. It was a good thing for us because they had experience which might have been useful if some problem relating to the building itself cropped up during a night shift. Of course, as they were already receiving a salary, they were asked to decline any additional payments.'

'Thank you. Leaving that aside, what were Mr Prys-Jones's duties in terms of days and hours of work?'

'All the night watchmen worked four nights on, three nights off. They took over from day security at 10 o'clock at night, and the new day shift relieved them at 6 o'clock the following morning.'

'How many watchmen were on duty on any given night?'

'Usually four, but we also had two on call in case we needed back-up. Of course, we could also call the police if we needed them.'

'In addition to looking at the passes of anyone who might want to enter the Castle, what else would the night watchmen be expected to do?'

'There would not usually be many visitors at night, so their main duties were to keep their eyes open for anything that didn't look right, anything suspicious, to make regular patrols of the interior of the Castle, and to join in patrols of the perimeter with police officers.'

'Do you know whether or not Mr Prys-Jones worked in accordance with his contract?'

'Yes, he did. Each watchman had to sign in and out, and we have Mr Prys-Jones's signature on the logs for each night he was expected to work.'

Jamie produced a file of documents with copies for the jury.

'Exhibit 6, please, my Lord.' He waited for the usher to distribute them. 'Are these the logs?'

'They are.'

'We needn't go through them all. But, for example, on page twelve does Mr Prys-Jones's name appear as one of those on duty on 18 June, and is there a signature logging in and out for that night?'

'Yes.'

'And we can see, turning over the pages quickly, that the records continue, four nights on, three nights off, as you said.'

'Yes.'

'And turning to the very end of the document, dealing with 30 June, the night before the Investiture, does the log show whether Mr Prys-Jones was at work on that night?'

'He was working. The record shows that he signed in, but there is no record of his signing out.'

'Were night watchmen free to come and go, to leave the Castle and return, during the night?'

'They were not supposed to absent themselves after signing in. No.'

'No. But might there be a reason why a watchman would leave during his shift?'

'As I said, some watchmen would go out on patrol around the perimeter, but with that exception, there would be no reason to go out. There would be nowhere open to buy anything to eat and drink at that time. They were expected to bring whatever they needed with them from home. If they did leave for any reason, they were expected to inform the shift supervisor. If they were missed, and were absent without leave, we would want to know why, and the man concerned would be in danger of being dismissed unless he had a good explanation.'

'Would Mr Prys-Jones's employment have ended on 30 June, apart from his arrest?'

'Apart from his arrest, no, probably not immediately. Even though the Castle re-opened to the public after the Investiture, there was an enormous amount of work to do to restore it to the condition it was in before – apart from the permanent improvements, of course – so we needed additional staff for some time.'

'Thank you. Lastly, Mr Siddell, we know that a thorough search of the Castle was carried out in the wake of the arrest of Caradog Prys-Jones and the other defendants in this case.'

'Yes.'

'No explosive devices or weapons were found, but I believe your attention was drawn to a large stone which had been displaced in the corridor leading from the Black Tower to the Chamberlain Tower. Is that correct?'

'Yes.'

'And did you inspect the site yourself?'

'I did. I was alerted by messages sent by Superintendent Rees, and made my way to the Castle as soon as I could. The immediate area had been sealed off, and two soldiers were guarding it.'

'What time was this?'

'Slightly after 3 o'clock in the morning, if I remember correctly.'

'Would you describe what you saw?'

'A large stone, or slab, more accurately, in the floor of the corridor, at the front wall, was loose and was resting in place, but in such a way that it could be lifted up.'

'When you say "loose and resting in place", would the slab usually have been held in place in some way?'

'Oh, yes. You must understand that, although parts of the Castle are original and very old, it has been altered, repaired, maintained and so on over the years, certainly during the last century and this century. The walls still have some of their original construction, but the floor stones are now held in place by modern materials. Apart from anything else, that is a safety issue.'

'What conclusion did you come to about why this stone was loose?'

'It had undoubtedly been loosened deliberately. It couldn't have lost all its bonding material all at once, and certainly not without someone noticing. My first thought was that it had been done during the installation of electrical cables for TV filming. Most of the broadcasting was taking place in that area. The commentators were given space in the Black Tower, where their control room was, and in temporary booths between the Black Tower and the Chamberlain Tower. But I couldn't find any reason for this particular slab to have been moved in connection with that. The cables were running well back from the front wall.'

'What did you do?'

'The first thing I did was to check whether we had anything on the closed circuit television. We had installed closed circuit television to cover parts of the seating stands, but there was nothing covering the area I was interested in. I then called in a police photographer to take photographs of the slab in place, and the space underneath.'

'Exhibit 7, please. Usher, if you would…'

Jamie waited for the blue-covered bundles of photographs bearing the arms of the Gwynedd Constabulary to be distributed.

'Are these the photographs you referred to?'

'Yes.'

'The first picture shows the slab in place. Very helpfully, some measurements have been added in ink. They indicate that the slab is three feet four inches in length, and two feet nine inches across. Is that right?'

'Yes.'

'As the slab appears to be lying flat, is it immediately obvious that there is nothing holding it in place?'

'No, not unless you step on it and make it move, or you get quite close to it. It fits the space exactly, and it is partly in the shadow of the front wall. The soldier who found it trod on it, I believe, while searching that area. But otherwise you would have to get almost on top of it and look closely at it. At night, of course, it would be especially hard to see.'

'The second picture is of the space underneath, with the slab removed entirely. Again, measurements have been added, which indicate that the space is about a foot deep. Is that what you would expect?'

'No, that would be unusually deep. I would expect an inch or two at most.'

'What conclusion would you draw from that?'

'I would conclude that someone excavated under the slab to the depth of one foot.'

'Yes. Finally, Mr Siddell, please look at this. Exhibit 8, please, my Lord… can you tell me what this is?'

'Yes. This is a plan drawn by members of my office. It shows the location of the temporary stands erected for assigned seating for the Investiture ceremony.'

'And do we see from this, blocks A, B and C, which are actually on the lawn behind the Royal dais itself?'

'Yes.'

'Then we have blocks D, E, F and G, which are immediately in front of the Black Tower and the corridor, continuing almost to the Chamberlain Tower?'

'Yes.'

'And we can see other blocks, spaces for the choir and orchestra and so on, at different points in the Castle?'

'Yes.'

'How far were blocks D, E, F and G from the loose slab?'

'A matter of a few feet.'

'How many people were accommodated in those four blocks? An approximate number will do.'

'I can tell you exactly,' Siddell replied. 'If you look at the plan, bottom right corner, there is a breakdown of seating by blocks. Doing a little quick addition, there would have been…60 plus 114 plus 175 plus 176, which if my arithmetic is correct, makes 525 people in all.'

'The jury may be interested to know how many people were in the Castle at the time of the ceremony?'

'The total number of guests was 4045, including the Royal Family. Then, when you add in the choirs, musicians and so on, you arrive at 4478. Then, of course you have the press, police, military and so on, who are not counted as guests or performers. A large number, obviously.'

'What route was taken by the Royal Family to reach the dais?'

'The Queen entered the Castle through the Royal entrance by the Eagle Tower, where she was met by the Constable, Lord Snowdon, and the Mayor of Caernarfon, and was formally presented with the keys to the Castle. Then, after returning the keys to the Constable, she processed to the dais with the Duke of Edinburgh and other members of the Royal Party.'

'So they were walking almost the entire length of the Castle?'

'Yes. But Prince Charles was accommodated separately. He had a robing room in the Chamberlain Tower, and walked from there to the dais.'

'Right in front of stands D, E, F and G, and right past the loose slab?'

'Indeed.'

37

JOHN STEVENSON HAD BEEN the shift supervisor at the Castle on the night of 30 June. He remembered Caradog Prys-Jones signing in for work as usual at 10 o'clock, after which nothing unusual occurred until all hell broke loose some time between 1.30 and 2 o'clock, as reports started to come in of a bomb found not far from the Castle walls. At that point, Stevenson said, no one knew what was going on, and people were running around like headless chickens. Eventually, a senior police officer restored some semblance of order and organised them into search parties, and when more police officers and soldiers arrived, the situation started to look more under control. He was involved in the floor-by-floor search of the Eagle Tower, and knew nothing of the loose slab in the Black Tower corridor until much later.

'I want to ask you two further things,' Jamie Broderick said. 'First, you had worked with Caradog Prys-Jones a number of times before this night, had you not?'

'Yes, sir.'

'Did you notice whether he used to bring anything particular with him to work?'

'Yes. Caradog always carried the same duffle bag with red, yellow and black markings.'

'The usher will show you a duffle bag. My Lord, this is Exhibit 4. Can you say whether this is similar or dissimilar to the one Caradog Prys-Jones used to carry?'

The witness looked closely at the duffle bag Geoffrey presented to him.

'It is very similar,' he replied. 'I can't say whether or not it is his or not, but...'

'No, of course...'

'It is certainly very similar.'

'Secondly, Mr Stevenson, did you have occasion to speak to

Caradog Prys-Jones at any time during the night of 30 June, after he had signed in?'

'Yes. Caradog was down to do a patrol of the perimeter including the Slate Quay at 12.30 with whichever police officer or officers were in that area at the time. He was supposed to leave the Castle at 12.25 to rendezvous with the officers, conduct the patrol, and be back by 1.15 to 1.20, depending on how it all went.'

'Did you see him leave the Castle?'

'No. I may have been dealing with someone else when he left. I didn't see him around anywhere in the Castle, so I assumed he had gone on the patrol, and I thought no more about it.'

'Did you receive any report from the police officers he was supposed to be with?'

'No. As far as I knew, the patrol had taken place as planned.'

'But with one difference. Caradog didn't come back, did he?'

Stevenson shook his head sadly.

'No, sir. He didn't.'

There was no cross-examination.

'My Lord, I have a few witness statements to read to the jury,' Jamie said, 'dealing with evidence which is not in dispute and which my learned friends have agreed may be read. After that, I will invite your Lordship to rise until after lunch to begin the point of law which arises.'

The judge turned to the jury.

'Members of the jury, as you may have gathered, I have to deal with a point of law. It is my job to deal with questions of law; you are not concerned with that. I am told it may take some time, so rather than keep you waiting unnecessarily, I will release you for the day after the agreed witness statements have been read. I will ask you to be back tomorrow morning at 10.30 to resume then.'

38

'MY LORD, BEFORE I call DCI Grainger,' Evan Roberts began, after the court assembled at 2 o'clock without the jury, 'may I hand up a new English translation of the statement under caution made by Caradog Prys-Jones?'

Geoffrey took it from him and passed it up to the judge.

'My learned friends already have copies. It was prepared overnight by PC Watkins, as my learned friend Mr Morgan-Davies suggested. It does make one or two changes to the translation we have been working with up to this point.'

Mr Justice Overton looked at Gareth.

'Does this help, Mr Morgan-Davies?'

'Yes, my Lord. In addition to correcting a number of points of detail, it replaces the passage about blood flowing through the streets of London for generations to come, with the somewhat more restrained statement that ignoring the Welsh problem might lead to acts of violence – which has the advantage of being what Prys-Jones actually said in the Welsh original. I am very grateful to PC Watkins for his efforts.'

'The Court is also grateful,' the judge said, looking at Watkins, who nodded politely.

'I now call DCI Grainger,' Evan Roberts said.

Grainger was a large, broad-shouldered man with a menacing demeanour, only partially mitigated by the fact that he was carrying a bit too much weight. He was dressed in a dark three-piece suit which must have been made to measure for a slightly slimmer version of the man, a white shirt, and a dark blue tie. He took the oath in a deep, gruff bass voice.

'Steven Grainger, Detective Chief Inspector currently attached to the Metropolitan Police Special Branch, my Lord.'

'Chief Inspector, I am going to ask you certain questions in the absence of the jury about the statements made during interview by the defendant Dafydd Prosser. I am doing this because his Lordship has to decide whether or not to admit those statements in evidence. You understand that?'

'Yes, sir.'

'Thank you. By way of background, is it right that you had been assigned to duty in Caernarfon during the three months leading up to the Investiture, as head of a team of Special Branch officers?'

'That is correct, sir.'

'What was the purpose of the team's deployment?'

'To work with local police, the Ministry of Defence, and other bodies to ensure the security of the Investiture, and of Caernarfon Castle, and to assist in the investigation of any serious offences which might be committed, linked to the Investiture.'

'And – I think there is no dispute about it – in the early morning of 1 July were you on duty in plain clothes commanding a team of officers in the light of certain information you received?'

'Yes, sir.'

'Were you involved in the arrest of these three defendants at a location near the town square and the Castle, and in evacuating the immediate area when an explosive device was found in Mrs Hughes' car?'

'I was, sir. I also called in the bomb squad, who were able to assess the device, and who found that it had not been armed.'

'Yes. We have other evidence about those matters, and I am not concerned with them for now. Let me take you back to the time when that had been done. Was it by then after 2 o'clock in the morning?'

'It was after 2 o'clock by the time the device was finally declared to be harmless, as I recall.'

'What did you do next?'

'My immediate concern at that point was to ascertain whether there was a continuing threat. We had failed to arrest one suspect, Trevor Hughes, who remained at large, and I was concerned that there might be one or more further devices out there that we didn't know about.'

'How did you go about making further inquiries?'

'My view was that the person most likely to provide the information we needed was Dafydd Prosser. He was suspected of having built the device we had recovered. He had been arrested by

DC Owen, and was still at the scene, and he had offered to assist by demonstrating to the bomb squad officers that the device was safe.'

'What steps did you take?'

'We immediately conveyed Prosser to Caernarfon Police Station. He was booked into custody and placed in a cell. This had to be done before I could interview him.'

'Did you interview him alone, or with any other officers?'

'DS Scripps was with me.'

Evan paused. 'In connection with what happened next, have you made any notes, and do you wish to refer to them?'

'Yes please, sir.'

'I don't know whether there is any objection?'

With a glance at Ben, Gareth stood.

'The answer to that is the same as it was in relation to a previous witness, my Lord. My learned friend should please ask the appropriate questions. There may or may not be an objection, depending on the answers the Chief Inspector gives.'

'Well, I will take it shortly,' Evan said, with some show of irritation.

'It would be better if you took it *properly*, Mr Roberts,' the judge intervened before Gareth could say any more. Gareth quietly resumed his seat.

For a moment, Evan seemed disposed to argue, but bit his lip and continued.

'As your Lordship pleases. Chief Inspector, at what time did you make your notes?'

'It was later that morning, a little after 8 o'clock, in the canteen in the police station.'

'Was that the first practicable opportunity you had to make notes?'

'It was the first opportunity of any kind I had to make notes. After interviewing Mr Prosser, I had to follow events at the Castle and elsewhere in the town. I was also directing the ongoing search for Trevor Hughes, which in the event was unsuccessful, but nonetheless took some considerable time.'

'Was anyone with you when you made your notes?'

'Yes, sir. DS Scripps was with me. Following the usual practice, we made our notes together, and pooled our recollections.'

'And does it follow that DS Scripps' notebook would be identical to yours?'

'I can't speak for DS Scripps, sir, and I have not looked at his notebook, but I would expect his evidence of these events to be substantially the same as mine.'

'Quite so. Then, with his Lordship's leave...'

'No objection,' Gareth said. 'I may wish to inspect the Chief Inspector's notebook at a later stage.'

'Very well,' Mr Justice Overton said. 'Chief Inspector, you may refresh your memory from your notebook if you wish.'

The Chief Inspector took out his notebook and laid it before him on the edge of the witness box. 'Thank you, my Lord.'

'Refreshing your memory as you need to, Chief Inspector, please tell us what happened.'

'I entered Prosser's cell with DS Scripps at about 2.50, sir. I cautioned him again, and told him that I proposed to ask him certain questions to ascertain whether he and his fellow suspects posed any continuing threat. DS Scripps then took him to an interview room. Prosser sat on one side of the table, and we sat on the other.'

'Was one of you making notes at the time?'

'Yes, sir. DS Scripps made a contemporaneous note. It wasn't totally complete because it all moved rather quickly, but it provided us with an aid to our memory when we made our notes later.'

Gareth stood. 'Exact words, from this point on, please.'

'Yes, sir. I said to Prosser: "Look, Dafydd, you don't strike me as such a bad bloke. I know the bomb wasn't armed, and you helped the bomb squad boys by showing them how it worked."'

'At this point, Prosser intervened and said: "It was never armed. You arrested us before I could arm it. I told them that."'

'I said: "All right, fair enough. But what we need to know now is, how many other devices are out there? We want to know how many, where they are, and when they are set to explode."'

'How did Prosser respond to that?'

'He said: "There aren't any more."'

'I said: "I'm not sure I believe you, Dafydd. See, the problem is that we don't know what you were up to earlier in the evening, and we don't know where Trevor Hughes is now. Perhaps you would like to start by telling me where we can find Trevor?"'

'His answer?'

'Prosser said: "I can't understand why you haven't found him.

He's bound to be either at home or at the *Tywysog* book shop in Palace Street."'

'I said: "No. We've tried both those places, and there's no sign of him."'

'He replied: "Well, he's bound to be around somewhere. I'm sure you will find him. In any case, there are no other devices. I should know. I was the one who built this one."'

The Chief Inspector turned over another page in his notebook.

'DS Scripps then said: "Even his wife says she doesn't know where he is, but someone has to know. She had her little boy with her in the car, for God's sake. Did any of you give any thought to him?"'

'At this point, Prosser suddenly appeared to become highly agitated. He said: "Look, I keep telling you. The bomb was harmless. It wasn't armed. I would never have exposed Arianwen and Harri to any risk."'

'DS Scripps said: "That's all well and good, Dafydd, but the way the bomb squad boys tell it is that some of the materials you had in the device are quite unstable. In other words, they might explode at any time if they were wrongly handled."'

'Prosser replied: "That's not true. It was all well assembled and insulated. There was no risk. In any case, Arianwen knows nothing about this. We never told her anything."'

He paused for a sip of water.

'I then said: "Look, Dafydd, I'm going to tell the judge what you did in helping the bomb disposal boys, and that's going to help you. But now, we have to talk about making the rest of Caernarfon safe. You don't strike me as the kind of bloke who would really want to kill anyone or cause them injury. Nobody has been hurt yet. Let's keep it that way. And it would look much better for you if you told us everything you know."'

'He replied: "I've told you everything I know. I don't know where Trevor is, and there are no more devices that I know of. If there are, they are nothing we are involved with."'

'DS Scripps said: "It's going to be very hard on Arianwen, losing contact with her son for so many years while she is in prison. If we could tell the judge she didn't know about anything else that might be out there, that would help her."'

'Again, Prosser seemed to become very agitated. He said: "I've told you. She knew nothing. We kept her out of it from the beginning."'

'DS Scripps said: "Well, I'm not sure a jury would necessarily believe that, Dafydd. I mean, driving around at that hour of the morning with a bomb in the back of the car. Do you know what I'm saying?"'

'Prosser was shaking his head violently. I said: "Look, Dafydd, help us out here. Tell us where we need to look, and I promise, I'll put in a good word for both yourself and Arianwen."'

'Prosser said: "Look, I'll tell you everything about what we did. But there is nothing more I can tell you about Trevor, or about any more devices, because there aren't any."'

'DS Scripps said: "Well, that's very unfortunate, Dafydd, for you and Arianwen, both, I would say."'

'What happened then?' Evan asked.

The Chief Inspector turned over another page. 'At this point, sir, Prosser suddenly jumped up from his chair, ran around the table and assaulted DS Scripps by punching him in the face.'

'Indeed? What did DS Scripps do?'

'He didn't do anything immediately, sir. We were both taken by surprise. DS Scripps lost his balance and almost fell backwards in his chair, but I was able to reach out and support the chair and return it to its upright position. As I did so, Prosser punched DS Scripps again several times, to the face and body, and I saw that he was bleeding from the nose.'

'What did you do, Chief Inspector?'

'I shouted at Prosser to stop it, jumped up and ran around DS Scripps' chair as quickly as I could to restrain Prosser from attacking him any further. He was able to land one or two more blows before I could stop him, and when I reached him, Prosser assaulted me by punching me in the stomach and kneeing me in the groin.'

'What happened then?'

'I was in considerable pain as a result of his actions, sir, but I was able to punch Prosser in defence of myself and my colleague and, by that time, DS Scripps had recovered himself, and was able to get up and assist me. Together, we were able to restrain Prosser. We sat him back down, and cuffed his hands together behind the chair.'

'Chief Inspector, how many times was it necessary for you to strike Mr Prosser in the course of restraining him and making sure he could not cause either of you any further injury?'

'Prosser continued to resist us, sir. I remember punching him at least twice more. I saw DS Scripps do so at least once, but then DS Scripps got him in a headlock, which was how we eventually got him back to his chair.'

'What did you do once you had restrained him?'

'I could see some marks around his eyes where we had punched him, and it was obvious that he had sustained some injury. Accordingly, I immediately left the interview room, found the duty sergeant, Sergeant Griffiths, and asked him to call the police surgeon to attend. DS Scripps indicated to me that he was fit to continue duty, and we remained with Prosser. It seemed pointless to continue to question Prosser further in the circumstances, and I decided to return him to his cell to await the police surgeon, and to make further inquiries elsewhere.'

'But at that point, Prosser, who seemed to have calmed down, said: "I'll tell you all about what we did. Give me something to write with."'

'I said: "Before we take the cuffs off, you are going to have to give me some assurance that you will not attempt to assault us further."'

'He replied: "I won't do anything else."'

'I then released Prosser from the handcuffs, and provided him with a form to make a written statement under caution. I read the caution to him and ensured that he understood it. Prosser then made a written statement, which I produce, my Lord.'

'Is the statement in English?'

'It is, sir.'

'Yes. Well as the jury are not here, I won't trouble you to read it, Chief Inspector. His Lordship and my learned friends have copies. Can I just ask you this? Did Prosser offer any further violence towards either you or DS Scripps?'

'No, sir. From that point he was completely cooperative.'

'Did he in due course receive treatment from the police surgeon?'

'Yes he did, sir.'

'Can you say what injuries, if any, he had received?'

'I don't know that myself, sir. The police surgeon would have reported to the duty sergeant after examining him.'

'And finally, is it fair to say that there is no evidence to suggest that Dafydd Prosser, or any of the defendants in this case, was

involved with any explosive device other than the device recovered
from Arianwen Hughes' car?'

'That is correct, sir.'

'Yes, thank you, Chief Inspector. Wait there, please.'

39

GARETH STOOD.

'So, am I to understand, Chief Inspector, that as you stand here today, you can't tell us what injuries Dafydd Prosser sustained at the hands of yourself and DS Scripps?'

'The police surgeon would have reported to the duty sergeant, Sergeant Griffiths.'

'Yes, so you told my learned friend Mr Roberts. My question is whether you know what injuries he sustained?'

'I have not seen the full report...'

'Well, let me help you. I have seen the report, as has his Lordship.' Gareth picked up a document from the pile in front of him. 'It indicates that Mr Prosser suffered a number of lacerations around both eyes, the nose, and the right cheek, and on the back of the head. Do you understand the term "lacerations"?'

'Yes, sir, I do.'

'Good. Would those lacerations have been the result of his being punched in the face by yourself and DS Scripps?'

'Yes, I would think so.'

'Well, would there be any other way they might have been caused?'

'Not that I can think of, no.'

'No? They were not caused, for example, by any blows struck by the third man who was in the interview room with DS Scripps and yourself?'

'A third man?'

'Yes. There was such a man, wasn't there? I suggest that he was tall, mid-to-late thirties, wearing a grey suit and a red tie, and that he was a Welsh-speaker with a South Wales accent.'

'There was no one in the interview room except DS Scripps, Prosser and myself.'

'Really? No one from the Security Services, for example? You were interviewing Prosser about a matter of high importance, as far as security was concerned, weren't you?'

Evan Roberts stood. 'I would ask that my learned friend proceed with caution, my Lord,' he said. 'I am sure he is aware that the Crown has a privilege about such matters.'

'The Crown has a privilege to protect the identity of officers of the Security Services,' Gareth replied. 'I have not asked for his identity, and I do not intend to do so. But the question of whether such a person was present during the interview is one I am fully entitled to explore, and it is one of obvious relevance.'

'Continue, Mr Morgan-Davies,' Mr Justice Overton replied, more or less ignoring Evan Roberts.

'I suggest to you, Chief Inspector, that such a man was present, and that he assaulted Dafydd Prosser by punching him.'

'No such person was present, sir.'

'The police surgeon's report also tells us that Dafydd Prosser suffered two broken ribs. Do you know how he came to sustain those injuries?'

'No, sir.'

'Really? This man was being interviewed by DS Scripps and yourself, and in the course of the interview he sustained two broken ribs, and you cannot help his Lordship at all about how that happened? Is that right?'

'I would assume, sir, that it happened when we were putting him back in his chair. I don't know that, but that's what I would assume.'

'And how exactly do you assume it would have happened during that process?'

'As I said earlier, DS Scripps put him in a headlock. He was walking Prosser back around the table to his chair. I was assisting by holding his arms and helping to drag him along. Prosser was still resisting and struggling quite violently. I think his chest may have come into contact with the table once or twice as we were struggling with him.'

'You think so?'

'Yes. I can't think of any other way it could have happened.'

'Prosser had to go to hospital later in the morning, did he not?'

'I understand the police surgeon recommended to Sergeant Griffiths that he be taken to hospital for a check-up, sir, yes. He was taken to the hospital later, in the custody of uniformed officers, and was returned to the police station later in the day.'

'Yes,' Gareth said. 'Now, let's talk about what really happened on that morning, shall we?'

'Oh really, my Lord,' Evan Roberts protested half-heartedly. Both Gareth and the judge ignored him.

'I don't know what you mean,' the Chief Inspector said.

Gareth paused. 'Chief Inspector, I want to make clear to you, and I recognise that it is an unusual thing to say, that I make no criticism either of you or DS Scripps for anything you did on that morning.'

DCI Grainger smiled thinly, then gave Gareth a look which suggested some scepticism about what he had just said.

'You believed you were dealing with a serious emergency,' Gareth said. 'I understand that.'

'We *were* dealing with a serious emergency.'

'You had every reason to believe that there were other explosive devices in play, which could have killed people, or caused serious injury, possibly during the Investiture itself.'

'That is correct, sir.'

'Yes. And that is why I make no criticism of you. It may be that what you did was not strictly proper but, for my part, I make no criticism and I believe it to be unlikely that anyone else would criticise you.' Gareth paused again. 'But for legal reasons, his Lordship must hear the truth.'

'His Lordship *has* heard the truth,' Grainger replied.

'I think not,' Gareth said. 'Firstly, as I have already said, you had with you an officer of the Security Services. That would have been perfectly natural. You were working with the Security Services all along, weren't you? I make clear again, I am not asking for this man's name, but such a man was present, wasn't he?'

'No, sir.'

'And I suggest to you that he – not you or DS Scripps – began questioning Mr Prosser about the whereabouts of Trevor Hughes.'

'Not at all.'

'And about whether or not there were additional explosive devices.'

'No. As I have already said, DS Scripps and I asked the questions about which I have already given evidence. No one else was involved.'

'I further suggest that Mr Prosser already had his hands cuffed behind his chair at that time.'

'No, he did not.'

'And when Mr Prosser was unable to assist with the information you wanted – which I think you now accept was genuine...?'

'I don't dispute that, sir.'

'When Mr Prosser was unable to assist, this man lost his temper, called Mr Prosser an "anarchist bastard" and punched him repeatedly in the face while he was unable to defend himself?'

'No, sir.'

'You and DS Scripps, I suggest, then joined in, and all three of you continued to assault Mr Prosser, punching him repeatedly to the head and body.'

'Not true.'

'You kept shouting questions at him, and he kept shouting that he had no further information to give you?'

'Not true.'

'Finally, the third man pushed Prosser's chair over, with him in it, and kicked him in the head, didn't he?'

'Not true.'

'At which point you stopped the man and pulled the chair up again?'

'This is all completely untrue.'

'You made so much noise about it that Sergeant Griffiths came in to see what was going on, didn't he?'

'I don't recall Sergeant Griffiths coming into the interview room until I went to fetch him after Prosser had assaulted us.'

'You and DS Scripps told Sergeant Griffiths not to interfere, didn't you?'

'No.'

'And when he protested again, the third man frog-marched him out of the interview room and warned him not to come back?'

'Nothing of that kind happened.'

'Prosser wasn't in any position to assault anyone, was he? He had his hands cuffed behind his back, didn't he?'

'Not until we had restrained him after the assault.'

'And when you finally realised that Prosser had nothing more to tell you about Trevor Hughes, or about additional devices, you ordered him to write a written statement under caution, making clear to him that if he did not comply, he would be beaten up again?'

'Absolutely not. He made the written statement voluntarily.'

'Sitting there with his hands cuffed behind his back, numerous cuts and lacerations, and two broken ribs? He volunteered to make a statement, did he?'

'Yes.'

'Didn't ask for medical treatment? Just said he wanted to confess it all in writing?'

'Yes.'

Gareth shook his head. 'Chief Inspector, let me say once again, I am not seeking to criticise you. You had a situation of the utmost seriousness to deal with; you had a responsibility to the public. I understand that. You had reasons, which I suspect most people would think were good reasons, for crossing the line. But you did cross the line, didn't you?'

Grainger breathed out heavily. 'We crossed the line in one respect, sir. I will admit that.'

'Indeed? What was that?'

'Both DS Scripps and I promised Prosser that we would do what we could to help both him and Arianwen Hughes if he told us the truth. It was obvious that he cared very much for Mrs Hughes, and we played on that. I know we are not supposed to offer inducements when questioning suspects. We are supposed to obey the Judges' Rules. We did cross the line to that extent.'

'I am suggesting you crossed the line to a far greater extent than that,' Gareth said.

'I don't accept that,' Grainger replied.

40

DS SCRIPPS WAS CALLED and gave evidence virtually identical to that of DCI Grainger. Watching Mr Justice Overton becoming restless as the afternoon wore on, Gareth decided to keep his cross-examination as short as possible. He questioned Scripps about the third man, and received the predictable answer that no such man had been present.

'Sergeant, according to your evidence, Dafydd Prosser assaulted you, punching you several times in the face. Is that right?'

'It is, sir.'

'As a result of which you were bleeding from the nose?'

'Yes, sir.'

'And he was able to do that before DCI Grainger could intervene?'

'Yes, sir.'

'Because there was no third man to come to your aid?'

'There was not.'

'But you told DCI Grainger that you were fit to continue duty?'

'I had to continue duty, sir. We were in the middle of an emergency.'

'And when the police surgeon, Dr Markey, came to the police station, you said you had no need of his services?'

'Dr Markey came to see Mr Prosser, sir.'

'Because of the two broken ribs, and numerous lacerations he received while you and DCI Grainger were restraining him?'

'Yes, sir.'

'You're not saying that Dr Markey would have refused to treat you if you had needed treatment? You're not saying that, are you?'

'No, sir. I am sure he would have examined me if I had asked.'

'And you are quite sure Dr Markey did not examine you?'

'Quite sure. I didn't ask him to.'

'You didn't ask because you had no need of Dr Markey's services, did you, Sergeant? Because all the violence came from the three of you, and was directed towards Dafydd Prosser?'

'I have given my evidence, sir, and I stand by it.'

'And he made a written statement because you told him to, and because you made it clear that he would be beaten up again if he failed to make a statement? Isn't that what happened?'

'I have given my evidence and I stand by it.'

41

IT WAS LATE IN the afternoon, and the combative cross-examination had brought about a tense, uneasy atmosphere in the courtroom. When Evan Roberts proposed that Mr Justice Overton should adjourn for the day, it was a suggestion that appealed to everyone in court, with the sole exception of Gareth Morgan-Davies. Gareth suspected that his best hope was to press home whatever advantage he had gained while the turbulence lasted, and before the witnesses had any chance to confer with each other overnight.

'My Lord, I agree that it has been a long afternoon,' he said. 'But I would ask that we continue. The two remaining witnesses will be quite short. I understand my learned friend has no questions for them, and calls them only to make them available for cross-examination. I don't anticipate being very long with either of them. That would also mean that they don't have to come back tomorrow – I am sure Dr Markey would appreciate that – and it would mean that we won't keep the jury waiting tomorrow morning.'

To one or two barely suppressed groans, the judge nodded his agreement.

Evan Roberts called Sergeant Griffiths, asked him his full name, and instructed him to answer any questions the defence might have.

'You were the duty sergeant at Caernarfon Police Station on the early morning of 1 July, is that right?' Gareth began.

'I was, sir. I was on duty in full uniform. I commenced duty at 10 o'clock the previous evening.'

'And I think, at that time, the senior officer on duty would have been Superintendent Rees?'

'Yes, sir.'

'But we have heard that Superintendent Rees had to leave the police station at about 1.30 to take charge of security at the Castle after an explosive device had been found?'

'That is correct, sir.'

'Which left you as the senior officer on duty at the police station?'

'Temporarily sir, yes.'

'All right. In any case, as duty sergeant, was it your responsibility to take charge of any suspects who might be arrested, and to be responsible for them while they were in custody at the police station?'

'That is correct, sir.'

'And did that include responsibility for their welfare and safety while they remained in custody?'

'Yes, sir.'

'Three suspects relevant to this case were brought in, having been arrested, is that right?'

'Yes, sir.'

'Do you have a copy of your custody record with you?'

'Yes, sir.'

'And did you record in that document anything of significance which occurred during their time in custody?'

'I did, sir.'

'Please look at the record as I ask you questions, Sergeant. Firstly, is it right that about 1.45 on that morning, Caradog Prys-Jones and Arianwen Hughes were brought in at more or less the same time, although by different officers?'

'That is correct.'

'And, as duty sergeant, you would take certain information from them to establish their identity, to ascertain what property they had with them, and to ensure that they were fit to be detained?'

'Yes.'

'Were both suspects fit to be detained?'

'They were, sir. The only difficulty was about Mrs Hughes' young son, who was with her. I had to make arrangements for the local authority to care for him while she was in custody, which was not easy at that time of night, and in the end we had to place him with a local family who had experience of fostering children, as a temporary measure, until the next day. Mrs Hughes was very distressed about the situation, needless to say.'

'And then, perhaps an hour or so later, was Dafydd Prosser brought in by DCI Grainger and DC Owen?'

'Yes, he was.'

'Was Mr Prosser fit to be detained at that time?'

'He was, sir.'

'He didn't complain of any injuries at that time, did he?'

'No, sir.'

'Were all three suspects placed in separate cells?'

'Yes, sir.'

'And did you remain available to them at all times?'

'I did, sir. I was up and down the stairs a fair bit until DCI Grainger came back to the station. Almost all my officers were out on duty somewhere, many helping with the search at the Castle, so we were a bit stretched, and I had to keep an eye on the desk as well as the suspects.'

'Yes. Did there come a time when DCI Grainger indicated that he wished to interview Dafydd Prosser?'

'I was present when he decided to interview Mr Prosser first with DS Scripps, to see whether information could be obtained about any further bombs. Superintendent Rees had asked that any further information be passed to him immediately. We all thought we had no time to lose.'

'Who else was present when DCI Grainger made that decision? DS Scripps?'

'As I remember, yes.'

'And that chap from the Security Services, you know who I mean, tall, mid-to-late thirties, wearing a grey suit and a red tie, spoke Welsh with a South Wales accent. He was there, wasn't he?'

Out of the corner of his eye, Gareth saw Evan Roberts hovering, unsure whether or not to say anything. By the time he had decided not to, the sergeant had already replied.

'I should think so, sir, yes.'

'You know the man I mean, don't you? I'm not asking for his name.'

'Yes, sir.'

'Yes, because you had been working quite closely with the Security Services, hadn't you? By "you" I mean the police, both the local force and Special Branch?'

'Yes.'

'It is not the usual practice for someone who is not a police officer to be present during an interview, is it?'

'No. Not unless it's someone whose presence is necessary for the welfare of the suspect, a parent or guardian for a young person, of course, or an interpreter.'

'Who is responsible for enforcing that rule?'

'I am, as duty sergeant.'

'In an emergency situation such as this, where it is urgent to obtain information which may lead to the prevention of a public outrage, might you make an exception to the general rule?'

Sergeant Griffiths considered carefully for some time.

'There might be occasions where I would, sir. I'm not sure what they would be, and I would certainly consult a senior officer before making such a decision.'

'But your senior officer was away, taking care of the Castle, wasn't he?'

'Yes, sir.'

'Sergeant Griffiths, I want to make clear that I am not criticising you in any way at all. You were faced with a very serious situation, and you no doubt felt you had to assist DCI Grainger in any way you could. But the court needs to know. You authorised the man from the Security Services to be present during the interview of Dafydd Prosser, didn't you?'

The sergeant began to say something, but then stopped.

'Can I make this easier for you?' Gareth said, not unkindly. 'If for no other reason, DCI Grainger needed an interpreter, didn't he? Nationalist suspects almost always insist on speaking Welsh to police officers, don't they?'

'Yes, sir.'

'And you didn't have anyone available to act as interpreter, did you? You couldn't do it yourself, obviously, being duty sergeant. Please understand, I'm not suggesting the man did actually interpret. The interview was conducted in English. I accept that. But that would have been one good reason at the time, wouldn't it?'

'I suppose it would, sir.'

'DCI Grainger and DS Scripps don't speak *yr hen iaith*, do they?'

Gareth's use of the Welsh phrase, "the old language", brought a smile to the sergeant's face.

'Not a word, sir.'

'Not a word. It would have taken time to find an independent interpreter at that hour, and time was the one thing you didn't have?'

'Yes, sir. That's quite true.'

'Well, then…?"

'I didn't formally permit the gentleman from MI5 to be present, my Lord. But I did nothing to prevent it. I looked the other way. There is nothing in the custody record about it.'

42

THERE WAS AN AUDIBLE gasp from various sections of the courtroom. In the dock Dai Bach, who had been sitting forlornly with his head between his hands, suddenly looked up. Mr Justice Overton sat up abruptly in his chair and asked Gareth to pause. He made a careful note of what had been said.

'Do I understand you correctly, Sergeant Griffiths?' the judge asked. 'Is it your evidence that this man from the Security Services was in fact present during Prosser's interview?'

'I can't say for certain that he was there all the time,' the Sergeant replied. 'I wasn't there myself, and he may well have been in and out of the interview room when I was attending to other matters. But I was aware that he was there at least some of the time.'

The judge made a further note and nodded to Gareth.

'There came a time, Sergeant,' Gareth continued, 'did there not, when you heard a disturbance coming from the interview room?'

'Yes, sir.'

'What was it that you heard, exactly?'

'I heard sounds which suggested to me that there was a fight or scuffle of some kind going on, furniture being knocked over or dragged around, some swearing, sounds which suggested that blows were being exchanged.'

'What did you do as a result of hearing these sounds?'

'I made my way to the interview room and opened the door.'

'What did you see when you entered?'

'I saw that Dafydd Prosser had his hands handcuffed behind him in his chair,' the sergeant replied. 'I saw that he was bleeding from his nose, and that he had cuts around the eyes, and a red patch on his right cheek, which was beginning to swell up. DCI Grainger told me…'

'That's all right, you can tell us. His Lordship has already heard it.'

'DCI Grainger told me that Prosser had become violent and

had assaulted both himself and DS Scripps, and that they had been obliged to restrain him.'

'What did you do?'

'It seemed obvious that Prosser was in a great deal of pain. I told DCI Grainger that I was going to call Dr Markey, the police surgeon, and that he should suspend the interview until the doctor had examined Mr Prosser.'

'What did DCI Grainger say to that?'

'Nothing, as far as I remember. I left the interview room to call Dr Markey, who arrived about forty minutes later.'

'Are you aware that after you had called Dr Markey and left the interview room, and after you had instructed DCI Grainger to suspend the interview until he had been seen by the doctor, Dafydd Prosser made a statement under caution, which the prosecution seek to persuade his Lordship was a voluntary statement?'

'I am aware of that, sir, yes.'

'Did DS Scripps ask to see Dr Markey?'

'Not as far as I remember. No.'

'Did you notice any visible injury to DS Scripps?'

'No, sir. I have nothing in the record about that.'

'What about the man from MI5? Was he there at this time?'

'He left the interview room hurriedly when I entered, sir, and I didn't see him again.'

Gareth paused.

'Sergeant Griffiths, what would you say if I put to you that the visit to the interview room you have just described was not the first visit you made, during that interview, but the second?'

'My second?'

'Yes. Is it not correct that there was a first occasion when you heard sounds that led you to interrupt the interview?'

'No. I don't think so.'

'Did you not enter the interview room and ask what was going on? DCI Grainger and DS Scripps asked you to leave and, when you refused, you were bundled out of the room by the man from MI5. Isn't that right?'

'I have nothing in the custody record about that, sir,' the sergeant answered, after a pause.

'That wasn't what I asked...'

'I do have a recollection that at some stage the man from MI5 asked me not to come in, or to leave, but I'm not sure whether that was the time I have already described, or another time. It was a very confused night.'

Gareth thought for a moment.

'I won't press it,' he said. 'Thank you very much, Sergeant Griffiths.'

Dr Markey told the court that he had been called to attend the Caernarfon Police Station by Sergeant Griffiths in response to an injury to a person in custody. He arrived at about 4.15 in the morning. He examined Dafydd Prosser and found that he had two broken ribs, and a number of cuts and lacerations on the back of the head, around both eyes, and on the nose. He had a very red, swollen right cheek. Prosser appeared to have many areas painful to the touch, and seemed greatly distressed and fearful. He refused to tell the doctor how his injuries had been caused. The doctor told Sergeant Griffiths that Prosser should be taken to hospital to be examined there, without delay. He initially suspected that Prosser might have a broken cheekbone, but an X-ray at the hospital revealed no fracture. He was later informed that Prosser had been returned to custody with heavy bandaging around his rib cage and a supply of analgesics. Doctor Markey suggested that he follow up the next day to check on Prosser's condition in custody, but was told that his services were no longer required.

'I am aware of the lateness of the hour,' Mr Justice Overton said.

It was now 5 o'clock and a general air of exhaustion had set in.

'But I think it is right to give my decision now, so that all parties, particularly the prosecution, can regroup and decide what adjustments should be made to their cases. I shall be very brief. I think it better, in the circumstances, not to express any specific views about the evidence I have heard.

'The test I have to apply is this. The prosecution has the burden of persuading me beyond reasonable doubt that the written statement under caution made by Dafydd Prosser was voluntary, and that it was not obtained by oppression. Based on the evidence I have heard, I am not so persuaded. A confession obtained by force cannot be said to be made voluntarily. There were also some admitted breaches of the Judges' Rules, the inducements made to Prosser to put in a good word for him and Mrs Hughes if he cooperated. Those breaches are not insignificant. But the main ground of my decision is that I am not sure that the statement was made voluntarily in the sense to which I have already referred.

'Mr Morgan-Davies has said, very fairly, that he does not seek to criticise the officers for their conduct during the interview, which took place in circumstances of particular urgency. The officers had every reason to believe that they were dealing with an exceptionally grave situation in which lives were under immediate threat. I agree with Mr Morgan-Davies that the officers were entitled to considerable leeway. Whether others will agree at some later time is another matter, but that is not relevant today.

'Whether or not there were circumstances which justified the conduct of the interview, its consequences as a matter of law are clear. The written statement under caution made by Dafydd Prosser is inadmissible. The oral statements he made to the police officers are likewise inadmissible. All this evidence is excluded, and will not be placed before the jury. I will now adjourn until 10.30 tomorrow.'

43

THEY HELD AN IMPROMPTU party in Chambers to celebrate a victory which no one, including Gareth, had expected. It was not every day that you managed to persuade a judge that a confession might have been obtained by means of force. Judges generally trusted the word of police officers, who were often the target of wild accusations by defendants who regretted having made incriminating statements while in police custody, and for Gareth, the exclusion of Dafydd Prosser's statements to the police was quite a coup. On Gareth's instructions, Merlin dispatched his junior clerk, Alan, to Fleet Street for a case of good champagne from *El Vino*, the Temple's wine bar of choice.

The party was a sign of how much Chambers had changed since Bernard Wesley had departed for the High Court bench. Wesley, while capable of great charm and warmth, had been a formal Head of Chambers. There were those, especially the younger members of Chambers, who found approaching him in his room an intimidating experience. His hospitality was also formal. There might be tea occasionally after court. He was known to keep a bottle of sherry in his room, which sometimes made an appearance at about 6 o'clock if anyone was with him. A rarer sight was the bottle of fine single malt whisky, which was produced only late in the evening, when he was alone or in serious conversation with one, or at the most two, others. In Wesley's day, any Chambers party would have been planned and announced months in advance, with great fanfare and great attention paid to the guest list. Informal gatherings of this kind, open to everyone in Chambers, were virtually unknown. Gareth had set out to change that culture. Members of Chambers needed a setting in which to talk to each other, and he was determined that no one should feel hesitant about coming to his room just because he was now Head of Chambers. On this evening, a number of members of Chambers had gathered for the celebration.

'I hear you talked my father into excluding a confession, Gareth,' Clive Overton said with a broad smile. 'Does that explain the flight of pigs I saw over Chambers on my way back from court?'

'I did indeed,' Gareth smiled. 'And, what's more, he was quite right to exclude it. But for God's sake don't tell him we are having a party to celebrate. He might change his mind.'

Clive laughed. 'Don't worry. He has refused to even see me until the case is over, just in case it gives someone the wrong impression. You know what a stickler for protocol he is.'

'He is quite right,' Gareth replied. 'You can never be too careful, especially with Evan Roberts watching our every move, and he will be out for blood after this. I don't think he expected to lose this one.'

'Your learned junior tells me that you played the role of a Celtic Lorelei,' Aubrey Smith-Gurney said, 'and shamelessly lured a poor little Welsh police officer on to the rocks by drawing him into a Welsh-speaking alliance against the wicked English.'

'I didn't say that,' Donald protested.

'Well, perhaps not exactly,' Smith-Gurney conceded, 'but as the second most senior chap in Chambers, I am allowed the occasional embellishment. Besides, I insist I'm not far off the mark.'

'He did charm him, though,' Donald said, 'like a bird from a tree.'

'That's only partly true,' Gareth smiled. 'Firstly, the witness was an experienced sergeant, not a poor little officer; and secondly, the wicked MI5 officer who started the beating up of my client, was a wicked Welsh-speaker, not a wicked Englishman.'

'I still believe the bit about the charm,' Harriet Fisk said.

'Thank you, Harriet,' Gareth said. 'Oh… was Ben in your room? I need to find him.'

'Yes. He was on the phone with someone. I think he is just on his way… in fact, here he is now.'

'Ah, yes.' He waved a hand in Ben's direction.

'Help yourselves to champagne, everyone,' he said to the room at large. 'Roger, see if you can find Anthony and tell him we are here. He may have been late getting back from court in Reading.'

He walked to the door, put an arm around Ben's shoulder, and steered him to the table where Alan was in charge of pouring champagne into glasses and opening new bottles as required.

'Merlin said you needed a talk,' he said.

'I'm not in a rush,' Ben replied. 'Enjoy your victory party. It is well deserved. For all the times I've seen you in court, during my pupillage and since, I am still impressed.'

Gareth smiled thinly. 'To tell you the truth, Ben, we won today mainly because of sheer good fortune. Apparently, they didn't send Sergeant Griffiths the script.'

Ben shook his head.

'Oh, he had the script,' he replied. 'He just didn't like it.'

'What? You think he has some sympathy with Dai Bach?'

'No. I think he resents having his police station taken over by ill-mannered, aggressive coppers from London who can't speak a word of the language, but push him around and behave as if they own the place.'

Gareth nodded. 'Yes, you may well be right. I'm sure that's not the way they usually do things in Caernarfon. In some ways, it must have seemed like having Edward I and his merry men back in town.'

'You still had to exploit it,' Ben said, 'which you did perfectly.'

'Thank you. So, what's up?'

'I've got Barratt in the clerk's room,' Ben said. 'Can we have a word with you and Donald? It's something we should talk about this evening.'

'Yes, of course. Let's use your room.' He called over his shoulder. 'Donald, bring an extra glass of champagne with you for Barratt, will you, and come to Ben's room.'

44

'WE ARE GETTING THROUGH the prosecution case quite quickly,' Ben said. 'There's not much left, now that the confession evidence in Dai Bach's case has gone.'

'Just the statements made by Caradog and Arianwen,' Donald confirmed, 'the scientific evidence about the device, and the search of the various addresses – a day, two days at most.'

'I don't think any of that is controversial,' Gareth said. 'I wouldn't be surprised if we finish the prosecution case tomorrow or Thursday.'

'There's the surveillance evidence,' Ben pointed out, 'about the Belfast trip. It doesn't concern Arianwen, but you may have a few questions about it.'

'One or two,' Gareth said, 'nothing much. Let's say two days.'

'And after that,' Ben continued, 'the natural order of business would be for Caradog to give evidence. The judge is bound to have him brought into court to offer him the opportunity to go into the witness box.'

'He's not going to give evidence,' Donald said. 'He will refuse to leave his cell; and even if he does grace us with his presence, he will just give another speech in Welsh about how dreadful the English are. The judge will have him removed again, complete waste of everybody's time, and we will move on to our case – not that we have a case, but still…'

'He might give evidence,' Ben said, 'if somebody asked him.'

Donald laughed. 'Why would he do that? And why would anybody ask him to? Even if he went into the witness box, it wouldn't really be evidence; it would be little more than a rant. It would be very dangerous for our clients. There is no telling what the man might say.'

Gareth was smiling towards Ben.

'But you're thinking about it, aren't you?'

'Yes.'

'For God's sake, Ben,' Donald said quietly. 'Why would you do that? What could you possibly have to gain by it?'

'It's simple, Donald,' Gareth replied, before Ben could say anything. 'He doesn't have Trevor Hughes. If he had Trevor Hughes, Trevor would say that Arianwen had nothing to do with any conspiracy to cause explosions, and was kept out of it from the start. But he doesn't have Trevor Hughes, and Dai Bach won't be giving evidence, so the only other possibility is Caradog.'

Ben was nodding. 'I am not sure how credible he would be. I am going to call Arianwen, but I would be much happier with some independent evidence to support her.'

'He's hardly independent,' Donald protested. 'He's her brother, and he's a co-conspirator and, given his performance thus far, I don't think the jury would believe a word he said. It would do her more harm than good.'

'I'm not so sure,' Gareth said. 'The jury may well think that Caradog is a ruthless extremist, but they might just believe that he wouldn't have dragged his sister into it, let alone her four-year-old son. It wasn't necessary to use her to carry the bomb. Dai Bach would back her up if he could, but you know I can't let him.'

'I know.'

'It might be worth a shot.'

'You have no idea what he might say,' Donald insisted. 'He is totally unpredictable, and don't forget, the prosecution would be entitled to cross-examine him.'

'Yes,' Gareth replied, 'and that does raise some practical difficulties. He is not represented. If he gives evidence, he will be cross-examined and he may incriminate himself. You would have to warn him of the risks.'

'He has incriminated himself as much as anyone could already,' Ben pointed out. 'Look at the statement he made at the police station.'

'Perhaps so, but you still have a professional duty to warn him.'

'I would point that out to him when I see him, of course,' Barratt said.

'That's not enough. If he decided to give evidence on his own, that would be one thing. But if *you* ask him, at a minimum, you would have to advise him to take independent legal advice about the risks of giving evidence. You can't advise him, Barratt. You're acting for Arianwen. You would have to have another solicitor waiting in the wings.'

'Technically, Barratt, you have a conflict of interest,' Donald said. 'If Caradog gives evidence, he could also make it worse for Dai Bach. As Dai's solicitor, that puts you in a difficult position. It may seem that you are advancing one client's case at the expense of the other.'

Barratt nodded slowly. 'Yes,' he said.

'It's not necessarily an insuperable problem,' Gareth continued, after a silence. 'It means we would have to speak to Dai Bach about it as well and give him the chance to object, but my guess is that he would be all in favour of it. He has been very protective of Arianwen from day one.'

'We can't advise him to agree to it,' Donald said. 'He would be taking the risk of making his case worse, without any chance of repairing the damage.'

'Certainly, we would have to make sure that he understands the situation fully,' Gareth replied. 'But we can tell him, quite truthfully, that the chances of Caradog making his case any worse are extremely remote.'

'Are they?'

'Donald, Dai Bach's case could hardly get any worse than it already is. Yes, we won a great victory today and kept out his confession, and we are all drinking this excellent champagne to celebrate. But what have we really accomplished? The fact remains that he was caught red-handed with a bomb in the company of Caradog Prys-Jones; he assured the police that he knew it was harmless; and he showed them how it worked. They have the search of the garage, and the trip to Belfast. And we can't call him to give evidence because he has effectively admitted his guilt to us. All in all, I would say that the chances of Caradog making it any worse for him are negligible, and I think that if we offered Dai Bach a chance to save Arianwen, he would jump at it.'

'I still think it would be wrong,' Donald persisted.

'Would it?' Gareth asked. 'Perhaps so, on a strict legal view. On the other hand, from a human point of view, if he can do something for Arianwen, it may be the one thing in this whole sorry mess that gives him some reason to be proud of himself, and perhaps at this point that might appeal to him.'

He turned to Barratt.

'If you can find out when they are bringing Caradog to court, we will see Dai Bach at the same time. Whatever you do, don't forget to take an independent solicitor with you.'

45

'CARADOG IS HERE AT court,' Barratt said. He was breathless after a run up several flights of stairs to join Ben, Gareth and Donald outside court one. It was only 9.30, but already the press and public, including the ever-present Welsh contingent, were preparing to take their places in anticipation of another morning of drama, and court one was already bustling.

'I spoke to the clerk of the court. The judge thinks he should give him a chance to cross-examine Grainger about his statement under caution and what happened to him at the police station, so he asked for him to be brought this morning.'

'That makes sense,' Ben said. 'After what Gareth did to the witnesses yesterday, the judge is going to be very wary of any evidence of what happened at the police station.'

'And,' Barratt continued, 'I understand that Caradog is indeed gracing us with his presence.'

'Then we should try to see him now,' Ben said, 'before court begins.'

'I wasn't expecting to see him quite so quickly,' Barratt admitted. 'I haven't got another solicitor lined up. But I did see Jack Ellis when I was coming into court. He's a good man. If I can find him, I could ask him whether he would help us out.'

'Why don't you do that now?' Ben suggested. 'If necessary, I will ask the judge to start a few minutes late.'

'Tell him I need to see my client too,' Gareth said, 'to advise him about his case in the light of what happened yesterday. Donald and I will go down to the cells and see him now. I will run it by Dai Bach in principle, and see what he says. Let me know how far you get with Caradog as soon as you can.'

'It's good of you to help with this, Jack,' Barratt said, as they walked together along the corridor to the cell in which Caradog Prys-Jones was being held before being taken up to court. 'I am sorry to snatch you away from your conference.'

'Don't mention it,' Jack Ellis replied. 'My clerk can deal with it just as well as I can. This all sounds far more exciting than three counts of supplying cocaine.'

'There are days when a routine drugs case seems very appealing,' Barratt grinned.

'Swap you?'

'If I wasn't in so deep, I would think about it seriously.'

A prison officer met them outside the cell.

'Good morning, sir,' he said brightly. 'I am given to understand that you gentlemen are not actually representing Mr Prys-Jones, is that right?'

'Good morning, Officer,' Barratt replied. 'You are quite right. We can't speak to Mr Prys-Jones without his permission, but we are here to ask him to see us. Here is my card. He knows who I am. Would you mind asking him, please?'

The officer grinned. 'You don't happen to know how to say all that in Welsh, do you sir? It might make it a bit easier.'

Barratt returned the grin. 'Afraid not. Sorry.'

'I'll do my best, sir.'

The officer unlocked the cell and returned within a short time. He looked surprised.

'Mr Prys-Jones's compliments, sir. He would be very pleased to see you. I'll have to lock you in, obviously. Bang on the door when you're ready to leave.'

They entered the small, sparse cell. As always, the stale, claustrophobic atmosphere of the cells was oppressive and, as always, it hit Barratt in the stomach the moment he walked in. As often as Barratt had experienced the motionless air, with its pervasive smells of tobacco, human sweat and the hint of urine, he had never become entirely accustomed to it. He tried to steady himself, leaning back against the door of the cell. Caradog Prys-Jones was standing by the wall to the left, holding Barratt's card. He was conventionally dressed in an open-necked shirt, blue jeans, and black shoes, and there was no sign of the bandana he had worn on the first day of trial, no sign of *y Ddraig Goch*. In fact, Barratt could see no hint of nationalist defiance in his dress at all.

'Mr Prys-Jones,' Barratt began. 'Thank you for seeing us. First of all, I must ask if we may speak in English. I know…'

Caradog smiled. 'That's perfectly all right, Mr Davis. I speak English jolly well, as it happens. I am sorry I can't offer you coffee.'

He laughed, and Barratt joined in, weakly, still trying to steady himself.

'This is Jack Ellis. He's also a solicitor. He's not involved in the case. I'll explain why he is here in a moment.'

'Mr Ellis.'

They shook hands.

'We may not have much time,' Barratt said, 'so I will come straight to the point. I represent both your sister and Dai Bach, as you know. Dai Bach will not be giving evidence in his defence, for reasons I needn't go into. But Arianwen will, and she is going to say that she knew nothing about the conspiracy to cause explosions, that she was kept in the dark all along.'

'That is quite true,' Caradog replied. 'That's what I said in my statement to the police.'

'Yes,' Barratt said. 'But strictly, what you say in your statement is not evidence in her case. The judge may give us some leeway on that; many judges do, because it's a silly rule. But… well, it would be much more persuasive if the jury were to hear that from you, rather than just from a statement read to them by the prosecution.'

Caradog was silent for some time.

'I see,' he said.

'I wouldn't ask you if it wasn't important. It may make a real difference to her case.'

'As you know, Mr Davis, I don't recognise the court. I didn't recognise it when the trial started, and I don't intend to recognise it today. My demand is to be taken to Wales, to be tried in a Welsh court, in the Welsh language…'

'Yes, I know. But we're not in the courtroom now, Mr Prys-Jones. We are down here in the cells and, down here in the cells, I am hoping that we can be honest with one another. So, being honest with each other, it's not going to happen. They are not going to take you back to Wales. You are stuck here, in this court. So, the only question is: is it more important to you to play to the gallery, and repeat a point you have already made very clearly, or to give your sister a fighting chance of being acquitted on a charge of which you and I both know she is not guilty?'

Again, Caradog was silent.

'If she is convicted,' Barratt continued, 'she will go to prison for a very long time, and Harri will grow up in a series of foster homes. The evidence against her is pretty damning. She was driving the car with the bomb in it, and she was arrested with you and Dai Bach. If her husband were here I would feel more optimistic about it but, right now, I don't have any evidence to put before the jury except her own word, and I am not sure that's going to be enough.'

He paused.

'I'm not here because I want you to surrender any of your principles. I'm here to ask for your help on behalf of your sister. I am here to ask you to give evidence for her.'

'I understand,' Caradog replied.

'I have brought Jack with me because, before you decide, you should take independent legal advice. You must be aware...'

'I can be cross-examined,' Caradog interrupted. He smiled – as the two solicitors seemed taken aback. 'I understand that. I've been filling the long hours at Brixton by doing some reading in the prison library. They haven't got a great selection of books, to be honest – there's not much there for anyone with a mental age of more than ten. I have offered to give them a list of possible acquisitions, but they don't seem very interested. Still, I've been doing my best, and I've been delving into that *Archbold* book you gentlemen use. Quite interesting in some ways – well, if you have nothing better to do on a fine spring evening.'

'You are entitled to consult privately with me,' Jack said. 'Barratt will withdraw, and I will explain the risks to you and advise you independently. I have no interest in this case. My only concern is for you, if you want my help.'

Caradog shook his head.

'I'm grateful, Mr Ellis, but it's not necessary,' he replied. 'I will give evidence. They are not going to get anything out of me that I haven't said already in the statement I made to the police. I'm not going to say anything against Dai Bach. You can put his mind at rest about that.'

'They can ask you questions about him,' Jack pointed out. 'I have a duty to warn you that if you don't answer, it may affect the credibility of your evidence, and you may be held in contempt of court.'

'What's the penalty for contempt of court?' Caradog asked.

It shouldn't have been a humorous moment, but all three suddenly laughed out loud.

'Nothing you need be worried about,' Jack replied.

'Even so, we can't advise you to commit an offence,' Barratt said.

'You haven't,' Caradog answered firmly.

'All right,' Barratt said. 'Thank you. Can I just confirm one or two points?'

'Fire away.'

'In your statement to the police, you said that Arianwen knew nothing about the conspiracy, and was kept in the dark from first to last. Are you sure about that?'

'Yes. Absolutely. Trevor insisted on it. He made it a condition of his getting involved with us, and he was very serious about it, believe me. If 'Dai Bach and I hadn't promised to leave her out of it, he would have had nothing to do with us. I can assure you that we were very careful to keep her well away from what we were doing – well, until Dai Bach panicked at the last moment.'

'All right,' Barratt said, scribbling a note. 'In particular, she has always insisted that she had no idea what was in the suitcase.'

'She didn't. She didn't even know about the garage.'

'What was the original arrangement for delivering the device?'

'Trevor was supposed to meet Dai Bach with the car outside the Castle Hotel and do the driving, out to Bangor, pick up the case, and back to the *Maes*. I found a reason to leave work. I told them I was joining a patrol of the Castle perimeter. I was to meet them at 1.15, which I did. My part of it worked like clockwork.'

'It must have been quite a shock when you saw that she was driving.'

Caradog did not reply for some time. He looked down at the floor of the cell, his hands folded tightly across his chest.

'I couldn't believe it. I just couldn't believe it. I thought I was seeing things. I've never been so angry. I was beside myself. I gave Dai Bach a real mouthful, believe me. I don't know what he was thinking. There were still plenty of taxis in the *Maes*. There was no need to involve Arianwen.'

'Mr Prys-Jones, do you have any idea what happened to Trevor Hughes?'

Caradog shook his head.

'No. I don't know to this day what happened to him. I thought for some time that he must have got cold feet at the last moment. But I no longer believe that.'

'Why not?'

'Trevor wasn't the type to bail out just like that. In all the time I knew the man, he always struck me as the steady type, someone who could be relied on, no matter what. He had serious reservations about getting involved at first. He asked a lot of questions. He didn't involve himself lightly. But once he agreed to join us, once he committed himself, he seemed whole-hearted.'

'So, now what do you think?'

Caradog did not answer immediately.

'Truthfully? I'm afraid he has come to some harm. Otherwise, someone would have found him by now.'

'Who would have harmed him,' Barratt asked, 'the Security Services?'

'The police, the Security Services, whoever. They may not have planned it that way, but those were dangerous times to be in Caernarfon. There was a lot of paranoia. It may be that Trevor was just in the wrong place at the wrong time.'

He held up a hand.

'Please don't tell Arianwen I said that,' he added. 'She has enough to worry about as it is.'

46

THE JURY WERE BACK in place, and so, to the general astonishment
of the court, was Caradog Prys-Jones. The first defendant was
sitting quietly in the dock, apparently concentrating on the
proceedings. The judge had not yet said anything to note his
presence, but there had been an outbreak of excited whispers
among the press and public when he was brought up from the
cells – with a guard of two burly male prison officers – which had
not yet entirely subsided. Caradog seemed oblivious to it. He had
no plans to cause any further disturbance, but he was not about
to acknowledge the court to the extent of speaking English, and
he had PC Hywel Watkins alongside him to interpret in case of
need.

Feeling bruised and battered as a result of the defeat he had
suffered on the previous afternoon, Evan Roberts had handed over
to Jamie Broderick to deal with DCI Grainger. The Chief Inspector
seemed subdued as Jamie led him effortlessly through the standard
questions about his notebook, and then about his involvement in
the evacuation of the area around the *Maes* after the discovery of the
explosive device.

'Chief Inspector, the jury have heard already about the arrest of
the three suspects, and I need not ask you to repeat it. But I take it
you can answer any questions about that if my learned friends have
any?'

'Yes, sir.'

'Thank you. Then let us turn now to events after you returned
to the police station. You accompanied Dafydd Prosser to the
station with DC Owen, the officer who had arrested Prosser, is that
right?'

'Yes, sir.'

'Did you then proceed to interview the suspects in company with
DS Scripps, an officer who was a member of your team?'

'I did, sir.'

'With the agreement of my learned friends, I'm going to lead you through the next few questions. Did you and DS Scripps decide that you should interview Dafydd Prosser first?'

'Yes, sir.'

'And was that because it was urgent to obtain as much information as you could, as quickly as you could, to ascertain whether there was any continuing danger to the public?'

'Yes, sir.'

'For one thing, Trevor Hughes had not been arrested, and his whereabouts were unknown?'

'Yes, sir.'

'And you were aware that other officers, under the command of Superintendent Rees, were searching the Castle for any possible further devices at that very moment?'

'Yes, sir.'

'Just answer "yes" or "no": did you and DS Scripps interview Dafydd Prosser?'

'Yes.'

'And did it eventually appear that there was no evidence of any continuing danger from the defendants in this case?'

'Yes, sir.'

'On the following morning, at about 10 o'clock, 2 July, the day following the Investiture, was Mr Prosser charged with conspiracy to cause explosions, and cautioned, and did he make no reply to the caution?'

'That is correct, sir.'

'Thank you. Going back to the morning of 1 July again, the morning of the arrests, did you and DS Scripps go to the cell in which Caradog Prys-Jones was being held at about 4 o'clock, with a view to interviewing him?'

'We did, sir.'

'Was anyone else with you?'

'Yes, sir. PC John, a local officer who spoke Welsh, accompanied us.' Grainger paused to look venomously towards Gareth. 'PC John had been involved in the search of the Castle, and had not been available as an interpreter before this point.'

Gareth smiled back amiably.

'What did you do on entering Mr Prys-Jones's cell?'

'I reminded Mr Prys-Jones of the caution, and asked PC John to translate it into Welsh, which he did.'

'What happened next?'

'There was then a prolonged exchange between Mr Prys-Jones and PC John in Welsh, at the conclusion of which Mr Prys-Jones handed to the officer what appeared to be a lengthy, hand-written document. PC John told us that the document was a statement Mr Prys-Jones had written about his involvement in the matter. He further said that Mr Prys-Jones had indicated to him that he would not answer any questions, and that the statement was all he had to say. I later ascertained,' the Chief Inspector added disapprovingly, 'that Sergeant Griffiths, the duty sergeant, had supplied Mr Prys-Jones with writing materials, at his request, without advising me of this.'

'What did you do on receiving this document?' Jamie asked.

'The document was in Welsh, sir, so there was nothing I could do before I had it translated. But I did ask Mr Prys-Jones, through PC John, whether he was prepared to sign the statement in the proper form for a written statement under caution, and I once again reminded him of the caution. He indicated through PC John that he would agree to this, and the appropriate language was added to the document in Welsh, after which Mr Prys-Jones signed it, and DS Scripps witnessed his signature.'

'Did you, in due course, have the statement translated, and do you now produce the original of the statement with an English translation?'

'Yes, sir.'

'Thank you. Exhibit 9, please, my Lord.'

'Yes,' Mr Justice Overton said.

'And on the following morning, 2 July, at about the same time as Dafydd Prosser, was Caradog Prys-Jones also charged with conspiracy to cause explosions and cautioned, and in reply to the caution did he say, in Welsh: "I have said all that I have to say"?'

'That is correct, sir.'

'Thank you. My Lord, with the usher's assistance, we have copies of Mr Prys-Jones's statement under caution, Exhibit 9, in Welsh and English, for the jury and for Mr Prys-Jones. If the usher would kindly distribute them...'

Jamie waited for this to be done.

'Chief Inspector, I will read the English translation. Please follow along with me and correct me if I make a mistake.'

'Very good, sir.'

47

I, CARADOG PRYS-JONES WISH to make a statement. I want someone to write down what I say. I have been told that I need not say anything unless I wish to do so, but that whatever I say may be given in evidence.

My name is Caradog Prys-Jones. I make this statement to clarify the events on 1 July 1969 which have led to my arrest. I am a Welsh man. My language is Welsh, and I take great pride in the history and culture of the Welsh people. For centuries, Wales has been subjugated by the English. Since the days of Edward I, if not before, they chose to make war on a peace-loving Celtic people. They destroyed the power of the great Princely Houses of Gwynedd and Powys, and imposed the rule of a foreign monarchy. I am not one to dwell on history. I am a man of my own time. But in my own time I have seen the continuing subjugation of Wales, the attempts to destroy her ancient language, the endless assimilation of everything distinctly Welsh into the culture of England.

Finally, I saw with my own eyes the forcible destruction of my family's homeland in the Tryweryn Valley. The Valley, containing the village of Capel Celyn, was flooded, over the objections of the Welsh people, to build a reservoir to supply water to the people of Liverpool, an English city. I have no hatred for the English people, or the city of Liverpool, but this act of rape against Wales in the interests of English expansion filled me with such desperation, such hopelessness, that I did not know where to turn. When your English Queen mocked us by proposing that her son should be the latest of his line to usurp the title of Prince of Wales, to which he has no right, I decided that action must be taken.

In the fifteenth century, Owain Glyndŵr took up arms against the English, not because he wished to do so, but because he was driven to it. He too had been a man prepared to live on good terms with England, but ultimately found it to be impossible. He was unsuccessful in his quest to throw off the English yoke. But in the end, it is not immediate success that matters, but to set in motion a train of events which, in the context of history, at the right time, when there is the necessary convergence of political intent, will bring about justice. I therefore determined to declare myself to be an heir of Owain Glyndŵr. I determined to stand against the oppressor as he did, even though I knew that I myself could not bring about justice, and that whatever I did was likely to fail to achieve the ultimate goal. Others worked with me as the Heirs of Owain Glyndŵr, but I shall say nothing of them. I shall speak only about myself.

I wish to make clear specifically that from first to last my sister Arianwen knew nothing of what we did, and had no knowledge of what was found when she was arrested.

I determined to place an explosive device within Caernarfon Castle, which I hoped would detonate either during the usurper's shameful ceremony, or before it, in such a way as to cause the ceremony to be abandoned. I did not make the explosive device myself, having no knowledge of, or aptitude for, such things. I planned to carry it into the Castle in the duffle bag I had with me when I was arrested. I was working at the Castle as a night watchman on the night of 30 June into the morning of 1 July. I had identified a location in which to place it, quite close to the green on which the ceremony was to take place. My intention was to demonstrate to the English Government and the Monarchy that it was possible to resist their abuse of Wales, and that there were those of us prepared to do so. I did not specifically intend to kill or injure anyone, but I knew that this would almost certainly be the result of what I did.

The people of England must understand that the people of Wales are not helpless victims. If they do not change their ways and recognise our nation, it is inevitable that violence and bloodshed will continue. On the other hand, if they will recognise us, there is no reason why we should not live in harmony together. The first step is for the people of England to tell their Saxon Monarch that she must keep her predatory hands off Wales, and renounce the pretensions of her family to the title of Prince of Wales, a title which only the people of Wales can bestow.

I have no regrets about what I did. I will account for myself further only to a Welsh court. Long live Wales!

I have nothing more to say.

I have read the above statement and I have been told that I can correct, alter or add anything I wish. This statement is true. I have made it of my own free will.

48

'Is THE STATEMENT SIGNED appropriately by Mr Prys-Jones, and is his signature witnessed by DS Scripps?'

'Yes, sir.'

'Chief Inspector,' Jamie continued, 'at about 4.45 on the morning of 1 July, did you go with DS Scripps to interview Arianwen Hughes?'

'I did, sir.'

'Did you have an officer with you to interpret?'

'We had a female officer with us, sir, WPC Marsh. But she was not called on to interpret. Mrs Hughes engaged with us in English throughout the interview.'

'How did Mrs Hughes appear when you saw her?'

'She was bitterly distressed, sir. She was crying, and appeared to be inconsolable. She kept asking about her son. WPC Marsh tried to reassure her that he was being well looked after and promised to keep her informed of his whereabouts, but this seemed to have little effect. She also asked several times about her husband, Trevor Hughes. I told her that we were looking for him, but that we had not yet found him. This also distressed her greatly.'

'Yes. Were you able to conduct the interview in those circumstances?'

'WPC Marsh did suggest that it should be postponed until Mrs Hughes had recovered her composure, and I was prepared to agree. But on hearing this, Mrs Hughes herself asked that we continue with the interview. She said she wished to make a statement, and she added that, once we heard what she had to say, we would realise there had been a mistake.'

'What did you do?'

'I then cautioned Mrs Hughes again, and asked her whether she would like WPC Marsh to write a statement under caution for her. She said that she would. She then made and signed a statement under caution, sir.'

'And do you now produce that statement, which will be Exhibit 10?'

'Yes, sir.'

'And again, just before we read it, on the morning of 2 July, at about the same time as the other defendants, was Mrs Hughes charged with conspiracy to cause explosions and cautioned, and in reply to the caution, did she say: "No. You're making a terrible mistake"?'

'Yes, sir.'

'Once again, there are copies for the jury... Chief Inspector, again, I will read it. Please correct me if I do so in any way incorrectly.'

'Very good, sir.'

I, Arianwen Hughes, wish to make a statement. I want someone to write down what I say. I have been told that I need not say anything unless I wish to do so, but that whatever I say may be given in evidence.

Yesterday evening at just before midnight I received a phone call from Dafydd Prosser, who is known to me as Dai Bach. Mr Prosser explained that my husband, Trevor Hughes, had offered to drive him in our car to Bangor to collect some personal effects, because he was going to stay with a friend. Trevor had not appeared, and Mr Prosser did not know where he was. I also did not know where Trevor was. I had expected him to be home by then. Because I felt badly that Trevor had let Mr Prosser down, I decided to drive him myself. I took our son Harri with me, because I could not leave him unattended in the house, and I drove to the Castle Hotel, where Mr Prosser had asked me to meet him. I picked him up and drove him to Bangor. Our car is a grey Austin 1100 saloon car.

As we entered Bangor, Mr Prosser directed me, not to his house, but to a garage. I do not know that part of Bangor well, and I cannot say where the garage is. I was surprised at this request, but I did as I was asked, and I saw that Mr Prosser retrieved a case of some kind from the garage and placed it in the boot of the car. I did not pay much attention to this as I was leaning over to the back seat to make sure that Harri was comfortable. We then returned to Caernarfon. Mr Prosser asked me to stop at the corner of New Street and Chapel Street, where he had arranged to meet his friend. By now it was just after 1 o'clock.

Mr Prosser got out of the car, and walked away down New Street towards Chapel Street. He did not tell me why he was doing this. After one or two minutes, I saw Mr Prosser walking back towards the car, and I saw that my brother, Caradog Prys-Jones, was with him, carrying his duffle bag. I was very surprised by this, because I had not expected to see him, and I believed that he was working at the Castle. On seeing me, Caradog appeared to become extremely agitated and I heard him shouting at Mr Prosser, though I could not hear what was said. The two of them walked past me to the rear of the car, and opened the boot.

I then got out of the car myself to see what was going on. When I walked to the rear of the car, I saw that Mr Prosser had opened the case he had brought from the garage, and I saw what appeared to be a number of sticks of dynamite and some kind of clock. There were a number of electrical wires of various colours. I remember thinking that it looked like one of those bombs you see in films, but then I thought: 'Don't be stupid. It can't be. Dai Bach wouldn't have a bomb.' I was completely confused. I tried to speak, but I found that I couldn't say a word. I was feeling faint. Then suddenly, a number of men arrived, and from then it is all a blur. One of them threw me hard against the driver's side of the car. I felt him place handcuffs on my wrist. I know now that these men were police officers, but I did not know this at the time. I remember one of the men talking about sending for the bomb squad and evacuating the area.

[Question for clarification from DCI Grainger: 'Was that me?' Answer: 'It might have been. Everything was so confused. I can't remember.']

Then I saw Harri through the car window and I found my voice for long enough to scream at the men to tell them that my son was in the car. One of the men took Harri out of the car, and took us both to a police car. I don't remember anything else.

I did not know that Mr Prosser had placed explosives in my car. I did not know that he, or my brother, or my husband, was involved in any plan to plant a bomb anywhere. I have no knowledge of anything like that. I am horrified by the idea. If I had known, I would have refused to have any involvement in it. In particular, I would never have put Harri in the car, or driven it myself, if I thought there was anything dangerous in it.

This is ridiculous. I don't even know why I'm saying all this. This is all nonsense. It's not true. It can't be true. I don't believe it. I refuse to believe it. I am sure there has been a mistake of some kind, and that it will be clarified. That is all I have to say.

I have read the above statement and I have been told that I can correct, alter or add anything I wish. This statement is true. I have made it of my own free will.

'Is the statement signed appropriately by Mrs Hughes, and is her signature witnessed by yourself?'

'Yes, sir.'

'Yes. Thank you, Chief Inspector. Wait there please in case there are any further questions.'

49

'MR PRYS-JONES,' THE JUDGE said, 'do you have any questions for the Chief Inspector? If you do, you may put them in Welsh, and PC Watkins will interpret for you.'

Caradog seemed to hesitate. Gareth stood.

'My Lord, if there is no objection, as Mr Prys-Jones is not represented, may I stand by him and make suggestions?'

Before the judge had any chance to reply, Evan Roberts had leapt to his feet.

'My Lord, I must object in the strongest terms. Mr Prys-Jones has chosen to represent himself. Not only that, he has persistently refused to recognise the court, and has sought to use the court, not to present a defence, but to make political speeches. It is quite wrong for my learned friend to provide informal representation to him in this way.'

Gareth smiled. 'My Lord, because of his greater experience in the civil courts, my learned friend may not be familiar with the principle on which we work in these courts, that counsel has a duty, wherever possible, to assist the court in ensuring that unrepresented defendants have a fair trial. There is no conflict of interest between my client and Mr Prys-Jones, and I have the advantage of speaking Welsh. That is why I offered to help. Of course, if your Lordship feels that I should not do so, then I will withdraw, but...'

'Please, Mr Morgan-Davies, stand by Mr Prys-Jones and assist him to the extent you can.'

'Yes, my Lord.'

Evan seemed poised to renew his objection, but Jamie pulled his arm and sat him back down before he could get the words out.

Gareth walked unhurriedly to the dock, gestured to Caradog and PC Watkins to come forward, and spoke quietly to them in Welsh.

'Mr Prys-Jones, ask these questions in Welsh and, Officer, please interpret the questions and answers for the court.'

'Yes, sir,' PC Watkins said.

'Chief Inspector, you have produced Exhibit 9, my statement under caution, in Welsh with an English translation.'

'Yes, sir.'

'The jury have the English translation. But that is not the first translation made of my statement, is it?'

'No, sir.'

'The first translation read rather differently. Do you have a copy of it?'

'Yes, sir, in my file.'

'Would you find it for us, please?'

Evan was already poised to get back on his feet, and he broke free of Jamie's now relaxed grip on his arm.

'My Lord, I fail to see how this can be relevant. An agreed translation has been put before the jury. Any inaccuracy which may have existed in an earlier translation has nothing to do with the case at all.'

Gareth raised his voice, to be heard from the dock.

'My Lord, that rather depends on the nature of the inaccuracy,' he replied.

'I agree,' Mr Justice Overton said. 'Continue, Mr Prys-Jones.'

'In the second paragraph from the end, the one just before: "I have no regrets…" do you see it?'

'Yes, sir.'

'Does it read as follows: *"The people of England will have no rest until they realise that the people of Wales are not helpless victims. If they do not change their ways and recognise our nation, we promise them a tide of blood in the streets of London which will flow beyond this generation and for many generations to come"*?'

'It does say that, yes.'

'Now, let's look at that same paragraph in the translation the jury have. *"The people of England must understand that the people of Wales are not helpless victims. If they do not change their ways and recognise our nation, it is inevitable that violence and bloodshed will continue."'*

'That is correct. Yes.'

'Based on what you have been told by PC Hywel Watkins, our court interpreter, do you accept that it is the translation before the jury which is the more accurate translation of the statement?'

'Apparently, sir, yes. PC Watkins looked at it again because of a suggestion Mr Morgan-Davies himself made, I believe.'

'Who made the original translation?'

'I would have to check...'

'Let me save you the trouble. It was done by a Mr Forrester of Caernarfon. We have his witness statement.'

'Ah yes, sir, that is correct. I remember now. The local force recommended him to us as someone they used quite often in the area.'

'Where is Mr Forrester now?'

'I couldn't say, sir.'

'Would you agree that Mr Forrester's translation has the effect of making me seem more fanatical and given to inciting far greater violence than PC Watkins' translation?'

'Wouldn't that be true, sir?'

Several gasps were heard around the courtroom. Gareth glanced at Mr Justice Overton and stifled his response.

'Chief Inspector,' the judge said, slowly and deliberately, 'I am rapidly losing patience with you. If I have cause to lose my patience altogether, you will have cause to regret it. I direct you to answer the questions put to you and to say nothing else. Do I make myself clear?'

'Yes, my Lord.'

'Let me try a different question. I have referred to Mr Forrester's document, charitably, as a translation. In fact, he has inserted words into the English text which are simply not there in the Welsh text. That's not making a bad translation, is it? That's a falsification, isn't it?'

'I don't speak Welsh, sir...'

'Then, let's forget about translations for a moment. If someone deliberately inserted words into a statement under caution which the maker of the statement did not use, after the maker of the statement had signed it, with a view to misleading the court, would that be an honest thing to do?'

'No, of course not.'

'Of course not. But that is what has happened here, isn't it? Did you ask Mr Forrester to do that?'

'I am shocked that you would even suggest such a thing.'

'Is the answer to my question "no"?'

'It is "no".'

'I have no further questions, my Lord.'
Gareth returned to his seat.
'My Lord, I have no questions on behalf of Mr Prosser.'

50

BEN STOOD.

'My Lord, may I inspect the Chief Inspector's notebook?'

Evan Roberts was on his feet yet again.

'My Lord, this is simply harassment of this officer, which…'

'Please sit down, Mr Roberts,' the judge replied.

DCI Grainger showed no resistance at all. He had already handed his notebook to Geoffrey, the usher.

'If your Lordship would allow me a moment…'

Ben flicked through the pages unhurriedly before returning the notebook to the usher.

'Thank you, Chief Inspector. You interviewed Arianwen Hughes and she made the statement under caution which you have produced as Exhibit 10, yes?'

'Yes, sir.'

'It would be fair to say that she has denied any involvement in this conspiracy throughout.'

'She has, sir, yes.'

'In particular, she denied any knowledge of the explosive device found in her car.'

'Yes.'

'As you said yourself, she was bitterly distressed throughout the interview, to the extent that you gave some consideration to postponing it until she had regained her composure.'

'That's correct.'

'Part of the reason why she was so distressed was the way in which you and DS Scripps questioned her about the whereabouts of her husband, Trevor Hughes. Isn't that right?'

The Chief Inspector affected to look surprised.

'I don't remember asking her about her husband, sir.'

'There is nothing about any such questions in your notebook, is there?'

'No. Exactly. If we had asked her about Mr Hughes, I would have recorded that in my notebook, as I recorded everything else.'

'Would you explain to the jury why you didn't ask?'

'I don't understand, sir.'

'The jury has been given the impression that finding and arresting Trevor Hughes was a high priority. Is that not correct?'

'Yes, it certainly was.'

'Well, why not ask the person most likely to know where he was?' The Chief Inspector seemed unsure how to reply.

'After all, you asked Dafydd Prosser where Hughes was, didn't you? Why not his wife?'

Evan Roberts rose again.

'My Lord, I would ask my learned friend to be careful with this line of questioning. The jury has not heard about any questions put to Prosser.'

'And they are not going to hear any details of it now,' Ben replied. 'I am merely asking whether questioning took place about Trevor Hughes in the interview with his wife.'

Evan reluctantly resumed his seat.

'Yes, we did ask Prosser about where we could find Trevor Hughes,' the Chief Inspector replied.

'Yes. You did so because it was urgent to find him. The jury have heard all this before, Chief Inspector. You didn't know whether there might be other explosive devices in play. You had to find him if you could.'

'That is correct, sir.'

'In fact, it was so urgent that you made Mr Prosser an offer, didn't you? You offered to put in a good word for him, and for Mrs Hughes, if he gave you information about Hughes' whereabouts, didn't you?'

'Again, my Lord, this is quite improper.' Roberts was raising his voice now.

'I have no objection to it,' Gareth interposed quickly.

'Whether or not my learned friend for Prosser objects, it is improper,' Evan insisted.

'It is a perfectly proper question,' Ben said.

'I agree,' Mr Justice Overton said. 'Continue.'

'Do you need me to repeat the question, Chief Inspector?'

'No, sir.'

'Then, would you please answer it?'

'Yes. We did say that to Mr Prosser.'

'Yes. And on another occasion you have admitted under oath that in so doing, you were in breach of the Judges' Rules, have you not?'

'Yes.'

'And, so that the jury will understand, the Judges' Rules are rules of conduct, binding on the police, governing the questioning of suspects by police officers.'

'They are, sir.'

'The Rules say you are not allowed to put any pressure on a suspect to answer questions or make a statement by the use of threats or inducements, don't they?'

'Yes, sir.'

'And the Rules are there to be obeyed. You are under a duty to obey them, aren't you?'

'Yes.'

'You broke the same rules again when you questioned Arianwen Hughes, didn't you?'

'No, sir.'

'Did you not say to her, almost as soon as you entered her cell, words to this effect: "There's no point in crying about your son. You're not going to see him again for a very long time, if ever"?'

'Certainly not.'

'Did you tell her that you might let her see her son if she told you where her husband was?'

'Certainly not.'

'And did not DS Scripps say this, and I'm putting his exact words to you: "By the time we've finished with you, you will be lucky to be out in time for his silver wedding anniversary"?'

'Certainly not.'

'And that's why Arianwen Hughes was so upset that you had to think about postponing the interview, wasn't it?'

'Certainly not.'

'And then you did the same as you had done with Dafydd Prosser, didn't you? You offered to put in a good word for her if she told you where Trevor Hughes was.'

'No, sir.'

'But she didn't know, did she?'

'I don't know whether she knew or not.'

'So, you thought she might know?'

'I... I didn't say that...'

'Why didn't you ask her?'

Ben moved on without waiting for a reply.

'No trace of Trevor Hughes was found, despite a very intense search, is that right?'

'That is correct.'

'What steps did you take to find him subsequently?'

'As soon as we realised that he was not in the immediate vicinity, we put out an immediate alert to all ports and airports to detain Mr Hughes on sight. We sent his picture and description to all police forces throughout the United Kingdom, and to the Irish Garda.'

'That was because there was some intelligence that Mr Hughes had fled to Ireland?'

'Yes. In the following weeks, there were some reports that he had been sighted in Ireland, although there has never been any confirmation of that, to my knowledge.'

'In the Republic or Northern Ireland?'

'The North. We also sent his picture and details to Interpol, in case he had somehow succeeded in travelling abroad, despite the ports and airports watch.'

'But as you stand here today, you have no idea where Trevor Hughes is to be found, is that right?'

'If I knew where Trevor Hughes was to be found, sir, he would be arrested and brought before a court.'

The Chief Inspector looked around the court to make his point.

'We will find Trevor Hughes. He can't hide for ever. It's only a matter of time.'

'But not in time for this trial, Chief Inspector?'

'Unfortunately not, sir.'

51

'I PUT MY LEARNED friends on notice,' Evan said self-importantly, 'that this afternoon I shall be calling an officer of the Domestic Security Service to deal with certain events which took place in Ireland.'

The court had heard from DS Scripps, who had been cross-examined only by Ben, and then very briefly. Ben had asked the prosecution to make WPC Marsh available for cross-examination on a later day, to which Evan had agreed with an ill-grace which served only to irritate Mr Justice Overton even further. The jury had already left court for lunch.

'Following the usual practice, the witness will not give his name, and will be referred to only as "Witness A". He will also give evidence while screened from everyone except your Lordship in order to protect his identity fully. I am sure your Lordship will readily understand that any public exposure would not only limit his professional effectiveness, but might well place him in danger.'

'That is the usual practice,' Gareth replied. 'I have no objection.'

'Nor have I, my Lord,' Ben added.

'Witness A, are you an officer of the Domestic Security Service, otherwise known as MI5?'

'I am.' The voice, coming from behind the curtained screen, sounded disembodied, and echoed eerily in the high empty spaces of the courtroom. 'I will not give my name publicly, but I will identify myself by presenting my identity card to the judge if required to do so.'

'Not necessary,' Gareth said.

'I agree,' Ben echoed.

'I am grateful to my learned friends. Keep your voice up, Officer, please. This is a big courtroom, and your voice may be lost otherwise.

In April 1969, were you assigned to duty in Northern Ireland?'

'I was.'

'As far as you can, and without going into details you are not at liberty to divulge, will you give the court a general idea of your duties at that time?'

'At that time, I was partnered with an officer of the Republic of Ireland's *Garda Síochána*. Our remit was to monitor certain arrivals into both the Republic and into Northern Ireland from other parts of the United Kingdom and Europe, and to track certain individuals and groups crossing the border between Northern Ireland and the Republic.'

'On or about 2 April did you have occasion to note the arrival of a particular individual in the Republic of Ireland by means of the ferry from Holyhead to Dublin?'

'I did.'

'Are you authorised to tell us his name?'

'No. I can tell you that this man is a West German national and, according to the West German Security Service, is closely associated with an anarchist group in that country generally known as Baader-Meinhof. This group is suspected of a number of violent crimes which have apparent political motivations.'

'Thank you. Since you are Witness A, let's call this man "Man B".'

'All right.'

'Did you observe Man B after his arrival?'

'Yes. My partner and I photographed Man B on arrival and followed him when he left the terminal. He was met by a man. We can call him "Man C" if you like…?'

'Yes.'

'Man C has been identified as a probable regional commander in the IRA, based in West Belfast.'

'When you say "met"…'

'Man C was driving a motor vehicle, the details of which I have, but am not authorised to divulge. My partner and I followed this vehicle from Dublin to Belfast, and kept observation on both men for the remainder of that day and the next day.'

'Did any of those observations have any bearing on the present case?'

'No. But on Friday 4 April, we made an observation which does appear to relate to this case.'

'Please tell my Lord and the jury about that.'

'My partner and I were keeping observation in a public house in West Belfast in the early evening, 6.30 to 7 o'clock. At that time, Man B was drinking there on his own. We had seen Man C leave the area in his car earlier in the day, but we decided not to follow, so that we could maintain observation on Man B. At about 7.30, Man C entered the public house in company with three other men, Men D, E and F, who were unknown to us. Man C introduced Men D, E and F to Man B. They shook hands and they all started to talk together. They were talking for about an hour, during which time they had three rounds of drinks. Just after 8.30, Man B and Man E left the group and went into a room behind and to the right of the bar. This is a private room, and we were not able to observe them. They were gone until about 10 o'clock, when they emerged from the room and re-joined the group. Man E was carrying a notebook of some kind. Men D, E and F left not long after this. We did not continue observation.'

'Were you able to hear anything said between the men?'

'Unfortunately, no. This was a high-risk surveillance in the sense that it was very intensive. There was a high risk that we would be identified as keeping observation on them just because of the frequency and duration of observation. We did not feel it would have been justified to move closer in an effort to hear. Frankly, we were not concerned with Men D, E or F at that stage. We knew nothing about them.'

'Thank you. You say that Men D, E and F were unknown to you. Did you later take any steps to identify them?'

'Yes. Since there had been contact, we did inquire. There was no relevant police or Security Service intelligence. But we were able to obtain photographs taken on their arrival by ferry at Dublin, and from the passenger list and other sources we were able to identify them as follows. Man D was identified as Caradog Prys-Jones, Man E as Dafydd Prosser, and Man F as Trevor Hughes, Man D and Man F having addresses in Caernarfon, and Man E having an address in Bangor.'

'What did you do with this information?'

'As there was no active intelligence involving these individuals, it was not regarded as a high priority. We filed a routine report, which meant that information about their contact with Man B and Man C would appear on any future response to an information request about any of them, or about Man B or Man C.'

'So when Mr Prys-Jones, Mr Prosser and Mr Hughes were named in connection with this case, information about their contact with Man B and Man C would have been available?'

'Available to my Service, yes. It would have been available to police forces only if specifically requested and in redacted form, but as my Service was actively involved in the events surrounding the Investiture, the information was made generally available as soon as those involved were identified.'

'Are you saying that, but for that coincidence, the contact might not have been known to the police?'

'It would not have been known.'

'It does sound as though there is a certain lack of communication between branches, all of whom have the same goals, doesn't it?' Evan asked.

'That is a fair comment,' Witness A replied. 'But that kind of procedural policy is rather above my pay grade.'

52

'WE HAVE HEARD THAT at some point, there was intelligence that Man F, Trevor Hughes, had escaped arrest and travelled to Ireland. Is that correct?' Ben asked. Gareth had indicated that he had no questions.

'Yes. Actually, that intelligence came from us. We passed it on to Special Branch. It never came to anything.'

'But there were subsequently some reported sightings of Hughes in Northern Ireland, were there not?'

'Yes, but I am very sceptical about them.'

'Why is that?'

'Because there were so few of them. Hughes is a very high-profile fugitive and you would expect a certain number of sightings in various places. I myself would only start to believe in them if they were frequent and reasonably consistent as to dates and places. We never had anything like that here. Actually, there has been a surprising lack of sightings everywhere, not just in Ireland. It's as if he has disappeared from the face of the earth.'

'So your Service can't really assist the court about Hughes' movements or present whereabouts at all?'

'I'm afraid not. But I can tell you this. We received the ports and airports alert, and we kept a close eye on things. If Trevor Hughes did escape to Ireland, it's very unlikely that he came by any conventional route – by that, I mean ferry or scheduled flight. We would have spotted him. It's far more likely that he had his own private means of transport, and it is almost certain that he wasn't using his real name. We will keep monitoring any fresh reports, of course. But I wouldn't hold your breath.'

After the judge had risen for the day and the barristers were gathering up their papers, Gareth leaned across to Ben.

'I tell you what,' he said. 'As far as Trevor Hughes is concerned, I am coming around to Caradog's view. I think he may have come to some harm.'

Ben nodded.

'It's hard to believe that he vanished into thin air so completely. He only had a couple of hours' head start, didn't he? He was with Dai Bach in the square for most of the evening.'

'Exactly,' Gareth said.

'Arianwen thinks he is alive and well,' Ben said.

'Wives generally do,' Gareth observed. 'That's what makes this kind of case so terribly sad when the truth finally emerges.'

'If you're right, I hope they don't find him for a long time,' Ben said. 'She can't cope with any more at the moment.'

53

'POLICE SERGEANT EMRYS PUGH, of the Gwynedd Constabulary, my Lord, attached to Caernarfon Police Station.'

'Thank you, Sergeant,' Jamie said. 'On the early morning of 1 July last year were you on duty in uniform in Caernarfon?'

'I was, sir.'

'Did you make a note of the events about which you are going to give evidence? Was that note made at the first practicable opportunity and while the events were fresh in your memory?'

'Yes, sir.'

'Unless there is any objection – I see there is none – please refresh your recollection using your notes. At about 1.30 on that morning, were you at Caernarfon Police Station?'

'I was, sir.'

'Did you receive any instruction from Superintendent Rees?'

'Yes, sir. Superintendent Rees told me that a suspect by the name of Trevor Hughes was at large, and that it was urgent to apprehend him because there was a danger of further explosive devices having been planted, or about to be planted, in Caernarfon, with which Hughes was likely to be involved.'

'When you say "further devices", Sergeant, I take it that you were aware that a device had been found in a car near the town square.'

'Yes, sir, I was aware of it.'

'Please tell my Lord and the jury what you did.'

'I rounded up every uniformed officer I could find – five in all. I found them in the canteen on their break having a cup of tea. I quickly briefed them that we needed to search for Hughes at two places. One was the *Tywysog* book shop in Palace Street, and the second was a residential address in *Penrallt Isaf*. These were Hughes' known place of work and home address. I told the officers that Hughes was to be arrested, and that he was to be regarded as dangerous. Superintendent Rees indicated that he would make armed officers available as soon as he could, but we were to proceed to these addresses immediately and attempt to locate Hughes without delay.'

'And is that what you did?'

'Yes, sir. I took two constables with me, and proceeded to the home address in *Penrallt Isaf.* I assigned the other three constables to the book shop.'

'What did you do on arrival at the home address?'

'We parked in front of the house. We saw that there were lights on inside. One of the constables gained access to the house.'

'I take it that he was not unduly gentle in doing that?'

'No, sir, he was not.'

'What happened once you gained entry?'

'We shouted as loudly as we could: "Trevor Hughes, police! We have armed colleagues on the way!"'

'Was there any response?'

'No, sir. We made a cursory search of the house. There was no one there.'

'You say a cursory search…?'

'We were aware that it would be necessary for scenes of crimes officers to search the premises at a later time, to search for evidence. We did our best not to interfere with the scene. We made no attempt to make a detailed search.'

'But in the course of your cursory search, did you see any evidence at all of a male being in residence at the address?'

'Yes, sir. In the wardrobe and chest of drawers in the main bedroom there were numerous items of male clothing – a complete male wardrobe as far as I could see – and in the bathroom there were razors, shaving cream, after-shave lotion and other male items.'

'What did you do then?'

'We secured the house as best we could, and I left one of my two constables on guard, in case Hughes should return, and also to prevent any unauthorised intrusion. With the other constable I then proceeded as quickly as I could to the *Tywysog* book shop.'

'What did you find there?'

'The other team of officers had gained access to the premises, but there was no sign of Trevor Hughes. I radioed in to the station to report this. The officers drew my attention to a number of documents which were potentially of interest to the inquiry. I instructed the officers to leave these items in place for a later search by scenes of crimes officers. We secured the book shop, leaving an officer on guard, and returned to the police station to await further instructions.'

'Sergeant Pugh, I don't think this has been done yet, so can I ask you please to look at the floor plan of the book shop, which the jury have. It is Exhibit 3. Can you confirm that it is an accurate plan of the layout of the *Tywysog*?'

'Yes, sir, I can confirm that.'

'Thank you. My Lord, my learned friends have indicated that there is no dispute about the later detailed searches made of the various premises the jury has heard about. So rather than take up time unnecessarily by calling each of the scenes of crimes officers, we have agreed that I may summarise their evidence through Sergeant Pugh, who was in overall charge of that phase of the operation.'

'That is correct, my Lord,' Gareth said.

'Yes, very well,' the judge said.

54

'SERGEANT PUGH, AS YOU have said, you made only a cursory search, leaving the more detailed search for evidence to specially trained scenes of crimes officers, is that right?'

'Yes, sir.'

'Those officers conducted a thorough search later the same day, and seized a number of items of evidence?'

'Yes, sir.'

'Those items were then sent for forensic testing where necessary. Are you able to help the jury with the results of those tests?'

'I am, my Lord.'

'Thank you. Let me begin with a scene you have not yet told the jury about, and that is Caradog Prys-Jones's home in Pretoria Terrace. Were those premises searched, and is it right to say that nothing relevant to the investigation was found there?'

'That is correct, sir. There were a few books dealing with the history of Wales and with Welsh nationalism, but these were books in general circulation published by highly reputable publishing houses, and they were not deemed relevant to the inquiry.'

In the dock, Caradog laughed briefly.

'All right. Turning then to the home address of Trevor and Arianwen Hughes in *Penrallt Isaf*, was that address searched, and is it right to say that nothing of relevance to the inquiry was found there?'

'That is correct, sir.'

'Turning next to the *Tywysog* book shop, you have already told my Lord and the jury that the officers who went there looking for Trevor Hughes drew your attention to some documents of interest?'

'Yes, sir.'

'And were those items later seized by the scenes of crimes officers?'

'They were, sir.'

'Very well, let's go through them. My Lord, may we give them sequential exhibit numbers, please?'

'Yes.'

'I am obliged. What is Exhibit 11?'

'Exhibit 11 is a passenger's copy of a reservation for the ferry between Holyhead and Dublin for travel on 3 April 1969, with a return date three days later, in the names of Caradog Prys-Jones, Dafydd Prosser and Trevor Hughes.'

'Exhibit 12?'

'Exhibit 12 is a cheque book for an account at Lloyds Bank in Caernarfon in the name of Trevor Hughes, with a stub for cheque number 2674 dated 14 March 1969, payable to the ferry operator, which appears to represent payment for the reservations on the ferry, Exhibit 11.'

'Thank you. Exhibit 13?'

'Exhibit 13 is an invoice from a company called the Secure Packaging Company Ltd, based in Sheffield, which relates to the purchase by Mr Hughes of a heavy steel carrying case, model number XT453, manufactured by the company.'

'And why is that relevant?'

'If you look at the invoice, sir, you will see a picture of the model XT453. The carrying case used to contain the explosive device found in Arianwen Hughes' car was an XT453. There was no serial number on that case, but there is no doubt about the model. And if you look back at the cheque book, Exhibit 12, you will see a stub for cheque number 2682 dated 4th May 1969, payable to the Secure Packaging Company for £150 – the amount of the invoice.'

'Thank you. Exhibit 14?'

'Exhibit 14 is a hand-written note purporting to be signed by Trevor Hughes and a man called Arthur Watts for the monthly rental of a garage in Glyncoed Road, Bangor – which is the address where the device appears to have been assembled – specifying a rent of £10 per month, payable in advance, in cash.'

'Yes, thank you, Sergeant. Now, turning to that garage in Glyncoed Road, was it also searched, and again were a number of items seized and sent for forensic examination?'

'Yes, sir.'

'What are Exhibits 15 to 19?'

'Exhibits 15 to 19 are typed documents with hand-drawn

diagrams purporting to be instructions for making home-made explosive devices.'

'What can you tell us about them?'

'Most of them are known to police and military experts already. They are typical of instructions which have been circulating among criminal and anarchist groups in this country, in Ireland, and in various continental countries, for some time now. No one knows who wrote them. They are in English, except for Exhibit 17, which is in German, but the standard of English suggests that they may have been compiled by persons whose first language is not English. They circulate in the underground market, of course, but someone determined to find them would be able to do so by making the right inquiries.'

'Are they sufficient to enable a person with reasonable intelligence and practical skills to assemble a home-made bomb?'

'Provided he – or she – has the necessary ingredients, yes. Bombs corresponding to these instructions have either been detonated or been disarmed on a number of occasions by the military in a number of locations. At the same time, it has to be said that, in the hands of the unskilled, there would be the potential for considerable danger.'

'You mean, in terms of blowing themselves up while trying to assemble the device?'

'Exactly. The instructions are not always as precise as you would wish as regards safety, and you have to remember that you are dealing with dangerous, and sometimes unstable, ingredients, and with electrical circuits which have to be wired carefully and precisely. If you know what you are doing you should be safe enough, but anyone coming to it for the first time would be at some risk.'

'Exhibits 20 to 29?'

'Exhibits 20 to 29 are small fragments of electrical wire, and trace quantities of dynamite found on small pieces of brown cardboard, possibly from a cardboard box of some kind, which appear to be identical with those incorporated into the bomb. Exhibit 30 is a pair of pliers bearing small fragments of the same electrical wire. Exhibits 31 and 32 are pairs of plastic kitchen gloves bearing traces of the same electrical wire and the dynamite used in the bomb. If I may go on, sir?'

'Yes.'

'Exhibit 33 appears to be a box for an electrical alarm clock of

Japanese manufacture, which is the same model used as a timing device in the bomb.'

'Thank you, Sergeant Pugh. Were there also other items which were seized, but have not been produced in evidence, including two trestle tables, two folding chairs, tea-making equipment, a tin containing biscuits, tea mugs and the like?'

'There were, sir, yes. They are available to be inspected, should anyone wish to do so.'

Jamie paused to consult a note.

'Did the scenes of crimes officers also search for fingerprints in the garage?'

'Yes, sir. On their arrest, fingerprints were taken from Dafydd Prosser and Caradog Prys-Jones. On the trestle tables, chairs, tea mugs, and other items in the garage, the officers found a large number of prints, which were submitted for comparison, and were found to be identical to those of Dafydd Prosser. There were a smaller number, I think seven or eight in all, on the trestle tables and one chair, which were also sent for comparison and found to be identical to those of Caradog Prys-Jones.'

'Has it ever been known for sets of fingerprints taken from two different individuals to be identical?'

'No, sir.'

'And does it follow that the prints that were found were indeed those of Dafydd Prosser and Caradog Prys-Jones?'

'That does follow, sir, yes. Other fingerprints were also found, but there is no evidence that they are related to the inquiry.'

'I take it you had no prints from Trevor Hughes to compare to those in the garage?'

'That's correct, sir.'

'And in fairness, you did have the fingerprints of Arianwen Hughes, and is it right that no prints were found corresponding to hers?'

'That is also correct, sir.'

'Did officers also search the home address of Dafydd Prosser in Bangor?'

'Yes, sir.'

'And were any items seized from that address?'

'Just two, sir, Exhibits 34 and 35, a green shirt and a pair of brown corduroy trousers, found on close examination to bear microscopic traces of a substance identified as dynamite. However, the traces were too small to enable any comparison to be made with the dynamite used in the bomb.'

'Thank you. Did the officers search the car which had been used to convey the bomb to the Castle?'

'Yes, sir. The car was impounded and subjected to a thorough search. There were a number of fingerprints on the steering wheel and dashboard, identified as those of Arianwen Hughes, and a number on the front passenger side door handle, the boot handle and door, identified as those of Dafydd Prosser. That was only to be expected, of course. Apart from that, nothing of relevance to the inquiry was found.'

'Lastly, Sergeant Pugh, after the bomb squad had examined the device and removed it from the heavy steel carrying case, was the case checked for fingerprints?'

'Yes, sir. No prints were found either on the case itself or on the timing device, except for one partial thumb print on the carrying case which was inadequate for comparison.'

'Yes, thank you, Sergeant Pugh. Wait there, please.'

'Sergeant Pugh,' Ben said, once Gareth had indicated that he had no questions, 'can you confirm, and I think it follows from what you have said, that the officers did not find Arianwen Hughes' fingerprints on anything relevant to the inquiry, except for the surfaces of the car itself?'

'That is correct, sir.'

'Not anywhere in the garage?'

'No, sir.'

'Not on the explosive device itself, or its carrying case?'

'Correct, sir.'

'Thank you. Going back to the search of the Hughes' home in *Penrallt Isaf*, did the officers find any note in the handwriting either of Trevor Hughes or Arianwen Hughes?'

'I'm not sure what you mean by a note, sir. There were a number of pages of handwriting in the music room which appear to be that of Arianwen Hughes, and a few pieces of paper elsewhere which might well be in the writing of Trevor Hughes, but none of it was deemed relevant.'

'I am sorry, Sergeant. My question was not very precise. Let me try again. Was there any note, either from him to her, or her to him, left somewhere like the kitchen table, explaining where he or she might be – saying, "see you later" or anything of that kind?'

'Oh, I see what you mean, sir. No. Nothing like that, as far as I am aware.'

'So there was no indication that Trevor intended to be away for any length of time?'

'No, sir.'

'Indeed, you indicated that all his clothes and personal effects seemed to be in place?'

'Yes, sir.'

'And generally, when you entered, you found a scene that suggested an ordinary family home, in use by an ordinary family on an ordinary evening?'

'Yes, I think that would be fair.'

'Lights on, as if they were not expecting to be away for long?'

Jamie stood.

'I'm not sure the sergeant can properly be asked to speculate quite that far, my Lord,' he said.

Ben nodded.

'I don't press it, my Lord. Thank you, Sergeant.'

55

'CAPTAIN JOHN RANDOLPH PERRY, my Lord, Royal Engineers, attached to the Explosive Ordnance Disposal Unit, popularly known as the bomb squad.'

The captain's uniform was pristine, and boasted three medals. He was a tall man with jet-black hair, well-built, but carrying no excess weight, and he had a ready smile. He joined his hands behind his back.

'Captain Perry,' Jamie said, 'for a month or thereabouts before the Investiture of the Prince of Wales, were you commanding one of three small EOD units assigned to Caernarfon to work in cooperation with the police and other bodies responsible for public security?'

'Yes, sir. Under my command I had Sergeant Ian McDonald and Corporal John Laud.'

'Before we come to the details of this case, can I ask you about this? I am sure you must have considerable training in preparation for the work you do.'

'Yes, sir. In addition to general military training, of course, both officers and other ranks have an intensive four-week training course, in which we have to learn about all kinds of ordnance, and how to make them safe. I am sure you understand, sir, there is far more to the job than dealing with the kind of home-made device we encountered in this case. In times of war, we are responsible for dealing with all kinds of unexploded ordnance on and around the battlefield, as well as making civilian areas safe in the aftermath of a battle.'

'It is always dangerous work, isn't it?'

'Yes, sir. It is.'

'What characteristics must a good EOD officer possess?'

The captain smiled.

'I suppose, first and foremost, the ability to remain calm, remember the training, evaluate the situation he finds himself in, and to work well with his team under pressure. In my own personal opinion, sir, it also helps to be stark raving mad.'

There was loud laughter in court, in which the judge and counsel joined.

'Indeed, Captain Perry,' Jamie said. 'In the kind of situation we have here, where a home-made device is found in a civilian area, what considerations come into play?'

'Oddly enough, sir, disarming the device in that kind of situation is not usually the most urgent task. The first and most important thing is the evacuation of the surrounding area, and the police need an assessment of how big an area must be evacuated. That can be of crucial importance because the greater the area, the more time it takes, and you can't assume that time is on your side. So first, we take a general look at the device, and try to form an opinion about its size, the potential damage involved, and how stable it seems to be.'

'Please tell my Lord and the jury what you mean by "stable".'

'By "stable", I mean that there appears to be no immediate risk of an uncontrolled, unpredictable detonation. If the device is unstable, there may be no guarantee that there is time to evacuate the area, and it may be necessary to attempt to disarm it immediately, despite the risks.'

'Whereas… if it appears to be stable…?'

'Wherever possible, we prefer to remove the device to a safe area and deal with it by means of a controlled detonation. This allows us to eliminate any risk to members of the public and ourselves. But of course, it may not be possible to do that safely. We may not have confidence in the stability of the device, or a timing mechanism may indicate to us that a detonation is imminent. If we don't think we can remove it to a safe area, we will allow the police whatever time we can to evacuate, but we will then attempt to disarm it *in situ*.'

'Thank you, Captain. Now, let me turn to the occasion with which the jury are concerned, 1 July 1969, the early morning on the day of the Investiture. Were you on duty at that time with the members of your team?'

'Yes, sir.'

'And were you called to the junction of New Street and Chapel Street, near the town square in Caernarfon, shortly after 1 o'clock that morning, following the report of a bomb being found in the boot of a car?'

'Yes, sir.'

'What did you do on arrival?'

'We parked nearby. Corporal Laud stayed with the vehicle and ensured that we were ready to remove the device to a place of safety if possible. Sergeant McDonald and I approached the rear of the car. We observed that the street had been cordoned off by means of police cars, and that an evacuation of the immediate area was taking place, from residential properties and the Castle Hotel. We then began to observe the device with the aid of powerful torches we use for night-time work.'

'As you were doing this, did anyone else approach?'

'Yes, a police officer, DC Owen if memory serves, approached with a man who was handcuffed and was evidently in the officer's custody.'

'Did this come as a surprise?'

'Not entirely. We had been told over the radio that one of the suspected makers of the device had been arrested and was prepared to cooperate by explaining how to disarm it.'

'How did you react to that information?'

'We are trained to be highly sceptical of offers of help from perpetrators. You have to think there is some chance they will give false information to keep you from disabling the device, or even trigger a detonation. Every army in the world has horror stories about that. The Americans have lost a fair number of EOD officers in Vietnam through relying on Viet Cong collaborators – apparent collaborators – and we had our share in Malaysia and elsewhere. So we prefer to make up our own minds. I'm not saying we might not ask a question or two if we had a tricky one, but we wouldn't rely on the answer unless it matched our own assessment.'

'Did Mr Prosser – you know, of course, that it was Mr Prosser – did Mr Prosser in fact give you useful information.'

'He did, although… I'm sorry I'm smiling. It's just that by the time Mr Prosser got there, Sergeant McDonald and I had already drawn our own conclusions.'

'Which were…?'

'We were dealing with a home-made explosive device of quite basic design, but competently made and almost certainly very stable. There was no immediate risk of detonation, and we were confident that it could be moved to a safe area without difficulty. In fact, we were looking around for the senior officer – DCI Grainger – to tell him he could call off the evacuation, as soon as he provided a police escort for us to remove the device to a place of safety.'

'What led you to think that the device was stable?'

'It was composed of military grade dynamite, which was in pristine condition. It was obvious that the maker intended to detonate the device automatically by means of a 24-hour electronic alarm clock, but this was not connected up and was not operating. There was no other source of ignition. There was no sign of any mercury-based or other mechanism to render the device unstable if handled. To be honest, anything like that would have been a few levels above the level of sophistication of the device, and even if you used such a mechanism, you would not install it until the bomb was in its intended place. The device was contained in a very snug, heavy, steel carrying case, which would also have guarded against the risk of an uncontrolled detonation.'

'So, Mr Prosser's advice was not really needed?'

'No. But in fairness, he didn't know that. He pointed out to us that the device was not armed, and he told us exactly how it was constructed. He made no effort to mislead us in any way at all. We clipped a few of the wires as he instructed us, just to show our appreciation. Once Mr Prosser had been taken away, we loaded the device into our vehicle and took it under police escort to a place of safety.'

'Did you destroy the device?'

'No, sir. The police asked that it be dismantled and the various components kept as evidence, which we did.'

'All right. Now, I know that you have not brought the dynamite to court today, for obvious reasons…'

'I am very glad to hear that, Mr Broderick,' Mr Justice Overton said. There was some laughter.

'Yes, my Lord. But is it available for anyone to inspect?'

'Yes, sir. The dynamite, of course, is in proper storage at a military facility, but I believe the police have the alarm clock, the carrying case and the rest of the components.'

'Yes. I am going to show you a number of items now, and ask that these be numbered sequentially as exhibits. With the usher's assistance… please look at this first item. Is this the steel carrying case in which the device had been placed?'

'Yes, sir.'

'Thank you.' Jamie smiled. 'I'm sorry, my Lord, I'm afraid I've lost track of where we are with exhibit numbers.'

'This will be 36,' Gareth volunteered.

'I am much obliged to my learned friend. Exhibit 36. Would you please look at the next item the usher is handing you, and can you tell us what this is?'

'This is a basic electronic 24-hour alarm clock of Japanese manufacture, readily available in shops.'

'Exhibit 37. And the next item?'

'A quantity of electrical wire, again readily available in shops. You can see that various parts of it are frayed and the wire is exposed at the ends where we cut it at the site.'

'Thank you. That will be Exhibit 38. And lastly, there is a small album of photographs which will become Exhibit 39. Please tell my Lord and the jury what these are.'

'These are photographs of the device, I think 20 in all, taken at various stages of the process of dismantling it. The first ones show it as we found it in the carrying case. Then we move to pictures with the case removed, and then various pictures which illustrate the stages of dismantling it. Finally, there are pictures of the dynamite and other components individually.'

'Yes. Let me ask you about the dynamite for a moment. Are you able to give the jury any further information on that?'

'Yes indeed. The dynamite is not only military quality, but it has been identified as being part of a batch stolen from a military establishment in Wales about 18 months ago. I am not authorised to say any more about the details of the theft, my Lord, for reasons of security.'

'No, of course,' the judge said.

'Finally, Captain Perry, I would like to ask you about the consequences which might have ensued if the device had been planted, as the defendants intended, inside Caernarfon Castle.'

Gareth stood.

'My Lord, I must object to this, and I do so on behalf of Mr Prys-Jones, who is not represented, as well as on behalf of my client. My learned friend has not shown that the witness is an expert in the area of how damage is caused by explosions, what kind of damage is caused, or over what area it is caused. And any such evidence would be little more than speculation, given that the Crown can do no more than speculate about where the device would have been placed. The evidence would be highly misleading to the jury.'

'My Lord,' Jamie replied. 'I will ask the captain about his credentials in that area if required to do so. But there is nothing speculative about his evidence. The Crown has already adduced evidence about the probable site chosen by Mr Prys-Jones for the bomb. If he, or Mr Prosser, wishes to dispute that evidence, they are free to do so.'

'I agree, Mr Broderick,' the judge said. Gareth quietly resumed his seat.

'Captain Perry, are you trained in evaluating the kind of damage and the probable extent of damage which may be caused by explosive devices?'

'Yes, of course. That kind of assessment is crucial to our work.'

'I ask the usher to show you Exhibit 7. Your Lordship and the jury will recall that these are photographs of a loose paving stone and the space beneath it, situated towards the front wall in the corridor leading from the Black Tower to the Chamberlain Tower in Caernarfon Castle. Captain Perry, I want you to assume with me that the device you found has been placed in the space under the paving stone, that it has been armed using the alarm clock, and that the paving stone has been placed back in position. Do you follow?'

'Yes, sir.'

'Please look also at Exhibit 8, the seating plan... from this you will see where the Black Tower and the Chamberlain Tower are, and you will see that there are banks of seats just in front of where the device is, and that just in front of those seating stands there is the dais where the ceremony of Investiture takes place. Do you see that?'

'Yes, sir.'

'Can you tell my Lord and the jury what scale and extent of injury and damage you would expect if the bomb were to detonate in that location during the ceremony?'

'Again, my Lord,' Gareth said, 'I must object that this is pure speculation.'

'You will have the opportunity to cross-examine, Mr Morgan-Davies,' the judge replied. 'Please answer the question, Captain Perry.'

'There would be a high probability of loss of life and very serious injury amongst those in the seating stands nearby, and even those on the dais. In addition, of course, there would be very considerable damage to the immediate area of the Castle building surrounding the site of the device.'

'Yes. Thank you, Captain Perry. Please wait there.'

56

GARETH WAS ABOUT TO stand when Donald Weston tugged on his gown.

'Gareth, let me take him.'

'Why?'

'I'll explain later.'

Gareth looked at Ben, who was smiling, and calculated briefly. There was little, if anything, to gain by the cross-examination, but also little to lose. He had objected to some of Captain Perry's evidence and felt obliged to put a few questions. Donald knew what they were, and they would come just as well from him. Why not?

'Yes, all right,' he replied. 'My Lord, my learned junior, Mr Weston, will question this witness.'

'Captain Perry,' Donald began, 'dynamite is not greatly used as a weapon by the Armed Forces these days, is it?'

'If you mean as a combat weapon, no. It was never designed for that purpose. Dynamite was designed, and has always been used primarily for blasting and other situations which demand controlled explosions. It is useful to the Army for sabotage purposes, of course, but there are other materials which are far more useful and adaptable for use in weaponry.'

'Thank you. Is it also correct that many factors may influence the extent and distribution of damage from a dynamite explosion?'

'Yes, I would agree with that.'

'Among them, the exact positioning of the device?'

'Yes indeed.'

'If you look at Exhibit 7 again, would you not agree that the floor of the space is far from even?'

'Yes.'

'And so there could be no guarantee that the device would be level, rather than on an angle, and there would be no certainty about the precise direction of the explosion?'

'That is true to some extent, but I would not expect it to be a significant factor.'

'So, would you expect the explosion to take effect in each direction?'

'Yes.'

'But you could not rule out that the device might veer in one direction or another on detonation?'

'I could not rule that out. But the force of the explosion would still be very considerable, and it would be more than capable of having catastrophic consequences in the seating areas in front of it, and on the dais.'

'Is it possible that the force of the explosion might be inhibited to some extent either by the carrying case, or the paving stone which, in my learned friend's example, was placed over the aperture, and so more or less on top of the device?'

Captain Perry shook his head.

'Perhaps to a very limited extent. But far more significant is the fact that both the paving stone and the carrying case would probably be blown apart, causing pieces of shrapnel to be propelled outwards with considerable velocity. Anyone struck by such a piece of shrapnel would have virtually no chance of avoiding death or very serious injury.'

Every eye in the courtroom was on Donald Weston. He appeared quite calm.

'Captain Perry, let me ask you about something else. You said, very fairly, that Dafydd Prosser did not try to mislead you in any way?'

'Yes, that is true.'

'Indeed, he offered whatever help he could give, not knowing, of course, that you already had the situation under control, but nonetheless, he tried his best, didn't he?'

'Yes, he did.'

'What state did he seem to you to be in at that time?'

The witness reflected for some moments.

'I think the best word would be distraught, sir. He was clearly very distressed. There were tears in his eyes, and he seemed to be speaking very rapidly. I had the impression that he was very anxious to do what he could to mitigate the situation, to make sure that everyone knew there was no danger.'

'This was a very basic device, wasn't it? Nothing to suggest that it was the work of anyone other than a first-time bomb-maker?'

'I would not disagree with that, subject to the observation that it was very competently made, and I was particularly impressed with the use of such a heavy carrying case, and the high grade dynamite. I would suggest that the maker probably had access to some written instructions of the kind found by the police in this case, which make the rounds via the underground network.'

He paused.

'There is also a certain neatness, a certain compactness, about it which makes me think that the maker may well have had some help from a more experienced collaborator. But I would have to concede that I am speculating to some extent there. It is certainly a device which could have been made by a first-time maker, if he had a certain aptitude, the right instructions, and good materials.'

'Thank you, Captain Perry.'

'My Lord,' Jamie Broderick said, after the jury had been dismissed for the day, 'as my learned friend Mr Schroeder requested, the prosecution has located WPC Marsh, the officer who was present when Arianwen Hughes was interviewed by DCI Grainger and DS Scripps. She will be available tomorrow morning, but not, I'm afraid, until then. We can't go any further until she has been called. I will have to ask your Lordship to rise until tomorrow morning. But we are making good progress.'

'I am grateful to my learned friend,' Ben said. 'If she has made a witness statement, I would very much like to see it before I ask her any questions.'

'She has not made a witness statement,' Jamie replied. 'The prosecution will not call her as a witness except to establish her identity, but will simply make her available to the defence for cross-examination. I should have called her former WPC Marsh. I understand that she is no longer a police officer.'

'Sorry,' Donald said, as they made their way back to the robing room. 'I'm afraid I didn't get very far, and I let him shoot me down.'

Gareth shook his head.

'There was nothing much you could have done. It was worth a try. It's all we can do. Why were you so keen to have a go at him yourself?'

Donald smiled.

'My father was an army officer before he retired,' he replied. 'I picked up a few bits and pieces about explosives from him. And Captain Perry is a rugby player. He plays second row for the Army. He didn't seem to remember, but I do. I played against him a couple of times when I was playing for the university. I thought it might just buy us a bit of sympathy.'

'Perhaps it did,' Gareth replied. 'He could have been a lot rougher on Dai Bach about his talents as a bomb-maker if he had a mind to.'

'What on earth am I going to do with the former WPC Marsh, who hasn't made a witness statement?' Ben asked.

'Take a leaf out of Captain Perry's book,' Gareth grinned. 'Proceed with extreme caution, remember your training, and remove to a place of safety if at all possible.'

57

THE FORMER WPC MARSH made her way to the witness box
hesitantly, looking around her constantly, as if to see who might be
watching. She was dressed in a plain blue dress and brown shoes
with low heels. Her face showed no trace of makeup. She was pale,
and took the oath so quietly that Mr Justice Overton had to ask her
to repeat it loudly enough for him to hear her.

'She looks a bit nervous, doesn't she?' Ben whispered to Gareth.

'She looks scared to death,' Gareth replied. 'And I see Evan is
dealing with her – an interesting choice, given that they have nothing
to ask her.'

'Please give the court your full name.'

'Sandra Marsh,' she replied, hesitantly.

'Thank you,' Evan said. 'Wait there, please. My learned friends for
the defence may have some questions for you.'

'None from me,' Gareth said. As he was sitting down, he turned
to Ben. 'Go easy on her.'

'Don't worry,' Ben replied.

He stood and faced the witness box.

'Is it Miss or Mrs Marsh?'

'Miss.'

'Miss Marsh. I represent Arianwen Hughes. You know Mrs Hughes,
don't you, because you were present when she was interviewed at
Caernarfon Police Station by DCI Grainger and DS Scripps?'

'Yes.' It was said very faintly.

'Miss Marsh, I'm sorry, but it's a big courtroom, and I'm going to
have to ask you to keep your voice up so that we can all hear.'

'I'm sorry.'

He smiled. 'That's all right. We all drop our voices sometimes.
Just do your best.'

She smiled back. 'I will.'

'Now, at the time when you attended Mrs Hughes' interview, you were a WPC based in Caernarfon, is that right?'

'Yes.'

'But I understand you have left the police force since then?'

'Yes.'

'What are you doing now?'

'I am looking for a job. I am living with my parents in Maesteg until I find something I want to do.'

'I see. Well, I may come back to that. But let me ask you to remember the interview. You were present, I take it, because it was a female suspect, and it was felt appropriate to have a female officer in the room?'

'Yes. Also, I speak Welsh, and DCI Grainger didn't know whether Mrs Hughes might want to speak in Welsh.'

'Yes, of course. I want to take this as shortly as I can. I am going to suggest to you that DCI Grainger and DS Scripps took an extremely aggressive line with Mrs Hughes. Would you agree?'

She did not answer for some time, looking down to the floor of the witness box.

'Miss Marsh...?'

She looked up, and seemed poised to speak, but suddenly burst into tears. Geoffrey, the usher, a veteran of many such situations, stepped forward unobtrusively with a box of tissues.

'Would you like a glass of water?' the judge offered.

She nodded. There was a pause while Geoffrey brought it.

'Miss Marsh' Ben said, 'obviously my question brought back some memories. I don't want to make it difficult for you. Tell us in your own words, if you prefer, what happened during the interview.'

She blew her nose several times, and looked back at Ben.

'They were brutal to her,' she said simply. 'I couldn't believe it. I had only been a police officer for a few months – less than a year – but I had never witnessed anything like it. I knew she was meant to have done something terrible, and they had to question her. I understood that. But it went beyond questioning.'

'In what way?' Ben asked.

'They started off asking her where her husband was,' Sandra replied. 'It was important to find him, of course, but they kept on and on at her.'

'What was their manner?'

'At first, they were trying to persuade her. They said they might let her see her son if she told them where her husband was. They even promised to put a good word in for her with the judge if she would give up her husband. I knew that wasn't allowed under the Judges' Rules, obviously, but in the circumstances...'

'In the circumstances you didn't think anything of that,' Ben said. 'Of course not. No one will criticise you for that.'

'But when she said she didn't know, they started shouting at her. Screaming, almost. It was so bad that I kept waiting for Sergeant Griffiths to come in and ask what was going on – but he didn't.'

'Can I ask you about one or two things that were said? Did they say words to this effect? "There's no point in crying about your son. You're not going to see him again for a very long time, if ever"?'

'Yes.'

'Did DS Scripps say this: "By the time we've finished with you, you will be lucky to be out in time for his silver wedding anniversary"?'

'Yes. He did. Words to that effect, anyway. I remember the bit about his silver wedding.'

'What effect did this appear to have on Mrs Hughes?'

The witness shook her head.

'She was already upset enough about her son when they brought her in. Sergeant Griffiths asked me to speak to her and try to calm her down. The son had already gone off to a temporary foster home, and she was beside herself. I managed to calm her down a bit, but when we went in for the interview she started asking me about him, asking if she could see him. It was terrible. Finally...'

She cried again, seizing a whole wad of tissues and holding them to her face.

'Are you all right?'

She made a huge effort.

'Finally, she was on her knees in a corner of the cell, begging them, pleading with them, sobbing and sobbing and sobbing, saying she would do whatever they wanted if they would bring her son to her. It was terrible...'

She cried again, dried her eyes, and looked up again.

'That is my memory of the interview,' she said.

'Why didn't you make a witness statement for this case?'

'I was told not to.'

'Indeed? By whom?'

'By DS Scripps. He said that I had nothing to tell the court that he and DCI Grainger couldn't say, so it would be better for me not to be involved.'

'What did you think about that?'

'I was very unhappy about it. I went to see Sergeant Griffiths because he was my immediate superior, but he said there was nothing he could do because it was a Special Branch investigation.' She paused. 'In fairness, I don't think he was happy about it himself, but he thought his hands were tied. You have to understand, Special Branch were everywhere during that week. They had virtually taken over the police station, and their word was law.'

Ben saw Gareth turn his head towards him, and nodded.

'And MI5 too, Miss Marsh. They were there too, isn't that right?'

Evan was getting to his feet. Ben ignored him.

'There was a man in a grey suit and red tie there from MI5, wasn't there, who was going in and out of the interviews?'

'Don't answer that!' Evan almost shouted.

'Mr Roberts,' Mr Justice Overton said, almost as loudly. 'It is for me to tell witnesses what questions to answer and what questions not to answer. If you are ever appointed a judge, you can do what you like in your own court. But while you are at the Bar, you will not presume to tell a witness in my court not to answer a question. Is that clear?'

'I'm sorry, my Lord, but…'

'I will not hear any ifs and buts,' the judge replied. 'You have been at the Bar long enough to know better, Mr Roberts. Now, please sit down.'

'My Lord…'

'I told you to sit down, Mr Roberts. Do not try my patience.'

Evan gradually subsided into his seat. The judge nodded to Ben.

'Let me ask again. Did you see the man I described?'

'Yes, he was there too. Sergeant Griffiths had to pull him out of one interview that same evening. I don't know which one, but I know Sergeant Griffiths was concerned about whatever was going on there. I wish he had come to see what was going on where I was.'

'Thank you,' Gareth whispered to Ben.

Ben paused for some time.

'Miss Marsh, when did you stop being a police officer?'

'About a week after the interview of Mrs Hughes.'

'And may I ask what led you to that decision?'

'What I saw in Mrs Hughes' interview,' she replied. 'Perhaps I'm just not cut out for the job. But I didn't become a police officer to see people treated the way she was, even if she was accused of a serious crime. I didn't think it was right, and I couldn't live with it.'

'You're here to lie to the court, aren't you, Miss Marsh?' Evan asked angrily.

It was all Ben could do not to leap out of his seat, but Gareth's arm restrained him.

'No,' she replied simply.

'You're angry at DCI Grainger and DS Scripps because you don't approve of what they did, and you're determined to make matters look bad for them if you can?'

'No. I'm here to tell the truth. A lot of pressure has been put on me not to, believe me. And it did keep me quiet for a while. But I am here now, and I'm telling the truth.'

Evan Roberts sat down angrily, and gestured to Jamie Broderick to deal with what remained of the prosecution case. This consisted of a long series of agreed facts – technical matters linked to the investigation, which were not in dispute – and a written statement prepared by Hugh James, a senior lecturer in Welsh history at Cardiff University.

Hugh James's statement took almost an hour to read, and consisted of a lengthy history of the rebellion against the English Crown led by Owain Glyndŵr in the fifteenth century. The judge and jury listened politely but, particularly towards the end, with waning attention. It had been a story of a reluctant rebellion, imaginative and courageous in its own way, but ultimately doomed to fail in the face of a greater force. Jamie Broderick then declared the prosecution's case closed and Mr Justice Overton adjourned for the weekend.

58

Monday 11 May 1970

'MR PRYS-JONES,' MR JUSTICE Overton said, once court was assembled, 'now that the prosecution case has been closed, you have three choices open to you.'

It was a moment everyone in court had been imagining and anticipating ever since Caradog Prys-Jones had made his re-appearance in court and, if possible, the courtroom seemed even more crowded than usual. The possibility of another drama, another outburst and scuffle in the dock, perhaps, was never far from anyone's mind. But Caradog had seemed composed throughout, and had said nothing, except for the occasional whisper to PC Hywel Watkins. Gareth had made a point of having a quick word as court closed on the previous Friday, asking Caradog whether he had anything he wanted Gareth to raise with the judge, but while Caradog thanked him politely, there had been nothing. But now the trial had entered a new phase, and things were no longer the same.

'The first choice is to remain silent. You are not obliged to say anything. You have the right to remain silent throughout the trial. The prosecution has the burden of proving your guilt if they can, and the jury may not hold your silence against you in any way, because that is your right. You do not have to prove your innocence. You are presumed to be innocent unless and until the prosecution proves your guilt. So you have no obligation whatsoever to give evidence, or to say anything. The second choice is to make what is called an unsworn statement from the dock. You may say anything you wish, as long as it is relevant to the case, and you cannot be asked any questions about it. Lastly, you may come into the witness box, take the oath, and give evidence. If you give evidence, it may well command more weight with the jury than an unsworn statement, but if you give evidence, you may then be cross-examined both by counsel for the other defendants, and by prosecuting counsel. What do you wish to do?'

Caradog spoke in Welsh.

'I will give evidence,' PC Watkins translated for him.

Caradog made his way slowly from the dock to the witness box with PC Watkins, flanked by the same two burly prison officers. A uniformed police officer had positioned himself unobtrusively by the door of the courtroom. Caradog was again conventionally dressed in a smart open-necked shirt, a dark brown jacket and light brown trousers, with no Welsh insignia in sight. He stood erect in the witness box. PC Hywel Watkins stood as close to him as he could, notebook and pencil in hand. The expectant murmurs, which had run around the courtroom since Caradog's announcement that he would give evidence, subsided as he held the New Testament and took the oath in Welsh.

'You may give your evidence in any way you wish,' Mr Justice Overton said. 'I will only interrupt if I think something may not be clear for the jury, or if you stray into irrelevant areas.'

Caradog nodded. He waited for the translation before starting to speak. It had taken him very little time to recognise that his interpreter needed him to speak slowly, and pause often, to allow the interpretation to catch up, and he had begun to sense the natural rhythm of words and interpretation. Caradog Prys-Jones and Hywel Watkins had settled into a flow; their speech was now fluent and easy to follow.

'First,' he said, 'I would like to apologise for having lost my temper and become involved in a fight with the prison officers on the first day of the trial. I do not apologise for refusing to recognise the court. That is still my position. I do not recognise this tribunal as a court which can try me legitimately. It is my right as a Welsh man to be tried in Wales, by a Welsh court, using the Welsh language...'

'Mr Prys-Jones...'

Caradog held up a hand.

'Nonetheless, I apologise for the way in which I conducted myself, which was discourteous and achieved nothing except to make people angry. I wish to add that, although I do not recognise the court, in my opinion you have conducted the proceedings fairly.'

'Yes, very well, Mr Prys-Jones,' the judge said. 'Thank you.'

'Despite my refusal to recognise the court, I have decided to give evidence today out of fairness to my sister, who has done nothing wrong and has been wrongly accused.'

Evan Roberts was on his feet.

'My Lord, it is not proper for the defendant to make comments to the jury about the guilt or innocence of another accused. Would your Lordship please admonish him…?'

'No, I will not, Mr Roberts,' the judge replied, cutting him off. 'Mr Prys-Jones is representing himself, and he will be given some leeway accordingly. If he goes beyond that leeway I will intervene, and I do not require your assistance in doing so.'

'As your Lordship pleases,' Evan growled. The judge seemed poised to reply, but checked himself.

'As far as my evidence on my own account is concerned,' Caradog continued, in the same measured rhythm with Hywel Watkins, 'the jury have the statement I made to the police. It contains a full account of my own actions and motivations, and I have nothing to add to it. I am content to be judged on the basis of that statement, so far as my own responsibility is concerned.

'So far as my sister Arianwen is concerned, I wish to add this. She knew nothing about what I was doing. I kept her in the dark deliberately because I did not wish her to be involved. She is a mother with a young child, my nephew. She is a person who has been opposed to violence in any form throughout her life. If she had known what I was going to do she would have refused to have anything to do with me. In fact, I would have expected her to take steps to prevent me. But that was not my concern. My concern was simply that she is my sister, and I would never have knowingly exposed her to the risk of becoming involved. She knew nothing on the night when she was arrested, or at any time before that.'

He paused for some moments.

'That is all I wish to say.'

There was silence for some time. In due course, Gareth stood.

'I have no questions, my Lord.'

Ben thought for a moment.

'Mr Prys-Jones, you said that Arianwen has always been opposed to violence. On what do you base that opinion?'

'I base it on what I have heard her say throughout her life.'

'Has she accompanied you on peaceful protests from time to time?'

'Yes, we attended protests together and we attended political rallies together.'

'Rallies on behalf of Plaid Cymru?'

'Yes.'

'And protests against what kind of things?'

'Various things, including the infamous ceremony conducted in Caernarfon Castle by Elizabeth Windsor for her son.'

'And including the flooding of the Tryweryn Valley and the destruction of the village of Capel Celyn?'

Caradog bowed his head and closed his eyes. It took him some time to reply.

'Yes, including that.'

'When you attended these protests and rallies, did you ever see her act in a violent way?'

'No, not once.'

'Is your sister a Welsh nationalist?'

'She does believe in independence for Wales, yes. But she is an artist, a musician, and her main concerns have always been the preservation of the Welsh language, and protecting our cultural identity. She is a member of *Cymdeithas yr iaith* – the Welsh Language Society. She is a gentle woman. She has never been involved with violence in any form.'

'Thank you, Mr Prys-Jones. I have no further questions, my Lord.'

59

'WELL, YOU SAY THAT you didn't want to get your sister involved, Mr Prys-Jones,' Evan Roberts said, springing to his feet immediately. 'But you didn't mind getting her husband involved, did you? He was one of your co-conspirators, wasn't he?'

'I am not here to speak about Trevor Hughes.'

'You are here to answer any proper questions I put to you, Mr Prys-Jones. Trevor Hughes is also the father of your nephew Harri, isn't he?'

'He is.'

'Yes. But you had no concerns about involving his father, your sister's husband, in your plans, did you?'

'I didn't involve Trevor Hughes in anything. Whatever he did, he did of his own volition. He must answer for himself.'

'Well, unfortunately, he is not here to answer for himself, is he? The jury has not had the opportunity to hear from him. Why is that, Mr Prys-Jones? Do you know where he is?'

'No, I do not.'

'And if you knew, I daresay you wouldn't tell us.'

'That is an improper comment,' Gareth said quietly, half standing.

'Yes, it is,' the judge agreed.

Caradog had given no sign of answering the question.

'If your sister was not involved, why was she driving the bomb and Dafydd Prosser to a rendezvous with you on the edge of the town square when she was arrested?'

'She was not meant to be doing that.'

'But she did, didn't she?'

'She was not told what was in the car.'

'How do you know what she was told, Mr Prys-Jones? You weren't there, were you?'

'There was a clear understanding that she was to know nothing.'

'Really? Well, even if that was clear to you, you don't know how clear it was to Dafydd Prosser, do you? Or to Trevor Hughes? You don't know what Trevor may have told her at home, do you?'

'It was Trevor who insisted that she should know nothing. He would never have told her, and he would never have tolerated anyone else telling her.'

'Trevor Hughes made that clear to you, did he?'

A pause.

'Yes, he did.'

'Was Dafydd Prosser present when Trevor told you that?'

Caradog began to answer, but then checked himself.

'I cannot answer for Dafydd Prosser. Dafydd is here, and he will speak for himself if he wishes.'

'I don't know whether he will wish to or not,' Evan replied. 'So I am asking you.'

'I am not going to answer for Dafydd.'

'Dafydd Prosser built the bomb for you, didn't he? The bomb you were going to take into Caernarfon Castle under cover of your job as a night watchman?'

'I will not answer.'

'Using his skill as a chemist, and the tips you picked up from the IRA and the Baader-Meinhof group when all three of you went to Belfast?'

'I will not answer.'

'Why else was he there with your sister when you arrived in the square to collect the bomb?'

'I will not answer.'

'It was because he was the one who knew how to set the timer, wasn't it? He was going to set it to detonate during the Investiture ceremony, wasn't he, because that was the plan?'

'I will not answer for Dafydd. I was the one who was to take the bomb and place it in the Castle.'

'Do you have the knowledge and the skills to make a bomb, Mr Prys-Jones?'

'No. I do not.'

'Does your sister?'

'No, of course not.'

'Would you have known how to set it to detonate, using the alarm clock as a timer?'

'No.'

'Would your sister have known?'

'No.'

'So, who was going to arm the bomb for you? Are you sure it wasn't your sister?'

'I am quite sure.'

'Of course not, because she is opposed to violence, isn't she? Her role was only to do the driving, is that it?'

'She had no role.'

'So who was going to arm the bomb?'

'I will answer only for myself.'

Evan turned to Mr Justice Overton.

'My Lord, having taken the oath, the witness is compellable to answer these questions, but he is refusing to do so.'

'Yes, thank you, Mr Roberts,' the judge replied. 'I had noticed that myself.'

'Then I would ask that your Lordship order him to answer the questions, and advise him of the possible consequences of refusing to do so.'

Jamie Broderick had closed his eyes and was leaning forward with his hands on the desk, folded under his chin. He opened his eyes, caught Ben glancing across at him, and raised his eyebrows with a shake of his head.

'Very well,' the judge replied. 'Mr Prys-Jones, you must answer the questions Mr Roberts is putting to you. If you refuse to do so, I will hold you in contempt of court, and you may be sentenced to time in prison. Do you understand?'

'I understand,' Caradog replied. 'But I am in prison already.'

'Yes, well, you may have to spend another day there.'

There was subdued laughter, some of it from the jury box.

'Do you have any further questions, Mr Roberts?'

Evan flung himself back down into his chair.

'No, my Lord.'

'Mr Prys-Jones, is there anything else you would like to say?' the judge asked.

'No,' Caradog replied. 'Thank you.'

'Is there any witness you would like to call, or any evidence you wish to place before the jury.'

'No. Thank you.'

'Very well. You may return to the dock.'

Slowly, the small procession wound its way back from the witness box to the dock as solemnly as it had come. As the door of the dock was locked behind them, Gareth stood.

'My Lord, I shall not be calling Mr Prosser to give evidence, and no evidence will be called on his behalf.'

The announcement caused a buzz around the courtroom, but if Mr Justice Overton was surprised, he did not show it.

'Yes. Very well, Mr Morgan-Davies,' he said. 'Do I take it that you will be presenting a case, Mr Schroeder?'

'Yes, my Lord.'

'Yes. Well, I don't suppose there will be any objection to a short break before you call Mrs Hughes. We will adjourn for half an hour, members of the jury.'

60

WHEN THEY ENTERED THE cell, Arianwen looked pale, but seemed composed enough. She gave everyone a hug, and was visibly pleased to see Eifion, who had returned from Cardiff to be at court with her. They exchanged a few quiet words in Welsh. As usual, she wore an ankle-length Indian cotton dress, today a light blue with a muted white floral design.

'So, the moment has come,' she smiled.

'Yes. Try not to be too nervous,' Ben said. 'I know you are bound to be a bit apprehensive, but I'm not going to let anyone ask you anything they shouldn't. There should be nothing to take you by surprise.'

'I'm sure I will be fine.'

'I'm sure you will, too. I just wanted to check you had no last-minute questions. You know that once you start giving evidence, you're not allowed to talk to any of us – Barratt, Eifion or me – until your evidence is finished?'

'I understand. It's so that you can't tell me what to say.'

'Exactly. And you understand what is going to happen in court?'

'I think so. You will ask me questions first, then I will be cross-examined, then the judge may ask me questions, and I will try to remember to call him "my Lord".'

'Don't worry too much about that,' Ben said. 'The main thing is to listen to the question. Answer what you are asked and don't go beyond that if you can help it. Don't worry about the judge too much. I doubt he will have much to ask you, if anything at all.'

'It's Evan Roberts you want to be careful of,' Eifion said. 'He's a snake in the grass, if ever there was one.'

'Actually,' she smiled, 'I'm not worried about him. I would be more concerned if it was going to be Mr Broderick asking me questions.'

'Oh?' Ben said, returning the smile. 'Why is that?'

'Evan Roberts is a bully,' she replied simply. 'He's the sort of boy we all remember from school, strutting around the playground as if he owns it, picking on boys smaller than himself. I've been watching the way he treats people – not only the witnesses, but everyone, including the judge. He tries to walk over them to get his way, and it doesn't work. The jury don't like him. I've been watching them.'

'You're quite right,' Ben said. 'Just keep that in mind, and don't get sucked into playing his game, trying to argue with him and so on. I will argue with him if anyone has to, but you mustn't. All you have to do is stay calm and answer politely and truthfully.'

'And don't be tempted into trying to provoke him,' Barratt added. 'He is quite capable of getting worked up on his own without any help. As Ben said, just stay calm.'

She smiled again, brightly. 'I can do that.'

61

'MRS HUGHES, PLEASE GIVE his Lordship and the jury your full name.'

'Arianwen Hughes.'

'How old are you?'

'I am 35.'

'Have you ever been convicted of any criminal offence?'

'No. Never.'

'I think you were born Arianwen Prys-Jones, and you are the sister of Caradog Prys-Jones. Is that right?'

'Yes.'

'Is Caradog older or younger?'

'He is my older brother. There are three years between us.'

'Where did you live growing up?'

'In Caernarfon, in the same house in *Rhês Pretoria* – sorry, that is Pretoria Terrace in English – where Caradog still lives. After our parents died, I lived there with Caradog until I got married.'

'Yes. We will come to that later. Following up on your last answer, you gave us the name of the street in Welsh. Is Welsh your first language?'

'Yes. Our parents always spoke Welsh at home. That's not unusual in North Wales. A lot of families are still Welsh-speaking. Of course, once we started school we learned English too, so I grew up with both. But Welsh is still more natural for me.'

Ben smiled. 'But you don't need PC Watkins to help you?'

She laughed. 'No, no. My English is quite good.'

There were some smiles among the jurors.

'I can take this quite quickly. You went to school locally in Caernarfon, and then to university at Bangor?'

'Yes.'

'What were your subjects?'

'Music and Welsh.'

'And after university?'

'I came back home. I started to take pupils at home, teaching music.'

'Yes. What instruments do you play?'

'The cello is my main instrument, but of course, I also play the piano. It's usual for musicians to play the piano in addition to any other instrument they may have.'

'I see. Did you think of teaching in a school?'

'I did, but at that stage I had some idea that I could play professionally, and I didn't want to commit to a school schedule.'

'When you say "play professionally", do you mean as a soloist?'

She smiled. 'That would have been wonderful, but no, I didn't think of myself as having that kind of talent. I did think I could hold my own in the cello section of a symphony orchestra.'

'And I think you did indeed hold your own in an orchestra for some time?'

'Yes. I auditioned successfully for the BBC Welsh Orchestra, and I was a member of the orchestra for two or three years.'

'Why did that come to an end?'

'I had to spend a lot of time away from home in Cardiff, where the orchestra is based. We had a very busy schedule of concerts and recording sessions, and of course there was a lot of rehearsal involved. My parents' health was failing and I was needed at home, so I went back to Caernarfon. Unfortunately, my parents then died within a short time of each other.'

'But you didn't return to the orchestra?'

'My position had been filled. It is not a big orchestra, and – well, I suppose I could have waited and auditioned again, but I never did. I settled down to taking pupils at home, and I play chamber music with friends from time to time to keep my hand in.'

Ben paused to consult his notes.

'Next I want to ask you this. What is your personal opinion about the political status of Wales?'

'You're asking me if I am a nationalist?'

'Yes.'

'Yes, I do believe that Wales can and should be an independent nation. I support Plaid Cymru. I vote for the Party and I work for them at election time.'

'Let me ask you this, then. Do you have anything against England, or the English people, or the Royal Family for that matter?'

'No. Not at all. We have lived together, Welsh and English people, for centuries. I have many English friends. I hope it will always be that way.'

'How do you reconcile that with being a nationalist?'

'My vision for Wales is not that we exclude people. I don't want to set up road blocks between England and Wales. I don't want to make English visitors apply for visas or produce passports. I don't even want borders. I want life to continue much as it is now. My vision for Wales is simply the freedom to govern ourselves, to make our own laws about things that concern Wales.'

'Have you attended demonstrations and rallies at various times?'

'Yes, I have.'

'What kind of things were you protesting about?'

'My protests were mainly about supporting the Welsh language. I joined the *Cymdeithas yr iaith* – the Welsh Language Society – while I was at university, and I have always supported it.'

'And, it may be a fairly obvious question, but what are the goals of that Society?'

'To preserve Welsh as a living language. English is so pervasive today, everyone has to speak English, and there is a danger that people may lose interest in Welsh, even if they speak it at home. If that happens, the language could be lost within a generation or two. It is an ancient and beautiful language, and if we don't do something now, it may soon be too late.'

'Did you also protest about political questions?'

'Yes, sometimes.'

'Can you give us an example of that?'

'I protested about the flooding of the Tryweryn Valley and the village of Capel Celyn.'

'It may be that the jury are not familiar with that episode. Could you tell us briefly what happened?'

'The Government decided to flood the valley and the village, and forcibly remove the inhabitants, in order to create a giant reservoir to increase the water supply to Liverpool. There were protests for several years, and all kinds of challenges to it. But of course, in the end the Government had its way, as it always does.'

'Yes. Did the Tryweryn question have any personal significance for you, apart from the obvious significance of a Welsh valley being destroyed for the benefit of an English city?'

'Yes. The Tryweryn Valley was where our family were from. My great-grandparents had a home there in the village, and although our branch of the family didn't live there in my generation, I have relatives who did, and we still thought of it as our homeland.'

'Did you protest against the Investiture of Prince Charles?'

'I did, as did many others in and around Caernarfon, and in Wales generally.'

'Why did you demonstrate against the Investiture?'

'I really think that if it hadn't been for Tryweryn and one or two other things, I wouldn't have been all that upset about it. But it started to feel personal, you know, the assumption that the Government can come in and out of Wales any time it likes, take what it wants, and not even try to help us in terms of conserving the language, protecting our cultural heritage. The Investiture just seemed like another example. It was so crass and insensitive.'

'In what sense, crass and insensitive?'

'The title of Prince of Wales has been used by the English monarchy for centuries to emphasise its control of Wales. I am not sure Wales wants a prince of any kind in this day and age. But, if we do, there are princely bloodlines in Wales, and we are quite capable of finding our own Welsh prince without having one imposed on us.'

Ben paused again.

'What is your attitude towards violence?'

'I am against the use of violence in any shape or form,' she replied. 'It horrifies me.'

'In all circumstances?'

'Yes. It upsets me even when I know there is no alternative, for example during the War when we had to stand up to Hitler.'

'Would you be prepared to use violence to bring about independence for Wales?'

'No. I would not.'

'Would you approve of the use of violence by others for that purpose?'

'No. I would not.'

'Would you condone it or agree to cover it up?'

'No. I would not.'

62

'I WANT TO ASK you next about your brother, Caradog,' Ben said. 'Of course, you have known him all your life. You have heard the evidence against him in this case. I'm not asking you to comment on that evidence, or express an opinion about it. But knowing Caradog as you do, how do you react to hearing what has been alleged against him in this case?'

She held her head in her hands for some time, before looking up again to reply.

'I've been in shock ever since the day I was arrested, and I am in shock now. I have looked at it from every point of view I can think of, and I can't account for it. Caradog is an intellectual, a man of ideas. His version of nationalism is rather more political than mine, I think. His idea of an independent Wales may involve a greater degree of separation from England than mine. But I have never heard him advocate violence to achieve independence – or for any reason. I can't believe what I have heard, even in court during the trial. I have been sitting in the dock in disbelief, and even now I don't know how to make sense of it.'

'You referred to the flooding of the Tryweryn Valley as something that affected you because of the link to your family. Was that something that affected Caradog, as far as you could see?'

'Yes. We were both very angry, greatly distressed by it. We demonstrated against it, and helped with a large-scale publicity campaign, all to no avail. Yes, we did feel extremely bitter about it, but even then, I never heard Caradog say anything that made me think that he saw violence as a remedy.'

'What about the Investiture itself?'

'As I said before, I felt it was a very crass thing to do, and I am sure Caradog felt the same. But the most I ever heard from him were some colourful remarks about the Royal Family. He never once led me to think that he was interested in taking any violent action.'

Ben paused again.

'At the same time, you have heard the evidence which has been given.'

'Yes.'

'And I must ask you this: did you have any knowledge of any plan in which Caradog was involved to plant a bomb at Caernarfon Castle?'

'No. I did not.'

'If you had known of it, would you have approved of, or condoned it?'

'No. I would not.'

'What would you have done?'

'I would have told him that unless he abandoned the idea, I would go to the police and report it myself.'

'Would you in fact have gone to the police?'

'Yes, I would, and Caradog knows me well enough to know that I would do it.'

'Did you know, before this trial began, of any group calling itself the Heirs of Owain Glyndŵr, or its name in Welsh, which I am afraid I am going to forget?'

'*Etifeddion Owain Glyndŵr*,' she replied. 'That would be the name in Welsh. No. I had never heard that name used.'

'Thank you. Next, I want to ask you about Dafydd Prosser, who you know as Dai Bach.'

'Yes.'

'Essentially I have the same questions about him. Please tell his Lordship and the jury how you met Mr Prosser.'

'I met Dai Bach through Caradog. I never quite understood how the two of them became such good friends. They are like chalk and cheese. Caradog is an intellectual, very reserved, aloof even, in his manner. Dai Bach is quite the opposite. It's not that he isn't clever. He is. But he is an extrovert, a rugby player, the kind of man who will talk to anyone and get on with them. I know Caradog met him when he was doing some work for Plaid Cymru at some point, and the two of them hit it off instantly, even though Dai Bach was living over in Bangor. They spent a lot of time together in the evenings, and Caradog would bring Dai Bach to the house for dinner quite often. He was living on his own, and we weren't sure how well he was taking care of himself. To be honest, I rather took pity on him. We both thought he would probably subsist on beer and baked beans if we didn't feed him a few times a week.'

There was some laughter. Turning around slightly, Ben saw Dafydd Prosser smiling and nodding in the dock.

'It's true, aye,' he said, loudly enough for everyone to hear. A warning look from the judge was enough for him to raise a hand in apology and sink back into his seat.

'Did you ever discuss questions of nationalism with Dai Bach?'

'Oh, yes, of course. But I think Dai Bach got whatever ideas he had from Caradog. He hung on Caradog's every word, and took his cue from him. He looked up to Caradog almost like an older brother.'

'Did you ever hear Dai Bach advocate violence to gain independence for Wales?'

'No.'

'Did you ever hear him advocate violence for any purpose, such as disrupting the Investiture?'

'No. Dai Bach came with us to rallies and demonstrations, and he was quite capable of shouting rude things at police officers. He could get very excited about rugby, but as far as I know he always took that out on the opposing loose-head prop. I never knew him advocate violence for any political reason, and again, I have been sitting through this trial in disbelief.'

'But again, you have heard the evidence?'

'Yes.'

'So, my question is: were you ever aware of any plan involving Dai Bach to construct a bomb or to plant a bomb at Caernarfon Castle?'

'No.'

'Did you ever hear that he was involved with the Heirs of Owain Glyndŵr?'

'No. Never.'

'And again, if you had been made aware of those things, what would you have done?'

'I would have told him that if he didn't give it up, I would go to the police myself and report it.'

'Again, would you in fact have gone to the police?'

'Yes, I would.'

Ben turned to Mr Justice Overton.

'My Lord, I am now going to turn to other matters. I wonder whether we might have a short break?'

'Yes, very well, Mr Schroeder. Twenty minutes, members of the jury, please.'

'So far, so good,' Barratt observed, as they were leaving court.

'Yes,' Ben agreed. 'But it's what's coming next that will tell.'

63

'PLEASE TELL THE COURT when you first met Trevor Hughes.'

She had prepared herself with a glass of water and a handkerchief. Ben saw that some of the confidence she had shown during the first part of her evidence had ebbed away, and her face was pale.

'In 1961. I went to the *Tywysog* book shop not long after Trevor had taken it over,' she replied.

'A bit louder, please, Mrs Hughes,' Ben said. 'It's a large courtroom and it's important that his Lordship and the jury hear what you say.'

'Yes. I'm sorry.'

'That's all right. The *Tywysog*, of course, the jury will recall, is the book shop in Palace Street.'

'Yes. It was at the end of October 1961. Trevor had just bought the shop from Madog. I called in one day.'

'Why?'

'Out of curiosity, mostly, I think. I wanted to see who could possibly have replaced Madog. Madog was an institution. He had been at the *Tywysog* for ever, or so it seemed anyway.'

'So you knew the book shop well before Trevor arrived?'

'Oh, yes, everyone knew the *Tywysog*. It was a landmark in Caernarfon. Caradog spent a lot of time there over the years, looking for books to buy, or just chatting with Madog. Books are such a big part of his life. It was difficult for him to stay away from there for long. I didn't go half as often as Caradog, but if I was shopping in town I would call in and browse for a few minutes. When Madog announced that he was selling up and retiring, it was like we were losing part of the town.'

'So you went in and introduced yourself to Trevor?'

'Yes.'

'And what happened?'

She smiled.

'That's a good question. I wasn't sure at the time. But something happened between us. We didn't say anything to acknowledge it, but it was there.'

'Looking back now, did you fall in love?'

'Yes. We did. There and then. I'm sure of it.'

'What did happen at that first meeting?'

'I heard him speaking to someone else. He spoke Welsh rather – well, uncertainly, as if he didn't have much confidence. It was only to be expected, really. He had lived in England for so long and he hadn't used his Welsh for a long time. He was doing the best he could, but I could tell that he was having trouble with the local accent in Caernarfon.'

'And what did you do?'

'I deliberately spoke to him slowly, in a very formal, almost literary Welsh. Spoken Welsh is very different from its written form. If I'd spoken to most people in Caernarfon as I did that day, they would have laughed at me. But it seemed to work. He responded to me. I think he was grateful I had taken the trouble. And oddly enough, to this day, I still speak Welsh with Trevor quite differently to the way I would speak with anyone else, even though he has no problem understanding Caernarfon Welsh now.'

'How did you meet again?'

'Caradog invited him home to dinner one evening, quite soon after our first meeting. Caradog had been in the shop and he had dragged Trevor out for a pint when he closed for the day. That wasn't unusual for Caradog. He quite often brought people he found interesting home for dinner – to be cooked by me, of course – often with no more than half an hour's warning.'

'I'm sure that must have been a challenge.'

She smiled. 'I got used to it over the years.'

'And how did you find Trevor on that occasion, your first dinner at home?'

'It was very strange. We were listening to Caradog holding forth as usual, and Dai Bach weighing in and agreeing with him as usual, and we were joining in, too. But it was as though we had our own private conversation going on in the background, a conversation only we could hear, consisting mostly of smiles and glances. I had the feeling that I was smiling all the time, and I was sure Caradog must have noticed. We shook hands when he left, and I think we both knew by then that something special had happened.'

'How did it progress from there?'

'As soon as Caradog brought anyone home for dinner, they became a family friend, and family friends were always invited back, so I saw quite a bit of him at home. After a while it became normal for him to be there, and after dinner he would often come into my music room and listen to me play, sometimes for hours on end. He would just close his eyes and listen. It meant so much to me, because no one else in my family had much of an interest in music.'

'Did you continue to call into the *Tywysog*?'

'I called into the shop as often as I could. Before long, I was there most days. I didn't stay too long, but I tried to call in almost every day.'

'So you started going out together?'

'Oh, yes. At first we went out for coffee or a drink after he closed the shop. Then we went out for a meal sometimes. After a few months, he started to look for classical concerts to take me to. That took some doing. There wasn't much going on in the Caernarfon area. We went to Chester, and to Aberystwyth once, and sometimes we even went down to Cardiff to hear the orchestra, which brought back happy memories for me. Eventually, we became lovers.'

'As far as you could judge, how did Caradog feel about your relationship with Trevor?'

'He seemed very happy for me. He seemed to like Trevor, and everything he said was very encouraging.'

'And did there come a time when Trevor asked you to marry him?' She laughed.

'As a matter of fact, *I* asked *him*,' she replied. 'I told him it was an old Welsh custom for a woman to propose to a man.'

'Is that an old Welsh custom?' Ben asked.

'There's no reason why it shouldn't be,' she replied. There was some laughter in the jury box, and even a smile on the bench.

'In any case, yes, we agreed to get married.'

'You were married in Caernarfon in a quiet ceremony in April 1963.'

'Yes.'

'And your son Harri was born in May 1965.'

She bowed her head.

'Yes,' she replied softly.

64

'BEFORE I COME TO what happened on the evening of 30 June and the early morning of 1 July, let me ask you this. In all the time you have known Trevor Hughes, have you ever had any reason to believe that he held any extreme nationalist views?'

'No.'

'In all the time you have known him, have you ever had any reason to believe that he would be prepared to use violence to protest against anything going on in Wales?'

'No.'

'What were his feelings about nationalism and events in Wales as far as you could tell?'

'You have to understand. Trevor is from a Welsh family, but he had spent most of his life in London, and I am not sure that his feelings have ever run as deeply as Caradog's, or even mine. He came with us to all the rallies and demonstrations; he worked for Plaid Cymru with us at election time; he did all those things. When we talked about Wales over dinner, which we often did, he always agreed with Caradog, but I never knew how much of that was simply politeness, because Trevor is a very polite and considerate man. It's one of the things I like most about him. I don't know how deeply he really feels about Welsh questions. I'm not saying his feelings aren't real; I'm sure they are. But you couldn't call him an extremist.'

'Did you ever see him act violently when you went to the rallies and demonstrations?'

'No. I don't know quite how to say this, but Trevor is the kind of man who wouldn't need to resort to violence.'

'What do you mean by that?'

'There is an air of confidence about him. He has a natural authority. It's hard to describe. There is just something about him. We had some tense moments at demos, of course, but he had a way of calming things down without even raising his voice. It is the way he holds himself and deals with people. He can get people to talk or back away, and so he can defuse situations which might get out of hand otherwise. I have seen him do it any number of times, but I still can't explain exactly how he does it.'

'You know, of course, from the evidence given at this trial, that in April of last year he went to Belfast with Caradog and Dai Bach?'

'Yes.'

'Did you know about that at the time?'

'I knew they were going to Ireland, yes. I didn't know they were going to Belfast, and I certainly didn't know they had plans to meet anyone.'

'What was your understanding about that trip?'

'Trevor told me…'

Evan Roberts had sprung to his feet.

'My Lord, I must object to that question. It calls for hearsay.'

'I am not asking it to prove what actually happened in Ireland,' Ben replied immediately. 'This witness has no knowledge of that. I am asking it only to show her state of mind, what she knew or didn't know. It is not hearsay for that purpose.'

'I agree,' Mr Justice Overton said. 'You may answer, Mrs Hughes.'

'Trevor told me that they felt they had all been working too hard, and they could do with a few days away to relax, have a few drinks, and so on. I had the impression that Ireland was his idea. It is a popular choice if you live in North Wales, because you are so close to the ferry at Holyhead.'

'So you approved?'

'It seemed like a good idea to me. They had been working hard, and I thought a break would do all of them good. I was glad that Caradog had agreed to go. It is hard for him to wind down, and I thought it might help.'

'Did you know where in Ireland they were going?'

'I assumed they would stay in Dublin. I'm not sure whether Trevor told me that, or whether it was just what I assumed. I may just have taken it for granted. Most people do stay in Dublin, if they are just going for a few days.'

'I want to ask you now about the events of the evening of 30 June and the early morning of 1 July last year. What were you doing on that day?'

She sighed deeply.

'It was a normal day, just a normal day. Harri had nursery school. Trevor dropped him off on his way in to the *Tywysog*. I had one pupil in the morning, an elderly lady whose house I went to once a week for a piano lesson, and I had two children in the afternoon who came to me, one for piano, one for cello. I made myself a sandwich for lunch in between and snatched a few minutes of practice for myself. After the second lesson, I picked Harri up from nursery, took him home and fed him, played with him until bedtime and put him to bed. That was my day.'

'Did you have any plans for the evening?'

'No. There was one final demonstration scheduled in the *Maes*. There had been one almost every evening for a couple of weeks as the day approached. But they were running out of steam. A lot of people had decided to leave town for several days as a final protest, so there didn't seem a lot of point. They had held a rehearsal that day at the Castle, I think, either afternoon or early evening, so the police were going to be out in force. In any case, I didn't have the energy to do it again, and I had no one to look after Harri. Trevor said he would show his face there for a while. He was going to meet Dai Bach. They would attend the demo, probably have a pint or two, and after that I was expecting Trevor to come home.'

'As far as you knew, where was Caradog that evening?'

'Working at the Castle, I assumed.'

'Did there come a time during that evening when you received a telephone call?'

'Yes.'

'From whom?'

'From Dai Bach.'

Ben glanced briefly at Gareth, who nodded.

'Do you remember what time that was?'

'I wasn't watching the time, but I am sure it was somewhere between 11.30 and midnight.'

'Had Trevor returned home?'

'No.'

'Were you at all worried?'

'No, not really. When you get going with Dai Bach over a couple of pints, it can turn into a bit of a long evening. So I wasn't worried about Trevor. But I was surprised when Dai Bach called, because I had assumed they were together.'

'What did he say to you?'

'He said something about having to meet a friend with his suitcase because he was going away for a few days. He said Trevor had agreed to pick him up in the car to drive him to Bangor for his suitcase, but he hadn't come. I offered to help.'

'Had Trevor said anything about driving Dai Bach to Bangor?'

'No, not a word. If he was going to do that, he would have to come back home to pick up the car, and I would have expected him to look in and tell me where he was going. I looked outside and the car was there, so I knew Trevor hadn't taken it.'

'Were you worried at that point?'

'I wasn't worried, exactly. I just didn't know what was happening. I thought there had probably been some mix up over the time, but I didn't have any way to contact Trevor.'

'What did you decide to do?'

'Dai Bach sounded very anxious, for some reason. It seemed strange to me. It wasn't that he was going away for a few days. As I say, a lot of people were doing that. It was more his tone of voice. Anyway, since he sounded a bit upset, I thought the simplest thing would be to drive him myself. It's not that far to Bangor. I knew I could take him over there, pick up the suitcase, and drop him off in the *Maes* within the hour, if the traffic wasn't too bad and there were no police roadblocks. We weren't expecting the police to close the town centre to traffic until later in the morning.'

'And did you do that?'

'Yes. I woke Harri and put him in his seat in the back of the car with a couple of toys, and drove to the *Maes*. Dai Bach had asked me to meet him outside the Castle Hotel, which I did.'

'Did you ask him about what was going on?'

'Yes. I asked him where Trevor was. He said he didn't know. He said they had got separated during the demo. He was expecting Trevor to meet him with the car, but he never came. Beyond that he didn't say that much at all.'

'Were you worried by now?'

'I'm not sure I would say worried. I did sense that something was not quite right. I did wonder what had happened to Trevor, but I wasn't really worried about him. Trevor can look after himself. I was mostly concerned for Dai Bach. He was on edge, quite agitated. That's not unusual in itself for Dai Bach, but this was different.'

'Did you drive to Bangor?'

'Yes. But that was another surprise. We drove to Bangor, but not to his house. Instead, he directed me to a garage.'

'Before he directed you, did you know where the garage was?'

'No. I had never been to that street before.'

'Did you ask him about why he wanted to go to the garage?'

'Yes. He said he used it for storage, and that was where he had left his suitcase.'

'Did you think anything about that?'

'Again, it seemed a bit odd. But by that time, I had had enough. I just wanted to take him back to Caernarfon and go home. Harri was awake again by the time we got to Bangor, and he wasn't happy about not being in bed, so I was trying to calm him down as well as concentrating on driving.'

'Did you see the suitcase when Dai Bach collected it from the garage?'

'No. I was turning round to attend to Harri. I was aware that he was putting the suitcase in the boot, and I saw him slam the boot door shut. Then he got back into the car and we drove back to Caernarfon. I'm not sure we said another word until we arrived back.'

'Where did you drop him?'

'When I turned off the Bangor Road towards the *Maes*, he asked me to turn down New Street, and we stopped just before the corner of Chapel Street.'

'Then what happened?'

She did not respond for some time.

'You will have to excuse me,' she said. 'I'm not feeling well. Could we stop for a while?'

Ben looked up at Mr Justice Overton, who nodded.

'We will rise for lunch,' he said. 'Two o'clock, members of the jury, please. Mrs Hughes, you know that you are not allowed to speak to your counsel or solicitors until you have finished giving evidence?'

She nodded. 'Yes.'

'Very well. Two o'clock.'

'She will be all right,' Eifion said, as they left court. 'It's just that you're getting to the really painful part now. Her memory still has gaps, and it really hurts her to talk about it. But she's a strong girl. She will get through it.'

'I hope you're right,' Ben replied.

65

'HOW ARE YOU FEELING now?' Ben asked, once Arianwen had returned to the witness box. 'Are you all right to continue?'

'Yes, thank you,' she replied. 'I am ready.'

'Before lunch, you told us you stopped in New Street near the corner with Chapel Street. What happened then?'

'Dai Bach had said that was where he was meeting his friend. Then, quite suddenly, he got out of the car, closed the door, and started walking down New Street towards Chapel Street. He walked across Chapel Street and then a short distance further down New Street. And then…'

She had closed her eyes and taken a deep breath.

'Take your time.'

'I'm sorry. I'm afraid my memory of all this is just bits and pieces. It was so horrible for me, and it all happened so quickly, and I can't always remember…'

'Take your time. Tell us as much as you can remember.'

'I saw Dai Bach coming back towards me, and I saw that he was with another man. I didn't see where the other man came from. I assumed it must be his friend, and I remember thinking: "Thank God for that", because I was anxious to take Harri home and go home myself. And then…'

This time Ben waited, and she recovered her composure.

'And then, I looked again and I saw that the other man was Caradog. They began walking back across Chapel Street towards me.'

'What did you think about that?'

'I was totally confused. I didn't know why Caradog would be there. He was supposed to be working. I still didn't know where Trevor was. I switched the ignition off, and I was going to get out of the car. But then I saw that Caradog was in a real state. He was shouting at Dai Bach, and Dai Bach was trying to get a word in edgeways and couldn't. You could tell from the way they were behaving, walking very quickly, flinging their arms all over the place.'

'Were you able to hear what either of them said?'

'No. By the time they were close enough for me to hear they had stopped talking. They made straight for the rear of the car. I got out and walked around the car to join them.'

'What did you see?'

'Dai Bach had opened the boot. There was something covered with an old blanket I kept in there. He took the blanket away and I saw a metal case of some kind. He opened it, and I saw…'

'Take your time.'

'I saw inside the case, and there was what looked like an alarm clock and strands of electrical wire, and what looked like sticks of dynamite. That was as much as I saw.'

'Did you say anything?'

'I tried, but I was speechless. Literally. I was staring at Caradog and Dai Bach, open-mouthed, and I couldn't find any words.'

'Why do you think that was?'

'I was in shock. And I've been in shock ever since that moment. I haven't been able to get over it.'

'What happened next?'

She shook her head. 'As best as I can remember a man appeared from nowhere, and put Caradog up against the back of the car, and another man came and did the same to Dai Bach. I still couldn't speak. Then from nowhere a man came and dragged me around to the rear door on the passenger side, and slammed me up against the side of the car. It winded me, took my breath away. Then I felt him pull my hands behind my back and I felt him putting handcuffs on me. I was aware of a lot of shouting going on.'

'You know, of course, that the men were police officers?'

'I know that now. At the time I had no idea what was happening.'

'Do you remember anything in particular that was being shouted?'

'Just fragments. I am sure I heard someone shout about a bomb, and someone else was shouting that they had to evacuate the area. I can't remember any more. I was totally confused.'

'Were you aware that you were being arrested?'

'On some level, I suppose I was, but as I say, nothing was making sense.'

'Then what happened?'

'The man who had put me up against the car was trying to drag me away, and it was then that I remembered I had Harri in the car. That's what brought me back to my senses, I think. I screamed at him, but he didn't seem to understand at first. After two or three attempts, he reacted. He shouted at the other men that there was a child in the car. He took my handcuffs off and told me to stay where I was. He went around and took Harri from the car, and told me to follow him, which I did.'

Ben paused.

'Mrs Hughes, before you went round to the back of the car to see what Caradog and Dai Bach were doing, did you have any idea of what was in the boot of your car?'

She sobbed.

'No. Of course not.'

'If you had known what Dai Bach was putting into the boot while you were at the garage in Bangor, would you have agreed to carry it?'

She suddenly looked up and stared Ben full in the face.

'Would I have helped him to take a bomb to Caernarfon Castle? No. No. I can't believe I have to answer the question.'

'I'm sorry. I have to ask...'

'No. And even if I had the inclination, would I do it with my child in the car? Do I seriously have to answer this? What kind of person do you think I am?'

She was almost shouting now.

'I have to ask.'

'No. I can't believe this is happening to me. It can't be real. I want my son back.'

She began to sob violently. Ben waited for some time before turning to the judge.

'My Lord, I wonder whether your Lordship would allow me to continue tomorrow morning? Mrs Hughes is obviously very distressed.'

'We are proceeding at a rather slow pace, Mr Schroeder.'

'Yes, my Lord, but I don't have very much left, and I would prefer to allow Mrs Hughes some time to recover rather than rush her when she is distressed. We have made good progress in the trial as a whole.'

'Yes, very well,' the judge replied reluctantly.

'I am most obliged to your Lordship.'

'I thought she did rather well,' Gareth commented, as they gathered up their papers for the day.

'I can never tell when I'm on my feet,' Ben replied. 'She didn't do Dai Bach any harm, did she?'

Gareth shook his head.

'No, not at all. Incidentally, I thought I would open the bowling myself tomorrow morning once you've finished with her.'

Ben looked at him blankly.

'I didn't know you had anything to ask her.'

'I don't really,' Gareth replied. 'But I thought I might start her off with an underarm delivery. Might help a bit.'

66

Tuesday 12 May 1970

COURT HAD ASSEMBLED AND Arianwen had returned to the witness box. She looked composed, and had put on a smart new pale orange cotton dress. Ben eyed her anxiously for any tell-tale signs of distress.

'Mrs Hughes, yesterday afternoon I was asking you about your arrest. I must now come to the time when you were at the police station. I know this will be difficult for you, and I will take it as shortly as I can.'

'Thank you,' she replied.

'Were you taken by car to the police station?'

'Yes.'

'It's not very far, of course. Was Harri with you?'

'Yes. Once we were in the car, the officer allowed me to travel with Harri sitting in my lap.'

'Please tell my Lord and the jury what happened when you arrived at the police station.'

She held her head in her hands silently for some time.

'I got out of the car with Harri, and I remember walking with him into the police station, holding hands. And then suddenly, this woman police officer, a uniformed officer, just came and yanked Harri's hand out of mine. She started to take him away. Just like that, without a word. I couldn't even say goodbye, or say something to tell him that it would be all right. She just grabbed him and took him off. Harri was screaming and calling for me...'

She started to cry.

'Take your time,' Ben said.

'That made me start to scream,' she continued. 'I was screaming at them to bring Harri back, and I was trying to go after them, but there were two male officers holding me back. They more or less dragged me, still screaming, to a cell, threw me inside, and slammed the door. I fell on the floor quite heavily. I noticed the following day that I had some bruising on my thigh, though I didn't feel any pain at the time. I was too upset.'

'What happened next?'

'Some time later – I don't really know how long – two plain clothes officers came into my cell with a female officer in uniform.'

'Did you know who they were at the time?'

'I am sure they introduced themselves, but I could hardly concentrate on anything for thinking about Harri.'

'Was the female officer WPC Marsh, who gave evidence to the jury?'

'Yes.'

'Was she the officer who took Harri away?'

'No. That was someone else. WPC Marsh was very polite to me, very proper.'

'Do you now know that the male officers were DCI Grainger and DS Scripps?'

'Yes.'

'And how did they behave towards you?'

She began to cry again.

'They were shouting and carrying on, demanding to know where Trevor was. I didn't know, so I couldn't answer their questions, but they wouldn't believe me. They went on and on.'

'Did they say anything in particular that distressed you?'

'Yes. They told me that I would never see Harri again unless I told them where Trevor was. They said that they had the power to keep him from me, that he would be put in a foster home until he grew up. On the other hand, if I cooperated, they would put in a good word with the court, and I might be able to see him and have him back one day.'

'Do you remember anything that was said specifically?'

'Yes. I remember the younger officer…'

'DS Scripps?'

'Yes. I remember him saying that they would lock me up and I would be lucky to get out in time for Harri's silver wedding anniversary.'

'This may be obvious to the jury, but how did that make you feel?'

She sat silently, shaking her head for some time.

'I lost my mind. I was beside myself. I remember screaming and even jumping at Mr Grainger at one point. Then, when he pushed me away, I just curled up on the floor and wailed and wailed, begging them for pity, asking them why they wouldn't believe me.'

'How did WPC Marsh behave during this time?'

'She was very upset by it all. She was trying to get them to stop, but of course, they wouldn't listen to her. She did her best to comfort me.'

Ben paused.

'You later made a written statement under caution, which the jury have. Is what you said in that statement the truth?'

'Yes, it is.'

'Do you stand by it today?'

'Yes. I do.'

'Thank you, Mrs Hughes,' Ben said. 'There will be some further questions for you.

'Yes, Mr Roberts,' the judge was saying.

Gareth stood.

'My Lord, if I may…'

'I'm sorry, Mr Morgan-Davies. I hadn't anticipated that you would have anything for this witness.'

'One very brief matter, my Lord. Mrs Hughes, Dafydd Prosser accepts that you knew nothing about any plan there might have been to cause explosions. But…'

'Oh, really,' Evan Roberts said loudly, springing to his feet. 'That is entirely improper. My learned friend is not asking a question, he is giving evidence. Dafydd Prosser has not given evidence, and it is not for my learned friend to…'

'Yes, Mr Roberts, I have your point,' the judge replied. 'Mr Morgan-Davies, if you have a question, please ask it.'

'Yes, my Lord, of course. My question, Mrs Hughes, is this. It is correct, is it not, that Dafydd Prosser did not direct you to the garage until you were already in Bangor?'

'That is correct.'

'No reference was made to a garage over the phone, or during the drive to Bangor?'

'None at all.'

'Yes. Thank you very much,' Gareth said, resuming his seat and ignoring stares from the judge and Evan Roberts. He grinned mischievously at Ben. 'How's that for an underarm delivery?'

'I can't believe you did that,' Ben whispered.

'Don't mention it,' Gareth replied. 'I just thought Dai Bach's evidence might help.'

67

'MRS HUGHES,' EVAN ROBERTS began, 'if I understand you correctly, your position is that you knew nothing, at any time, about any plot to plant a bomb in Caernarfon Castle, is that right?'

'That is correct.'

'And you were blissfully unaware that you were driving from Bangor to Caernarfon in the early morning of 1 July with a bomb in the boot of your car?'

'There was nothing blissful about it, but I had no idea that the bomb was there.'

'You had known your brother, Caradog Prys-Jones, all your life, of course?'

'Of course.'

'You had known Trevor Hughes since 1961, and you had been married to him since 1963?'

'Yes.'

'You had known Dafydd Prosser for many years also?'

'Yes.'

'Would it be fair to say that you were close to all three, in different ways, naturally?'

'Yes, that would be fair.'

'You had dinner with all of them on a regular basis at home?'

'Yes.'

'And it would be fair to describe all three as having nationalist views?'

'That would depend on what you mean by nationalist. If you mean violence, no, that would not be fair.'

'All right. Let me be more precise. Leave any question of violence aside. All three men believe that Wales should be a nation politically independent of England and the rest of the United Kingdom?'

'Yes, it is fair to say that.'

'And you share that belief?'

'Yes. I do.'

Evan paused to consult his notes.

'You have been in court and heard the evidence in this case, haven't you?'

'Yes.'

'And you now know that your brother, your husband, and Dafydd Prosser were involved in a conspiracy to plant a bomb in Caernarfon Castle on the occasion of the Investiture, don't you?'

Gareth and Ben stood simultaneously. Gareth won the race to intervene by a short head.

'My Lord, perhaps my learned friend would find it easier to show the witness the indictment and ask her to return the verdicts, to save the jury the trouble. This is the very question the jury has to decide.'

'Yes,' Mr Justice Overton said. 'Ask it in a different way, please, Mr Roberts.'

'As your Lordship pleases. Mrs Hughes, you know that on the occasion you were arrested, there was a bomb in the boot of your car. That's right, isn't it?'

'Yes.'

'You didn't put it there, did you?'

'No.'

'Because your case is that you didn't know it was there.'

'That is correct.'

'Would you agree, then, that there are only two ways in which the bomb could have got into the boot of your car: either your husband Trevor Hughes put it there at some earlier time; or Dafydd Prosser put it there when you stopped at his garage in Bangor?'

'Yes, I would agree.'

'Thank you. And of those two possibilities, is it not far more likely that Dafydd Prosser took it from his garage and put it in the boot of your car? Why else would he have asked you to drive him to Bangor and back? There was no other suitcase in the car, was there?'

'No. I would agree.'

'Thank you. And when you were arrested, Dafydd Prosser and your brother were present by the boot of your car, and the lid of the carrying case was open, revealing the bomb for you all to see. Is that also right?'

'Yes.'

'Your brother was supposed to be at work as a night watchman at the Castle at that time, wasn't he?'

'As far as I know, yes.'

'Does it not follow that your brother was there to collect the bomb and carry it into the Castle?'

Gareth rose again.

'Whether or not that follows is a matter for the jury,' he objected, 'not for this witness to speculate about.'

'I'm suggesting there is nothing speculative about it as far as this witness is concerned,' Evan replied. 'You knew all about that, Mrs Hughes, didn't you?'

'No. I did not.'

Evan paused.

'You heard evidence that your brother, your husband and Dafydd Prosser went together to Belfast in April of last year, and met with a member of the IRA and a member of the Baader-Meinhof group. You heard that evidence, did you not?'

'Yes, I did.'

'You say your husband told you they were going on a boys' excursion to Dublin, to relax for a few days, sink a few pints of Guinness, that kind of thing?'

'That is what he told me.'

'Can we agree that the meeting in Belfast must have been connected to the plan to build an explosive device for use on 1 July?'

'I wasn't present at the meeting. I can't say what was discussed.'

'No, of course. Did your husband ever tell you that he had contacts in the IRA?'

'No.'

'What about your brother?'

'No.'

'Did either of them ever say that they had contacts in the Baader-Meinhof group?'

'No.'

'Can you think of any reason why either your husband or your brother would have had contacts of that kind, given what you know about their activities?'

'No. No reason whatsoever.'

'So the evidence of that meeting must have come as quite a shock to you?'

'Everything in this case has come as a shock to me.'

Evan paused again.

'That isn't true, is it, Mrs Hughes?'

'It is true.'

'You were close to all these men. It must have taken months for them to draw up plans for this conspiracy; to get hold of the ingredients for the bomb; take advice from those more experienced in such matters in the IRA and Baader-Meinhof; build the bomb, presumably during evenings and weekends; and decide how and where to plant it…'

Ben stood. 'My Lord, perhaps my learned friend would clarify which of those various speculations he is asking the witness to comment on.'

'If my learned friend would allow me to ask the question…'

'It wasn't a question; it was a series of assumptions. And, once more, he is asking the witness to comment on the very matters the jury has to decide.'

'What is the question you wish to ask, Mr Roberts?' the judge asked.

'I am suggesting that it would have been impossible for her to be unaware of what they were up to, my Lord. That is my point.'

'Then perhaps you could put that to her without the preamble?'

'As your Lordship pleases. Mrs Hughes, you must have been aware, and you were aware, that your husband, your brother, and Dafydd Prosser were hatching a plan to place a bomb in Caernarfon Castle on the occasion of the Investiture. That is right, isn't it?'

'No. I didn't know.'

'You were turning a blind eye, perhaps, because you were close to them?'

'No. I wouldn't have done that. If I had known, or even suspected anything like this, I would have spoken out.'

'You shared their belief in nationalism, didn't you?'

'I don't share any belief in violence.'

'So you say…'

'My Lord…' Ben began, rising.

'Enough, Mr Roberts,' the judge said.

'You drove Dafydd Prosser to Bangor and back because you

thought that was a contribution you could make to the conspiracy, didn't you?'

'No.'

'Far from being ignorant of the plan, you knew all about it, and you were quite willing to help if you could?'

'No.'

'Indeed, you were so devoted to the cause that you placed your son, Harri, at risk, didn't you?'

'No!'

'By putting him in a car which had dynamite in it…'

There was suddenly a loud bang as she brought both hands down with full force on the top of the witness box.

'No!' she shouted. She made a conscious effort to calm herself. 'If you think I would do that, you don't know me at all. You know nothing about me at all.'

'But it all went wrong, didn't it?'

'No.'

'And when it all went wrong, where was your husband? Where was Trevor Hughes?'

'I don't know.'

'He deserted you, didn't he?'

She hesitated.

'I wouldn't say that.'

'Really? Well, he disappeared into thin air, leaving you holding the baby or, perhaps I should say, holding the bomb.'

'I don't accept that.'

'Well, where is he, Mrs Hughes?'

'I don't know.'

'I suggest that you do.'

'You can suggest whatever you want…'

Ben was on his feet now, trying to intervene, but they spoke over him.

'I am suggesting you know exactly where he is. Why don't you tell us?' His voice was raised, almost to shouting.

'Why don't *you* tell everyone where my husband is?' she shouted back.

For a moment, there was total silence in court.

'Why don't *I* tell you where he is?' Evan asked incredulously.

'Yes. You've had every police force in this country, in Ireland,

and God only knows where else, looking for him ever since I was arrested, and you don't know where he is? He's not Houdini. He's a book seller, for God's sake. He didn't just disappear into thin air.'

'What are you suggesting, Mrs Hughes?'

'I'm suggesting that you, or someone, know very well what happened to Trevor. What have you done with him?'

Suddenly, Evan Roberts lost his temper.

'Don't talk to me like that,' he shouted. 'I am not some police officer you are yelling at on one of your demonstrations. I am prosecuting counsel in this case.'

'My Lord...' Ben intervened.

'That's enough, Mr Roberts,' the judge said.

'You're not a prosecutor,' Arianwen shouted. 'You're a school-yard bully. You are no better than the police who threatened to keep my son from me for the rest of my life.'

'That will do, Mrs Hughes,' Mr Justice Overton said.

She did not even hear him.

'And you claim to be Welsh,' she shouted finally. 'You're no more Welsh than Charles Windsor.'

Finally, a silence, this time a shocked silence, descended again on the court. Arianwen sighed and bowed her head. Evan Roberts took his seat with a vindictive smile. Ben sat down slowly, his eyes closed.

'Don't react,' Gareth whispered.

'Do I take it that you have finished your cross-examination, Mr Roberts?' the judge asked.

'I have, my Lord.'

'Then we will adjourn for half an hour. I am sure the jury have had enough, as have I.'

The vindictive smile returned.

'I am sure the jury will not hold Mrs Hughes' outburst against her,' Evan said with exaggerated magnanimity.

The judge paused before leaving the bench.

'I wasn't talking about Mrs Hughes,' he replied venomously.

When the judge returned to court, he found the atmosphere sombre. Arianwen was sitting in the dock with her head in her hands.

'Will you be calling any witnesses, Mr Schroeder?'

'No, my Lord, I close the case for Mrs Hughes.'

The judge nodded. 'Very well. We will have closing speeches tomorrow and I will sum up on Thursday. Members of the jury, please be back to resume at 10.30 tomorrow morning.'

68

Thursday 14 May 1970

MR JUSTICE OVERTON GAVE the jury a firm direction that they could not convict any defendant unless the evidence satisfied them of guilt beyond reasonable doubt. He defined a conspiracy as an unlawful agreement to commit a criminal offence. He warned them that Dafydd Prosser's decision not to give evidence was a decision every defendant in a criminal court was entitled to make, and that it must not be held against him in any way. It was certainly no evidence of his guilt. There were only a few other matters of law to deal with, and he dealt with them succinctly and clearly. He then spent a good deal of the day reminding the jury of the evidence they had heard, and putting it in context. It was a long, but necessary, task. Towards the end of the afternoon, he was ready for his concluding remarks.

'Members of the jury, what does it all come down to? The Crown say that Caradog Prys-Jones and Dafydd Prosser, with the absent Trevor Hughes, made an agreement to plant a bomb in Caernarfon Castle, set to detonate during the Investiture, with an obvious risk of loss of life and serious injury to many people, including the Queen and Prince Charles. The Crown say that they recruited Arianwen Hughes to carry the bomb in her car from the garage factory in Bangor to the square in Caernarfon, for Caradog Prys-Jones to collect, using her young son to give the impression of a normal family activity. Caradog Prys-Jones had ready and unquestioned access to the Castle because of his job as a night watchman, and had already selected a site for the bomb to be placed, close to the Royal dais and to several seating stands for guests.

'Members of the jury, this is a case in which it is impossible not to have strong feelings about the evidence you have heard. Any act of planting a bomb, especially where there is a strong probability that lives will be lost or terrible injuries caused, must cause revulsion in any right-thinking person. When those lives might have been lost and those injuries caused during a joyful national celebration, when the victims might have included the Queen, or Prince Charles, or another member of the Royal Family, the act becomes one which strikes at the very heart of British life, the very fabric of our government. No one in this court expects you not to have strong feelings about that. That would be impossible, wouldn't it?

'That makes what I am about to say all the more difficult. But I must say it. I must and do direct you now, not to disregard your feelings, not to deny them, but to put them to one side for a time while you deliberate about this case. I say that, because the law requires you to do what you have taken an oath to do, that is to say, to return a true verdict in accordance with the evidence. You cannot return a true verdict according to the evidence if you start with any prejudice against these defendants. Every defendant who comes before our courts is innocent until proven guilty, and that applies whether the charge is one of a minor theft, or a crime of the utmost gravity, as in this case. That principle applies to this case just as much as it would to a case of shop-lifting. It applies to every case which comes before the criminal courts of this country. You must, therefore, put whatever feelings you have about the case on one side and decide on the basis of the evidence.

'I also want to make this clear: that none of these defendants is on trial for believing that Wales should be an independent nation, or for engaging in lawful political activities to further that cause. None of the defendants is on trial for believing that England has in the past acted with aggression against Wales, or for believing that England has been indifferent, if not actively hostile, to the preservation of the ancient Welsh language as a living language. Indeed, having heard the historical evidence presented to you, you may think that in some ways they have a legitimate grievance. I make that clear because both Caradog Prys-Jones and Arianwen Hughes have told you frankly that they are nationalists. They are perfectly entitled to hold those views and to promote them in every lawful way. They are not to be convicted because of their beliefs, and you are not to be prejudiced against them because of their beliefs, even if you may personally disagree with them.

'Nor are you to be prejudiced against Caradog Prys-Jones because of his behaviour earlier in the trial, which led me to have him taken down to the cells. Indeed, you may well regard his refusal to recognise the court as no more than another protest against all things English – an ill-advised and ill-timed protest, you may think, but perhaps no more than that. He returned to court subsequently. He has made no further protest and, indeed, he has given evidence, although more on behalf of his sister than on his own account.

'The Crown say, of course, that this was not simply a matter of holding beliefs or promoting them by lawful means. The Crown says that this was a serious crime, which would have been a serious crime even if it was not committed in a political cause. It is illegal to cause explosions in these circumstances, regardless of the motive of the person who causes the explosion.

'Let me deal first with the case of Caradog Prys-Jones. I have reminded you of the prosecution's evidence. It is said that he was the leader of the Heirs of Owain Glyndŵr; that he commissioned Dafydd Prosser to build a device capable of being detonated during the Investiture ceremony; that he found a place to plant it, making use of the access he had to the Castle as a night watchman; and that he was prevented from carrying the plan out only because of his arrest. When interviewed by the police, he gave them a written statement under caution. It is not disputed that this was a voluntary statement. You may think – of course, it is a matter for you to say – but you may think you would be perfectly entitled to regard that statement, not only as an admission of guilt, but as a defiant statement of self-justification. Indeed, you may think that, on its own, it is more than enough to convict him, and certainly when it is taken together with the other evidence you have heard. But that is a matter for you.

'Turning to Dafydd Prosser, he has not given evidence, but for the reasons I have explained, you will not hold that against him. The Crown say that he is linked to the bomb by a good deal of circumstantial evidence found in the garage in Bangor, fingerprints and fragments of dynamite and electrical wire, and by the fact that he collected the bomb in the car driven by Arianwen Hughes and delivered it to Caradog Prys-Jones in the square in Caernarfon. When the bomb disposal officers arrived, he continually assured them that the device was not armed, which the disposal officers soon confirmed for themselves.

'The Crown say that there can only be one reason why Dafydd Prosser would know whether or not the device was armed, and that is because he built the device and was familiar with its condition when it arrived in Caernarfon. Obviously, it would be a sensible step not to arm it until the last possible moment, which was just before Caradog Prys-Jones put it in his duffle bag to take it into the Castle; and you will bear in mind Mr Morgan-Davies's observation that it was obvious to the bomb disposal officers almost immediately that it was not armed. But that, of course, does not begin to explain the fact, if you accept it as such, that he brought the device from the garage in Bangor to Caernarfon.

'Turning lastly to Arianwen Hughes, she has given evidence, supported by her brother, that she knew nothing about the plot to plant a bomb in the Castle, and that she had no idea that the item she carried back from Bangor was a bomb. As I said earlier, members of the jury, if that account is true, or if it may be true, then you cannot be satisfied beyond reasonable doubt that she had knowledge of the plan, and without proof of that knowledge she cannot be convicted of conspiracy.

'The Crown's case, you may think, turns on the argument that she knew all three men well, and well enough that she must have known what they were planning – that it is, from a practical point of view, impossible that she could not have known after such close contact with them over such a long period of time. It is for you to say where the truth lies, but I remind you that the test is not what she *must* have known, but what she *did* know. You must bear in mind, as Mr Schroeder reminded you, that her husband is absent from this trial, and that Mr Schroeder has not had the opportunity to cross-examine him about what his wife knew or did not know. That is a point to consider, but I remind you that you may not speculate about evidence that has not been given. You must try the case on the basis of the evidence you do have. The Crown do not suggest that she did anything other than carry the bomb to further the goals of the conspiracy. It is not suggested that she participated in any way in the planning, or in building the device.

'You have heard evidence, not only from Mrs Hughes herself, but from a number of prosecution witnesses, about her distress, particularly about being parted from her son. You cannot, of course, base your verdict on any sympathy for her about that, assuming that you have any such sympathy. But you may take her distress – which was, you may think, quite obvious when she gave evidence – into account; and you may take into account the feelings she has about her son when you ask yourselves whether she would have allowed herself to become mixed up in this plot, or whether, as she herself told you, she would have gone to the police herself if she had known of it. The Crown say that the fact that Harri was in the car when she drove from Bangor with the bomb in her boot is evidence of her fanatical devotion to the conspiracy. But you must remember also Mr Schroeder's argument that it could equally well show that she did not know what was going on. He suggests to you that no woman would expose her son to a risk of being blown up, however slight that risk might have been.

'As in the case of the other two defendants, you must not be prejudiced against her because of her nationalist views and, as in the case of her brother, you must not be prejudiced because of the way she expressed herself in court – in her case when, during her evidence, she referred to the Prince of Wales as "Charles Windsor". That may have been a deliberately slighting or insulting remark, or simply one made in the heat of the moment in the course of what was certainly a very heated exchange during Mr Roberts' cross-examination. But, members of the jury, it has nothing to do with the evidence in her case. The only question for you is whether you are satisfied beyond reasonable doubt that her act of driving the car in the early morning of 1 July was a knowing act of participation in the conspiracy, or whether it may be that she did so not knowing what it was she was carrying.

'Members of the jury, I am not going to send you out this afternoon. I know that you may be out for some time, so we will start fresh at 10.30 tomorrow morning. We are adjourned for the day.'

69

THE JURY RETIRED TO begin work the next morning just after 10.30 without undue ceremony. Ben made his way down to the cells to see Arianwen, but the tension made it impossible for either of them to say anything meaningful, and before long he left Barratt and Eifion to wait near the court for news, and returned to the Bar Mess. He found Gareth sitting in an armchair with a cup of coffee, reading *The Times*. He smiled.

'You look very calm. Where's Donald?'

'He went for a prowl around somewhere,' Gareth replied. 'He couldn't sit still for very long.'

'I'm not sure I can,' Ben said. 'Does it ever get any easier waiting for juries?'

'Not in the 20-plus years I've been doing this job,' Gareth replied. 'Mind you, it's not too bad when you have a client like Dai Bach, who's going down like a lead balloon. Not much drama in his case, I'm afraid, or in Caradog's. But they may be out for some time with your girl. I think she has a shot. Your closing speech was very persuasive and much as I hate to admit it, I thought Overton treated her very fairly in the summing-up.'

'Too fairly,' Ben said, seating himself in the armchair next to Gareth's. 'I'm not sure he's left me anywhere to go on appeal if she goes down.'

'I'm not sure he has. I have to say, I have been quite impressed with Miles in this case. After all the years I've known him as one of the most combative and opinionated Silks in the business, he seems to have become the model judge. Perhaps he is behaving himself because he's in the public eye. Perhaps he will show his true colours when he has to buckle down to the everyday business of the Queen's Bench Division.'

'How is Bernard enjoying life on the bench? Do you hear from him? I've hardly seen him since he started. Harriet was in front of him last week on a short matter and she said he was his usual formal self, very business-like.'

'He is thoroughly enjoying himself. We have been in touch about chambers matters, my taking over as Head of Chambers and so on, and the impression I get is that he's in his element.'

'Well, at least standards will be maintained at the Bar with Bernard on the bench,' Ben grinned. 'Woe betide anyone who appears in his court with wrinkled bands or his waistcoat unbuttoned. Can I get you some more coffee?'

Gareth shook his head. 'No thanks. It's ghastly stuff, isn't it? I don't know why I drink it – to pass the time, I suppose. Let's hope we're not here too long.'

Leaving Gareth to *The Times*, Ben poured himself a strong coffee and returned to sit and wait. Members of the Bar involved in other cases came and went, and he chatted to one or two, but most of the morning was spent sitting in the armchair, trying without much success to concentrate on an article about the reform of the criminal law which he had optimistically brought with him. Lunch time brought some relief, the chance to enjoy the hubbub of the Mess, to hear tales of what was going on in other courts. But when 2 o'clock came, the Mess emptied again and they were left alone with the silence.

The worst time was at about 5 o'clock, when the courts had risen for the day. The barristers in other cases had returned to chambers; the building was deserted; and the cleaners wandered dispiritedly through the rooms, clearing away the coffee cups and gathering up discarded newspapers, trailing humming vacuum cleaners behind them, and circling the chairs where they sat with an unspoken resentment about having to clean around them, so that they felt like intruders in their own Bar Mess. At 6 o'clock, Geoffrey the usher entered and disrupted the crushing silence by asking them to return to court.

'Mr Roberts,' the judge said. 'I have been told that the jury has reached a verdict in the case of two of the three defendants, but not the third. Unless there is any objection, I propose to take the two verdicts now, and then allow the jury further time to deliberate about the remaining defendant.'

Evan looked along counsel's row and saw no reaction.

'My Lord, I do not think anyone would seek to persuade your Lordship otherwise.'

'If any of the defendants is convicted,' the judge continued, 'I propose to sentence this evening.'

Evan looked along the row again. This time, Gareth stood slowly.

'My Lord, I can't object to that, of course,' he replied. 'But I do invite your Lordship to consider whether it might be better to adjourn until tomorrow morning. Inevitably, a verdict of guilty in the case of any defendant will be a stressful and emotional moment, not only for the defendant, but also for counsel and solicitors. It may be that a short adjournment would allow both counsel and your Lordship some time for reflection about mitigation and sentence.'

'I don't think I need any time for reflection,' Mr Justice Overton replied. 'I have had plenty of time for that during the trial, and I imagine that counsel have had ample opportunity during this long afternoon.'

'As your Lordship pleases,' Gareth replied. He resumed his seat, and turned to Ben. 'I take back all the nice things I said about him,' he whispered.

'I didn't think they were all that nice,' Ben whispered back.

At a nod from the judge, the clerk of court stood and asked the defendants to stand.

'Members of the jury, who shall speak as your foreman?'

The foreman of the jury stood. He was a precise-looking man, who had worn a pinstriped suit and a tie throughout the trial, and had taken copious notes of the evidence. In everyday life he was a high-ranking executive of a City bank.

'I am the foreman, my Lord.'

'Members of the jury, in the case of Caradog Prys-Jones, has the jury reached a verdict on which you all agreed?'

'We have, my Lord.'

'Do you find Caradog Prys-Jones guilty or not guilty of conspiracy to cause explosions?'

'We find the defendant guilty.'

'You find the defendant Caradog Prys-Jones guilty, and is that the verdict of you all?'

'It is, my Lord.'

'Members of the jury, in the case of Dafydd Prosser, has the jury reached a verdict on which you all agreed?'

'We have, my Lord.'

'Do you find Dafydd Prosser guilty or not guilty of conspiracy to cause explosions?'

'We find the defendant guilty.'

'You find the defendant Dafydd Prosser guilty, and is that the verdict of you all?'

'It is, my Lord.'

'Members of the jury, in the case of Arianwen Hughes, has the jury reached a verdict on which you all agreed?'

The foreman coughed.

'No, my Lord.'

There was a silence. After some time, the judge nodded.

'Then, please retire again, members of the jury, and continue your deliberations as to Mrs Hughes.'

When the jury had left, he added: 'I will remand Caradog Prys-Jones and Dafydd Prosser in custody for sentence.'

As the judge left the bench, Ben turned around to see all three defendants sitting, pale and motionless, in the dock.

70

THE BROKEN SILENCE OF the cleaners had now been replaced by the relentless silence of the night. The court was a daytime place, and at night its empty rooms seemed hostile and forbidding. The lights had been dimmed automatically at 8 o'clock by some central timing system over which those who remained in the building had no control. The portraits and certificates on the walls were reduced to ghostly shadows; even reading was a strain. Gareth and Donald were huddled in a corner, making spasmodic notes for a plea in mitigation which would be virtually devoid of mitigation.

Ben sat alone, refusing to think about mitigation, focusing only on the hopes raised by the fact that the jury had not reached a verdict. Arianwen's case was not straightforward. There was no way to tell what was troubling them. There was no way to tell whether they were divided and, if so, what the numbers were on either side. He had given them something to think about, but would it amount to reasonable doubt? And what if they failed to reach a verdict? It was certain that the prosecution would seek a retrial. But at least it would buy Arianwen further time, and perhaps in that time they would find Trevor Hughes. These thoughts, and others, circled through his mind as if on an endlessly revolving tape. The usher returned to fetch them just after 10 o'clock.

The late night finish had not deterred the public and the press at all, and the court was still packed. There was a nervous hush, as though all those present in the courtroom were holding their breath together in a concerted effort to cope with the stress of waiting. Of the three defendants, only Arianwen had been brought up to court. Ben smiled as encouragingly as he could, but she stared blankly ahead of her.

'Members of the jury,' the clerk asked, 'in the case of Arianwen Hughes, has the jury reached a verdict on which you all agreed?'

The foreman turned to the judge.

'We have, my Lord.'

PETER MURPHY

'Members of the jury, do you find Arianwen Hughes guilty or not guilty of conspiracy to cause explosions?'

'We find the defendant guilty.'

'You find the defendant Arianwen Hughes guilty, and is that the verdict of you all?'

'It is, my Lord. But if we may…?'

'Yes?' the judge asked.

'If we may, we would like to ask for some clemency in her case.'

Mr Justice Overton nodded. 'Thank you, members of the jury.'

Ben felt as if the courtroom had gone dark before his eyes, and he held on to the hard surface of counsel's row in front of him for support. He heard a whisper of condolence from Gareth, and a barely suppressed oath from Barratt behind him. But his concentration was on keeping his composure. He heard nothing from the dock, and when he eventually turned towards her, he saw the same steady stare ahead.

71

'LET THE OTHER DEFENDANTS be brought up,' Mr Justice Overton said.

Ben was not conscious of their arrival until he felt Gareth rise to his feet next to him. Slowly, his eyes readjusted to the light of the courtroom, and he began to regain his bearings.

'My Lord, there is little to say by way of mitigation in the light of the jury's verdict, and what little there is, I think I can say quite shortly both on behalf of Dafydd Prosser and, if your Lordship will allow, on behalf of Caradog Prys-Jones. Both men have been convicted of a dreadful crime, which could have had the most horrendous consequences. There can be no possible mitigation for that. At the same time, it is a tragic case, because these are young men of considerable intelligence and ability, who might have gone on to great things on behalf of Wales if they had not chosen this destructive path. I say only three things more.

'Firstly, they did what they did, not for any personal gain or advantage, but in pursuit of personal ideals – misguided ideals, certainly – but ideals nonetheless. Those beliefs are sincerely held and they run deep, and underlying them is a desire for freedom and justice – defined, of course, in their own flawed terms, and taking insufficient account of the freedoms of others – but beliefs in freedom and justice nonetheless.

'Secondly, they are both young men, whose immaturity and inexperience of life outside North Wales may have made them more susceptible to the beliefs they held than others might have been. Recognising as I do that your Lordship must sentence these young men to a long term of imprisonment, I ask that the sentence be such as to give them some hope that they may eventually re-emerge into the world, rehabilitated and with the opportunity to use their undoubted talents in a constructive way, for the benefit of society.

'Thirdly, I urge your Lordship to take account of the absence of

Trevor Hughes. The Crown has said that Caradog Prys-Jones was the intellectual leader of the conspiracy, and has defined the roles of all three conspirators from that starting point, with that assumption in mind. But in my submission, there is no basis for any certainty about that assumption. Your Lordship does not know, there is no evidence, about the role played by Trevor Hughes, and your Lordship cannot exclude the possibility that Hughes played a leading role and influenced the others to follow him, at least to some extent. Until Trevor Hughes is arrested and brought before a court, no one will know the full truth about what happened during those early months of 1969, or on the morning of 1 July itself.

'In conclusion, I urge your Lordship to show the defendants that justice administered in England, while necessarily severe in a case such as this, may still be tempered by a degree of mercy.'

Ben stood in his turn.

'My Lord, I am bound to accept the jury's verdict, and that, of course, means that I must accept that they did not find Mrs Hughes' evidence to be persuasive. Therefore, like my learned friend Mr Morgan-Davies, I must also accept that there is, and can be, no mitigation for what she did, in itself. But I respectfully adopt the observations made by my learned friend, which apply in equal measure to Arianwen Hughes. I ask your Lordship to reflect in particular that we will never know what difference the absence of Trevor Hughes may have had on this trial. Your Lordship has no way of knowing exactly what part he may have played in the events of the early morning of 1 July, and no way of knowing exactly what role he played in his wife's life that brought her to the situation in which she finds herself today.

'But it is not unreasonable to assume that his role in her life was a major one. There is no indication in her past record, or in the evidence she gave, that she would behave as I must accept she did. She is a musician, a teacher, a woman dedicated to her culture and her language. She does not share the harder-line view of nationalism which may appeal to others. There is no reason why your Lordship cannot accept her evidence on that score. She wishes for no political separation from England, she wishes for no borders, passports, or other trappings of a nominal independence. She is a woman whose Welsh identity is expressed through her language and her music.

'I remind your Lordship that the prosecution has never contended that she did anything more than transport the bomb. She was not involved in planning any part of the operation; she was not involved in building the bomb; she did not go to Ireland; she did nothing except that one journey to Bangor and back to Caernarfon, and she did not even do that on her own initiative, but because she was asked to do so. Your Lordship would be entitled to say that, if Trevor Hughes had been here, and we had heard from him, it is likely that your Lordship would be sentencing Arianwen Hughes on a very different basis, a basis which would reflect the influence her husband must have had on her life.

'As my learned friend said of the other defendants, there is no suggestion that they acted for any personal gain or advantage. Indeed, in the case of Arianwen Hughes, what she did could only cause her huge losses, and the most terrible loss is that she will be unable to bring up her son while he is young. She has lost the chance of seeing him grow up; of passing on to him her love of music and of her language; of seeing him emerge into the boy who will soon approach manhood. I submit that it was obvious to everyone in court that her grief over the loss of her son is genuine and that it is a devastating loss. She must feel that the cruel prediction made by DS Scripps during her interview is coming to pass.

'My Lord, I accept that your Lordship will pass a prison sentence of some length. But I urge your Lordship to accept the jury's recommendation in favour of clemency. I ask your Lordship to make a clear distinction between Mrs Hughes and the other defendants, both because of her limited role and because of the overwhelming likelihood that she is here today in large part because of the actions of Trevor Hughes. I urge your Lordship to allow her the realistic hope that she may be reunited with her son before time elapses to such an extent as to leave them as no more than strangers to each other. I even urge on your Lordship not to take away any hope that she may become a mother again, if circumstances permit.'

'Stand up,' Mr Justice Overton said.

The three defendants stood, white and tense.

'You have all three been convicted on the clearest evidence of a crime which ranks with the worst in the annals of British criminal history. If your deadly plan had not been discovered and interrupted by the outstanding work of the Gwynedd Police, Special Branch, and MI5, you would have succeeded in concealing a lethal explosive device under a flagstone in Caernarfon Castle, only a few yards from the dais where the Queen and the Prince of Wales were to be engaged in the ceremony of Investiture, and only a few feet from where seating stands had been erected for the use of guests. The device would have been set to detonate during the ceremony, at a time when the maximum damage would be caused. There was potential for substantial loss of life, and terrible injuries. You intended that result, or at least were content to accept it.

'I accept that you were motivated by what you considered to be the idealistic goal of resisting what you saw as the unjust treatment of Wales by England. I accept that you felt a sense of grievance, and I accept that you saw yourselves as the 'Heirs of Owain Glyndŵr', throwing off the yoke supposedly placed by the English, or the British Government, around the neck of the Welsh people. I do not doubt that your sense of grievance was, and is, genuine. Indeed, I will go further and say that it is to some degree justified, certainly by the lack of respect shown to the Welsh language and culture, which in my view reflects no credit on Great Britain or on our Government. But these are matters which must be resolved through political channels, not by the use of deadly violence.

'I also have my ideals, and one of my ideals is this: that neither the British people, nor the courts which uphold the law on behalf of the people, can for one moment give in to the use or threat of violence. On the contrary, it must serve only to strengthen their resolve to uphold the rule of law and the democratic process throughout the United Kingdom.

'In the light of what I have said, even bearing in mind the points made in mitigation, it follows that the court must pass sentences of the greatest severity. Caradog Prys-Jones, Dafydd Prosser, the sentence of the court in each of your cases is that you go to prison for 40 years. Arianwen Hughes, in your case, bearing in mind the lesser role you played and bearing in mind the recommendation of the jury, the sentence of the court is that you go to prison for 22 years. Take them down.'

The prison officers had been instructed to remove the defendants before any protest could be made, but any anxiety they might have had was unnecessary. They were led away like lifeless statues. The shock which permeated the courtroom as the sentences were announced was tangible. There was total silence in the courtroom for some time, and only after one or two minutes did a hesitant exchange of whispers begin in the press box and the public gallery. None of the lawyers in court moved a muscle. If the judge noticed the sense of shock, he did not show it.

'Members of the jury, you are entitled to the grateful thanks of your fellow citizens for your work in what must have been a most distressing and difficult case. In recognition of this, I will exempt you all from further jury service for life.'

The foreman stood again.

'Thank you, my Lord.'

'Mr Roberts, it is my intention to ensure that some officers receive appropriate commendations for their work in this case, which has not only led to the conviction of these defendants, but also prevented almost unimaginable harm befalling this country and our way of life. Because of the lateness of the hour, I shall say no more about it this evening, but I shall ensure that steps are taken so that the officers receive the recognition they deserve.'

Even Evan Roberts seemed to have difficulty in stirring himself.

'I am most grateful, my Lord,' he replied, managing to stand only half way up.

The judge was already almost out of court, and there was no one to hear the sigh of relief he gave as he gained the sanctuary of his chambers, gratefully tore off his wig, and threw it down on top of his desk.

72

BEN TOOK A TAXI home, and opened the front door as quietly as he could. It was after 1 o'clock by now, and he assumed that Jess would be asleep. She had left the downstairs lights on for him, and she had uncorked a bottle of Burgundy, leaving a wine glass and a plate with crackers, cheese and olives by its side. He dropped his briefcase and the bag containing his robes on the floor, and walked quietly upstairs. The upper floor was in darkness, but her reading lamp was on, and she opened her eyes and sat up as soon as he entered the bedroom. He sat by her side on the bed.

'You've heard, I suppose?'

'Yes. Barratt called. He told me that he was going to take you and Eifion out somewhere and get you both drunk. I left the wine downstairs in case it didn't work.'

'None of us felt like getting drunk by the time we had been down to the cells to see Arianwen.'

He bent over and kissed her. She started to get out of bed, reaching for her dressing gown.

'She must have been devastated.'

He shook his head. 'We couldn't even talk to her. She wasn't in the same room with us, except in body. They will have to give her a sedative to knock her out when they get her back to Holloway. I don't know how long it will be before she recovers, if ever. I don't even know how long it will be before we can talk to her about an appeal. She couldn't have taken any more tonight.'

'Is there any realistic ground of appeal?'

'Nothing comes to mind right now. But I'm in no better state to think about that tonight than she is.'

She had put on her dressing gown.

'Come on,' she said. 'If Barratt couldn't get you drunk, perhaps I can.'

They made their way downstairs together, and she brought a

second wine glass. Ben filled the glasses, she switched off the main lights, switched on two floor lamps, and they sat together on the sofa in the mellow light and the quiet of the early morning. He drained a glass of the Burgundy, and allowed his head to sink into his hands. She put her arm around his shoulder and pulled him gently against her. He began to cry, and she held him for a long time. When he eventually pulled himself up, she refilled the glasses.

'Was it the "Charles Windsor" thing? It couldn't have been just that, could it?'

He shook his head, and wiped his nose. He did not reply for some time.

'No. It wasn't just that. I think we have to face the fact that her brother, her husband, and Dafydd Prosser had every intention of killing the Queen or Prince Charles. In time of war they would all have been charged with high treason. Any jury would want to punish anyone involved in that, if there's any evidence at all. And there was evidence. She was in the car with the bomb. Her husband escaped, and I think the jury decided they weren't about to give the whole family a free pass just because she said she knew nothing about it.'

Jess nodded.

'But you believe her, don't you?'

He nodded. 'Yes. I believe her.'

'Is that why you're crying?' she asked gently.

He was silent.

'Before you say anything,' she said. 'I understand, and it's not a problem.'

He turned to her. 'What isn't a problem?'

'The Arianwen effect,' she replied.

'What?'

She smiled. 'I heard about it from Barratt and from Eifion,' she replied, 'the effect Arianwen has on men. She is very beguiling...'

'Jess...'

'No. Let me finish. I don't mean beguiling in any sinister way. She's not what you call beautiful in the classical sense, but there's something about her that draws people to her. I don't know what it is exactly, a kind of animal magnetism, an intense emotional connection. I'm a woman, but even I felt it in the short time I was with her. I'm sure men must feel it far more strongly. She has this gift of connecting with people almost instantly, and on a very deep level. You were representing her in a case in which everything was at stake for her – her freedom, her son, her whole life. How could you not feel connected to her? How could you not feel devastated when she is convicted? I've seen you lose cases before, and you get over it almost straight away. It's something I learned from you that I'm trying to apply to myself in my own practice. Losing happens; it's part of the job. You move on. But not this time. All I'm saying is: I understand why.'

He turned and kissed her.

'I am right, aren't I?' she asked.

'It is really bizarre,' he replied. 'When I went to Wales with Gareth, I had this feeling that I couldn't shake that she was with me in some way. Obviously, that's silly. But I couldn't shake it. I would be standing there looking at something in Caernarfon, especially when we were in the Castle, and I had the sensation that she was pointing things out to me. And even when we went to watch the rugby in Cardiff, she was telling me to immerse myself in the atmosphere, in those overwhelming waves of sound and passion all around the ground when they were singing. It was as if she wanted me to understand something. But I could never quite work out whether it was something about her, or about Wales. It was… well, it was something I've never experienced before. I wasn't going to say anything because…'

'Because you didn't want me to think you had fallen in love with her?'

'Yes.'

'Have you?'

'No,' he replied. 'There was a connection, there still is, but it's not about falling in love. I got too close, I suppose. It's just that I desperately wanted to win. I wanted to set her free, and I wanted you to get Harri back for her.'

She nodded. 'So did I. But things don't always work out the way we want them to. And I don't think there is anything silly about what you felt when you were in Wales. I think it was something real.'

She poured more wine.

'I really wouldn't blame you at all if you felt some attraction to her.'

'Jess…'

'No, I'm serious. I think I would, if I were a man, and I know Barratt did – I know him too well for him to hide it from me.'

'Jess…'

'Why shouldn't you?' she said. ''Just because you're married doesn't mean you can't find a woman attractive.' She kissed him. 'Don't you know that? I won't mind if you tell me you find someone attractive, as long as you don't do anything about it.'

He kissed her back and smiled.

'But what if I did do something about it?'

'Well then, I'd have to kill you, obviously. Come on, let's finish this bottle and go to bed for a couple of days.'

73

Wednesday 20 May 1970

BEN HAD ASKED MERLIN for the first two days of the new week out of court. He told the clerk that he needed time to prepare for a fraud case at the Old Bailey which was scheduled to start within the next few weeks. The reason was plausible enough, but the real reason was not the case he had coming up, but the case he had just finished.

He had asked for time off because he felt tired and drained, and no amount of sleep seemed to repair the damage. Jess had taken care of him throughout a long weekend, sitting or lying quietly with him when he needed her, leaving him alone with his thoughts when he wanted to be alone. But on Monday she had a child custody case in the High Court, and the reality of a new week had set in for both of them. Being at home by himself on Monday and Tuesday did not improve matters. The case of Arianwen Hughes would not go away, and he had not yet come to terms with the fact that he could see no ground of appeal which had any real hope of success. He had made a mental note to consult Gareth about it when he returned to Chambers, but he harboured no illusions that Gareth could magically produce a ground he had overlooked, like a rabbit from a hat. He had enough experience to know a solid conviction when he saw one.

When he returned to Chambers on Wednesday, he found it difficult to concentrate on the fraud case for more than a few minutes at a time. His client had allegedly defrauded one of the London Boroughs of a large sum of money over a period of several years. His small family firm had a contract to repair the Borough's paving stones, and it was alleged that he had systematically invoiced for work his workmen had not done, and inflated invoices for work that had been done. The prosecution had supplied several binders filled with schedules of invoices, and reports by employees who had inspected the work. The client had supplied a confusing account, justifying some, but by no means all, the invoices he had submitted. Under normal circumstances, Ben would have made good progress by now on a chart showing the differences between the prosecution's allegations and his client's version of events, but he had barely started on it, despite sitting resolutely at his desk for most of the day. It was some relief to him that, just after 4.30, his phone rang. He was hoping to hear Jess's voice telling him her case had ended well, and suggesting an early dinner.

'I have Mr Barratt Davis on the line, sir,' Merlin said. 'May I put him through?'

'Yes, of course, Merlin,' Ben replied automatically. There was an eerie, echoing silence on the line for a moment before Barratt's voice came through.

'Ben, I'm sorry to disturb you,' Barratt said, 'but something has come up.' He sounded hesitant and tentative; Ben had the impression that he was making an effort not to speak too loudly. 'I know you're busy, but can you spare a few minutes?'

'Yes, of course, Barratt,' Ben replied. 'What is it? Have you heard from Arianwen?'

'No. Holloway are still keeping her fairly heavily sedated. I'm hoping I may be able to see her on Friday.'

'I'm still wrestling with possible grounds of appeal,' Ben said. 'We can talk about it now if you like, but…'

'No, it's not that. Well, not directly. Actually, I would prefer not to go into it over the phone,' Barratt replied.

'All right, come to Chambers. I don't have any conferences this afternoon.'

'Ben… I know this is a bit irregular, but could you possibly come to my office?'

Ben hesitated. 'Irregular' was no exaggeration. Professional etiquette demanded that Barratt come to Chambers for a conference of any kind. Attending a solicitor's office professionally was not permitted in any but the most exceptional circumstances. Besides, Barratt's office held the uncomfortable memory of just such an exceptional circumstance. It was in that office that Ben, Jess and Barratt had held an all-night vigil for their client Billy Cottage: first while waiting for the Home Secretary to decide whether or not to commute the death sentence imposed on Cottage for a brutal murder; and later, during the few but interminable hours after they had learned of the Home Secretary's decision that the law must take its course. Only when the execution was announced on the morning radio news did the dreadful night at last come to an end. It was a memory which still haunted Ben occasionally, even though it was now almost six years ago.

'I have someone here you should meet,' Barratt was saying. 'He is not keen to venture out to Chambers, and in the circumstances I can't say I blame him. I don't want to say any more.'

Ben glanced down at the schedule he had been staring at unproductively for the past hour and suddenly realised how grateful he was for any excuse to leave it behind.

'Give me ten minutes,' he replied.

The clerk's room was at its busiest at this time in the late afternoon and, without interrupting, Ben opened the door just wide enough to wave to Merlin to indicate that he was leaving. He made his way down the building's main staircase on to Middle Temple Lane, turned left, and cut across in front of Middle Temple Hall to leave by the Little Gate, then left again by the Devereux into Essex Street, where the firm of Bourne & Davis had its offices. Barratt was waiting for him by the main door.

'Thanks for coming, Ben,' he said, as he held the door open for him.

'We are not to be disturbed,' he called out to Mandy, the receptionist, as he led Ben across the entrance hall towards the door of his office, 'unless World War Three breaks out.'

'Yes, Mr Davis,' Mandy called back.

'Actually, not even then,' Barratt added, shepherding Ben inside.

Ben smiled. 'It must be important if we can't be disturbed even for…'

His voice suddenly trailed away as he saw the man standing, facing him, by the bookcase to the left of Barratt's desk. There was no need for Barratt to introduce him. They had never met, but his face was familiar from any number of photographs.

'Trevor Hughes,' he said quietly.

Barratt had closed the door and made his way to his desk.

Hughes nodded, and tentatively approached Ben, his hand outstretched. Just as tentatively, Ben took it, and they shook hands briefly.

'Why don't you both sit down?' Barratt suggested. 'Ben, Mr Hughes came to my office about two hours ago. He…'

Ben held up a hand to silence him.

'No,' he said. 'Barratt, Mr Hughes is a fugitive from justice. There is a warrant out for his arrest. We can't talk to him.'

'Just hear me out, Ben. I had my hand on the phone myself the moment he walked in, believe me. But that was before I heard what he had to say.'

'It doesn't matter what he has to say,' Ben insisted. 'He is an indicted co-conspirator in the case we have just tried. If he says anything, it should be to the police – and to his own solicitor, if he has one.'

'Don't you want to hear why I came to see Mr Davis instead of my own solicitor, Mr Schroeder?' Hughes asked.

'It's not a matter of what I want, Mr Hughes,' Ben replied. 'You are a fugitive. Mr Davis and I can't talk to you. In fact, we have a duty to inform a police officer…'

'I *am* a police officer,' Hughes interrupted, quietly. 'For the time being, anyway.'

74

BEN STOPPED ABRUPTLY. HE felt himself going hot and cold in turn. For some moments, he was completely speechless. Very slowly, he sat down.

'What?' he whispered.

'My name is Trevor Finch. I am a detective constable in the Met, but I have been working in Wales on assignment with Special Branch since 1961.'

Ben stared blankly, first at Finch, and then at Barratt.

'This is not possible,' he said eventually.

'DC Finch brought this with him,' Barratt replied. He handed Ben a large brown envelope and two sheets of white paper, stapled together. 'This is a copy of the first two pages of his personnel file at Scotland Yard. I believe it is genuine. I have represented one or two police officers in disciplinary matters and I have seen forms like this before.'

Ben studied the papers carefully. The copy of the photograph was indistinct, but recognisable. The form contained a good deal of personal information, all of which could easily be checked. If it was a forgery, it was a completely pointless one which could be exposed very easily. As Barratt had said, it was very likely to be genuine. He tried to speak, but no words would come.

'Please tell Mr Schroeder what you told me earlier,' Barratt said.

'I was seconded to Special Branch in 1961 because they were worried about the rise of militant nationalism in Wales,' Finch began. 'I'm not sure why, really. Most of it was harmless enough at that time. Almost all the activity was in support of the Welsh language, and it was mainly peaceful protests, a bit of low-level property damage at worst, nothing the local police couldn't handle.

'It started to get a lot more serious after the flooding of the Tryweryn valley in 1965. It was a stupid thing for the Government to do. Many people in Wales — not just the extremists — were appalled by it, and, as we know, nationalist activity has continued since then, lawfully and otherwise.'

'I understand why the police would want to have someone in place,' Barratt said. 'But why you? Why not a Welsh police officer?'

'I am Welsh. I grew up in England and I'm with the Met, but I am from a Welsh family. I was given to understand that Special Branch didn't trust the Welsh forces a hundred per cent, and they wanted someone from outside.'

'And obviously, you speak Welsh,' Barratt said.

Finch smiled.

'Yes, though when I first went to Caernarfon my Welsh was rusty, to put it mildly. They talk ninety to the dozen up there, and the accent was strange to me. My family is from South Wales, and the accent there is very different. Even the language is different to some extent. Arianwen came to my rescue. She spoke Welsh to me which was straight out of *Teach Yourself Welsh*. Nobody actually speaks Welsh like that, but hearing real grammatical Welsh spoken slowly made the language come back to me, and once I got the language back, it all fell into place.'

Ben tested his voice.

'Were you sent to keep watch specifically on Caradog Prys-Jones and Dafydd Prosser?'

'No, no. That was pure chance, and actually, I don't think they had any thoughts of violent resistance back then. That came much later. They certainly weren't on our radar when I arrived in Caernarfon. But then, back in 1961, not much *was* on our radar. Back then, we were fumbling in the dark – we had hardly any worthwhile intelligence at all. We had no real idea who we were dealing with. We got the occasional tip from one of the Welsh forces but, as I said, Special Branch never really trusted them and half the time they didn't even bother to pass it on to me.

'It was total chaos at first. Most of the time, we didn't even know who the players were. There was the Free Wales Army, but they didn't have any real structure. Any two or three lads who could get hold of a couple of air rifles could call themselves FWA. There was no real chain of command that we could ever find. Then you had the *Mudiad Amddiffyn Cymru*, the Movement for the Defence of Wales – the MAC, we used to call them. They were much better organised, so they didn't give much away. And it wasn't only the groups who had military-style names. You also had cultural groups like *Cymdeithas yr iaith*, the Welsh Language Society, and there were even some people on the fringes of Plaid Cymru we suspected of having violent tendencies. And then there were people who belonged to groups that didn't have names at all, or at least none they talked about in public.

'Such as the Heirs of Owain Glyndŵr?' Ben asked.

Finch smiled and shook his head. '*Etifeddion Owain Glyndŵr.* Yes. As I say, they weren't on the radar at all in 1961. They came much later. They came from nowhere, out of the blue, and they took me completely by surprise.'

75

FINCH SAT DOWN IN a chair by the side of Barratt's desk and leaned back.

'Because we didn't have much to go on, Special Branch decided on deep cover, a long-term assignment. They set me up with a detailed legend – a personal history – and threw me in at the deep end in Caernarfon, to see what I could come up with. Some bright spark found out that the *Tywysog* book shop was up for sale and convinced the High Command that it would be a good idea to fork out a large sum of the taxpayers' money to set me up in it.'

'Quite an assignment,' Barratt said quietly.

'You can say that again.'

'According to your legend you had spent years in the book trade at Foyles.'

Finch laughed. 'Right. One week of training, that was it. The manager did his best, but how much can you learn in a week? They did give me a contact at Foyles to call if I needed to know something, and believe me, I made a lot of use of him. The rest I learned by running the shop.'

Barratt shook his head. 'And then what? You just kept your ears and eyes open?'

'Yes, basically, that was it. I wasn't getting much guidance from London. At times I got the feeling that Welsh nationalism wasn't exactly at the top of the urgent list. But as it turned out, the shop was a brilliant idea. Most nationalists are not talkative people. It takes a long time to gain their trust, if you ever do. And the book shop brought them in. The previous owner, Madog, knew all of them. God only knows what they talked about in the basement in his day. Actually, Madog was a lovely old guy. He loved the shop and his books, and there was always a twinkle in his eye. I really liked him.

'So, I made sure I continued to stock the same radical titles – books and magazines, Welsh, English, whatever; and I sat back and waited for someone to come and talk to me, waited for something to report back to London.'

'Like moths to the candle,' Barratt said.

'Yes. You might say that. It was the same with everyone who came into the shop. I didn't push. I just gave them space to cultivate me if they wanted to. Look, all the nationalists, whether it was the *Mudiad* or anyone else, wanted two things from the *Tywysog*. They wanted a place where they could find radical publications, including the real hard-core stuff – revolutionary and anarchist materials, even materials about weapons and explosives. And they wanted a place to meet where the police weren't likely to pry too much. I was able to offer them both.'

'But they had to make sure it was safe before they opened up to you,' Barratt said.

'Exactly. They had to come into the shop time after time. They would buy innocuous stuff at first – Welsh translations of crime novels and the like. Then, if they felt safe with that, they would graduate to overtly nationalist authors. And all the time they were trying to read me, trying to find out how I felt about nationalism, a question here, a question there, what did I think about this or that thing the Government was doing? What did I think about the Welsh language protests or about Plaid Cymru? And I would give them the answers they wanted to hear, and eventually they would show their hand.'

He laughed.

'But they had a lot of questions for me. Believe me, I was very grateful for the legend Special Branch had given me. It was very detailed, and it was based on people and places I know. It's the only way to make a story work. You have to be able to answer questions without thinking about them too much.'

'And were Caradog and Dai Bach a couple of moths?' Ben asked.

Finch nodded. 'Undercover work is like that,' he replied. 'Sometimes, you can toil away for months, or years, and come up with nothing, and then the next day it falls into your lap.'

'But there was nothing to make you suspect them when you first met them?'

'No. Perhaps I just didn't know what to look for then, so perhaps I missed it, but I don't think so. Unless I totally misread them, I don't think they had any violent intentions until much later. You know, they were nothing like the FWA types – antisocial 20-year-olds with air rifles trying to act like hard men, like something out of a bad film. You could see them coming a mile away. These two were nothing like that. They were thinking men, reasonable, cultured. Caradog invited me to dinner at the house as soon as he met me, and they made no effort to hide the fact that they were intellectual nationalists. They weren't shy about their nationalism at all. But violence wasn't on their agenda then, I'm sure of that. Something changed for them later.'

'But you didn't see it coming? If anyone had sensed a change, it would have been you, surely?' Barratt suggested. 'After all, they became your friends, and Caradog became your brother-in-law. You were close to them, weren't you? You saw them every day?'

'Yes. But I swear, Mr Davis, I didn't see it coming. One day everything was normal, and we're talking about family and work and rugby and having a couple of pints, and the next day, there we are in the basement and they are talking to me about planting a bomb in Caernarfon Castle.'

'That must have come as something of a shock, then.'

'That doesn't even begin to describe it. I was completely blown away. And the worst thing was… I could see my job and my life colliding head on. I could see it as clear as day, and there was nothing I could do about it.

'On the one hand, it was the kind of opportunity undercover officers dream about. That's when the job gets really easy, when the suspects take you into their confidence and you know exactly what they're going to do, where and when, every step of the way. It doesn't get any better than that. Caradog and Dai Bach didn't know it, but their fate was sealed the moment they tried to recruit me. We were going to monitor their every move, and when the time was right we would jump. And it wasn't as though I had a choice. What they were planning was as serious as it gets. I was a police officer. I had to take action.'

He paused.

'But at the same time, I hated it. I wanted to talk them out of it, I tried to talk them out of it, I tried to reason with them, I gave them every reason to think again, to back out. I shouldn't have. I wouldn't have done that for anyone else who approached me with a proposition like that. But I couldn't help myself. I liked these men. They were friends, family, they were a big part of my life…'

There was a silence for some time.

'You were too close to them,' Barratt said.

Finch nodded. 'Not intentionally,' he replied, 'but I was too close.'

'And then there was Arianwen', Ben said.

'Yes,' Finch replied. 'Then there was Arianwen.'

76

BEN SUDDENLY BROUGHT HIS fist crashing down on the arm of his chair.

'You deceived her,' he almost shouted, pushing himself up violently out of the chair. 'You betrayed her.'

'It wasn't like that,' Finch replied quietly.

'Oh, really? How was it then?'

Finch was silent for some time.

'I love Arianwen,' he replied. 'I always have, and I always will.'

Ben's emotions, personal and professional, were in turmoil. He struggled to control himself.

'For God's sake, man. You were an undercover police officer, keeping surveillance on anyone and everyone who came into the *Tywysog*. That included Arianwen. Yet you led her on, you married her, and you fathered a child by her. But when she was arrested and tried, you were nowhere to be seen. You betrayed her completely.'

'It wasn't like that.'

'Well, what *was* it like?'

'I know how it looks,' Finch replied. 'That's why I am here now. If you will let me explain…'

'What explanation can there possibly be?' Ben interrupted.

Barratt walked across to Ben and put a hand on his shoulder.

'Let him speak, Ben,' he said.

Ben reluctantly held himself in check and made himself sit down again.

'Arianwen took me completely by surprise,' Finch said. 'I wasn't expecting her, and I wasn't ready for her. You think about a lot of things when you are planning an undercover assignment, but falling in love is not one of them. She came into the shop one afternoon, not long after I arrived in Caernarfon. And I know this is going to sound daft, but it really was love at first sight. She was in one of those Indian-style shirts with a shawl and sandals as usual, and she had that long, black hair going just the slightest bit grey around the edges, and those soft blue eyes. She looked at me, and I looked at her, and that was it. I fell in love with her, and I have loved her ever since.'

Despite his anger, Ben understood what Finch was saying all too well. He had travelled some distance down the same path himself, and he could not honestly condemn Finch for that. He thought he sensed Barratt's eyes on him. He cast around for something to say.

'But that must have been against every rule of undercover work,' he protested. 'Why didn't you tell someone in London and get yourself pulled out?'

Finch nodded.

'I know. I should have. But you have to understand, Mr Schroeder, I had no concrete reason to suspect Caradog of anything when it started. I knew early on that he and Dai Bach were nationalists, of course. As I said, they made no secret of it. They recruited me to the nationalist cause, up to a point. I went on rallies with them, and I helped with political campaigns for Plaid Cymru, but that was all legal and above board. I had no idea of the lengths they were prepared to go to, and I'm not even sure when they turned that corner. It wasn't until long after Arianwen and I were married. By then, I suppose, they thought I was safe, or at least that I was hooked in, now that I was a member of the family.'

'They were right about that,' Barratt said, 'weren't they?'

'Yes. There came a point when it was probably too late, I suppose. Even then, I could have said something. I came up with crazy ideas to extract myself from the situation. I even thought of spiriting Arianwen and Harri to London in the dead of night, removing all trace of my cover.'

'But that wouldn't have worked, would it?' Ben said. 'Not by then. You were in too deep. And you would have had to separate Arianwen from Caradog.'

'Yes,' Finch agreed. 'And by then, there was another reason. After Tryweryn, Welsh nationalism moved up the Special Branch agenda rather quickly. After four years or more of sending monthly reports to London which no one even read, hearing nothing back from them, suddenly I was the centre of attention. They made me send reports every week instead of every month, and there were constant questions, constant requests for more information. And, of course, once the date of the Investiture was announced in 1967, it all went mad. Actually, we knew the date before anyone else. The Queen had agreed to the date of 1 July 1969 three months before the public announcement. They kept it quiet until arrangements could be put in place.'

'Arrangements for what?' Barratt asked.

'For surveillance, for putting security procedures in place. Special Branch was feeling the heat from MI5 by then. Obviously, they knew they might have a serious problem. There was bound to be trouble, and those who wanted to cause trouble had a long time to plan it. MI5 wanted constant surveillance on anyone we knew of who might think about taking action.'

'So from that point on, you had to stay in place,' Barratt observed. 'You had no choice.'

'I had suddenly become indispensable. By then, I was not only supplying information to London myself; I was also coordinating information from other officers. If I had left then, I would have given the game away to Caradog and Dai Bach, and we would have lost them. Not only that, once my cover was blown, word would have spread and we would have lost every suspect we had. If I had revealed myself then, they would have gone underground and stayed there.'

He looked at Ben and Barratt in turn, holding up his hands.

'I honestly believed that they had every intention of trying to kill the Queen and the Prince of Wales, or at least do incredible damage around them. I couldn't let that happen. What was I supposed to do?'

Ben stood and walked slowly to Barratt's desk. There was a long silence.

'But after the arrest,' he said eventually, 'you could at least have tried to help Arianwen, couldn't you? You could have distanced her from Caradog and Dai Bach in some way. Instead, you just ran away and abandoned her to her fate. And now she will spend a very long time in prison and Harri will grow up in a foster-home. I am having some trouble understanding how that squares with your loving her.'

Barratt reached out a hand and touched Ben's arm.

'Before you go too far down that road, Ben,' he said, 'there is something else you need to see.'

77

BARRATT PICKED UP THE large brown envelope which had been lying on his desk, and took out a thick document, which he handed to Ben.

'This is the other thing DC Finch brought with him,' he said. 'It is a very long sworn affidavit, almost 60 pages, which covers the whole history of his deployment in Caernarfon. And I understand that DC Finch would be prepared to give evidence to the Court of Appeal.'

The mention of the Court of Appeal set Ben's heart beating faster.

'That is correct, Mr Schroeder,' Finch confirmed. 'One of the things I deal with in the affidavit is what happened on the morning of the Investiture. I had kept Special Branch informed of the plans to plant the bomb up to the minute. I had to, just in case anything happened to me.'

'So they knew exactly where to find Arianwen to arrest her?' Ben asked.

Finch exhaled heavily.

'That wasn't the way I planned it. My first plan was to intervene and make the arrests before the bomb could even be moved. That was the safest thing to do. But my superiors wouldn't listen. They wanted to catch them red-handed. So then my plan was to drive Dai Bach to Bangor myself; drive back to the square in Caernarfon; and make an excuse for going somewhere else before Caradog and Dai Bach were arrested in possession of the bomb. If I couldn't make an excuse, I would be arrested with them. That's the way I wanted to handle it, and it could have been done. But...'

'But...?'

'But at the last moment, my superiors got nervous. As soon as the protest in the square ended, they whisked me away, and told me to leave Dai Bach to his own devices. They gave me no advance warning. Change of plan. Don't argue. Just do it.'

'But that might have meant that he would call the whole thing off, or change the plan completely,' Ben said.

'Exactly, Mr Schroeder. That's what I kept telling them. I didn't think Caradog would just give up, but it meant that we then had to try to keep them under observation without knowing what they were up to. Why do that when I could have followed every move? With the stakes being so high, I thought it was madness. But they wouldn't listen to me.'

'So Dai Bach was telling the truth,' Ben said. 'He was waiting for you outside the Castle Hotel, and you didn't show up.'

'Yes. I thought he would hire a taxi. There are always taxis around in the square. I swear to you, it never occurred to me that he would involve Arianwen. I insisted from day one that they leave her completely out of it. I made it a condition of my joining them, and I was pretty clear about it, I can tell you. It never occurred to me in my wildest dreams that Dai Bach would involve her. If it had, I would have gone home and taken the car somewhere so that she couldn't have driven it.'

'You must have been beside yourself when she was arrested,' Barratt said.

'That would be an understatement,' Finch replied. 'If I had seen Dai Bach that night, I would have killed him.'

'So, what did happen to you after you were whisked away?' Barratt asked.

'I was instructed to make myself scarce with immediate effect – do not pass go, do not collect £200 – and to remain out of circulation until otherwise ordered. So far, I have not been otherwise ordered.'

Ben looked at him in astonishment.

'But the prosecution told the court that you had gone on the run. There was supposed to be intelligence that you had fled to Ireland. There was even a veiled suggestion that you had been given sanctuary by the IRA.'

Finch scoffed.

'Yes. I'd like to know what genius came up with that one. It was complete nonsense. They had a car waiting for me. I drove down to London immediately, and I have been in London ever since – keeping my head down, yes, but not in sanctuary and certainly not with the IRA. I'm amazed that anyone bought that story. How would I have had time to catch a ferry to Ireland, even from Holyhead, even if the ferries were running normally that day, which I doubt? Look, the

first thing any police officer would do would be to put an alert out
to all ports and airports. I would never have made it to Ireland – not
that day, I assure you.'

78

'AND THAT'S THE KEY to it, Ben,' Barratt said. 'Someone decided to create the fiction that Trevor Hughes was a co-conspirator who had got away. That meant that they couldn't allow him to be arrested or put on trial. That's why they had to keep him under wraps.'

'That's why they had to change course at the last moment,' Ben said, 'even at the risk of endangering the public by allowing someone to move the bomb from Bangor all the way to Caernarfon. DC Finch's plan of arresting everyone before the bomb was moved was obviously far more sensible, but they couldn't do it. They couldn't let him be arrested with the others, so they couldn't have him driving the car.'

'Exactly.'

'They misled the court, Barratt,' Ben added quietly. 'They deliberately misled the court.'

'Yes,' Barratt agreed, 'and the worst of it is, I am not sure that they could ever have allowed DC Finch to re-emerge under his real identity. If he hadn't come to us today, we might never have known.'

'They couldn't let him come back now, certainly,' Ben said. 'It would prove that the trial was conducted under false pretences.' He stopped abruptly, as another light came on in his mind.

'And that means that some of the evidence... well, the invoices for the rental of the garage and the carrying case for the bomb...'

'Fabrications,' Finch said. 'I mean, I haven't seen them. I read about them in the papers while the trial was going on. But I definitely did not keep records like that. I did rent the garage in Bangor because I had to be in control; I had to be in a position to pull the plug at any time if I needed to. It was the only safe way to do it. But that was just a monthly agreement by word of mouth. There were no documents.'

'Would you be prepared to give us a sample of your handwriting?' Ben asked.

'Not a problem,' Finch replied.

'All right,' Barratt said. 'Let's think this through. The key question, as far as Arianwen is concerned, is the question of what, if anything, she knew. Her defence would not necessarily have succeeded, even if we could have called him to give evidence at the trial. Arianwen had the bomb in her car. You could argue that the jury would have convicted in any case.'

'Yes,' Ben agreed. 'But the test the Court of Appeal has to apply is: whether they can be sure that the verdict would have been the same even with his evidence; and I don't see how they can possibly be sure of that. Let's not have that discussion now. I don't want to risk contaminating his evidence.'

He turned back to DC Finch.

'You will give evidence on Arianwen's behalf?'

'Yes. It is the least I can do. I had always planned on coming forward if she was convicted. I hoped the jury might give her the benefit of the doubt, but now that she has been convicted, I will do anything I can.'

'The Court is bound to criticise you for the way in which you handled the undercover operation,' Ben said. 'You do understand that?'

'My career as a police officer ended on the day I decided to commit myself to Arianwen,' Finch replied. 'They would never have forgiven me for that, ever. I broke a cardinal rule of undercover work. But that is water under the bridge. It doesn't matter now. All that matters is helping Arianwen.'

'How will we contact you?' Barratt asked.

'I will keep in touch. I will contact you every few days,' Finch said. 'There's a number inside that envelope in case you need it. Just don't give it to anyone else, please. I am close by in London. If you need to see me again, just ask.'

'The Court of Appeal may want to look at the convictions of Caradog and Dai Bach too,' Ben said. 'I will have to speak to Gareth.'

'I will wait to hear from you when you've spoken to Gareth,' Barratt said. 'Then I will arrange a conference with Arianwen, and we will start the ball rolling.'

'I will make sure I see him this evening,' Ben said.

79

GARETH SHOOK HIS HEAD. It was late now, after 8 o'clock. Ben had told Jess he would be late home for dinner, but not why, and he had taken a copy of DC Finch's affidavit to Gareth's room as soon as he returned from Barratt's office.

'I knew something was wrong,' Gareth said quietly, dropping the affidavit on to his desk, 'but I couldn't put my finger on what it was. I feel so bloody stupid. Now that I think about it, the story of Trevor Hughes vanishing so mysteriously into the mists of the Menai Strait...'

'Yes, I know,' Ben replied. 'I feel the same.'

'This explains everything, doesn't it?' Gareth said. 'It never made sense that Trevor Hughes would have walked out like that. Dai Bach was completely baffled. He kept telling me that Trevor was totally reliable. He and Caradog never had any reason to doubt him. By the time the trial started, they thought MI5 had probably disposed of him. It never occurred to them that Trevor was grassing them up. But all the time, he was sending every detail of what they were planning to Special Branch. The police were watching their every move. They were sitting ducks. The police could have taken them whenever and wherever they chose.'

Gareth stood and walked over to his bookcase, and opened the two doors of the base section. He extracted two heavy glasses and a bottle of a good single malt whisky.

'Bernard left this for me as a parting gift,' he smiled. 'I haven't opened it yet, but this seems an appropriate occasion.' He poured a generous glassful for both of them. 'We need to give some serious thought to how we manage things.'

'Gareth, do you think this helps your man, or Caradog?' Ben asked. 'It obviously gives Arianwen hope, but I'm not sure about them.'

'I'm not sure, either,' Gareth agreed. 'His affidavit doesn't suggest that he crossed the line on entrapment by instigating an offence which otherwise would not have been committed. He is clear that they approached him with the plan, not the other way around. But, on the other hand, we can confront the Court of Appeal with the fact that the prosecution conducted the entire trial on a false basis. We don't know what the judge, or the jury, would have made of it if Hughes – or Finch – had given evidence, do we?'

'It's difficult to argue that it would have made no difference,' Ben suggested.

'Yes. So tomorrow, I will get Donald started on the law, and you and I will draft grounds of appeal and an application to the Court of Appeal to hear Finch's evidence.'

They toasted each other with a clink of glasses.

'The other thing we will do, I think,' Gareth said, 'is to pay a visit to our good friend Evan Roberts.'

'Oh? Why?'

'Because someone should make him aware of the deception he was led to practise on the court,' Gareth replied.

'Are we assuming that he was not aware of it at the time?'

'Evan, whatever his faults, is a member of the Bar,' Gareth replied, 'as is Jamie Broderick, and so we are going to assume that neither of them would knowingly have deceived the court. Privately, we have to reckon with that possibility, but we have to observe the conventions, and at the end of the day, it may not matter.'

'How so?'

'Because even if he didn't personally mislead the court, somebody did, and that is probably enough. But it will do no harm to point out a few home truths to Evan at this point.'

'Such as?'

'Such as that his career may be in jeopardy. Ben, if the Court of Appeal so much as suspects that he was a party to this kind of deception, they are going to drop him on his head from a great height. It's only fair to warn him of what is coming. In addition to that, it may focus his mind on the attitude he should take to our appeals. It may be in his best interests, as well as ours, for him to think about not resisting us. He was leading for the Crown after all, and it's not going to be easy for him to explain what happened, is it?'

Jess hugged and kissed him. She pulled him down on to the sofa, and sat beside him.

'Ben, this is marvellous news. Does Arianwen know?'

'Not yet, but Barratt has made an appointment to see her. He will take her a copy of Finch's affidavit and the grounds of appeal.'

'She is going to take this very hard,' Jess said. 'I mean, I know the appeal is good news, but when she knows the truth about her husband...'

'Yes,' Ben agreed.

'Do you think Finch is for real? Is there any chance he will run away and leave her in the lurch again?'

'I suppose it's always a possibility. But I don't think so. He says he loves her. I don't think he would have come forward and given us the affidavit if he didn't intend to do his best for her. He's not going to come out of this looking too good, whatever happens. No, I may be wrong, but my sense is that he is with us, and with her.'

She nodded.

'Ben, I need to see her too. Perhaps not at the same time you do, but before too long.'

'Yes, of course. You need to start thinking about Harri.'

'We can't do anything formally until the appeal is resolved, of course. But if she is freed, we need to start planning what her life will look like, and how we are going to persuade the local authority, and perhaps a judge, that she is a safe pair of hands for him.'

Ben nodded. 'Yes.'

'We will need every moment,' she added, 'just to allow her time to deal with how she feels. She will have to work out where Trevor Finch fits into all this, if he fits in anywhere at all. He is Harri's father, so she can't ignore him entirely. But how does she relate to him now? She will have to work that out so that we know where he fits into Harri's future. She is going to need time just to come to terms with all that emotionally, and decide where she goes from here. I don't envy her that. And even then, getting Harri back is not a formality.'

'But surely, if her conviction is overturned...?'

'Even if the conviction is overturned – on what your average local authority social worker may see as a technicality – she is still a woman who was driving her son around late at night with a bomb in the boot of her car. That's a fact, Ben, regardless of what

Trevor Finch may have to say about it now. I'm not saying we won't get Harri back. But it's not going to be easy, and it's not going to happen overnight. She needs to know that.'

80

Friday 22 May 1970

AS FAR AS HE could recall, Ben had never before had the experience of counting off ten minutes on his watch in perfect silence, just sitting and waiting, without anything happening or anyone speaking at all. But he and Barratt had that experience now, sitting in an austere conference room in Holloway prison, facing the woman, who from now on would call herself Arianwen Finch, across the battered and stained metal folding table. A copy of DC Trevor Finch's affidavit lay on the table in front of her, untouched. When she finally spoke, Ben was not sure whether she was speaking to them, or to herself, or simply to the opposite wall.

'I suppose I should hate him,' she said quietly. 'That's what I would have expected. I would have expected to find myself running around the room, screaming and cursing him and wishing him dead. That's how any woman in my position would feel, isn't it? But I don't. I don't hate him. I can't. I don't know why, but I can't.'

She suddenly focused on them.

'Perhaps it's because I haven't heard it from him. Do you think that's the reason?'

'I don't think there is any right or wrong way to feel,' Barratt replied. 'This must have come as a terrible shock. You will need time to sort your feelings out. We understand that, and I'm sorry it had to come from us, but you had to know as soon as possible. There are steps we have to take now.'

She nodded.

'Yes. You're right. I can't think about Trevor now. I have to think about Harri. Do you really think this will make a difference?'

She paused.

'Please tell me honestly what you think. The last thing I want is to have my hopes raised, only to have them dashed again later. I've spent every moment since the verdict trying to come to terms with what has happened to me. I've been to some very dark places in my mind... they had me on suicide watch for several days. Did you know that?'

'I suggested it,' Barratt replied apologetically. 'I...'

'No, you were right,' she said. 'You were right to assume the worst. I would never have done it, not while Harri is out there waiting for me, not while there is any hope at all that I might see him again. But I am sure you were worried about me, and if it hadn't been for Harri, I might have been tempted. I can't even begin to tell you what it's been like – the hopelessness, the despair, the emptiness, the feeling that my life was over, that I would spend what was left of it here, or somewhere like here. They have had me pumped full of sedatives and God knows what else ever since the trial ended, but it hasn't kept the darkness away.'

She looked directly at each of them in turn.

'So, all I ask is that you tell me the unvarnished truth. I can take the truth, but I can't take having to confront the hopelessness again.'

Ben leaned forward in his chair. He thought for some time.

'Arianwen, there is no such thing as certainty in the law, so I would never tell any client that their case is bound to succeed. I think Barratt would agree with me there.'

'One hundred per cent,' Barratt said.

'What I will say is that you have a very good chance of having your conviction overturned. The prosecution misled the court and the jury about Trevor, particularly about his role in the case, and the reason why he wasn't present at trial. If he had been present, as a witness, we could have cross-examined him, and his evidence may well have made a difference to how the jury saw your case. That should be enough to convince the Court of Appeal, because they have to be sure that the verdict would almost certainly have been the same, even if the jury had known the truth about Trevor and even if he had given evidence. I don't think the prosecution will be able to persuade them of that.'

She nodded.

'Will I have to go through another trial?'

'No. I don't think it would be possible to re-try this case, given the false way it was presented to the jury, and the huge amount of publicity it generated. It would be difficult to find twelve people in England to sit on a jury who aren't aware of the evidence given at your trial. I think the Court would simply quash the conviction.'

'How does this affect Caradog and Dai Bach?' she asked suddenly.

'Gareth is not sure it does,' Ben replied.

'But why not? Surely, the prosecution lied to the jury in their case, just as they did in mine?'

'That's true. But it's not as clear in your case why Trevor giving evidence would have helped them. The prosecution can point to all the other evidence against them. Remember, Caradog admitted what he did, and there was a lot of evidence against Dai Bach to suggest that he built the bomb.'

'But if Trevor put them up to it...?'

'If Trevor had done that, then that might make a difference. But there is nothing in his affidavit to indicate that he crossed that line.'

'He will give evidence to the Court of Appeal,' Barratt added, 'so Gareth will have the chance to cross-examine him, and something may come out. If so, they may be in with a shout, but we are not counting on it.'

'What you need to focus on,' Ben said, 'is your case. And, by the way, Gareth agrees with us about your case.'

'That's good to know.'

'I have heard what you have said about not getting your hopes up,' Ben said, 'but if you can let yourself do it, Jess wants you to start imagining what your life would look like if your conviction is overturned and you are a free woman.'

She shook her head.

'I'm not sure...'

'Only to this extent: where would you go? How would you take care of Harri? What kind of home can you make for him? Where would the money come from, and so on? Jess thinks you need to be as clear as you can about that now, so that we don't waste any time in trying to get Harri back for you when the conviction is overturned. You will need to satisfy the local authority, or a judge, that you have a safe and stable home ready for him to come to. Don't worry for now about where Trevor fits into the picture, if he fits in at all. But she would like you to have an idea of what kind of life you could make for yourself and Harri.'

'I haven't dared to let myself think about anything like that,' she replied. 'I will try, but I can't promise. I feel too fragile to imagine too much, and I'm afraid of jinxing the appeal.'

'I understand,' Ben replied. 'Just think about the basics. Even that will help.'

'All right,' she said. 'How long will it take for the appeal to be heard?'

'We have the paperwork ready,' Ben replied. 'We will ask the Court of Appeal to expedite it, and it is a high-profile case, so I would hope they would list it within a month to six weeks, depending on how busy they are. That's all I can say for now. Barratt will let you know as soon as we hear anything.'

'Thank you,' she said. 'Thank you both, very much.'

81

'GARETH, BEN, PLEASE COME in. Have a seat. Would you like something to drink? Tea? Coffee?'

Ben nodded their thanks to the junior clerk who had shown them into Evan Roberts' room in Chambers. He and Gareth sat down in the two formidable armchairs in front of Roberts' desk. The armchairs were covered in a dark red leather. The room was formally furnished throughout, with solid dark wood bookcases, old fashioned standing lamps with long, dark grey shades, and thick rugs with only the suggestion of a red border to offset their austere grey fabric. The whole room exuded a confidence in the occupant's exalted place in the legal world.

'No, thank you, Evan.'

Evan sat back in his chair expectantly.

'To business, then. To what do I owe this unexpected pleasure?'

As always, Ben found the man's formal politeness with the merest veneer of charm thoroughly irritating, but he did his best to remain calm. He had agreed that Gareth would do most of the talking. As a Silk, he more than matched Evan Roberts in stature and experience, and that was important to what they had to say.

'Well, it's a courtesy visit really, Evan,' Gareth began. 'You will receive the papers from the Director's office in a day or two, I'm sure. But Ben and I wanted you to hear this from us without delay. We have filed appeals against conviction on behalf of Arianwen Hughes and Dafydd Prosser, together with an application that the Court of Appeal should hear some new evidence which has only just come to light.'

The trace of a smile passed over Evan's face.

'Really?'

'Yes, really. I imagine the Registrar of Criminal Appeals will invite the Court of Appeal to consider the case of Caradog Prys-Jones also. He probably won't want to recognise the Court by appealing himself, but given the importance of the issue, I think the Court will want to hear his case in any event. That remains to be seen.'

'My only concern is with Arianwen, of course,' Ben added. 'In her case, I am confident that the Court will allow the appeal and overturn her conviction.'

Evan picked up a paperweight with practised nonchalance and passed it gently from one hand to the other several times.

'Well, I must say, Ben, that shows an admirable optimism on your part, even if rather misplaced.'

'You think so?'

'I do.' He paused with the paperweight in his right hand. 'As I recall, your client was caught by the police – bang to rights, as I believe the phrase is – with a competently constructed explosive device in her car, on her way to delivering it to her brother, who would then have planted it in Caernarfon Castle, in a position where it would have caused serious injuries if detonated during the Investiture.'

The paperweight began its rhythmic exchange of hands once more.

'So, yes, I do think an appeal against conviction sounds a little optimistic. Profoundly optimistic, actually.'

'It's not a question of optimism, Evan,' Gareth said. 'I also believe that Arianwen's appeal will be allowed, her conviction will be quashed, and she will walk away from the Royal Courts of Justice a free woman as soon as the Court of Appeal has delivered its judgment. I'm not so sure about Caradog or Dai Bach, but even in their cases, I think it is possible that the same result will follow. I can't be sure of that, but I do feel confident about Arianwen's case.'

'I see,' Evan smirked. 'Well, a certain misplaced optimism is only to be expected in juniors, but I am surprised that an experienced Silk such as yourself should succumb to it, Gareth. I assume you are going to enlighten me?'

'We are,' Gareth replied. He opened his briefcase and extracted the large envelope he had brought with him. He reached out and placed the envelope in front of Evan Roberts on his desk.

'This is a long and detailed affidavit dealing with the history of this case, written and sworn to by – well, I will call him Trevor Hughes for the moment. When you have read it, I think you will agree with me about the effect his evidence is likely to have on the Court of Appeal.'

Ben saw that the mention of Trevor Hughes' name had an immediate and startling effect on Evan, which he tried, in vain, to hide. The violent movement of the head and widening of the eyes were all too obvious. He swallowed hastily, and replaced the paperweight on his desk, but made no effort to pick up the envelope.

'How do you come to be in possession of such a document?' he demanded. 'Trevor Hughes is a fugitive from justice. It can't be right for you to…'

'The first and most important point made in the affidavit,' Gareth continued, talking over Evan and giving every impression of not having heard him, 'is that the man we all referred to during the trial as Trevor Hughes is in fact Detective Constable Trevor Finch, an officer of the Metropolitan Police who had been on an undercover assignment for Special Branch in Caernarfon since 1961, and remained so until the morning of the Investiture, when his wife, her brother, and Dafydd Prosser were arrested.'

Evan Roberts suddenly collapsed backwards into his chair. The blood seemed to drain from his face.

'That's absurd…' he began weakly.

'As I'm sure you recall, the prosecution presented the case to the jury on the basis that Trevor Hughes was a co-conspirator who had somehow managed to escape the clutches of the police on that fateful morning. Dark hints were dropped that he had managed to flee to Ireland. I can quote the exact words you used in your opening speech, if you wish to be reminded of them. I made a note at the time.'

'I do not need to be reminded of what I said,' Evan protested.

'In fact, you were right about one thing. DC Finch did escape that morning; but not to Ireland, and not because he was a co-conspirator. On the orders of his superiors, he returned to London, where he was ordered to lie low until the coast was clear; by which I think they probably meant the time when the trial was over, all three defendants had been convicted, and the case was beginning to fade from public memory.'

Evan stared blankly at Gareth and Ben in turn. Gareth allowed some time to pass before continuing.

'Unfortunately for them, there were some things his superiors didn't know about DC Finch – or so I assume. They didn't know that he had fallen in love with Arianwen, married her, and had a child by her. They really didn't know the man at all. Trevor Finch broke every rule in the book, of course, by marrying Arianwen without telling his superiors. That was a terrible error of judgment on his part, and it will cost him his career. But Trevor Finch is a man of principle, and his superiors reckoned without that.'

'You see, Evan,' Ben added, 'Trevor Finch's marriage to Arianwen was not a marriage of convenience; it was not a way to get closer to her brother or to spy on the Heirs of Owain Glyndŵr. On the contrary, Finch loved Arianwen very much – he still does – and he was never going to allow her to spend the best part of her life in prison without doing whatever he could to prevent it. He is prepared to give evidence about all of it, and I think the Court of Appeal will find him very credible.'

Evan was still staring blankly. His arms had fallen down to his sides.

'I'm sure the implications of all this are obvious enough, Evan,' Gareth said, 'but just in case of doubt I will spell them out for you. Arianwen's defence was that she had no idea she had the bomb in her car. Whether or not that is true, neither you nor I, nor the jury, will ever know. But the fact of the matter is that Trevor Finch, alias Hughes, was a witness vital to Arianwen's defence, who was spirited away and falsely painted as a missing co-conspirator. She was deprived of the opportunity to put her defence fully and fairly to the jury. The court and the jury were misled. The case was presented on a wholly false basis. In fact, I think one might even go so far as to say that the conviction of Arianwen Finch was obtained by fraud.'

He paused briefly again.

'Finch also says, by the way, that the evidence of the paperwork relating to the garage, and the purported invoices for the carrying case and so on, is fabricated. He has supplied a sample of his handwriting, and we expect our expert witness to confirm his evidence once she has had a chance to look at it.'

At last, Evan seemed to breathe again, but the false bonhomie had vanished now, and his voice was barely audible.

'I knew nothing about any of this,' he said.

'I am very glad to hear that,' Gareth replied. 'But perhaps you see now why we are confident that Arianwen's appeal will be successful.

We are also confident that once the Court of Appeal has given its judgment, the career of one or more senior police officers will end abruptly in disgrace.

'What we are not sure of is whether or not the career of anyone in the office of the Director of Public Prosecutions, or the careers of one or two members of the Bar, will end in a similar way. We assume, of course, that you and Jamie Broderick, as members of the Bar, had nothing to do with the fraud, and that you knew nothing about Finch's true identity. I am very glad to have that confirmed – for the sake of the profession, as much as for your sakes.'

'If this is true, I knew nothing about it at all,' Evan said, 'and I am quite sure that the same applies to Jamie.'

'In that case,' Gareth said, 'I would like to suggest that you take certain steps, in your own interests, to make that clear to the Court of Appeal. That is why we are here this afternoon.'

'Steps? Such as…?'

'Such as telling them that you will not object to them hearing Trevor Finch's evidence, that you do not challenge that evidence and, therefore, that you cannot in good conscience resist Arianwen's appeal. I will not ask you to roll over in the other cases, Caradog and Dai Bach. I recognise that there is an argument to be made in their cases. But Arianwen's appeal is unanswerable, and I hope you would agree that it would be unconscionable to allow her to remain in prison a day longer than she has to.'

Evan stared at Gareth for a long time. Gareth returned the stare impassively, apparently in no hurry to continue. Evan made a monumental effort to recover his composure.

'Gareth,' he said at length, 'all three of these defendants were, and are, as guilty as sin. Caradog Prys-Jones masterminded the plot, Dafydd Prosser constructed the device, Arianwen drove the car, and all three of them planned to plant and detonate it during the Investiture.'

'Let's focus on Arianwen for the moment,' Gareth replied.

'She is just as guilty as her brother and Prosser.'

'Her defence was taken away from her by the fraud perpetrated on the court by the prosecution,' Ben said calmly. 'The only question remaining is: who knew that the case put forward by the prosecution was fraudulent? It may be that the truth will emerge during the appeal, regardless of what you or I do. But I need hardly point out to an advocate of your experience that the way in which the appeal is presented may have a considerable effect on that, one way or the other.'

'What do you mean?'

'I mean what I said: that the way in which I present the appeal is bound to affect the Court of Appeal's view about who knew what, and when.'

'I sincerely hope,' Evan said, pulling himself up in his chair, 'that you are not trying to threaten me in some way; because if you are…'

'Don't try to take the moral high ground, Evan,' Gareth interrupted. His voice remained calm, but there was no mistaking his intent. 'Not in this case. It's not appropriate. It is not on. Ben is absolutely right. The fact is that there are two ways in which he can open this appeal to the Court. Whichever way he chooses, the appeal is going to succeed, so there is no particular reason for preferring one over the other.

'The first way is for him to lay the blame fairly and squarely on the police, and stop there. That would be a perfectly reasonable approach. After all, on any view, the main responsibility lies with the police. Following the usual gentlemanly practice, Ben could probably persuade the Court that there is no ground for assigning blame to counsel. Barring any unexpected turn of events, that would probably be enough to insulate you and Jamie – though not necessarily those in the Director's office. I am sure the Court would be quite relieved if it could be dealt with in that way.'

Evan did not reply. Gareth looked briefly at Ben before continuing.

'The second way to open the case,' he said, 'is to imply that the police could not have perpetrated such a fraud on their own. There are too many unanswered questions. How, the Court may wonder, could counsel have been blissfully ignorant of who DC Trevor Finch was and what role he played in the case? The Court will know that we have no way of proving how high, or how far, the deception went. For Ben's purposes, that does not matter. The Court is bound to allow the appeal. But once the seed of deception at the highest level is planted in their minds, they will have no alternative but to order a full inquiry… and once that happens… well, all bets are off, aren't they?'

Evan was silent for some time.

'If the prosecution does not resist my appeal,' Ben said, 'I have no incentive to say any more than is strictly necessary. I can't guarantee that the Court may not decide to probe further, of course, but I can give the impression that I see no need for it to do so.'

'This is blackmail,' Evan said.

'It's nothing like blackmail,' Ben replied. 'I keep forgetting that crime is not really your field, so I will not make a point of arguing with you about the law. I am perfectly content with my own moral position. The question is whether you are content with yours.'

'We are here as a matter of courtesy to you,' Gareth added, 'and to ask for justice for Arianwen, of course. We are simply suggesting that justice for her is in your interests as well as hers.'

There was a long silence.

'Do you actually think that I would have been party to misleading the court?' Evan asked. His voice shook with emotion.

'Speaking for myself, I take members of the Bar at their word,' Gareth replied. 'But what I or Ben may think is of no consequence. Once word of this fraud is breathed in open court, and comes within earshot of the press, it will no longer be a question of professional courtesy. This case will become a national scandal, and the public will demand that those responsible be held to account. At that point, it will no longer be within Ben's power, or mine, or even that of the Court of Appeal, to control it.'

He stood, and Ben followed his lead.

'I suggest that you read DC Finch's affidavit,' he said, 'and then ask yourself: what is the right thing to do, in the interests of justice? That's all I'm asking, Evan. Just ask yourself that one question. Even better, suggest to the Director of Public Prosecutions that he invite someone else to ask it – someone who has not been involved in the case before.'

They turned and walked without undue haste towards the door.

'Don't get up,' Gareth said. 'We will see ourselves out.'

82

THEY HAD BROUGHT ARIANWEN into the Royal Courts of Justice with no fanfare, through a side entrance some distance from the imposing arched main door by which the public entered. She was waiting for them in a small conference room adjacent to the court in which her appeal against conviction was to be heard. Although a serving prisoner, she was escorted, with a noticeable lack of concern for security, by a single female prison officer who seemed very relaxed and was sitting unobtrusively beside her. Arianwen had a white handkerchief clenched tightly in her right hand. Her face was even whiter than her normally pale complexion; the lines below her red eyes betrayed her anxiety and lack of rest all too clearly. She stood to greet her visitors. As Ben and Barratt took her hand in turn, they felt it shake. But she smiled and gave each a kiss on the cheek.

'When you came to see me at Holloway, you said it would be a good sign if they let me come to the hearing,' she said, searching their faces for the slightest hint of any good news, any cause, however tenuous, for hope.

'It *is* a good sign, Arianwen,' Ben replied, 'but as I said before, there are no guarantees. Everything depends on what happens today. We can assume that they have read Trevor's affidavit and they think you have a seriously arguable ground of appeal. That in itself is good. But they will probably want to hear from him and have him cross-examined by the prosecution, and we can't be absolutely sure what effect that will have on them.'

She had quietly resumed her seat next to the prison officer.

'So Trevor is here then?'

'Yes. He is waiting in the witness room.'

She nodded and closed her eyes for some moments.

'I don't know what effect it will have on me when I see him,' she said. 'I only hope I can cope… that it doesn't throw me off balance too much…'

Ben took her hand again.

'It's going to be important that you keep calm,' he said. 'I'm not asking you not to react at all. That would be impossible, and the Court will understand that. In fact they would probably think it was a bit odd if you didn't show some reaction when he comes into court. The important thing is not to suggest to the Court that you are trying to contact him or get his attention. The last thing we want is for you to look as though you are playing on his emotions, trying to encourage him, or anything like that. You don't need to look away altogether. You should appear interested in his evidence. But don't give the impression of cheering him on.'

She nodded. 'I understand. It's just that… you know, after you told me the truth about Trevor and brought me his affidavit, I felt…'

'I understand,' Ben said.

'I felt betrayed, so completely and utterly betrayed and abandoned. It took me days of reading his affidavit, time after time after time, even to begin to comprehend the scale of what he had done to me, and to Harri. Even now, there are days when I just can't believe it. I can't believe that I could have allowed myself to be deceived so completely.' She shook her head silently for some time. 'Ben, how could this have happened to me?'

'For what it's worth, Arianwen,' Ben replied, 'I don't think Trevor set out to deceive you. It was something that just happened. He wasn't expecting to fall in love with you.'

'That doesn't excuse what he did,' she insisted, her voice breaking.

'No, of course not,' Ben agreed. 'But you have to forget about that for the moment. What matters today is that Trevor is here, and he is here to do whatever he can to help you. It's not about making excuses for him. It's about accepting the help you have every right to expect. You must remember that, Arianwen. Let's get today over with. You will have plenty of time to think about the past later.'

She looked up at him.

'I will be fine,' she replied, her voice suddenly stronger.

'I know you will,' Ben said. 'You won't be waiting very long. We are first in the list at 10.30. They will be calling you into court in a few minutes. Eifion is here, of course.'

'Good. Is Caradog here?'

'No,' Ben replied. 'They haven't brought him, or Dai Bach. Even if they tried, I would bet good money that Caradog would refuse to leave his cell to come to court.'

'It's still an English court,' Barratt smiled.

She returned the smile wistfully, turning her head to the side.

'He always was a silly boy,' she said quietly. 'Always. From a little mite, my grandmother used to say.'

They met Evan Roberts outside Court 4. Barratt glanced at Ben, and saw him take a deep breath.

'Good morning, Evan. I hope you're well.'

'Perfectly well, thank you, Ben.'

Ben looked at Evan closely. His face was inscrutable; the usual thin smile was missing. He was giving nothing away, but Ben detected a hardness in the face he had not seen before.

'We have DC Finch here,' Ben said, as lightly as he could. 'Do I need to call him, as far as you're concerned?'

'It's a matter for you how you conduct the appeal,' Evan replied coldly. 'If the Court allows you to call Finch, we shall have some questions for him which he may prefer not to answer.'

Ben turned to look at Barratt before replying.

'Do I take it that you will be objecting to his evidence? I have to say, I find that rather surprising.'

'I will be resisting the appeal and objecting to Finch's evidence,' Evan replied. 'These three appellants are guilty of the offence charged, and they were rightly convicted. Your client is no less guilty than the other two, and in a case of such gravity, there can be no question of allowing her conviction to be overturned. Frankly, I will be astonished if the Court does not agree with me. But however that may be, I will present the Crown's side of the case.'

Ben stared at Evan for some moments.

'Come on, Barratt,' he said. 'Let's go into court and get ready.' They walked briskly through the huge wooden doors.

'We don't seem to have made much impression on him, do we?' Barratt commented as they took their seats.

'Apparently not,' Ben agreed, quickly removing the pink ribbon which bound together the papers in his brief.

'Did you think you might have changed his mind?' Barratt asked.

'I thought we might have. But you never know when you put someone in the position we put Evan in. Sometimes they cave in. But sometimes they see no way out except to fight tooth and claw for their lives. You don't know until the decision is made. It seems Evan has chosen to fight.'

'So, what now?' Barratt asked.

'The gloves come off,' Ben replied. 'If he wants a fight, we will give him a fight.'

83

'MAY IT PLEASE YOUR Lordships,' Ben began, 'with the agreement of my learned friend Mr Morgan-Davies, I will address your Lordships first. All the counsel who appear before your Lordships today also appeared at the trial. I represent the woman who will be known in this appeal as Arianwen Finch.'

The three judges of the Court of Appeal sitting in Court 4 at the Royal Courts of Justice, the Lord Chief Justice's court, had found it packed to the gunnels, the atmosphere highly charged. The Lord Chief Justice, Lord Parker, took his seat in the centre of the bench, flanked by Lord Justice Carver to his right and Mr Justice Melrose to his left. They looked down impassively on the unusually large throng before them. In addition to those involved in the case, a good number of barristers who happened to be free before appearances in other courts, and who had learned of potentially sensational revelations, had attended court early to make sure of a seat. Reporters representing the national and international press had spilled over from the seating usually reserved for journalists and, with no discouragement from the court staff, found space wherever they could, notebooks and pencils poised for action.

In addition, there were as many members of the public as space would allow, many of whom had made the journey from Wales. A number of police officers and court security officers had taken their places among them in the hope of heading off any trouble that might develop; though they had all been carefully searched before being allowed into court, and their general mood seemed calm and optimistic, not at all threatening. Arianwen and her escort had taken their places discreetly at the back of the courtroom, visible to the judges but screened from the public by a curtain.

The last, and only, time Ben had appeared in Court 4, he had lost the appeal of Billy Cottage, a client who was later hanged for a brutal murder. Even more eerily, the three judges of the Court of

Criminal Appeal on that occasion had been the same three judges
who now sat in judgment on Arianwen. The Court had changed its
name since then – it was now the Criminal Division of the Court
of Appeal – but it was still an intimidating tribunal. Cottage had
been Ben's first experience of appellate argument, and even though
everyone had assured him that he could not possibly have done
any more for his client, the memory of listening to the adverse
judgment, with the terrible consequence that soon followed, was
one that still haunted his dreams from time to time. Today, he
hoped, both Court 4 and the three judges sitting on high would
bring him better fortune.

'I thought, Mr Schroeder,' Lord Parker said, 'that your client was
indicted under the name of Arianwen Hughes?'

'Your Lordship is quite right,' Ben replied. 'That is one of many
unfortunate aspects of this case. At the time of the trial she believed,
as she had ever since her marriage, that she was Arianwen Hughes.
She is, in fact, Arianwen Finch, and that is important to her appeal.
With your Lordship's leave, I will refer to her by her correct married
name.'

'Yes, very well,' Lord Parker said.

'I am obliged. My learned friends Mr Morgan-Davies and Mr
Weston appear on behalf of Dafydd Prosser. My learned friends
Mr Roberts and Mr Broderick appear on behalf of the Crown. My
learned friend Mr Morgan-Davies has also been assigned by the
Registrar of Criminal Appeals to address your Lordships on behalf
of Caradog Prys-Jones. Mr Prys-Jones did not take any steps himself
to appeal against his conviction or sentence. He is an appellant today
only because the Registrar found that his case raises important issues
which he has invited your Lordships to consider.'

'I understand that he would have preferred to be tried in a Welsh
court, and in the Welsh language,' Mr Justice Melrose said, with a
smile.

'His appeal will receive the fullest and fairest consideration from
this English Court, Mr Schroeder,' Lord Parker said, joining in the
smile. 'But the proceedings will be conducted in English.'

'I am relieved to hear that, My Lord,' Ben said. 'My learned friend
Mr Morgan-Davies could address the Court in either language, but
I'm afraid I am restricted to English. This may be a good moment
to mention that we do have a Welsh interpreter in court – PC Hywel
Watkins who performed the same role at the trial, in case any

question arises about any materials or evidence of conversations in Welsh.'

'Yes, thank you,' the Lord Chief Justice said.

'My Lords, before I present the substance of the appeal on behalf of Mrs Finch, I have an application. I first invite your Lordships to rule that my learned friends Mr Roberts and Mr Broderick should play no part in this appeal as advocates. One or both of them may be witnesses to certain facts on which the appellants rely, and of course, it would not be proper for them to act professionally if their evidence is required.'

Evan Roberts jumped indignantly to his feet.

'My Lords, this is an outrage. We have been given no notice of any such application, and your Lordships have not even decided to hear any further evidence. We strenuously oppose the further evidence as being irrelevant and designed solely to deflect the Court from the facts of the case.'

Deliberately, Ben turned to smile at him.

'If my learned friend would allow me to finish,' he said, 'I will explain to your Lordships why the application I make is essential to the proper hearing of the appeal.'

Lord Parker conferred briefly with Lord Justice Carver and Mr Justice Melrose.

'We will hear your application, Mr Schroeder,' he said.

84

'I AM MUCH OBLIGED. My Lords, may I ask whether your Lordships have had the opportunity to read the affidavit of Detective Constable Trevor Finch, which was submitted with the application to adduce his evidence?'

All three judges nodded.

'We have,' the Lord Chief Justice confirmed.

'I am obliged. In that case, I will not take up too much of your Lordships' time with background matters. The essence of Arianwen Finch's appeal is that the prosecution's case at trial was put before the jury on a wholly false basis. The prosecution insisted from first to last that Trevor Hughes – the name DC Finch was using during his undercover assignment – was also a guilty party. They told the jury that he was a party to the conspiracy who had evaded arrest and remained a fugitive from justice at the time of trial. That was untrue.

'It follows that certain individuals on the prosecution side – and your Lordships will understand that I choose my words with the utmost care – must have known that it was untrue. That, I am afraid, is an unavoidable reality. These individuals knew that DC Finch had been working undercover, and that arrangements had been made on the morning of the arrests for him to escape the police net and return to London, where he was to remain in hiding. The involvement of DC Finch was relevant to the case as a whole, but it was obviously crucial to Arianwen Finch's defence.'

Ben paused deliberately as the three judges exchanged glances.

'Mr Schroeder,' Lord Parker asked, 'do you suggest that Mr Roberts or Mr Broderick knew that the man calling himself Trevor Hughes was in fact DC Finch? I must say, that would be an exceptionally grave allegation to make against any member of the Bar, and it would require the clearest possible proof before this Court would entertain it.'

Ben felt every eye in the courtroom on him.

'My Lords, I do not suggest that. My learned friend Mr Roberts assured me personally some time ago that he and Mr Broderick had no knowledge of the deception. That, of course, is exactly what I would have expected, and I accept his word for it without hesitation.'

Lord Parker nodded.

'On the other hand, I cannot say what conclusions your Lordships may be compelled to draw from the evidence, and I would be failing in my duty to Mrs Finch if I did not invite your Lordships to consider every possibility. The fact is that my learned friend Mr Roberts chose to present the case to the jury in the way I have indicated, and the Court may feel that it cannot avoid inquiring into why he did so.'

Evan was on his feet again immediately.

'This is outrageous,' he said. 'My learned friend must consider the possible consequences of what he is saying.'

'I have considered them,' Ben replied. 'It might have been better if my learned friend had done the same at the beginning of the trial.'

'I will not be spoken to in this way…'

'Counsel will kindly address the Court, not each other,' Lord Parker intervened quietly. 'You will have your opportunity, Mr Roberts.'

'Yes, my Lord,' Ben said. 'I am not asking your Lordships to assume anything at this stage. Even if there has been no misconduct on their part, my learned friends may have evidence to give about who knew about this fraud, and who perpetrated it on the trial court. It may be evidence they do not even realise they can give, some detail it has never occurred to them to mention until now.

'The prosecution must be represented by counsel who has not been involved in the case before, and so cannot be a witness. That is the only course which would be fair to the prosecution itself. It would be desirable, for obvious reasons, that new counsel should be instructed and in place before the appeal proceeds any further.'

Lord Parker turned towards Gareth Morgan-Davies.

'Mr Morgan-Davies, what do you say about this?'

Gareth climbed deliberately slowly to his feet, exchanging a look with Ben.

'My Lord, I must confess that I am taken somewhat by surprise. My learned friend had not indicated to me that he would be making such an application. But as I have listened to the reasons he has put forward, I am bound to say that I find them persuasive, and I would join in the application on behalf of Dafydd Prosser.'

Lord Parker turned back to Evan Roberts.

'My Lords, the application is outrageous,' he spluttered. As Ben had calculated, the calm veneer had vanished. Evan was close to the edge. 'It's all very well for my learned friend to disclaim any intention of accusing me, but the application itself is an accusation.'

'I don't think that's true at all, Mr Roberts,' Mr Justice Melrose replied. 'You have read DC Finch's affidavit, as we have. If he is telling the truth, some police officer must have known. It stands to reason. But it doesn't follow that you would have known. Indeed, you might be the last person they would tell. They might very well have foreseen that, if any hint of Finch's true involvement reached you or Mr Broderick, you would be bound to come forward and say so immediately; in which case the game would be up.'

'I agree,' Lord Justice Carver added. 'If there was a plan to mislead the trial court, its success may well have depended on them keeping it from you.'

'Be that as it may, my Lords,' Evan insisted. 'If my learned friend Mr Broderick and I were to be removed from the case, it is bound to reflect badly, not only on us, but on the prosecution, and it would deprive the prosecution of the advantage of having counsel in this appeal who were present throughout the trial.'

Lord Parker nodded. He gestured to his colleagues. Lord Justice Carver leaned in towards him. Mr Justice Melrose left his seat and stood between them so that they could confer in a series of whispers without being heard. After what seemed a considerable time, they resumed their positions.

'We have decided to grant the application in part,' Lord Parker said. 'We think it is important that Mr Roberts and Mr Broderick should continue to act for the Crown, having done so at the trial. We also think it unlikely that we would call on either of them to give evidence in the appeal. But we cannot exclude that possibility.'

He paused.

'We must ensure that our decision is not only correct, but is seen by the public to be correct, that it is seen to be one in which they can have full confidence. For that reason, we conclude that the Court should also have input from prosecuting counsel who has not been involved in the case previously, only – and I stress this – only so that we can satisfy ourselves that we have not overlooked anything that may be important.'

Evan slammed his pen down on the desk. Lord Parker ignored him.

'Accordingly, we will adjourn this appeal until 10.30 tomorrow morning, and we will direct the prosecution to have new counsel available to assist the Court, with Mr Roberts and Mr Broderick, at that time.'

Evan Roberts stormed imperiously out of court as soon as the judges had risen, leaving his junior to gather up his papers.

'You weren't joking about taking the gloves off, Ben, were you?' Barratt smiled as they stood to leave court.

'I'm just warming up,' Ben replied.

85

ANDREW PILKINGTON HAD THEATRE tickets for the evening. He was all set to see an acclaimed new production of *Lear* in the West End. Not only that, he was taking a young woman he was very anxious to get to know better, and there were tentative plans for a light supper after the show. Consequently, when John Caswell, a senior member of the staff of the Director of Public Prosecutions, made an unscheduled appearance in Treasury Counsel's room at the Old Bailey to tell him that the Director needed him urgently, he was very far from pleased. But when he was told what the assignment was, he was intrigued and, despite his irritation, agreed to start work without delay. A series of clerks carried a vast array of documents into his room in brown cardboard boxes, and left them behind his desk. He phoned his clerk and asked him to send a note of apology, and twelve red roses, to the young lady he was obliged to stand up; and to send the junior clerk to bring him some sandwiches. He started work at 5.30.

Andrew was now one of the more senior Prosecuting Counsel to the Crown at the Old Bailey. He was trying to prepare a drug importation case, but now he had to read up, on short notice and with very little time, on the case of Caradog Prys-Jones and others. Like almost everyone in the country, Andrew had followed the trial in the press, but he had never seen the evidence for himself. Now, he not only had to see it; he had to become thoroughly familiar with it overnight. In addition to being a first-rate lawyer and a highly competent courtroom advocate, Andrew was an intuitive prosecutor. He could often read as much between the lines of a witness statement as he read in the lines. His reading of this case disturbed him. He was barely ten pages into Trevor Finch's affidavit when he concluded that Finch was undoubtedly telling the truth. Before reading any further he sat back and thought about what that meant. He then set about reading the remainder of the affidavit, several volumes of witness statements and exhibits, and some transcripts of evidence from the trial, including the evidence of Arianwen Finch. At 2.30, he took off his shoes, and his collar, set his alarm clock for 6.30, and stretched out on his sofa, where he turned the case over in his mind until he fell asleep.

The question in Andrew's mind was: what had gone on after Finch had reported back to Special Branch on the activities of Caradog Prys-Jones and Dafydd Prosser? Plans had, of course, been made for the arrests on the morning of 1 July, and it was understandable that some arrangement had been put in place so that Finch was not caught up in the net. But to Andrew's mind, it then became obvious that the prosecution had to take a decision – a decision which was by no means easy, but was one which had to be made. The police had a legitimate interest in protecting the identity of an informant, but not where withholding his identity would prevent a defendant from receiving a fair trial. That presented a stark but unavoidable choice: either disclose his identity, or drop the case. The one option not open to the prosecution was to hide the truth from the defence, and paint Trevor Hughes as a conspirator who had somehow managed to escape the clutches of the law. But that was what had happened.

As two members of the Court of Appeal had pointed out, that was very far from implicating counsel in any wrongdoing. Indeed, leaving counsel in ignorance might have been the only way to ensure that Finch remained the police's secret. But Andrew, putting himself in the position of prosecuting counsel at trial, was certain that he would have asked some hard questions before committing himself to that version of events. He was also as certain as he could be that Evan Roberts and Jamie Broderick had not asked those questions. Even with the advantage of hindsight, Andrew could not understand why. They were, it seemed to him, questions that must have been obvious even to the most inexperienced advocate. It all left him with a very sour taste in his mouth.

When he awoke at 6.30, he called John Caswell at home, to request that the conduct of the appeals should be taken out of the hands of Evan Roberts and put in his own. That decision, Caswell explained, was one which only the Director could take. In that case, Andrew insisted, the Director must be informed immediately. Caswell reluctantly woke the Director and, within an hour, Andrew had the authority he wanted.

The Director had also asked Evan Roberts and Jamie Broderick to make themselves available in the Crypt Café in the basement of the Royal Courts of Justice at 9 o'clock, in case Andrew had questions. At 8.30, when he gulped down a final cup of black coffee before making his way to court along Fleet Street and the Strand, Andrew had a lot of questions, but he had not decided how many of them he would put to Roberts or Broderick. When he arrived, feeling tired and uneasy, at the Crypt Café, Evan Roberts was very uncommunicative. He seemed unwilling even to accept that Andrew was now on board as one of the prosecution's counsel, much less that the Director had given Andrew the final say in how the appeal should be conducted. Jamie Broderick, seemingly out of his depth now, said not a single word. To Andrew's frustration, Evan seemed unable or unwilling to take the Court of Appeal's concerns seriously. He began to wonder whether Evan had lost the plot or, for that matter, whether he had ever understood the plot. It was a frosty and unproductive meeting, and eventually Andrew abandoned the attempt and made his way to court.

Outside Court 4, he saw Ben Schroeder and took him aside. They talked quietly for several minutes.

86

'MY LORDS,' BEN BEGAN, 'I now proceed to my application to call the evidence of Detective Constable Finch and other evidence, including the evidence of a handwriting expert, whose opinion, I am told, is not disputed. My Lords, in May of this year, all three appellants were convicted by a jury at the Central Criminal Court of a conspiracy to cause explosions at Caernarfon Castle, on the occasion of the Investiture of His Royal Highness Prince Charles as Prince of Wales. The Investiture took place on 1 July last year.'

As he began to open the facts to the Court, Ben turned slightly to his left and nodded to Andrew Pilkington, who was sitting behind Evan Roberts. It was a huge relief to know that Andrew was now in charge of the prosecution's case. Ben and Andrew knew each other well. Andrew had prosecuted in Ben's first serious trial, a rape case at the Old Bailey. He had also prosecuted Billy Cottage, and argued successfully to uphold Cottage's conviction in this very courtroom almost six years earlier. But he and Ben liked and trusted each other, and Ben felt a new surge of energy as he threw himself into his argument. The Court seemed receptive, and he decided not to be too long in his remarks.

'My Lords,' he concluded, 'your Lordships cannot answer the questions raised by these appeals without the evidence of Detective Constable Finch. The Crown is not prepared to admit the facts stated by the officer, and so there is no way for the appellant to present that evidence except to call him as a witness. He is present, and ready to give evidence when called.'

Ben resumed his seat. Evan Roberts stood.

'My Lords, may I first say that the prosecution has no objection to the evidence of the handwriting expert, and as my learned friend has said, her opinion is not disputed. The prosecution accepts that the various handwritten passages and signatures she refers to are not in the handwriting of DC Finch.'

'I am much obliged,' Gareth interjected, only half rising to his feet.

'Yes, very well,' Lord Parker said.

'But, my Lords, I submit that there is no basis for admitting the evidence of DC Finch. In the first place, insofar as Finch was acting as an informant, the prosecution was entitled to withhold, not only his identity, but any details of his activities as such. That has been the law at least since the last century, when it was confirmed by the case of *Marks v Beyfus*.'

Out of the corner of his eye, Ben saw Andrew look down and shake his head.

'But that is not an absolute principle, surely,' Lord Parker protested. 'The point of that very case was that it has to give way to the interests of justice, if the evidence is necessary to establish the defendant's innocence.'

'It was not necessary for that purpose in this case,' Evan replied. 'These appellants were caught red-handed in circumstances which clearly suggested their willing involvement in the conspiracy. Even if you leave Trevor Hughes out of it altogether, the evidence against them was overwhelming.'

'But you didn't leave Hughes out of it, did you?' Lord Justice Carver interrupted. 'If you had, that would have been one thing. But you didn't. You painted a picture of Hughes as being just as guilty as the appellants. You made him part of the prosecution's case. I am having some difficulty in seeing how the prosecution could have done that without being frank with the jury about who he was, and what he was doing.'

'It's not as though there was any threat to his safety,' Mr Justice Melrose added. 'That's one reason for the identity rule, isn't it? That doesn't seem to me to apply to this case in any real way.'

'Those are my submissions, my Lords,' Evan replied, resuming his seat abruptly. Ben saw Andrew lean forward and tug urgently on Evan's gown. Evan shook his head without turning round.

Lord Parker glanced at Ben.

'The only thing I would seek to emphasise, my Lords,' Ben said, 'is that the evidence was obviously crucial to Mrs Finch's defence. The jury had to hear what he knew about any involvement, or lack of involvement, on her part. It went directly to her state of mind

– what she knew or believed about what she had in the car. For the prosecution to withhold Finch, to deny her the opportunity to question him about it, cannot have been right. I am not seeking to prove what she knew in this appeal, because in my submission, I am not required to do so. I am simply seeking to show why it was wrong to allow the trial of Arianwen Finch to proceed without the jury knowing the truth about Trevor Finch.'

The judges conferred briefly, Lord Justice Carver leaning over towards the Lord Chief Justice, and Mr Justice Melrose standing behind and in between them.

'The Court will hear the evidence of Detective Constable Finch,' Lord Parker said. 'We are persuaded that it is necessary for a fair hearing of the appeal – particularly in the case of Mrs Hughes, or Finch, but also in the case of the two other appellants.'

87

'I SWEAR BY ALMIGHTY God that the evidence I shall give shall be the truth, the whole truth and nothing but the truth. My Lords, I am Detective Constable Trevor Finch of the Metropolitan Police, currently attached to Special Branch.'

Trevor Finch handed the New Testament back to the usher and folded his arms behind his back. He was smartly dressed in a restrained blue suit and tie. If he was nervous, he gave no sign of it. In demeanour, he might have been giving evidence about a routine traffic stop at his local magistrates' court.

At the back of the court, Arianwen suddenly realised that she had been holding her breath ever since he had come into view on the opposite side of the courtroom, making his way to the witness box. She released her breath in one sudden, violent exhalation which was audible throughout the courtroom, and which caused all three judges to look briefly in her direction. The prison officer put a glass of water into her hands, and she drank gratefully. She knew that she was unprepared to see Trevor again after all that had happened, but the jumble of memories and emotions that flooded her left her confused. She had expected to feel something straightforward – hatred, loathing, even contempt – which would have concentrated her mind and enabled her to channel all her energy into silently sending in his direction the rejection he deserved. But to her surprise, while the sight of him made her angry – angry enough to hit him if she had been close enough – she also felt the remains, feeble but still real, of her feelings for him as her lover, her husband, and the father of her child. To her dismay, there was to be no clean, convenient, pathway for her feelings. This man had done such violence to her life, but still she could not hate him. She had been trying to hate him ever since she had learned the truth about him, but she was not capable of it. Nor could she simply erase him from her emotional memory. She stared at him helplessly.

'Detective Constable Finch,' Ben was saying, 'Do you have a copy of your affidavit with you?'

'Yes, sir.' Finch had carried the affidavit with him into the witness box. He now laid it out in front of him.

'Are the contents of that affidavit true, or when you state an opinion, true to the best of your knowledge, information and belief?'

'Yes, sir.'

'Thank you. Officer, the Court has read your affidavit, and so I am not going to take up time unnecessarily by taking you through it in detail. But there are a few matters I want to ask you about. After that, my learned friends may have some questions.'

'Yes, sir.'

'You joined the Metropolitan Police in 1954, and became a Detective Constable in 1959, is that right?'

'It is, sir.'

'At that time, you were attached to Holborn Police Station, carrying out inquiries as a member of the CID?'

'That is correct.'

'But in 1961, you were asked to undertake an assignment for Special Branch, is that right?'

'Yes, sir.'

'For what period?'

'The period was not specified. It would depend on events. As long as I was needed in the role, I would remain attached to Special Branch.'

'The role being an undercover assignment in Wales?'

'Yes.'

'And taking it briefly, was this assignment the result of certain concerns Special Branch had about the rise of more militant forms of nationalism in Wales?'

'Yes, sir, it was.'

'Please tell their Lordships what your qualifications were for such a role?'

Finch turned towards the judges.

'My parentage is Welsh, my Lords, and I speak Welsh, though in all honesty, having lived in London for many years, my Welsh today is mainly due to what I learned in Caernarfon from Arianwen. Before that, it was only just about adequate.'

'Arianwen being your wife, one of the appellants in this appeal?'

'Yes, sir.'

Arianwen saw Trevor's eyes turn to her and, to her amazement, felt herself returning something approaching a smile.

'In addition to that, sir, the fact that I had lived most of my life in London and had little background in Wales, made it easier for them to give me a legend that would work.'

'A legend being a fictitious identity and personal history, to be used for the purposes of your assignment?'

'Exactly, sir. It has to be very detailed, because you have to anticipate that someone may inquire into it if you attract suspicion while on assignment, and it's a lot easier if the legend takes the inquirer into places farther from home, where inquiries may be more difficult for him.'

'And as a result, in October 1961, you were provided with a position as the manager, and apparent owner of the – you must forgive me if I mangle the pronunciation, as I am told I usually do – the *Tywysog* book shop in Palace Street in Caernarfon?'

Finch laughed. 'Your pronunciation is very good, sir, and yes, that is correct.'

'Where in due course, you met Caradog Prys-Jones, his sister Arianwen, and Dafydd Prosser, known to his friends as Dai Bach?'

'Yes, sir.'

'What name did you use for the purposes of your assignment?'

'Trevor Hughes.'

Ben paused and turned over some pages in his notebook.

'I'm going to jump forward in time. Did there come a time in April 1963, when you married Arianwen Prys-Jones?'

Arianwen saw his eyes flash in her direction again.

'I did, sir.'

'And, so that there is no doubt in their Lordships' minds about the lawfulness of that marriage, were both of you free to marry?'

'Yes, sir.'

'Where did the marriage take place?'

'At the Register Office in Caernarfon.'

'Was it celebrated with all due formalities, witnesses, and so on?'

'Yes, sir.'

'Are you and Arianwen still husband and wife?'

'Yes, sir.'

'In May 1965, did Arianwen give birth to a child?'

'Our son, Harri, yes.'

'And – forgive me, I don't mean to be crass, but it is important to be precise – are you Harri's father?'

'Yes, sir. I am.'

88

BEN PAUSED AGAIN.

'Officer, I am sure this will not be an easy question for you to answer, but there is no way of avoiding it. Getting married while working undercover, to a woman who was a potential subject of your surveillance, is not something your superiors would have approved of, is it?'

'It was against the rules,' Finch replied immediately, 'completely against the rules, and I knew that at the time.'

'Did you tell your superiors what you were doing at the time?'

'No, sir.'

'When, if ever, did you tell them?'

'Not until after the police had interrupted Caradog's plot to plant the bomb at the Castle on the day of the Investiture, and Caradog, Dai Bach and Arianwen had been arrested. I returned to London that day, and over the course of the next few days I was debriefed about the events leading up to the Investiture.'

Ben looked up at the judges.

'My Lords, subject to your Lordships' approval, my learned friends and I have all agreed that no names of DC Finch's superiors shall be mentioned in open court. There may in due course be other proceedings, including disciplinary proceedings, and we are agreed at the Bar that there should be no risk of prejudice to the officers concerned because of any premature publication of their names. The names are given in DC Finch's affidavit.'

Lord Parker looked to both sides, and saw both Lord Justice Carver and Mr Justice Melrose nod.

'Yes, very well, Mr Schroeder.'

'I am much obliged. Your Lordships should have before you a schedule of officers who may be referred to, each of whom is assigned a letter of the alphabet. Your Lordships will see references in particular to four senior police officers, referred to as officers A, B, C and D.

There are also references to two other persons, who are not police officers, but who work for another governmental body concerned with the prosecution process, who are assigned the letters E and F.'

Lord Parker nodded. 'Yes.'

'Officer,' Ben continued, 'you will also find a copy of that schedule in front of you. Using the letters provided in the schedule, would you tell their Lordships which officers conducted your debriefing?'

'Officers A and B,' Finch replied, without hesitation.

'Did you tell Officers A and B about your marriage to Arianwen?'

'Yes, sir.'

'Did you tell anyone else?'

'No, sir.'

'Do you have any reason to believe that anyone else knew about your marriage at that time?'

Finch thought for some time.

'I really can't say. There was nothing stopping anyone from finding out. There was no secret about it. Arianwen and I were living together openly in Caernarfon. We had a child. We were well known in the community. If anyone had come to check up on me, they would have found out immediately. I assume that nobody ever did because, if anyone had checked up, I would have heard about it, but I really don't know.'

'But as a result of the debriefing? Based on what you know of the command structure, would it be likely that other officers would have known?'

Evan Roberts stood.

'I must object to that, my Lords. The witness cannot be asked to speculate about what other officers may have known.'

'I will re-phrase the question,' Ben volunteered, seeing the Lord Chief Justice nodding. 'I ask because in your affidavit, you referred to the possibility of Officers C and D being made aware of your marriage. What did you base that on?'

'Officers C and D were in the chain of command with respect to my assignment, because I directed my reports to them, and they passed them up to Officers A and B. So it would be strange if they were not made aware of the results of my debriefing. But I can't say any more than that. Obviously, I haven't seen any of the paperwork.'

'Have you ever spoken to the individuals referred to in the schedule as E and F?'

'No, sir.'

'Do you know either of them, or anything about them?'

'No, sir. But I know that Officers A and B reported to them or they were supposed to, anyway.'

'How do you know that?'

'They told me.'

Ben paused.

'What was the reaction of Officers A and B to your revelation about your marriage?'

Finch laughed. 'I think it's fair to say that they were not very impressed.'

'What did they say, exactly?'

'They made it clear that my conduct was unacceptable, and that my career as a police officer was over, certainly as far as the Met was concerned, once the trial came to an end. It was a fair enough comment. It was no more than I deserved.'

89

'DID OFFICERS A AND B give you any instructions at the time of your debriefing?' Ben asked.

'Yes, sir. When the debriefing ended, I was told that, until further notice, my undercover assignment was to continue. I was to remain available if needed, but apart from that I was to find a place to live in London and keep my head down until otherwise ordered. I would continue to receive my salary until my assignment was terminated.'

'What do you mean by keeping your head down?'

'I was to go to a part of London where I was not known, avoid contact with other police officers and, most importantly, have no contact with anyone in Wales.'

'Did you do that?'

'Yes, sir.'

'How did you conduct yourself?'

Finch smiled. 'I found a quiet place to live; changed my appearance in terms of hair colour, facial hair and so on; dressed in ways no police officer would. I spent a lot of time sleeping. I read quite a bit, improved my snooker game a fair bit, and generally tried to pass the time. That's about it, really.'

'Were you ever ordered to come out of hiding, or told that you could?'

'No, sir.'

'Have you ever been ordered or told that you were free to come out of hiding, to this day?'

'No, sir.'

'Not even at the conclusion of the trial in this case?'

'No, sir.'

'About a month ago, Officer, you visited the office of my instructing solicitor, Mr Davis, who sits behind me, did you not?'

'I did, sir.'

'You had a conversation with Mr Davis, and very briefly with me, and you left with Mr Davis your affidavit and a copy of one or two documents from your personnel file to prove your identity?'

'Yes, sir.'

'And you indicated your willingness to give evidence about the matters dealt with in your affidavit if Arianwen appealed against her conviction?'

'Yes.'

'Was that in accordance with the instructions you had been given at the time of your debriefing, or any instructions you were given subsequently?'

'No, on the contrary. I was deliberately disobeying the instructions I had been given.'

'Why did you do that? Why did you go to see Mr Davis? Were you not worried about your position as a police officer?'

'My career as a police officer had ended long before then,' Finch replied. 'That was the last thing on my mind.'

'Then, why did you do it?'

'Because what had happened to Arianwen was wrong, and I had to do something to put it right if I could.'

'When you say "what had happened to Arianwen", what are you referring to?'

Finch was silent for some time. Lord Parker was about to order him to answer the question when he eventually replied.

'Arianwen didn't know she had a bomb in her car,' he said. 'It is my fault that she was arrested and convicted.'

90

'PLEASE TELL THEIR LORDSHIPS what happened on the evening of 30 June 1969,' Ben said.

'Caradog and Dai Bach called a meeting at Caradog's house to discuss how to transport the bomb from the garage to a place where Caradog could collect it. It was the only detail they hadn't agreed on.'

'What time was the meeting?'

'It was early evening, about 6 o'clock or 6.15, a few hours before Caradog went to work.'

'He was working as a night watchman at the Castle at that time?'

'Yes. Dai Bach and I were then going to attend the final demonstration against the Investiture in the town square later in the evening.'

'Who was present at this meeting?'

'Caradog, Dai Bach, and myself.'

'Not Arianwen?'

'No.'

'How did you feel about attending that meeting?'

'It went against every instinct I had as a police officer.'

'Why was that?'

'I thought it was an unnecessary risk to allow the bomb to leave the garage.'

'What alternatives were there?'

'The alternative was to raid the garage and seize the bomb before it could go anywhere. I recommended this course of action to Officers C and D as soon as I knew Dai Bach had finished work on the bomb. I wanted them to raid all our houses at the same time. I had made sure there was nothing at home to incriminate Arianwen or me. They could have arrested Caradog and Dai Bach and seized the bomb there and then. It would have avoided exposing the public to any danger.'

'What did Officers C and D say about that?'

'They said they had passed my suggestion on to Officers A and B, and that A and B weren't sure they had enough evidence for an arrest. They wanted to wait until they were on the move and they could catch them in the act. I kept on asking them to change their minds.'

'Why?'

'It was too dangerous. I didn't know whether Dai Bach would try to prime the bomb before transporting it. If he did, they would have to call in the bomb squad to disarm the bomb in public, evacuate the area, and there would be unnecessary risks to officers and the public.'

'Did it also cause you other problems as an undercover officer?'

Finch tightened his lips and looked down. Again, Lord Parker was on the brink of ordering him to answer.

'Yes, it certainly did.'

'Tell their Lordships about that, please.'

'When I got to the meeting, Caradog and Dai Bach told me the plan was for me to drive the bomb to a rendezvous near the town square, so that Caradog could pick it up during the early morning, at 1.15, before the local police closed the town centre to traffic. Caradog would find a reason to leave his post in the Castle to meet us and collect the bomb. He would then convey it into the Castle in his duffle bag.'

'What did you do?'

'I agreed to do what they had asked. But I contacted my superiors – Officer C, to be precise – as a matter of urgency by phone and asked again for the garage to be raided without delay. I couldn't imagine why they would need any further evidence before making the arrests.'

'How did you anticipate the evening ending?'

'I hoped that Caradog and Dai Bach would be arrested, and the bomb seized before it could be armed. I always assumed I would probably be arrested to keep up appearances, and that later I would be disclosed as an informant. But apparently, that wasn't how they saw it. That was when I knew that they were going to pull me out.'

'Were you given any instructions by your superiors?'

'Yes. I was told that I was to fail to show up for my appointment to drive. I had arranged to meet Dai Bach at the Castle Hotel on the square. I would then drive him to Bangor, pick up the bomb, and return to Caernarfon in time for the rendezvous with Caradog. I was

392 PETER MURPHY

ordered not to meet him, to leave him in the lurch, effectively.'

'Did you do that?'

'Yes.'

'What further instructions were you given?'

'I was ordered to meet another officer at a different rendezvous. This officer made a car available to me. I was ordered to drive straight to London and report to Officers A and B as soon as possible.'

'Did you do so?'

'Yes. I left at about 10.30 that night.'

'Without seeing your wife or son?'

Finch bowed his head.

'Yes,' he replied quietly.

'And you were gone, never to return to Caernarfon?'

There was a ripple of whispering around the courtroom. Arianwen had been looking down, but suddenly raised her eyes sharply. Finch felt her gaze.

'Yes. I was ordered to remain in London, as I said before.'

Ben paused.

'Officer, did you give any thought to what Dai Bach would do when you failed to appear at the Castle Hotel?'

'Yes, sir. It was possible that he would try to call the whole thing off, of course, but he would have known that Caradog would not want to give up that easily. So I thought Dai Bach would probably hire a taxi and transport the bomb to the rendezvous that way. It would be more risky, of course, but that was what I would have expected.'

'Did you have any idea that he would ask Arianwen to drive?'

'No, not at all.'

'Is there any reason why you assumed he would not ask her?'

'I made it clear when they first approached me that Arianwen must be left out of it. I insisted that she not be involved in any way. They both agreed to that.'

'Why should that stop them from involving her if it became necessary at a critical moment in your absence?'

'I can be quite forceful when I want to be,' Finch replied, 'and I gave both Caradog and Dai Bach every reason to think that they might come to harm if they did not respect my wishes.'

'But in fact, Dafydd Prosser did not respect your wishes, did he?'

'He panicked,' Finch replied. 'That's the problem with making people change their plans at the last moment. That was the wild card my superiors introduced into the situation. If I had driven myself, or if they had raided the garage, there would have been no problem.'

'Did Arianwen ever know about the bomb?'

'No. She did not.'

At the back of the court, Arianwen barely stifled a sob and held her head in her hands.

'Did Arianwen ever know about the Heirs of Owain Glyndŵr, or about the plan to plant a bomb in Caernarfon Castle?'

'No. She did not.'

'Is Arianwen the kind of woman who would have set out in the car with her son in the back seat, knowing that there was a bomb in the boot?'

Evan stood.

'Really, My Lords, is my learned friend inviting the witness to speculate about Mrs Finch's character?'

Ben was about to reply when Lord Parker cut Evan off.

'I would hardly call it speculation, Mr Roberts,' he said, 'and I can't think of anyone better qualified to give us an opinion on that subject. Answer the question, Officer.'

'She would never have done that, my Lord,' Finch replied. 'Not in a million years.'

'Did Arianwen play any part at all in the conspiracy to cause explosions at the Investiture?' Ben asked.

'No. She did not.'

'Is Arianwen a nationalist?'

'Yes,' Finch replied, 'in many ways she is. She is passionate about the Welsh language, and she campaigned constantly to have the language properly recognised. She supported Plaid Cymru at election time, and she campaigned for other Welsh causes. But violence? No. She had no truck with violence, ever.'

Ben allowed some time to pass.

'Looking back now on what happened, with the advantage of hindsight, how do you feel about the conclusion of your assignment in Wales?'

Finch smiled a bitter smile. It took him some time to reply, and this time, Lord Parker did not seem anxious to press him.

'I have a certain professional pride in the work I did – keeping my legend intact for such a long time. I am glad that I played a part in preventing what could have been a very serious act of violence directed against the Royal Family at the Investiture; and, frankly, I am glad that we were able to get Caradog Prys-Jones and Dafydd Prosser off the streets. But...'

He paused and bowed his head again.

'But I am ashamed of what I have done to Arianwen. I feel sick every time I think of her being convicted when I wasn't there to defend her. I wish I could rewind the clock and do things differently. I mean, everything, from the day I met her.'

'What would you do differently if you could rewind the clock?' Ben asked. 'Would you avoid any entanglement with her to protect your work?'

'No,' Finch replied immediately. 'I would marry her, and we would have Harri, but I would tell her who I am before we married, and I would find another job.'

He glanced to his left and saw Arianwen raise her head slightly. She looked at him, and he returned her look.

'I am sorry, Arianwen,' he said to her. 'Truly sorry.'

'Is any part of your evidence today connected to trying to keep your job as a police officer, or to justify your actions?'

'No,' Finch replied. 'There is no justification for what I did to Arianwen. I shall be resigning from the Met as soon as these proceedings are over, assuming they haven't fired me first.'

Ben nodded.

'Thank you, Officer. Wait there, please. There may be further questions.'

Trevor glanced in her direction again, and their eyes met.

91

'OFFICER,' GARETH BEGAN, 'IN your affidavit, you say that Caradog and Dai Bach approached you to become involved in an act of violence against the Investiture. Is that right?'

'Yes, sir.'

'So none of it was your idea?'

'No, sir.'

'You never suggested a target, or a plan of action? After all, your legend was as the owner of a rather radical book shop with nationalist connections. Are you sure you didn't get a bit carried away, get a bit too enthusiastic?'

'I never suggested any plan of action to them, sir, no. The only plans or actions I discussed with them were those they had come up with and asked for my assistance with.'

'Did you not encourage them in their plans at all?'

'Only as far as was necessary to protect my legend, sir. I did not encourage them to do anything they were not planning to do already.'

'But you made the arrangements to rent the garage didn't you?'

'Yes, sir.'

'Why did you do that, if it was not an act of encouragement?'

'Dai Bach needed a secure place to assemble the parts and construct the device. I had to have control over that place. I had to make sure that I could get into it, or allow other officers to do so, at any time.'

'You wanted control? Why should you have control, if it was not your plan?'

'There were going to be dangerous materials there, sir. If Dai Bach had been totally incompetent, or if I had any worries about safety, and it became necessary to pull the plug, I needed to be able to get in there without delay.'

'Who arranged the trip to Belfast in April of last year? Didn't you have something to do with that?'

Finch smiled. 'Let's just say that I had some input. Dai Bach thought he needed some help in constructing the timing device. He said the written instructions he found in the basement at the *Tywysog* were not clear enough. Caradog said he had met a couple of men who had connections with the IRA when they came to Caernarfon to sound out some of the local nationalists a year or so before. That was true. MI5 had documented that visit, and they had briefed me on it. The initial approach was made by Caradog. I agreed to go along with them.

'But I did ask my superiors to have colleagues in MI5 check all the arrangements, and make sure the trip was as safe as it could be. They were watching us as far as they could. But that wasn't to aid the conspiracy. It was to keep us as safe as we could be in the circumstances. I'm not sure Caradog or Dai Bach ever realised how dangerous it was. My MI5 colleagues tell me that West Belfast is not a place to visit as an outsider these days unless you have a very good reason.'

'Was the trip really necessary?'

'To be honest, sir, I think that Dai Bach would have worked it out on his own, left to his own devices. He is an intelligent man. But there were safety considerations. If he did make an error, it might have been very serious, and I couldn't lend assistance myself. So, dangerous as it was, it was decided to let him go to Belfast to learn from those more experienced in the art of bomb-making.'

'Which also meant,' Gareth said with a smile, 'that your colleagues in MI5 stood to gain some knowledge of IRA bomb-making techniques which they might not otherwise have had?'

Finch returned the smile.

'And Baader-Meinhof methods also, in this case, sir. I think that was an unexpected bonus.'

'I'm sure it was,' Gareth said. 'Are you sure that wasn't the main purpose of the visit?'

'I assure you, sir,' Finch replied, 'that I would not have taken civilians into West Belfast just to gain information about terrorist methods for MI5. That's their job.'

Gareth paused.

'Officer, you were undercover in Caernarfon for the best part of eight years, were you not?'

'Yes, sir.'

'During which time, you ran an important community bookstore?'

'Yes.'

'You married a local girl, became part of her family, had a child, and made friends?'

'Yes, sir.'

'You undertook political activities with them on behalf of Plaid Cymru, and attended demonstrations and the like – all perfectly legal, let me make that clear – but you did those things, didn't you?'

'Yes sir.'

'You understood the particular distress caused to your wife and to Caradog by the flooding of the Tryweryn Valley, where their family's home had once been?'

'Yes.'

'And you are of Welsh parentage yourself?'

'Yes.'

'This is a distasteful phrase in some ways, Officer. I don't mean it to be, but it is the most graphic way of putting this to you. Did you perhaps go native?'

Finch hesitated.

'If you mean…'

'I am asking whether you perhaps gained some sympathy for the views of Caradog Prys-Jones and Dafydd Prosser during the almost eight years you spent undercover with them. I am asking whether you acquired something of a new legend, whether you were tempted to change sides?'

'I did sympathise with some of the things they were aggrieved about,' Finch replied, after some thought. 'The flooding of the Tryweryn valley appalled many people in Wales, people who would not advocate violence. It appalled many people in England. But if you are suggesting that I became a terrorist, or had sympathy with terrorism, the answer is no. Not at any time.'

'You weren't tempted, even slightly, to become the person you pretended to be for those almost eight years?'

'No, sir. I remained a police officer, and I did my job.'

92

'I HAVE SOME QUESTIONS on behalf of the Crown,' Evan Roberts said. But before he could begin, Andrew Pilkington stood up almost directly behind him.

'No, my Lords,' Andrew said. 'The Crown has no questions.'

'We certainly do,' Evan insisted.

'No,' Andrew replied, 'we do not.'

The three judges exchanged looks of astonishment. Ben glanced to his right and saw Gareth burst out laughing. He could not help joining in.

'Well, make up your minds,' Lord Parker said. 'Who speaks for the prosecution?'

'I do.' Andrew Pilkington and Evan Roberts spoke at almost exactly the same time.

'This is extraordinary,' Lord Parker said, his voice betraying some irritation. 'In all my years of experience on the Bench and at the Bar, I have never known a case in which two members of the Bar argued about who was in charge. Never.'

He looked at the two other judges in turn. They both shook their heads.

'My Lords,' Andrew said, 'I would be grateful for a short adjournment so that my learned friend and I can discuss the matter. I am speaking now as Treasury Counsel who received authority to conduct this appeal earlier this morning from the Director of Public Prosecutions personally.'

Lord Parker considered for several seconds.

'Very well,' he replied, with some show of reluctance. 'We will adjourn for twenty minutes, at the end of which we shall expect this unseemly squabble to have been resolved.'

He turned to DC Finch. 'You can step down for the moment, Officer, but don't talk to anyone about your evidence during the adjournment.'

As Lord Parker was about to lead the other judges out of court, Lord Justice Carver touched his arm and whispered into his ear. Mr Justice Melrose stood and moved behind the Lord Chief Justice's chair, so that he too could hear. There was a whispered conversation between all three judges for some time. Ben looked questioningly at Gareth, but Gareth could only shrug his shoulders. It was impossible to tell what they were saying. Eventually, the three judges resumed their seats.

'Mr Schroeder,' Lord Parker said. 'We have discussed the evidence we have heard thus far. Without in any way prejudicing our decision in Mrs Finch's case, we think it right to grant her bail pending the conclusion of the appeal. She may sit with her solicitor behind counsel without being supervised by the prison officer.'

There was a spontaneous burst of applause which lasted for some seconds, and one or two shouts from the public gallery in Welsh, which the judges ignored. Ben turned towards Arianwen and saw her raise her hands to her face. As she made her way through the court to sit beside Barratt and Eifion, he felt tears welling up in his eyes.

93

TWENTY MINUTES LATER, ANDREW Pilkington rose to address the Court of Appeal. Evan Roberts remained in his seat, his hands clenched in front of him, a look of pure fury on his face.

'My Lords,' Andrew said, 'I am grateful for the time. As a result, I can be very brief. Having heard the evidence of DC Finch we do not propose to cross-examine him, and the prosecution no longer resists Arianwen Finch's appeal against conviction. We cannot exclude the possibility that, if the jury had heard DC Finch's evidence, they may well have reached a different conclusion, and we agree with the defence that it would not be safe to allow her conviction to stand. We therefore invite your Lordships to allow her appeal.'

Ben glanced behind him. Arianwen was holding Eifion's right hand between hers, and her eyes were filled with tears. Barratt was smiling, elated. There was further sustained applause and shouting in Welsh from the public gallery. Again, the judges said nothing and allowed them to run their course.

'*Diolch yn fawr iawn,*' Arianwen said to Ben. 'Thank you so much.' He turned back towards the judges, now barely able to suppress tears of his own.

'We do wish to be heard on the appeals of Caradog Prys-Jones and Dafydd Prosser, which are resisted,' Andrew was saying. 'And we would respectfully invite your Lordships, at the conclusion of your judgment, to make observations about the proper means of holding an inquiry into the facts surrounding DC Finch's absence from the trial, and the information given about that to the trial court and to the defence.'

'We have already allowed Arianwen Finch's appeal against conviction and ordered her immediate release,' Lord Parker began. It was by now almost 1 o'clock, and the Court had heard from Gareth Morgan-Davies on behalf of Dai Bach and Caradog. Andrew Pilkington had replied on behalf of the prosecution. It was clear that the Court had no intention of breaking for lunch at the normal time and was determined to bring the case to an end as soon as possible without adjourning.

'I need not repeat what was said. The Court agrees that in the absence of DC Finch, and more importantly, in the light of the inaccurate and misleading basis on which the case was put to the jury, her conviction cannot be regarded as safe. The law is clear. The prosecution is entitled to withhold the identity of an informer or undercover police officer, for the obvious purposes of ensuring his safety and not compromising his professional effectiveness. But there is one clear exception to that rule: namely, that where the identity of the informer is essential to the defence of an accused person, the prosecution must either disclose the identity or abandon the case. There was no evidence against Mrs Finch apart from the fact that she was arrested in apparent possession of the bomb. The question for the jury was whether it was possible that she was ignorant of what she had in the boot. Clearly, the jury might have taken a very different view of that question if they had known the truth about DC Finch, rather than the prosecution's version of events.

'As we have been invited to do, we call on the Attorney-General to set up an inquiry to investigate, as thoroughly as possible, the circumstances under which the case was put to the jury in the way it was. We will make no other comment about that for now, except that no stone should be left unturned, and no one – and we mean no one – should be regarded as above suspicion.

'I now turn to the other appeals. Mr Morgan-Davies, to whom we are indebted for his very able argument, not only addressed us on behalf of his own client, but also, at the behest of the Registrar of Criminal Appeals, on behalf of Caradog Prys-Jones. Mr Prys-Jones, of course, has only himself to blame for the fact that he did not have his own counsel. But we have a duty to consider his appeal just as carefully as if he were present and represented, and we are grateful to Mr Morgan-Davies for assisting the Court in that task.

'Mr Morgan-Davies invites us to say that the false story the jury was told about DC Finch infects Mr Prys-Jones's case, and Mr Prosser's case, just as it does that of Mrs Finch. He invites us to find that all three convictions are unsafe and must be quashed. In essence, he says that Trevor Finch was an informant, and that his identity should have been disclosed to the defence because it was necessary for a fair trial, as it was in the case of Arianwen Finch. We do not agree.

'That was the position in Mrs Finch's case, but that was because her state of mind was the key to her case, and DC Finch would have been an important source of evidence on that question. We have considered anxiously whether it is also true of the other two defendants. We do not think it was. Ironically, the prosecution's case would probably have been a good deal stronger than it was if DC Finch had been disclosed and called as a prosecution witness. But that was not done. We repeat that there is no excuse for the court being misled. But there was evidence against both Caradog Prys-Jones and Dafydd Prosser which did not depend on DC Finch at all.

'Mr Prys-Jones, in essence, admitted the offence to the police in a statement under caution. Even if he had not, there was the clearest possible evidence that he chose the site at which the bomb was to be placed, and he arranged the perfect cover for himself by getting a job as a night watchman with access to Caernarfon Castle at all hours.

'There was the clearest possible evidence against Dafydd Prosser to implicate him in the construction of the explosive device in the garage at Bangor, consisting of debris from the dynamite and electrical wire, the instructions for building such a device, and his fingerprints. In addition, both men went to Belfast in circumstances which make it clear that they intended to – and apparently did – receive valuable technical information from those in other organisations who were more experienced in such matters, information of which Prosser no doubt made good use when he returned to Bangor.

'It is true that certain evidence given to the jury should not have been given to them. It is now agreed that certain passages and signatures in documents, which the prosecution said were in the handwriting of Trevor Hughes, were in fact written by someone else. That is not in dispute. The written report of the hand-writing expert, Miss Bailey, makes it clear. The evidence of these documents should never have been given to the jury. It was a serious irregularity. We must consider whether it renders these convictions unsafe. We do not think it does. There was a great deal of other evidence against both the appellants.

'There is no evidence at all to suggest that Mr Prys-Jones and Mr Prosser were entrapped by DC Finch into committing an offence they would not otherwise have committed. We are unable to see that the identity of DC Finch was essential to the defence of Mr

Prys-Jones or of Mr Prosser. Accordingly, we conclude that there is no ground on which their appeals against conviction can succeed. Those appeals are accordingly dismissed.

'We have not been invited in any serious way to interfere with the sentences passed by the learned judge. They were severe sentences, but the judge was right to be severe. These men were convicted of a conspiracy to cause an explosion which might have caused death or serious injury to the Queen, Prince Charles, or other members of the Royal Family, or to other persons present at the Investiture. It was an offence of the utmost gravity. The sentences were fully merited, and are beyond criticism.'

He paused.

'But we cannot exclude the possibility that, if the learned trial judge had known of the part played by Trevor Finch, he might have viewed the matter of sentence in a somewhat different light. We have no way of knowing whether that would have been the case or not. It may very well be that it would have made no difference at all. But it seems to us important to avoid any possible appearance of injustice arising from the prosecution's conduct of the case, and accordingly for this reason alone – and I stress, for this reason alone – we have decided to reduce the sentence of Caradog Prys-Jones and that of Dafydd Prosser from one of 40 years to one of 20 years.

'We will say no more about this case, leaving to others to decide what further steps, if any, should be taken.'

94

It was after 2 o'clock when Ben and Barratt left court with Eifion, and made their way to the small room where Arianwen was waiting for them. It was the same room in which she had waited for the appeal to begin, more than four hours earlier, but this time, there was no prison officer and the door was not locked. She embraced all three men warmly, holding them in her arms in turn for a long time without speaking. She was still crying softly.

'We asked for you to be brought here so that the court security staff can smuggle you out of the side entrance,' Barratt explained. 'The press are gathering like vultures by the front entrance, and we thought you would prefer not to have to deal with them.'

'Thank you,' she replied. 'I am in no state to answer questions. I just want to go home and hide away for a long time.'

'I will arrange that for you,' Barratt said. 'We will get you back to my office, and when you're ready, one of my staff will take you to Euston and travel home with you, just to make sure you don't get any unwelcome attention. Her name is Mandy, and she is well able to look after you.'

Barratt paused.

'Then, when you are strong enough, we will talk to the local authority about getting Harri back for you.'

Arianwen looked at Barratt anxiously.

'Please tell me that won't be a problem,' she said. 'I couldn't bear it if he has to stay in a foster home.'

'You've been cleared,' Ben said. 'They can't have any legitimate reason not to give him back, as far as this Court is concerned. Barratt will arrange a conference with Jess to discuss where you go from here, but it's one step at a time.'

'I will be writing to the local authority immediately,' Barratt said. 'It may take some time to get him back, but I am sure you will be able to see him very soon, and that's a start. Look, try not to worry about it. We will be there with you every step of the way.'

She embraced all three men again, and held each of them tight.

Barratt hesitated.

'Arianwen, it shouldn't be more than another ten minutes or so before we can go. But I promised to tell you that there is someone who would like to see you, just for a minute or two.'

Her jaw dropped.

'Trevor?' she whispered.

'Yes. I told him you probably wouldn't want to, especially today. It's entirely up to you. I only agreed to tell you because he insisted. He said he understood that you might tell him to go to hell. If you like, I will slip out now and give him his marching orders.'

She thought for a long time.

'I will see him,' she said.

'Are you sure?'

'Yes.'

They left her alone.

95

'HELLO, ARIANWEN,' HE SAID.

She got to her feet, almost involuntarily, as he entered the room, her hands clasped tightly in front of her. She looked at him. He was standing before her abjectly, in complete misery, his hands in his pockets. It was painfully obvious that he had told the Court of Appeal the truth when he said that he was ashamed of himself. He was looking down, but he raised his eyes for a fraction of a second, and she saw nothing but pain and regret. Once again, she found herself confused by the hopeless assortment of feelings inside her. Again, she found herself wanting to despise, even hate this man who had betrayed her; yet once again her mind and emotions would not cooperate with her. Even more confusingly, there was still a fondness, perhaps even a love for him. Most of all, something about his despair and hopelessness moved her in ways she could not account for. But she did not speak.

'I am going to resign from the police force,' he said hesitantly, after some time. 'I have no idea what I am going to do. I haven't been able to think about anything except the case until today. I will have to find myself a job eventually. God knows what it will be. I don't know anything except being a police officer...

'I thought I might take some time off, go away, maybe to Europe somewhere, for a while, and think it through...

'The thing is, Arianwen... what I want to ask you... and I am not asking you to say anything now...

'I know it's hopeless for us,' he said at last. 'I know it's over. I know that it is my fault, and I know there is nothing I can do about it. I know all that.'

His words struck her like a physical blow. She sat down abruptly, afraid that she might fall if she remained standing. She still did not speak.

'I am sure you are ready to tell your solicitor to get you a divorce.

I don't blame you at all. I won't fight it. All I ask is that you let me see Harri sometimes. I don't ask any more than that. I will provide for him, of course…

'I am truly sorry, Arianwen. I have no excuse for what I did. I know that doesn't mean much now. But I am truly sorry.'

His voice trailed away once more. She stared at him, and they looked at each other for a long time. At length he took his hands from his pockets, where they had been since he had entered the room, and nodded.

'I understand,' he said. 'I didn't expect anything else really. I will go now. I just wanted to say sorry.' He turned towards the door and opened it.

Suddenly and unexpectedly, her voice returned.

'Is it true?' she asked. 'What you said in your affidavit about still loving me? Is that true, or were you just trying to make yourself feel better about what you were doing?'

'It is true,' he replied quietly. 'I have always loved you, and I always will.'

They were silent together for some time, she in her chair, he half way out of the door with his back to her. Abruptly, she stood and walked over to him and took his hand.

'I will never stop you seeing Harri,' she said. 'You are his father. He loves you and he needs you.'

'Thank you.'

'As far as Trevor Hughes is concerned, my relationship with him is over for good. There is no way back. You must understand that.'

'I understand…'

He bowed his head, his eyes closed, but to his surprise she lifted his head gently and waited until he opened his eyes.

'But I don't know about Trevor Finch,' she said. 'I don't know Trevor Finch, you see. I saw him do something good this morning. I watched him rescue a woman he cared about who was in terrible danger, and I think I would like to meet him. So, go wherever you are going to sort yourself out, and don't come back too soon. But when you get back, find me and introduce me to Trevor Finch.'

96

Friday 17 July 1970

BEN WAS PORING OVER the prosecution's latest schedule of false and inflated invoices when Gareth came into his room at about 5 o'clock. His fraud trial was now in its third week, and the end of the prosecution's case was not even in sight. His life seemed to have become an endless round of arithmetic and futile efforts to reconcile huge bundles of invoices. But the fraud had served to take his mind away from Wales and from Arianwen Finch, and for that he was grateful. That case had too many ghosts, the ghosts of Wales, and he was glad that their hold on him was beginning to fade. He and Jess had discovered a new closeness, a new gentleness, since the case ended. She had never asked him any more about Arianwen. She knew that she had nothing to fear.

'Still drowning in paper?' Gareth smiled. 'Can I drag you away for a pint?'

'I wish I could, Gareth,' he replied. 'But I have to be on top of this to cross-examine another of the prosecution's accountants tomorrow.'

'What does it look like?' Gareth asked.

'I think the ship is going down with all hands.'

Gareth laughed.

'Well, you can't win them all, you know.' He brandished a newspaper he had been carrying under his arm. 'Anyway, I won't interrupt. I just wanted to ask whether you had read *The Times* today?'

'No. Please don't tell me there is a new case on fraud.'

'No, no,' Gareth replied. 'I'm not talking about the law report.' He turned to the page he wanted, and laid it before Ben. 'I'm talking about the Court Circular.'

'Oh?'

Ben picked the paper up and read the passage Gareth had circled in red ink.

The Queen has been pleased to approve the appointment of Evan Lloyd Roberts to be a Judge of the High Court of Justice. The Lord Chancellor has assigned Mr Justice Roberts to the Queen's Bench Division.

Ben sat back in his chair.

'They are rewarding Evan Roberts for that fiasco? Please tell me this is some kind of joke.'

'Apparently not,' Gareth said.

Ben sat silently, shaking his head, for some time.

'My God, they're kicking him upstairs to cover it all up, aren't they?' he said. 'This will immunise him against any inquiry. There's going to be a cover up. And what's the betting Jamie Broderick will get Silk in a year or two? This is unbelievable.'

Gareth smiled. 'My word, you are getting cynical in your old age.'

'Well, what else can it mean?'

Gareth spread his arms out in front of him.

'It may not mean anything at all. Evan was senior civil Treasury Counsel. It's not unusual for someone to go up to the High Court after some time in that role. It may have been planned for quite a while, and our case may have nothing to do with it.'

'It is a bit of a coincidence that he should be appointed now, though, isn't it?' Ben replied. 'I know the Court made no findings…'

'They couldn't,' Gareth interjected. 'There was no evidence.'

'I know,' Ben said. 'But Roberts didn't exactly come out of it smelling like roses, and the Court said no one should be immune from suspicion when they set up the inquiry.'

'*If* they set up an inquiry,' Gareth corrected him. 'It is only a recommendation, and the recommendations of the Court of Appeal are not always followed.'

Ben shook his head.

'So, this isn't a reward for a job well done?'

'Well, in a sense it may be,' Gareth replied. 'Let's not forget that he did successfully prosecute two would-be bombers, who got their just deserts. The powers that be are always impressed by that. I know Arianwen got caught up in it all. I know it was very murky in some ways, and what happened to her shouldn't have happened. But the Court of Appeal straightened it out for her, and what I had to say didn't even make a dent in the case against Dai Bach or Caradog – well, except for the sentences, I suppose. You can't insist on seeing conspiracy in everything, Ben, otherwise you will drive yourself mad.'

'I know, but I would hate to think that they are trying to protect him or, even worse, buying his silence.'

'That did occur to me, of course,' Gareth said, 'but after some reflection I have decided that I have not yet become a complete cynic and, accordingly, I have decided to give the Lord Chancellor the benefit of the doubt.'

'You are more charitable than I am,' Ben replied.

He brooded for some moments, then threw the newspaper down on his desk and smiled.

'To hell with it. I never asked you, Gareth. As a Welshman, what effect did the case have on you? Are you a nationalist at heart?'

Gareth laughed.

'I love my country, of course, and my language, and I applaud all the efforts to promote Welshness, whatever that may be. But we can't live in the Middle Ages. Edward I is dead and gone, and so is Owain Glyndŵr. We have to let them go.'

He turned back on his way to the door.

'Besides,' he said, 'we can still give you English a good kicking at the Arms Park, or even at Twickenham, and as long as we can still do that, as far as I am concerned, Welsh honour is more than satisfied.'

'I'm not sure Caradog would agree with you about Glyndŵr,' Ben said.

'Glyndŵr was a freedom fighter,' Gareth replied, 'but he wasn't an extremist. He was a civilised man. He did what he thought he was driven to do, but it wasn't out of any sense of ideology. That's something later writers ascribed to him. Personally, I don't think the likes of Caradog and Dai Bach would have been welcome in his army.'

He paused with his hand on the door handle.

'And they certainly wouldn't have been his heirs.'

Author's Note

Two books in particular were of great assistance to me in my research for this novel. *Investiture: Royal Ceremony and National Identity in Wales, 1911-1969*, by John S. Ellis (University of Wales Press, Cardiff, 2008) provides a detailed history of the two recent Investitures held in Caernarfon Castle, that of the future Edward VIII (and Duke of Windsor) in 1911, and that of Prince Charles in 1969. Ellis offers an intriguing analysis of public attitudes to the two events, both in England and Wales, and shows how those attitudes changed or evolved from one period in history to the other. He also offers an interesting, if necessarily incomplete, account of the rise of Welsh nationalism, the emergence of extremist elements, and of the resort to violence in Wales in response to certain events.

The Investiture of HRH The Prince of Wales at Caernarvon Castle 1 July 1969: Record of Procedures adopted by the Ministry of Public Building and Works, Central Office for Wales (MPBW, date and place of publication not stated) may be the single most staggeringly useful publication I have had available to me for research for any book I have written. It is a complete record of every facet of the planning, organisation and conduct of the 1969 Investiture, and includes details of: everyone involved in any capacity, from the Earl Marshal to the lowliest chorister or trumpeter; every committee appointed; every security measure taken; every piece of equipment used; every contract entered into; every piece of pomp and ceremony adopted; and every expenditure made; down to the last penny and paperclip. It also has wonderfully helpful photographs and plans, showing who was where, and when, on the day. It was a veritable treasure trove for an author.

But best of all were the people I myself met in Caernarfon. One lady, who insists on remaining anonymous, recounted several intriguing stories of events surrounding the Investiture. But my main insight came from a fortuitous, and fortunate, meeting with

Emrys Llewelyn, town guide *extraordinaire* of Caernarfon who, once he understood my purpose in being there, gave me, not only an extended tour of the town, but also the benefit of his lifetime of residence there. He took extra time to show me many things I suspect tourists rarely see, and to tell me of his own experiences of the time of the Investiture, which were invaluable. He took me to a bookshop, whose layout inspired my imagination of the physical structure of the *Siop Llyfrau'r Tywysog*, and where I purchased his book, *Stagio Dre*, which I intend to read as soon as my Welsh is up to it. Emrys has remained in touch ever since, sending me contemporary pictures of Caernarfon, and patiently answering any questions I cared to put to him.

I have consistently used the Welsh spelling for Caernarfon, with the Welsh F rather than the English V, because this is a book set in Wales, even though much of it takes place in London, if that makes sense, and because I think the Welsh spelling is more elegant. There is inevitably some Welsh in the book, hopefully explained and hopefully not enough to put non-Welsh speakers off; I count myself among that group, though I intend to remedy it. Emrys and his wife Mari, who teaches the language, gave me some help with my Welsh, but any errors which remain are my own.

Finally, this is the time to thank those involved with the Ben Schroeder series, without whom Ben would never have made his first appearance in a courtroom. First, thanks to Ion Mills and Claire Watts at No Exit Press, for their faith in my writing. It was Ion's idea, not mine, that Ben would make a good protagonist for a series – he was a relatively minor character in my original draft of *A Higher Duty* – and it is such a pleasure to have a publisher who is happy to hold our business meetings at the pub we both regard as the best in London, where we can chat about things over a pint or two. Thanks, too, to fellow author Clem Chambers, creator of the Jim Evans series, who introduced me to No Exit after a chance meeting at dinner; and to my agent, Annette Crossland of A for Authors, who diligently promotes Ben to a wider audience. I owe so much to my editor, Irene Goodacre, whose eagle eye and painstaking fact-checking, not to mention her extensive knowledge of a wide variety of subjects including rugby, have saved me from many an error. It's a shame she can't be a Wales supporter, but her skills and her fierce support for the characters in the series, especially Jess Farrar, more than make up for that. Last, but of course not least, my wife Chris.

Without her love and support over many years, I would not have been able to write as I do, and in many ways these books are hers as well as mine.

About Us

In addition to No Exit Press, Oldcastle Books has a number
of other imprints, including Kamera Books, Creative Essentials,
Pulp! The Classics, Pocket Essentials and High Stakes
Publishing > oldcastlebooks.com

For more information about Crime Books go to > crimetime.co.uk

Check out the kamera film salon for independent, arthouse and
world cinema > kamera.co.uk

For more information, media enquiries and review copies please
contact > marketing@oldcastlebooks.com